SIGNS OF OUR TIMES

KARL BOYD

PublishAmerica
Baltimore

© 2007 by Karl Boyd.
All rights reserved. No part of this book may be reproduced, stored in a retrieval system or transmitted in any form or by any means without the prior written permission of the publishers, except by a reviewer who may quote brief passages in a review to be printed in a newspaper, magazine or journal.

First printing

All characters appearing in this work are fictitious. Any resemblance to real persons, living or dead, is purely coincidental.

At the specific preference of the author, PublishAmerica allowed this work to remain exactly as the author intended, verbatim, without editorial input.

ISBN: 1-4241-7865-7
PUBLISHED BY PUBLISHAMERICA, LLLP
www.publishamerica.com
Baltimore

Printed in the United States of America

To: Judy & Jerry,   21 JAN 08

Thank you for supporting our wonderful and dedicated troops through "The Wounded Warrior Project", and helping my writing habit move along. Enjoy the story and tell <u>ALL</u> your friends about it. Let's make it a #1 seller. When you've read my novel, please give me a review at <u>www.karlboyd.com</u>

Karl Boyd

CHAPTER 1

(One)

As Katie Adkins, a twenty-one year old student in her junior year at Southern Colorado University, (SCOU), sat behind the wheel of her badly dented, no-longer white 1989 Volvo, her mind raced.

The information she possessed was so vital she knew it couldn't be reported over a landline or sent by e-mail. She must deliver it and the proof to the FBI.

For the hundredth time since she began this desperate, last ditch action, she asked herself, "Will the FBI believe me, or will they think I'm a nut? How can I convince them the threat of a terrorist attack on the President and hundreds of thousands of Americans is real?"

When Katie first heard the horrific plot and told her co-workers at the research laboratory, they shared a laugh at her expense. Even in this day and age of mayhem and murder, no one wanted to believe her, especially when she told them the source of her discovery.

In a way, she couldn't blame them, but why wouldn't even one of them listen and offer to help? No, they were too worried about saving their own asses and not looking like fools.

So she took action on her own, knowing when she was vindicated, they'd laugh out of the other side of their stupid mouths. A fleeting smile came to her lips as she thought, "screw 'em."

As she nervously tapped her short red fingernails on the steering wheel and waited for a break in the traffic so she could turn left onto Mulberry Street, Katie glanced at her two companions.

"I've got you as my witnesses," she said aloud and both passengers turned her way and nodded in agreement. For a few moments, Katie felt better, but a nagging doubt still made her stomach churn.

"Dear God, they have to believe us," she prayed.

Using one hand to shield her eyes from the rays of the rising sun, Katie edged her aging wreck closer to the oncoming stream of traffic and silently pleaded, "Come on, someone. Give me a break."

Her male passenger tugged at Katie's sleeve. When she glanced his way, he told her he was hungry, but Katie replied, "You'll have to wait."

Then her other companion indicated she needed to go to the bathroom, but again, this wasn't the time or place, and Katie told her so.

Neither of them was upset, but they squirmed in their seats as youngsters are apt to do when they don't get their way.

Just then, a large moving van pulled to the curb and partially blocked Katie's view of the traffic from the left.

Shaking her head in disgust, she thought, "If it isn't one damned frustrating thing this morning, it's another."

Cautiously easing the old car out onto the pavement until she could see around the truck, she measured the oncoming traffic.

Without asking first, the female passenger undid her seat belt, pushed the window control button, and the glass slid downward with a sound like a wiper blade swinging across the windshield on a rainy day. Because it was chilly and she feared for her passengers' safety, Katie started to tell her companion to raise the window and buckle up.

Just then a Good Samaritan stopped his white Cadillac a few feet behind a tan Oldsmobile van, leaving enough space for her to pull out, so she decided to wait until they were on the way.

If the woman driving the van would roll forward a few feet, Katie could move into the second lane. Looking left, she saw a tanker truck approaching a half-block away, misjudged its speed, made a quick decision and pulled out. The engine compartment of the old Volvo fit into the vacant space, but the driver's area sat exposed to oncoming traffic.

Thankfully, the line of vehicles moved on, but the driver of the minivan either didn't notice or was preoccupied.

Glancing apprehensively in the direction of the fast-moving fuel truck, Katie cried out in frustration and fear, "Come on lady, move it or park it," and tapped the horn to wake the old gal up. But the vehicle remained where it was, as if it was pegged to the ground.

There was no way Katie could know the female driver was unable to respond to her pleas.

(Two)

The driver of the fully loaded, five-thousand-gallon-capacity fuel truck was Ted Branski, a young brown-haired black-eyed thirty-five year old father of two children, Liz eight and David five. Ted was listening to and singing along with country music on the radio, and when he saw Katie's vehicle pull out of the driveway, he began to let up on the accelerator, but didn't complete the maneuver.

He never heard the shot that killed him, didn't see the side window of his truck explode in a hail of shattered glass or feel the bullet enter his skull above his left ear and blow his head apart. One moment Ted was alive and the next he was stone-cold dead.

The driver of the van was a petite brunette, Nora Smith, a mother of three-year-old twin boys, Erin and Darren. Ten minutes ago, she dropped them off at day school and although she didn't know it, she kissed her boys goodbye for the final time.

Five seconds before Ted's murder, Nora met the same fate, so in spite of Katie's urging, she couldn't move her van.

As Katie watched in helpless horror, the gas truck roared down the street and smashed into her car. A piercing scream tore from her throat, but it was lost in the noise of a powerful explosion.

(Three)

It had been a long cold night for the paid assassin, Claude Werner, who shivered in his hiding place and tried to shift his six-foot frame around so the cold, damp, hard ground wouldn't hurt as much. His medium-long coal-black hair was wet from the morning dew and although he was tired, his black eyes stood out like holes drilled in marble as he peered through the high-powered scope of a rifle.

It was a cloudless sunny day, featuring the azure blue sky of late summer in

Colorado. After the chill of the night, the heat from the orange orb blazing its way upward warmed Claude's weary back. He was glad it hadn't rained. He hated to work when wet and miserable.

His features were above average and his suntanned face was handsome, but not on a par with any well-known movie star or rock musician. If you passed him in a crowd, you would never remember him, and that was what he wanted—anonymity.

Although he had no idea who ordered the "hit" on his three intended victims, Claude didn't give a damn. The main objective for him was the money, five hundred thousand dollars for a clean contract.

This was his last job and he was anxious to complete it. Five years ago when he became a hired gun, he set a goal of ten million dollars in the bank and retirement. When he received his pay from this job, his aspirations would be met with an extra one hundred thousand in his account.

Claude hoped to kill and be on his way in a few minutes, but things didn't work out that way. Throughout the night his targets remained hidden behind closed blinds in an apartment on the top floor three hundred yards away.

It was too risky for him to enter the building, kill them there and make his escape. There were too many variables he couldn't control.

This was supposed to be a clean kill, but it had turned ugly already, and neither of his two victims was one of the intended targets. His purpose was to first eliminate Katie's two companions and then her, but so far he hadn't had a clear shot.

Knowing she would leave soon, his plan was to take out the two passengers as they got to the end of the driveway and then kill Katie. When the door to her garage slowly creaked its way upward, he shifted his weight, took a deep breath to steady his nerves and achieved a good sight picture.

As the Volvo eased out of the garage, the sun reflected off the windshield and temporarily blinded him. Before he could acquire his target again, a large moving van pulled to the curb and blocked his shot. It was something he hadn't planned for. For a moment he feared he might not complete his mission and cursed in frustration, "Damn it!"

Glancing at the flow of traffic again, the chance came to finish the job and make it appear to be an accident. While the head of the driver of the van was a clear shot, the position of the truck driver relevant to Claude's lair was an awkward one. But he was a marksman and well paid for his expertise, so he took the chance and the results paid dividends far beyond his expectations.

His first bullet hit Nora in the forehead, killing her instantly. Her body jerked backward, recoiled forward, and slumped against the wheel. Two seconds later he killed Ted.

Eight seconds later the fuel truck crashed into the Volvo and crushed it against the front of the Cadillac. One and two seconds after impact, two separate bullets struck the cargo compartment of the truck and the volatile mixture exploded in a tremendous fire ball.

From where Claude hid on a hill across the street, he could feel the heat. Calmly breaking his weapon down, he packed the rifle into a custom-made container, closed the lid, stood up and walked nonchalantly through the small brush and weeds to the sidewalk running through the tree-shrouded park. Claude never looked back to check his work. It was his first mistake.

(Four)

If the fire department weren't located two blocks away, an entire city residential area may have gone up in smoke. Even with the fast response and yeomen work of the fire department, after the fire was extinguished, six victims were dead and twelve injured. The fire destroyed three apartment buildings, seven cars, and two trucks. It also injured three firemen, none seriously.

Eight hours later, with the fire out and a fleet of wreckers working feverishly to clear the road of burned vehicles, District Fire Chief Hiram Fletcher leaned back and rested his sore tired back against the fender of a fire truck, looked toward heaven and said, "It's a miracle we don't have more dead."

(Five)

The sun seemed to wink as it slid behind a narrow white cloud on the far horizon and said goodnight, filling the sky with a spectacular display of pink, orange, rose and grey tints spreading across the thin trails. As far as Sergeant Joe Francone was concerned, it was the perfect ending to a rather shitty day.

Wearing a set of civilian clothes that looked like they came from a local Salvation Army recycling center, Joe was a five foot, seven inch tall, worn-out cop. Although he was only thirty-nine, he looked older. He had long unkempt black hair that needed a trim badly and large blue eyes that seemed to stare off into the distance at nothing in particular.

Surprisingly, Joe missed nothing that happened around him.

He wasn't overly handsome, one of the semi-rugged indoor people who struggle daily to maintain their weight. But women still liked him and he enjoyed his share of romance, when he felt like it, and he hadn't for some time. The job and the people he dealt with wore him down, little by little, day by day.

Overweight for his height and twice warned about his appearance by his shift captain and immediate supervisor, Joe tried in a half-hearted way, but the pounds kept piling on. The only exercise he got was bending over backward to please his boss; jumping to conclusions too soon and lifting a cold one in the local hang out.

Ever since his wife, Shirley, left him three hard years ago, he drank too much, ate junk food and little else. Something had to give soon or he'd be out of a job.

After climbing out of his bruised and battered blue and white, Joe walked to a green metal door set into a grey concrete and red brick wall, stopped and reached into a pocket of his long brown coat.

Knowing what faced him inside and having had enough of smelling roasted flesh today, he stood outside the door to the county medical examiner's room and pulled a jar of Vaseline from his coat pocket. Twisting off the cap and holding it and the jar in his left hand, he scooped out a goodly portion with his right index finger and pushed the light-green grease into his nose.

Since he possessed a large hooked beak, it took several attempts to fill both nostrils. Then he replaced the cap and returned the jar to his pocket.

From another, he took a white handkerchief with an embroidered blue F on one corner and wiped his hands. To save time as he cleaned his fingers, he leaned his elbow against the doorbell button and pushed.

Inside the examination room at the rear of the building, Chief Forensic Scientist Sarah Gruber examined a shattered skull with shards of charred skin still clinging to the bone. A few moments earlier, as Sarah removed the torn remains of the victim's brains and placed them in a chromed bowl, a crumpled and smashed bullet clunked against the side. Using a small pair of tweezers to lift the lump of metal, she placed it in a thin manila evidence envelope.

Although she was small in stature, what she lacked in height, she made up for in pure guts. No one else could do the things Sarah did and smile at the same time. If she was pissed at you, her green eyes could dissect you like a scalpel, or grant you absolution when you deserved less.

Those who knew her well said she had a heart as big as Wyoming. Those who didn't thought she was a heartless bitch, who loved to cut up people just for the hell of it.

At the sound of the doorbell, Sarah looked around the room where four forms, three large and one small lay under stiff white sheets on cold metal tables with their remains half-exposed.

Fluorescent lights overhead glared down on the bodies like floodlights on a hot burlesque stage and their burned skin shined like burnished copper. Working at two of the tables, Sarah's assistants attempted to identify what little remained. Another helper, Judy Eskew examined something red and bloody under a microscope.

Judy was a former operating room nurse and Sarah's favorite co-worker. They first met when Judy was seriously injured in an automobile accident which killed her husband, and three days after the wreck, she hobbled in on crutches to claim his body. It was instant admiration for their shared determination and had remained that way for years.

"Can you get that, Judy?" Sarah asked.

"Sure," Judy said, limping briskly to the door.

Opening it, she saw Joe as he finished wiping his greasy hands and said, "It's just Joe."

As he walked in, Joe said, "Hi, Judy, I hear you've got some crispy critters for me."

Leading him to where Sarah stood holding the skull, Judy said, "Joe, sometimes you're too gross for words."

Smiling, Sarah said, "Come in, Just Joe."

Glancing down at Ted's burned corpse and then looking at Sarah, where she stood as if she was on stage, Joe said, "You look like a character straight out of Macbeth, who should be saying, 'Alas, poor You're Icky, I knew him well'. You know what I mean?"

Without waiting for a reply, he asked, "What have you got for me this time, Doc? It smells like a wiener roast gone haywire in here."

Shaking her head, Sarah's brown eyes flashed in momentary anger, but she couldn't stay upset at her favorite cop, so she said, "Stop it, Joe. It's not funny to make sport of the dead."

"Okay, Doc. I apologize. What've you got?"

Pointing to the stiff on her table and nodding at the still smoldering body on the adjacent one, she said, "This man and the woman over there weren't killed by the fire. They were shot."

"No shit!" Joe exclaimed, and then he asked, "Did you find the slugs?"

"Yes, we recovered both of them, but there wasn't much left. They were head shots and the bullets were crushed. Your crime lab experts will have to dig deeper to determine the caliber."

Looking around the room, Joe asked, "What about the rest of them?"

"The other woman died from the fire."

"How about the vic on the last table?" he asked.

"That's what's really strange, Joe," Sarah said. "It's not a person; it's a monkey or a chimp."

"No shit?"

Laughing at his limited vocabulary, Sarah said, "No shit, Joe. How does that grab you for suspense? You should write a novel."

(Six)

Worn-out, hung-over and sleep-deprived, Officer "Fad" Dean, one of Sulfur Springs' finest, ended his second fruitless attempt at sleep. Yesterday he and his salt-and-pepper team partner, Joe Francone, worked the graveyard duty tour and before they knew it, their night ran into the day shift.

On top of that, just before their tour ended, they covered the big gas truck explosion and fire. It took all day to process the scene and Joe was presently talking to the medical examiner.

After twenty-four straight hours on the job, Fad was bushed and Joe knew it. He told Fad to take off and get some Zs and that's what he was trying to do.

Because Fad missed breakfast and lunch as he worked the grisly accident scene, he didn't go directly home. After smelling singed hair and roasted flesh for ten hours, he didn't feel like eating supper and doubted if he did that he could keep it down.

Initially, his intentions were honorable. Stopping off at O'Grady's Bar, he plopped his six foot, three inch frame on a stool for one little drink to unwind after a horrible day.

To the surprise of no one, including him, with the bar a hangout for cops, there were several other officers and patrolmen there talking trash or bullshitting as they hefted a brew or two.

Somewhere along the line he lost count and his one Coors Light turned into four or six. On an empty stomach, they hit him harder than usual, so he was lucky to make it home in his beat-up Chevy without getting a DUI hung on his record. Now as a result, he was wired and wide awake.

For an estimated four and one-half hours since 2400 hours yesterday or 0001 today, (take your pick), he tossed, turned, rolled, kicked off the covers and pulled them back on. Fighting bravely and cursing silently, he failed miserably in his quest for forty winks.

Finally he gave up, but sat on the edge of the bed with his eyes tightly

SIGNS OF OUR TIMES

closed, because he was afraid to open them and confirm his greatest fear. Although he knew it was irrational, he believed his mind was actually a complicated computer controlled by an ugly, green, four-eyed and three-armed Martian.

In his mind, this alien monster worked the graveyard shift on the red planet downloading useless informational updates onto Fad's hard drive. When the Martian's supervisor wasn't watching, this spaced-out outer-space dweeb played violent video games.

The rationale behind Fad's strange belief was that after his first stint in the sack, which he knew had to be four hours long and being unable to sleep, when he peeked out at the clock, he found it was only one a.m. and wondered, "How the hell can that be?"

Raising his ancient left arm and extending his left nail-bitten index finger, he worked carefully but diligently with the wrinkled digit as a broom, and swept away two and one-half pounds of sand from his left eye deposited there by the fairy Sandman.

From past experience and the few clues he left behind, Fad knew the Sandman was a weirdo. The guy's strange M.O. of performing breaking and entering, (B & E's), every night throughout the city while carrying nothing but a gunny sack of sand and a tiny coal scoop told Fad that. Add to that the Sandman's fetish for leaving sand in his victim's eyes instead of hauling off any loot, plus his love of anything gritty and you had a real nut on your hands.

As far as Fad knew, the Sandman was never busted and didn't have a rap sheet. Over the years two sightings were reported, but both came from little old widows with a vivid imagination and a long time in-between being laid, so he thought it was wishful thinking on their part.

Let's face it, if the Sandman possessed the power to cloud men's minds, (and women's), he would choose the homes of young, good-looking and well-built broads. After gaining entry, he would crawl into the beds of his victims, jump their bones and leave them with a smile on their face and a kiss on their eyelids, instead of some crappy sand.

Turning his head toward the clock radio, Fad's sore and bloodshot left eye peeked out through a sand-encrusted slit, latched onto the glowing face of the clock and he said aloud, "Damn, it's only two thirty. The frigging Alien must be working overtime."

Running his hands through his thinning, kinky black hair, he wondered what to do.

Fad wasn't actually the black cop's name. It was a nickname laid on him by one of his fellow officers of the law, and he wished now he never told the asshole the story behind his name. He might as well have sent an e-mail to everyone in the department, because within fifteen minutes Fad's entire shift and some others he didn't know had heard the tale. Ever since, he was known as Fad.

His given name was actually composed of three first names, Frank, Albert and Dean. His unmarried and not-too-bright mother, Ruby Dean gave him the moniker. In one of her movie magazines, she misread an article proclaiming the latest FAD was to use three first names to make up a "trendy" name for a baby and thought this meant the three names must begin with F, A and D. In a drug induced fog, she knew her baby would have a foot up on the competition. Hell, his last name already began with a D.

A child, a seventh-grade graduate and eighth-grade flunkee, at the ripe old age of fifteen years, ten months and three days, Ruby got knocked up. Throughout the ghetto, it was rumored she could read fairly well and actually possessed a three-hundred-word vocabulary, (some of which contained as many as three syllables), and which were also sprinkled with a wide variety of colorful curses. If Ruby had to, she could even scrawl a few misspelled phrases.

Published through a poorly construed interpretation of the First Amendment, Ruby's prestigious reference library consisted of a twelve inch high, equally-divided pile of pure unadulterated trash.

The bottom section contained supermarket scandal sheets with glaring headlines and suggestive photographs; while the middle area was sub-divided into vivid tell all movie magazines and torrid romance novels. The last, but by no means least portion was a well-rounded collection of small black-and-white sex books.

These rare literary treasures depicted comic characters such as Popeye with a well-endowed elongated penis. Since Olive Oyl's rail-thin, stick-figure body could not entertain such a weapon, Popeye chased after other wider-hipped, seductive sirens-of-the-sea and land. These definitely were not the type of books found in your local library.

Believing every bold statement and overblown story in the scarlet tabloids, Ruby copied her favorite star and starlet's bizarre behavior and tacky dress codes to the letter and hoped someday to meet her Prince Charming as the romance book idols did. By the apparent heavy wear and tear to the small comics, it was evident she also studied them diligently.

When Ruby died of an apparent drug overdose three days before her twenty-first birthday, the police canvassed the neighborhood for clues. Nosy neighbors reported she faithfully practiced every sexual act and position contained within her "little books" with a wide variety of partners, but no one was ever connected to her premature death.

If a movie critic panned Ruby's motherhood portrayal, his review would read: "While Ms. Dean shone as a fertile producer, she underachieved in a role where countless others starred and flourished. When the final curtain descended, this critic was left with a sour taste in his mouth and sorrow in my heart for a life wasted, and those left behind."

Fad's aching mind could stand no more reminiscing. Deciding to take one more chance at catching some much-needed Zs and crawling back under the covers, he raised his head skyward and said, "It's time to take a break, my Martian friend."

On Mars, a third-level computer engineer, Allie N. Moon-star focused his fourth eye on the watch wrapped around the wrist of his third arm. It was quitting time, so Allie grasped the "mouse" with the suction cups at the end of the fingers on his second arm, moved the cursor to the "log-off" icon and left-clicked. His computer screen blinked and went dark as Fad finally drifted off to sleep.

CHAPTER 2

(One)
(EIGHT DAYS PREVIOUSLY)
Rushing out the door and down the blacktopped parking lot to his car, Larry Holgram thought, "Damn, I'm late."

Two hours ago, Larry called his wife, Carol to say although he was working late, he wouldn't miss the party, but time got away from him and now he was in trouble for sure.

A few steps from his vehicle, Larry, a Lab Technician, GS-8 pay grade, who was employed by the National Nuclear and Chemical Commission at the old Camp Shaffer Army Base outside Sulfur Springs, Colorado, stopped, slapped his palm against his head and said, "Oh no, I forgot Claire's present."

Since he had no voice box, Larry didn't actually say the words aloud. When he was eight years old, he and a friend, Billy played catch with a piece of pipe. So far they managed to snatch it out of the air with no problem, but then disaster struck.

Billy climbed a flight of stairs, and Larry was in the middle of a shout of joy, when with no warning, Billy turned and threw the pipe at Larry's head. When the pipe struck him in the mouth and ran down his throat like a buzz saw, it tore loose everything in its path.

SIGNS OF OUR TIMES

After several hours of surgery, when Larry woke up in a hospital bed, the doctors told his parents he would never speak again. It was a shock, but Larry was a "gamer," so he thanked God he was alive, learned sign language, never looked back in anger and went on to earn a college degree as a chemical engineer.

Standing five feet, eight inches tall, he weighed in at one hundred and seventy pounds. His body was trim and muscular from exercise and he always wore a smile. Even though he was forced to use a computer or hand-written notes to communicate with his co-workers if they didn't know sign language, he found them easy to work with.

Ten years ago, he met a brown-haired and brown-eyed beauty named Carol, and within six months they were married. A day shy of a year later, their daughter, Claire, was born. She made his heart sing, and tonight was her eighth birthday party. Earlier in the day, Larry bought her a gift of a small computer game she wanted, but in his haste to get away, he forgot it.

Turning back, he hurried to his office located on the fourth floor, two doors away from one of the deadliest places on the face of the earth, the laboratory where they tested nerve gas back in the seventies and eighties when the Cold War ran hot.

Now it was used for a different purpose, to neutralize and burn the same volatile mixture. It was not a job for the squeamish and Larry enjoyed his work.

Although the guard, Grady O'Reilly, knew Larry on sight, he took the time to double check his identity and badge. Security was tight before 9-11, but now it was ratcheted up a notch and Larry didn't mind at all. If there was one place in the world where terrorists couldn't gain entrance, it was here.

After passing muster, Larry logged himself in, hurried to the elevator, rode up to the fourth floor and walked down the hall to his office.

Knowing Claire's gift was located in the bottom left-hand drawer of his desk, he didn't bother to turn on the lights. Walking quickly to his station, he opened the drawer, removed the box and set it on his desktop.

Pushing the drawer closed, he turned to go and heard someone enter the office next door occupied by Felix Mendez. There were at least two men whispering in hushed voices, but Larry heard every word and it caused his voiceless throat to constrict.

(Two)
An unknown voice asked, "How much nerve gas did you siphon off so far?"
"Thirty-two ounces," Felix said. "It took me months, but I couldn't take more than a portion of an ounce at a time or it would be missed."

"How many people can we kill with that much gas?"

"If it's delivered correctly, an ounce will wipe out a town of several thousand," Felix said, "but we're after more. At least two hundred thousand people will be at the Cotton Bowl. With any luck, we'll kill half of the population of Dallas and Fort Worth."

"The main target is the President," the stranger said, and then he asked, "Are you sure he'll be there?"

"His alma mater is the University of Texas and he never misses a game, so what do you think?" Felix asked, and then answered his own question. "He'll be there."

Then Felix asked, "Can you replace the fire extinguishers on schedule? I think changing out thirty-two would take some time."

"It won't be a problem," the unknown person said. "We have three months until the game and one of our men works for the fire department. Let's collect the gas and get out of here before someone comes in."

"Don't worry, no one works at night," Felix said.

"You're sure?"

"They're not supposed to, but you never know about these nuclear nerds. I hope a lot of them go to the game. I won't miss them."

Larry couldn't believe anyone could be planning such a horrible scheme, but he knew he must get away before they found him. Starting for the door, his arm brushed against the gift box and it fell to the floor with a thud.

"What was that?" The stranger asked,

Felix replied, "I don't know, maybe we're not alone."

Opening his office door as quietly as possible, Larry ran out and down the hallway toward the elevators. Behind him he heard footsteps on the hard surface of the floor as Felix and his companion pounded after him.

Luck was with him and when he hit the "down" arrow, the door to the elevator opened immediately and beckoned him in like a warm mountain cabin on a cold winter day. Quickly punching the letter L for lobby, he watched as the doors slid shut and the car dropped three floors.

Running past Grady, Larry was out the door before he could say anything. He thought too late that he should have stopped and told him what happened, but then he wondered how the stranger gained entrance to the building at night.

"Was Grady in on it?"

SIGNS OF OUR TIMES

(Three)

Since his car was too far away and he knew pursuit would be swift, Larry turned right and ran toward the next building, which housed the research and experimental laboratories of SCOU.

Hurriedly punching in the entry code, he slipped inside. As the door closed behind him, he caught a glimpse of two men running out of the chemical laboratory. Praying silently that they hadn't seen him, he moved down the hallway to the first doorway, which opened into a large room filled with cages of all sizes and shapes.

Running to the first aisle, he ducked down to hide behind a large enclosure. To his surprise, when he looked up, the occupant of the cage said "Hello" in sign language. Although he thought he was seeing things, Larry automatically returned the greeting.

When the chimp signed, "My name is Wilbur. What's yours?" Larry was so amazed he didn't answer immediately, so Wilbur asked again.

Then like a magician turning a card, a plan took shape in Larry's mind. As he passed along the information about the terrorists to his new friend, his fingers and hands flew like sparrows after a handful of corn.

Wilbur sat, watched, "listened" and shook his head, either in fear, disbelief or as a natural habit.

Wondering if Wilbur truly understood the message or what he meant by his gestures, Larry thought, "All you have to do is remember and repeat it to someone."

Then from out of a corner of the cage, a female chimp appeared by Wilbur's side, grinned widely and repeated Larry's message. When she finished, she signed, "My name is Sadie."

Signing as fast as he could, Larry told her, "You're very smart, Sadie. Can you remember what I told you?"

Wilbur and Sadie replied positively in unison.

Then Larry remembered the fire extinguishers and attempted to pass on that information too. But before he could finish, the door to the room opened, and Felix and a swarthy man entered and saw him.

Jumping up from his hiding place, Larry ran, but it was no use. Felix tackled him by the legs and they fell to the floor.

Pulling him to a sitting position, Felix cocked his fist back as if he wanted to take his head off and asked, "What did you hear?"

When Larry didn't answer, the stranger moved quickly to Felix's side and slapped Larry across the face with the back of his hand, knocking him backward.

As he pulled Larry to a sitting position again, Felix suddenly recognized him and said, "Wait a minute Mohammed. This is the dummy from the office next to mine. He can't talk."

"Using my name wasn't smart. Can he hear?"

"Yeah and I bet he heard everything."

"That's too bad," Mohammed said, and shot Larry in the head behind his left ear.

For an instant while there was still life in his body, Larry's eyes seemed to smile, but Mohammed didn't notice.

The sound of the shot booming off the walls startled the chimps and monkeys and they screamed in fear. After grabbing nearby vines, Wilbur and Sadie swung high into a concrete tree to hide. Their screams joined those of the other animals and it sounded like a zoo gone wild.

Shouting over the noise, Felix asked, "Damn, Mohammed, why'd you do that?"

"He can't hear or talk now, can he? Quick, wrap his coat around his head to soak up the blood. Grab his legs and we'll haul him out the back door, dump his body in the lake and it'll be days before they find it."

Shaken at the sudden turn of events, Felix did as he was told. As they carried the lifeless form of Larry from the building, they left behind a small pool of blood and a trail of drops leading from the side of the cage to the rear door.

(Four)

When Larry didn't arrive on time for Claire's birthday party, Carol shook her head in disgust, reached for the phone and thought, "Dedication to his job is one thing, but this is inexcusable."

When Larry didn't answer and the phone rang and rang, Carol grew worried. By ten p.m. she was frantic, but when she called the local hospital there was no report of an accident involving his car.

Finally at midnight, she called the police and filed a missing person report. The officer who took her call, Sergeant Bert Collins was pleasant, but from the tone of his voice, Carol knew he thought she was worried over nothing.

Replying to Bert's latest question, she said, "No, Larry doesn't drink. And before you ask; no we didn't have a fight. It's our daughter's birthday and Larry dotes on her. There's no way he'd miss Claire's party unless something happened to him."

Trying to reassure her, Bert said, "We'll do our best to find him, but there isn't much more we can do than you've already done. I'll call around and see if anyone in the adjacent towns has any information and get back to you."

As Carol's eyes misted over, she said, "Larry can't talk. He can only communicate by sign language. If he's hurt, no one can hear him."

"I'll pass the information along to the patrolmen in the squad cars."

"Thank you," Carol said, hung up, broke down and cried.

After completing the missing person form, Bert sent it up the line to the detective in charge of those types of reports. Then he made the calls he promised, but discovered nothing to help. When he phoned Carol to inform her of no progress, he could tell she'd been crying.

CHAPTER 3

(One)

When she was younger, Katie Adkins was an introvert, very shy and unsure of herself around others. At five feet, four inches tall and chunky for her size, she was cute in a wholesome way, but not as beautiful as most women in the magazines she read.

Her coal-black hair was long and shiny and her matching eyes were set into a face that reminded viewers of Pocahontas. She had a small waistline, but not as tiny as she would have liked.

"Too many tacos at lunchtime," she thought and promised God she'd give them up soon.

Although she knew her limitations, still life frightened her most days, at least until she entered college and found there was existence beyond the small town of Shiprock, New Mexico.

During her high school days, she earned good grades, did her best to get ahead and saw her hard work pay off, when she became the first full-blooded Navajo to be awarded a complete four year scholarship to SCOU.

And then as a bonus, there was Wilbur and Sadie, who made school fun as well as educational.

SIGNS OF OUR TIMES

(Two)

Since her grandmother was deaf, Katie learned sign language at an early age. When she saw the advertisement in the school bulletin for volunteers to teach chimpanzees to sign, she couldn't believe it.

She was majoring in social science, hoping to work with animals to better their lives and those of humans. Now there was a chance her wish could come true.

After an interview the next day, she was hired and discovered the school would actually pay her to teach the chimps. At the same time she'd get to work in the research laboratory of her dreams.

That's when she first met Wilbur and Sadie and it was instant attraction for them all. She loved working with them, so she spent nearly every free minute at the lab, teaching and learning at the same time.

The only downer was being so close to the nerve gas laboratory next door. When she thought of what a few drops of that toxic potion could do to a town like Sulfur Springs, it was enough to make her skin crawl.

According to the scientists, because of the safety features they'd installed, there was no chance of the gas escaping. Still, the thought of an accident that could kill everyone in a few seconds frightened her, and every night she prayed that nothing would ever happen. But there were times when the threat caused bad dreams.

CHAPTER 4

(One)

Ramon Sanchez was a conscientious worker, who loved his job as a janitor at the research laboratory on the outskirts of Sulfur Springs. The old Army base sat out in the wilds below some medium-sized mountains and was almost deserted now, but Ramon thought the place was beautiful.

Lines of large oak trees marching down the main drive and flowers running wild where once thousands of troops drilled and paraded always put pride in his step.

Smiling to himself as he walked up the stairs to the lab, Ramon opened a side door with his own personal key. Although he knew the access code for the front door, he felt having a key to this entrance and being trusted with so much responsibility made him someone special.

It was a habit of his to always arrive several minutes before everyone else, make sure the coffee was perking and empty the trash can in the break room. Usually he had a cup of coffee and a doughnut, and then, even though he swept it before he left last night, he'd sweep the floor outside the monkey cage again. Sometimes the chimps got frisky and scattered fruit peelings everywhere.

SIGNS OF OUR TIMES

Thin as a rail from the time of his youth, Ramon had a dark face with black eyes and wore the mandatory moustache favored by most "macho" men of his race. As a naturalized U. S. citizen, he fought in Vietnam and was proud of his service.

He walked with a slight limp due to a piece of shrapnel he took in his calf during one unforgettable battle. Now, after seeing his share of blood and guts, he never wanted to leave the United States again.

During his tenure with the lab, Ramon had taken a special liking to the two chimps they were teaching to sign. Sadie was lovable and cute in her own way, with a grin as wide as the Bay Narrows Bridge. She had a full set of teeth that glistened when she smiled.

On the other hand, Wilbur was contrary, mean as hell at times and had a wicked set of molars that could chew chrome off a bumper hitch. He always wanted to be the leader, but Sadie stood up to him and made him behave, which was more than Ramon could do, but they got along well.

Today for some reason, his two favorite chimps were preoccupied or frightened. They paid no attention as he walked by and said, "Good morning, you two."

When he accidentally dropped his broom and the handle hit the floor with a sound like a shot, they screamed and ran to the back of their cage, where they huddled together with their arms wrapped around each other.

Feeling something was wrong, he asked, "What's with you guys?"

But they both ignored him, so he said, "Okay, if that's the way you want it, I'll leave you alone."

As he moved behind the cage to sweep, Ramon wasn't paying attention to where he stepped and almost fell to his knees when his foot slipped on something slick. Looking down, he saw a small pool of reddish-brown liquid and spots of the same fluid leading toward the back door.

After serving as a medic in Vietnam, he knew the sight of dried blood when he saw it, but this puzzled him and he wondered, "It looks like blood, but where'd it come from. I hope none of the chimps hurt themselves, but if one did, how would the blood get all the way out here."

This was a mystery, but Ramon was thorough in his work and knew this was something out of the ordinary, to be reported to the person in charge. Leaving the liquid where it was, he stepped around it, walked to the office of Doctor Wilson and knocked softly on her door.

Looking up and smiling, Doctor Mona Wilson asked, "Yes, Ramon, what is it?"

Mona Wilson was one sharp-looking lady with a set of knockers a lot of women would die for. She had a pair of deep blue eyes, luxuriously-coiffured blonde hair, long shapely legs that ran all the way up to the delicious cleft between her hips and a marvelously-curved body. No wonder half the male staff was in love with Mona or lusted after her in their dreams.

"I found something at the back of Wilbur and Sadie's cage that looks like blood. They acted funny this morning. I hope they haven't hurt themselves."

As she stood up and walked around her desk, Mona said, "That is strange. Please show me what you found."

After leading her around the cage, without saying anything, Ramon pointed at the stain and spots.

Bending over and looking where he indicated, she said, "I see what you mean, it does look like blood. Let me get some swabs and take some samples."

After hurrying to the rear of the laboratory, Mona returned a few minutes later with her assistant, Jerry Grimes, in tow. He was carrying several glass beakers in a small chromed rack and looked inquisitively at Ramon, but didn't say anything.

Donning a pair of rubber gloves, Mona held a fistful of long, thin wooden swabs in her left hand. Kneeling down and leaning over as she ran six of them through the fluid one at a time and placed them in individual beakers, she treated both of the men to a fascinating view of more cleavage than they could handle.

Seeming oblivious to the fact, she looked up at Jerry and said, "Run a blood test on two of them and see if it's animal or human."

After putting his tongue back in his mouth, he said, "Yes, ma'am."

Looking back at the spots, Mona said, "Refrigerate the others in case we have to report this to the police. They may want samples."

"Yes, ma'am," he repeated.

Then Mona ordered, "Ramon, get some tape from the storage area and make a barrier so no one walks back here. No matter how inquisitive they may be, keep everyone away. I don't like the looks of this."

Turning toward Sadie and Wilbur's cage and signing the same message, she called, "Come here you two."

Sadie ran to where Mona was and reached through the bars to hold her hand, but Wilbur remained aloof, so Mona signed, "Stubborn to the end, aren't you?"

Turning his back on the proceedings and ignoring her, Wilbur climbed slowly up and into a nearby tree.

As Jerry walked off, he said, "That's not like Wilbur. Something must have upset him."

"Sadie seems nervous too," Mona said. "I can feel her pulse and it's higher than normal. I wonder what went on here last night. Neither of them appears to be hurt or bleeding. Let me know your findings as soon as possible, Jerry."

Turning to Ramon, she patted his back and said, "Good job, Ramon."

His face flushed with pride, or did he blush because of her touch?

(Two)

An operator answered the phone and asked, "Sulfur Springs Police, how may I help you?"

"This is Doctor Wilson at the University Research Laboratory on the Army Base. I want to report something suspicious that happened in our department last night. Is there a detective I might talk to?"

"Hold on, ma'am and I'll connect you with the detective bureau."

While she transferred the call, Mona listened to Neil Diamond sing part of his hit, "Coming to America" and hummed along with the tune.

Thirty seconds later, Joe took the call and said, "This is Sergeant Francone. How may I help you?"

After identifying herself, Mona said, "The janitor in our building found a small pool of blood on the laboratory floor and a trail of drops leading to the back door. I took samples and determined it's human.

"No one here injured himself, so it's a mystery as to where the blood came from. In case something happened during our off duty hours, I thought I should call the police."

Joe liked this dame's voice and pictured her as something special as he asked, "Are you sure there isn't some other explanation?"

"No, we're sure the blood didn't come from any of the employees."

Continuing to build an imaginary picture of her in his mind from her sexy voice, Joe asked, "How long was the laboratory unoccupied?"

"The last person left at six p.m. yesterday. The janitor, Ramon Sanchez, was the first to arrive at six a.m. this morning, so the building was empty for twelve hours."

"Don't let anyone touch the evidence and keep everyone away from the scene," Joe said. "I'll come right out and take a look. Give me a few minutes to locate a forensic scientist."

"I had Ramon tape off the area and guard it," Mona said.

"Good work. Let me have your address again."

"It's seven fourteen General Sherman Drive, out on the old Army base, right next to the chemical research laboratory."

Joe knew the place well. The thought of the nerve gas often gave him nervous gas, so he said, "Oh, yeah, I know the place; it's where they burn the nerve gas."

The nearness of the chemical lab also caused Mona anxiety, and she said, "Yes, I'm sorry to say."

"Thank you Doctor Wilson, I'll see you in a few minutes."

After he hung up, he stared at the phone and wondered, "Is Doctor Wilson as sexy as her voice?"

(Three)

When Joe walked into Captain Hugo "Red" Hopper's office without knocking, Red was seated at his desk with his feet resting on an open drawer, reading a report. He wore a nicely cut two-piece blue suit with a snow-white crisply starched shirt, but his collar was open and a paisley tie pulled down. His plain face, which was highlighted by a large nose, seemed to be permanently blushed a dark scarlet color, hence the nickname Red.

Looking up, he asked, "What's up, Joe?"

"I got a call from the research lab out at the old Army base. A doctor claims there's blood on the floor they can't explain and wants someone to come out to take a look. I called Bill Favor in the forensic lab and he's going with me.

"The facility is next door to the lab where they burn the nerve gas. I don't think it'll amount to much, but as sensitive as the place is, we'd better check it out."

Red put his report down on the desk and said, "Yeah, you're right. Keep me advised. Let's hope someone cut themselves shaving and didn't report it."

Laughing, Joe said, "It sounds like more blood than that, Red. The doctor said there's a trail of drops all the way to the rear door. If someone got whacked, they chose a hell of a place for it."

Red nodded and said, "Do a good job."

(Four)

Bert spent the morning talking to Carol Holgram at her home. Larry still hadn't been found or heard from, and Bert felt something bad happened to the young husband. Carol reiterated Larry was a devoted father and no way would he have missed Claire's birthday party.

Through her tears, she told him Larry phoned yesterday at four p.m. to say he was working until six, but assured her he would be on time for the party at seven.

Although he was having doubts, Bert said, "I'm sure he'll call soon."

"Could you check his office?" Carol asked, giving him the address.

Hoping his co-workers might shed some light on Larry's disappearance, he said, "Sure."

When Bert pulled into a parking space outside the chemical lab, he was surprised to see Joe Francone's cruiser parked three spaces away and wondered, "What's Joe doing out here?"

He flashed his badge at the rent-a-cop on duty, but it didn't get him past the security post.

The guard, Fred Wilkins by his nametag, held up his hand and asked for Bert's I. D. After taking his badge and identification and checking them carefully, Fred asked, "What can we do for you Sergeant Collins?"

"I got a report of a missing person, one of your employees, Larry Holgram. I'd like to talk to his co-workers to see if they know where he is."

Pointing toward three green, scraped and stained, steel and plastic chairs that looked like they'd been there for a decade and hated every minute, Fred said, "Have a seat over there and I'll call Mister Holgram's supervisor."

"Thanks," Bert said, but didn't mean it.

He tried two of the offered seats and both had uneven legs and wobbled like a shopping cart with one wheel off the ground. The third was almost level, with the back worn and bent, but it looked as if it was the best he'd find, so Bert sat on the edge and leaned his arms on his legs.

Knowing he looked like a tardy schoolchild waiting to explain why to the principal, Bert thought, "Millions of dollars for nerve gas and not a few spare bucks for some decent chairs. That's our government and my tax dollars at work."

(Five)

Next door to where Bert sat on an uncomfortable chair, Joe leaned back in a nice, soft cushioned recliner, as he drank a cup of coffee in Mona's office. Her workplace was spacious with windows on two sides and outfitted with modernistic furnishings. The main attraction was an outstanding view of the surrounding mountains and forested slopes, where snow-capped peaks beckoned skiers to come and try their luck.

Tipping his cup to Mona, he said, "You were right about the blood; it's human."

She nodded and asked, "What do you think happened?"

"I don't have a clue. How many people have access to this building?"

"Probably a hundred or more," Mona said. "There are twenty-three people on staff and fifty volunteers from the college working with the chimps, monkeys and other animals. Our front door is controlled by a four-digit access code, but I'm sure it's common knowledge among the students. Many of them come to watch our training sessions."

After taking another sip of coffee, Joe said, "Well that narrows it down to less than the number of citizens in Sulfur Springs."

He liked the way Mona's hair hung down over one eye. As she brushed back her mane, her bright red fingernails glistened in the overhead light.

Red was Joe's favorite color, but he stopped checking out her body and said, "I need a list of your staff, volunteers and anyone else who might have the combination. Right now all we have is a lot of blood, but no body or indication there was foul play. But if things turn ugly, I'll have to talk to them."

Flashing him a dazzling smile, she said, "My assistant, Jerry Grimes, will get the information for you."

He was trying to pay attention, but at the same time, Joe was busy thinking how her teeth were perfect and shone like ivory. Then the tip of her tongue slipped through them and she licked her upper lip in a sexy way that made him have a daydream of jumping her bones.

As if she could read his thoughts, her eyes twinkled and he thought, "I'd give up doughnuts for a year to spend an hour in the sack with her."

Returning to business at hand, he said, "Then I'll let you get back to work and go see what Bill has come up with."

They shook hands and he thought she held his a moment too long. As they parted, her long nails trailed across his sweaty palm and her smile seemed wicked, but then it changed to the same one he earlier saw her give Bill, and he thought, "Maybe I'm reading this broad wrong, but I hope not."

Walking back through the lab, he discovered Bill squatted on the floor, taking pictures of the various blood spots and splatters. Little numbered plastic triangles sat beside each, and without looking up, Bill asked, "Can you smell the cordite?"

Joe sniffed the air and inhaled fumes telling him a gun was fired here sometime within the past twenty-four hours. He and Bill were blessed with big beaks and took a lot of ribbing from other cops, but they could smell gunshot residue when others couldn't, and ninety-nine times out of a hundred they were right.

"Yeah, I can. Last night someone got shot here."

Pointing toward a man in his mid-forties with brown, shoulder-length hair, who was wearing a white lab coat over tan slacks and a light-green polo shirt, Bill said, "The assistant over there, Jerry Grimes, told me the animals were all shook up this morning. I don't doubt it. If you fired a gun in here the noise would make anyone go bananas."

Chuckling at the pun, Joe looked around the room, noted two chimps in the cage closest to the scene and asked, "Is there anything special about these chimps, Jerry?"

Walking over to where they were, Jerry said, "Only the fact they're being taught to sign."

"Sign?" Joe asked. "You mean like deaf and dumb people?"

Sounding like a nerdy professor, Jerry said, "People aren't deaf and dumb, Sergeant. They're handicapped and we try to help them. We think the chimps will aid us by teaching children how to communicate by sign language. The kids have fun as they 'talk' to the chimps and learn at the same time."

"Okay, I stand corrected. It's a cute idea. No wonder the students volunteer."

"Here's one of them now. Sergeant Francone, meet Katie Adkins."

Joe saw a young student in a light-green dress standing next to Jerry. Her plain face was dark, but she wasn't black. Her hair was thick and long and he thought, "More like an Indian."

Sticking out her hand, she said, "Pleased to meet you."

As they shook hands, Joe said, "Likewise."

"What's going on, Jerry?" she asked.

"Ramon found some blood on the floor we can't explain. It's nothing to worry about, Katie. Go ahead and work with your two chimp friends. They're upset this morning and we need you to calm them down."

"Maybe they saw something they can tell you about," Joe said.

Jerry shook his head and said, "I doubt it, but you might ask, Katie."

"I'll see what I can do. It was nice to meet you Sergeant."

"Likewise," Joe repeated, and then he asked, "You all done here, Bill?"

"Yeah, I'll type the blood back at the lab and do a DNA to see if we can match it up to anyone reported missing."

Nodding to Ramon who was standing by the edge of the chimps' cage and listening, but who so far hadn't said a thing, Joe said, "If you want to, you can clean up this mess now."

Pushing his bucket from under the rail near the cage without speaking,

Ramon wrung out a mop with his hands. Joe saw him shake his head as if he was disgusted and for some reason, he knew it wasn't the first time Ramon cleaned up blood. Unknowingly, at the same time they both hoped it would be the last.

(Six)
So far Bert had got nowhere fast in his investigation, but at least now he was seated in a more comfortable chair in the office of the director, Hershel Witte, who asked, "Would you like a cup of coffee?"

Wearing a three-piece blue suit, with wire-rimmed glasses covering his brown eyes, Hershel was a half-bald bookish type, small-framed and short, probably not over five foot five inches. His fingers were small and as he spoke, he had a nervous habit of clicking his pen.

Bert smiled and said, "No, I'm fine. Are you Larry Holgram's supervisor?"

"Yes, I am." Click. "I was surprised when he didn't show up this morning." Click. "Larry has been a pillar. He always arrives for work on time and when it was necessary, stayed late. It's not like him to not call in." Click, click.

Tuning out the sound of the pen, Bert asked, "In the past years how many times has Larry been late?"

"Only twice, and those were due to weather or an accident on the highway. Both times Larry used his cell phone to call."

"I thought you said Larry couldn't talk. How'd he call in?"

Pointing to his cell phone on the desk, Hershel said, "He text-messaged me. It's how he carried on most of his conversations, that and instant messaging on the computer. Only a few of us here know sign language, but one way or another, Larry always got his message across."

"Was there any hanky-panky with a co-worker?"

"Larry?" Hershel asked. Then he said, "Hardly, he's a devoted family man. All he talks about is his wife and daughter."

"Is there any other reason he would just up and vanish?"

"None I can think of," Hershel said. "Would you like to see his office?"

"Yeah," Bert said.

They walked down the hallway, and Hershel pulled out a set of keys to open the door to Larry's office. He tried the knob and said, "Why it's open."

Pushing past him, Bert said, "Let me go in first."

A gaily-wrapped package meant for Claire sat on the floor three feet from the desk. A lump as big as Garfield's hairball came into Bert's throat and his eyes watered for a moment.

Pointing toward the package, he said, "We better let the experts look at this. It seems Larry left in a hurry. There's no way he would leave the present for Claire behind."

Nodding, Hershel said, "It is strange."

After taking a fast look around and not seeing anything else out of the ordinary, Bert said, "Lock the door and keep everyone out until the crime scene unit arrives."

"Yes, sir," Hershel said.

"Who has the offices on both sides of this one?" Bert asked.

"Felix Mendez has the one to the left, and Harold Stockman is on the right."

"I need to talk to both of them. Can you ask them to report to your office separately, so I can question them?"

"Yes, sir," Hershel repeated.

"After-hours, how does someone get into the facility?"

"They're checked in by the guard," Hershel said. "An access code is required and each entry is logged."

"I want to see the log and the guard who was on duty last night," Bert said.

"Grady's off now, but I'll telephone and tell him to come in."

"Is Grady the name of the guard?"

Hershel nodded and said, "Yes, Grady O'Reilly. He's an Irishman all the way down to his green socks."

After writing Grady's name in his notebook, Bert said, "Have him stop by our office this afternoon before he goes to work and ask for me. That way he'll be fresh and perhaps he can remember something to help us."

(Seven)

Talks with Felix and Harold produced nothing to aid Bert in the investigation. According to their statements, neither worked late last night and after leaving the building they hadn't seen Larry again. The log book authenticated their stories, as it indicated Larry was the only person logged in after working hours, just a few minutes after he left for the day.

Bert thought, "Larry must have forgotten something—the present. But what happened in those few minutes?"

Turning to Hershel, he asked, "Doesn't everyone have to log out when they leave?"

"Yes, they're supposed to. Why do you ask?"

"I don't see any notation on the log to indicate Larry checked out," Bert said. "According to you, it's not like him."

"No, it isn't. I'll ask Grady about it."

"When I see him this afternoon, I'll ask Grady myself. Thanks for your help, Hershel. The crime scene team will be here shortly. When I find anything, I'll let you know. I hope Larry shows up alive and well, but it doesn't look good."

"I hope so too. Carol must be terrified."

"She's hanging in there," Bert said, "but she is worried."

CHAPTER 5

(One)

Bert stood beside his car in the parking lot, in a brisk wind, waiting to see why Joe was on the Army base. While he was inside, the wind direction changed and now blew cold out of the north. Overhead, thin clouds sailed by on their way to a warmer clime.

His hands grew numb and he was about to climb into his squad car to turn on the engine and heater, when Joe walked out the door of the research lab. He waved and said, "Hey, Joe, I thought that was your vehicle. What's up?"

Jerking his thumb over his shoulder to indicate the laboratory, Joe said, "Nothing much. They found some human blood on the floor inside and no one seems to know why or how it got there. Why are you out here?"

"It's a strange coincidence. I got a missing person next door in the nuke lab. His name's Larry Holgram. It didn't come up in your investigation, did it?"

Joe checked his notes and said, "No, no one mentioned Mister Holgram's name. How long has he been gone?"

Looking through his own notes, Bert said, "Last night Larry was a no-show for his daughter's birthday party and his wife called it in. I checked his office and there's a package on the floor, probably a gift for the little girl. It appears Larry left in a hurry, his door was unlocked and he didn't log out."

"Maybe our cases are connected, Bert. You think the wife would go along with a blood sample of the daughter so we could do a DNA match?"

"At this point in time, I think Carol would do anything to help us locate Larry. I'll call and ask."

"Thanks, Bert. I'll see you back at the office."

(Two)

When Katie signed, "Good morning," to her two friends, only Sadie replied. Frowning instead of displaying his usual toothy grin, Wilbur stayed high in his fake tree.

Waving to make sure he saw her, Katie signed, "Feeling moody today?"

When she received no reply from him, she signed to Sadie, "Well Sadie, it looks like we'll be working by ourselves. Did anything happen last night?"

Without warning, Wilbur swung down from his perch and landed in front of Katie. As his hands flew, she made out, "Bad men, loud noise, frightened."

Surprised, she asked, "What bad men?"

"Two," He replied. Then he held his hands over his ears and spun around in a circle, with his head tilted back and teeth tight together, chattering to the roof in chimp language.

As Katie thought, "Something has really upset him," Sadie tugged at her sleeve. Looking down, she watched Sadie's fingers move almost too fast to follow, but she caught the word terror and gas along with bad man. Then Sadie made a motion like a gun with her fist and signed "loud bang".

She thought, "Sadie and Wilbur may have seen someone shot last night. Either that or someone made a loud noise to frighten them. Jerry said there was blood on the floor and I don't like the sound of it."

Shaking her head in disbelief, but wanting to know more, Katie signed, "Calm down. Speak slower and tell me what you saw."

As she read their signs incredulously, Sadie began her story and Wilbur mimicked her.

(Three)

On a crisp, clear autumn day, Sally Wright sat on her usual bench, enjoying a beautiful morning. Although the sun tried to shine through a thin, wispy layer of clouds, the weather was cool, but Sally didn't care. She was used to the cold and couldn't wait for the first snow of the year.

Another thing she loved was her ducks. Well, they weren't really her ducks. They were wild and didn't belong to anyone, but Sally enjoyed watching them on the lake behind her house.

"When they're feeding, all you see is duck butts," she told her husband, Sam, who laughed appreciatively.

Every morning when the ducks were migrating, Sally walked down to the edge of the lake, sat on her bench, threw corn to the birds and talked to them as they fed. It helped to calm her inner spirit and she felt as one with nature, especially on a cool autumn day when the sun was rising in the east, promising good things for the remainder of the day.

But today something was wrong. Her friends weren't in near the shore where they usually waited. The ducks were farther out, swimming in circles and chatting among themselves like magpies.

They seemed excited about something, and when Sally threw a few kernels of corn into the water, the birds didn't come close to feed. It was puzzling and she couldn't understand their behavior, but she thought, "Since they won't come to me, I'll move closer."

Standing up and walking to the edge of the high bank, she glanced down and saw something large and brown bobbing in the water. At first thinking it was a roll of carpeting someone discarded in the lake, she silently cursed the litterbugs of her generation. But then she saw it was a man's coat.

As she watched in horror, with the action of the small waves, a body rolled over, and the wrinkled white face of a man with dead, dark-black irises stared up at her. Screaming in fear, Sally dropped her bag of corn and ran toward home to call the police.

The noise frightened her ducks. Rising majestically from the water in a huge raft, they flew in ragged formation to a spot farther down the lake and settled uneasily to the surface. From that day forward, they would never return to the spot near Sally's favorite bench.

(Four)
By lunch time, Katie was worn out from the long morning session with Sadie and Wilbur, but felt she must share their story with someone. It had taken more than three hours of continually asking her friends to repeat the message before she had it all and it was too much for her to handle alone. She needed help to determine which law enforcement agency to contact.

Across the room, Katie saw Mona's assistant, Jerry Grimes, and thought, "He'll know what to do."

Rushing over to him, she said, "Jerry, you'll never believe what Sadie and Wilbur told me."

As if he really wasn't interested, Jerry asked, "What did your two primates have to say this morning?"

Referring to her notes, she said, "They said last night a man was shot here by two bad men, who plan a terrorist attack on the United States."

Jerry laughed and said, "Whoa, a terrorist attack predicted by two chimps. That'll make the six o'clock news for sure. Where did they dream up that scenario or have you been reading science fiction to them?"

It wasn't the reaction Katie expected to her news and she said, "No, they're sure. Why don't you talk to them?"

"Not me. Can you believe the bad publicity such a crazy story like this would bring to the lab? The government would probably cancel all of our grants for the next ten years. You can't be serious."

"Jerry, they don't have any reason to make up a story. Can't you at least talk to Sadie and Wilbur and hear what they have to say?"

"I told you, it's something they concocted or heard on TV. We let the chimps watch way too much garbage on the boob tube."

Persisting, Katie said, "I believe them."

"Well you can keep your thoughts to yourself. You're just a part-time volunteer, but the rest of us depend on this place for our livelihood. Don't make a big stink or you'll be sorry. Hell, Katie, Sadie and Wilbur are just chimps."

Even though she thought, "They're probably one hundred percent smarter than you are, Jerry Grimes," she kept her temper, acted as if he put her down and said, "Okay, Jerry, if that's the way you want it."

As he walked away, Jerry said, "Now you're making sense."

Knowing there was no way she could let this go, she thought, "There must be some way to get the story out to someone who will believe it, or even if they didn't, would investigate to see if it was true."

"But who," she wondered and the answer struck her—"the FBI." Her mind raced, and as she made plans, she forgot about lunch.

(Five)

Felix was worried because he didn't think Larry's disappearance would be noticed so soon. When Bert questioned him this morning, he knew he gave all the right answers. Grady made sure the log didn't reflect his entry into the lab, so if the authorities checked, Grady's actions would back up his story.

When he woke Grady up to tell him about the cop, Grady told him the director called earlier and told him to report to Sergeant Collins this afternoon.

"That wasn't very smart of you," Felix said, "Letting us in without telling us Larry was upstairs."

Grady didn't sound truly apologetic as he said, "I forgot all about him. I'm sorry."

Deciding to ream his ass, Felix said, "Sorry won't cut it, Grady. Get your act together and your story straight. No one came into the lab except Larry, and before you could stop him, he ran out. No, you don't know what frightened him or even if he was scared. Maybe he was in a hurry to get home for his daughter's birthday party. When Larry came back in, he told you about it. You got it?"

Still the braggart, Grady said, "Don't worry, I can handle the cops. The one you should be concerned about is Mohammed. He's too fast on the trigger for me. Why'd he have to kill Larry in the lab? You could have taken him someplace where they wouldn't have found any blood."

Backing down a little, Felix said, "I agree, Mohammed is too high strung, but he's instrumental in getting the job done. In the future, I'll try to keep him under control."

"You better. All we need now are cops nosing around."

"Tell your story the way we discussed," Felix said.

"I told you, I can handle this guy. Stop sweating it and go back to work."

(Six)

The cooler weather forced the brown-bag brigade inside, so when Felix walked in at noon, the cafeteria was packed with workers and he was lucky to find a seat near three employees from the research lab next door. Although he usually hated to listen to their "nerdy" talk, today he was astounded when he heard Jerry tell his two companions, "You wouldn't believe what Katie came up with this morning."

"What?" One of them asked.

"She says her chimps saw someone killed last night. They were two bad men, who are terrorists and plan an attack on the USA."

"Where does Katie get this stuff?"

With a smirk on his face, Jerry said, "A vivid imagination, I guess. I told her they watch too much CNN."

The older man shook his head slightly and said, "Maybe next we'll be invaded by Martians."

Continuing to smile, relishing every moment of putting her down, Jerry said, "Katie says the chimps know all about this terrorist attack and she wanted me to call the FBI. Can you imagine what the government would do if we reported this lunacy? I can see our grants going down the drain and all of us being laid off."

With a small chuckle, the younger one said, "Maybe that's what Katie needs."

"What?" Jerry asked.

"To get laid more often," he said and laughed.

Felix was amazed at his luck and choice of seats. The gods of fate smiled on him today as he thought, "Amazing, the dummy in the next office had enough smarts to pass on his story to two chimps. But I doubt if anyone will believe this woman, Katie, whoever she is. To be sure, I'll have to find and eliminate her and the two chimps.

"But how can I accomplish it? We can't have any more killing tied to the nerve gas or they'll get suspicious. It has to look like an accident. I'll contact Mohammed and he'll come up with something."

CHAPTER 6

(One)

At Joe's request and with Bert's blessing, Fad handled the interview with Grady O'Reilly.

"If he's connected with this in any way, it'll tick him off to have a black man ask him questions," Joe said. "Lately there are too many of these Irish guys ranting and raving about the IRA. I don't like it."

Nodding in agreement, Fad said, "Okay, if you say so. I'll ask Grady a bunch of personal questions about his sex life. It always makes their hot Irish blood boil."

"That's the idea," Joe said.

(Two)

Sauntering into the room, as if he was some cool cat from a rap group, looking for a new song to sing about the injustice of the system, Fad said, "Good afternoon, Mister O'Reilly."

Looking up from studying his fingernails, Grady said, "Hi. Are you Sergeant Collins?"

"No, Bert's been unavoidably detained."

Pulling out a chair, Fad put his left foot on the seat, bent over and looked Grady in the eye. His opponent was about six feet tall with muscular arms and from the looks of things, Grady had more in his head. Although Fad knew Grady worked indoors, his face was darkly tanned.

Continuing to stare at him, Fad said, "I understand you were on duty last night out at the chemical lab. Is that correct?"

"Yeah, I worked last night."

"Do you happen to remember Mister Holgram?"

"Yeah, he was the guy who left and then came back because he forgot his kid's birthday present."

"Did he seem depressed or unhappy?" Fad asked.

Grady picked at a scab on his wrist and said, "No, he was in a hurry to get home. I guess it's why he ran out of the elevator and forgot to log out. If he was late for the party, his old lady would give him hell."

"There wasn't anyone chasing Mister Holgram?"

Grady's brown eyes blinked and Fad noticed it. It was the sign of a lie about to be told.

"No, Mister Holgram was the only one in the building at the time. No one else came in while I was on duty. It was a long, boring night."

Changing his tone of voice, Fad asked, "Do you know anything else about Mister Holgram? Did he run around on his wife with some chick out at the plant?"

Shaking his long brown locks, Grady said, "No, he was straight arrow. I don't think he even noticed any of the good-looking women out there. Some of the young student chicks are always trying to get it on with the staff—you know, trade a little pussy for a higher grade."

"You ever hook up with any of them?" Fad asked.

"No, why should I? I've got a good woman at home."

Staring him down, Fad asked, "You take any drugs, do a little coke, smoke some pot or drink in excess?"

"No, I don't, and you're beginning to piss me off."

With an insincere smile and displaying an even set of sparkling white teeth through his full, dark lips, Fad said, "Gee, I'm sorry."

"Yeah, I'll bet you are."

"You're a tough guy, 'eh?" Fad asked.

"I'm tough enough."

"You got any connections with the Irish Republican Army?"

"No," Grady said, "I don't."

"Are you sure? We can check it out through Interpol."

"I told you no. How many times are you gonna ask?"

"As many as it takes to get a straight answer," Fad said. "I think you're hiding something, Grady. What is it? You play around with college boys? You look the type."

Standing up, his fist cocked and ready to fight, Grady said, "You son of a bitch."

The next thing he knew, Grady was on his back with Fad straddling his stomach and one of his elbows pushed down on Grady's throat until he could barely breathe.

Smiling, Fad said, "I take offense at your portrayal of my mother as a bitch."

Continuing to smile wickedly as if he was enjoying his work, he said, "Try it again and I'll kick your ass all over this room."

Through a constricted windpipe, Grady choked out, "Get off me."

"In due time. Now, where were we? Oh yeah, you were about to answer my question about whether you played around with young school boys. What about it?"

"I'm straight," Grady said. He coughed and spittle flew from his lips. "Let me up."

"You promise to be a good little boy?"

His eyes blazing with raw hatred, Grady said, "Yeah, get off me."

Jumping up, Fad stood back and watched as Grady slowly pulled himself up off the floor and back onto the chair. He could tell the Irishman was steamed, but he also knew he had the upper hand, and said, "So you aren't gay, don't do drugs or chase the teeny-boppers out at the University. What do you do for fun, play with yourself?"

Staring up at Fad with loathing in his eyes, Grady didn't reply, so Fad said, "Tell me again about last night."

"I told you. Mister Holgram left, came back a couple of minutes later and said he forgot a present for his daughter. I logged him in and he was upstairs maybe five minutes. Then the elevator came back down and he jumped out and ran as if his ass was on fire. He didn't even stop to log out. I yelled at him, but he didn't hear me. What else can I tell you?"

"And no one else was in the building or came into the facility during the time you were on duty. Is that right?"

Almost snarling, Grady said, "Yeah, it's what I told you. How many times do I have to repeat it?"

"Until I'm satisfied you're telling the truth," Fad said.

Staring at Fad with unabashed fury shining in his eyes, Grady said, "I am."

But then his eyes blinked a different story and Fad knew, "Grady's lying," and said, "Sit there and don't move until I get back."

After walking out the door to where Joe stood watching the interview through one-way glass, Fad asked, "So, what do you think, Joe?"

"I don't like his looks, but it's not enough to put him in the slammer. Grady's story is pretty pat—too pat for me. Something went down out there last night and he's not about to share it with us. When Larry ran out he was spooked. If he didn't fear for his life, he wouldn't have broken company policy."

"Yeah," Fad said. "When I read your report, I got the same feeling. This asshole is lying like whale shit on the bottom of the ocean, but I doubt if we'll get anything out of him tonight. I'll cut him loose and see what falls out of the trees."

"Go ahead. We always know where to find him. As ugly as Grady is, he can run, but can't hide."

Fad laughed and said, "It's the truth."

Opening the door to the holding pen, where Grady still sat looking as if he'd like to kill, Fad said, "You're free to go, asshole."

Standing up quickly, Grady strode out of the room so fast he didn't hear Fad laugh again.

(Three)

After four days, Katie came up with a viable plan to steal Sadie and Wilbur and take them to the FBI. With the rebuke she received from Jerry, she knew she couldn't trust any of her co-workers or so-called friends to help.

She thought, "To hell with them. When I'm vindicated, they'll be the ones with egg on their faces. Screw them and their high-priced jobs. What's more important, their cushy positions or the fate of the United States? I believe Sadie and Wilbur, and the FBI will too."

Early this morning, she called the FBI, talked to an Agent named Kris Hefner and told him she overheard two men planning a terrorist attack.

"Do you have any other witnesses?" He asked.

"Yes, I have two others who can back up my story."

She didn't dare tell him they were chimpanzees. She knew he'd think she was some kind of nutcase and blow her off.

"Is there somewhere we can meet and talk?"

"I'd like to bring my witnesses to your office," Katie said. "They're both handicapped, so you'll need a person who can use sign language."

"I'll take care of it. When would you like to meet?"

"Would tomorrow at nine a.m. be convenient?" She asked. "I know where your office is located."

"Sure, it's no problem. I'll leave your name at the desk. Just ask for me and the guard will call."

"I'll see you tomorrow morning," Katie said and hung up before he could ask for more information.

(Four)

After being on the phone until late last night to set up a contract to get rid of the little Indian pest and her two primate friends, when Mohammed called Felix early the next morning, he was tired.

When Felix answered, Mohammed said, "I'm worn out and not in the mood for any crap this morning, Felix, so listen up. Our little problem with this Katie person will be solved shortly. Give me her address and I'll pass it on to our man, 'Mister Jones'."

Felix knew when to keep his mouth shut, so he said, "Her name is Katie Adkins and she lives at seven forty-two Mulberry Street, Apartment Four-C. The license number of her old white Volvo is seven three Baker, six four Zebra."

"When does she work at the lab?"

"She's only a volunteer there and her hours are unpredictable, but this week she spent a lot of time with her two friends."

"We have to take care of the chimps too," Mohammed said. "Perhaps our man can arrange for some fried monkeys with an 'accidental' fire."

"I don't think it would be wise. If too many strange things happen, it would only reinforce her story and make the police suspicious. I think our man should tail her and hope she tries to take the chimps to the FBI."

"Why would she do that?"

"Her co-workers think she's crazy and the chimps have watched too much TV," Felix said. "There's no way she'll go to the local cops with a story like that. They'd put her in a loony bin, but the FBI would check out her story before they called her nuts, and I'm sure she knows it."

"Okay, we'll do it your way. I'll have Mister Jones tail her and try to take them all out at the same time."

"Good luck and keep me advised," Felix said.

(Five)
For the past two days, after first locating Katie, Claude maintained a constant surveillance of her movements. Each day she spent several hours at the research laboratory and he saw her sitting outside in the warm sun, writing notes in a journal.

As he waited for the right moment, he wondered, "Katie's a pretty girl. Why does someone want her dead? But it's not my call. Do the job, Claude and forget it. This is the last one and for the rest of my life, I'm on easy street."

Ten minutes ago, at eight forty-five, as he sat in his rental car on the opposite side of the street watching the laboratory, he saw his quarry enter the building alone. When only one small light came on, he thought, "She's up to something. Maybe tonight's the night and she's taking the chimps somewhere."

A few minutes later, as the light went out and Katie walked out the door holding the hands of two chimpanzees and moving fast, his suspicions were confirmed. He watched her hurry to her car, and then she helped the chimps climb into the back seat. He saw her hands moving, but had no way of knowing she was signing to tell them to stay down and out of sight on the floor. Then she threw a blanket over them, got into the driver's seat and drove off.

As Claude waited for a break in the traffic to make a U-turn, he thought, "She'll take them to her apartment."

When the opportunity presented itself, he pulled out and successfully made the maneuver. But as he began to speed up, he saw red and blue lights reflecting in his rear-view mirror and thought, "That was stupid. I turned right in front of a cop. I'll never catch her now. I hope she does head home. If she goes somewhere else, I'm screwed."

Thirty minutes later, after a lecture by a local cop about the accidents caused by people who did what Claude did, and receiving a warning ticket, he parked across the street from Katie's apartment.

Walking quietly, he made his way along the sidewalk until he could see into the interior of her garage and was relieved when he saw her vehicle parked inside.

The lights were on in her apartment, but she'd pulled the three window blinds down and he knew there was no way he could get inside without causing a disturbance.

His contact warned him about just such an occurrence when he said, "If you can, make their deaths appear to be an accident. But no matter what, this woman and her two friends must be killed within the next week. Your fee depends on it."

"I'll fulfill my end of the bargain," Claude said. "You be sure to pay my money to the controller."

"Don't worry, Mister Jones," Mohammed said. "You'll get what's coming to you."

(Six)

At nine fifteen p.m., Jerry arrived at the lab to check on three experimental vaccines he was working on, and the cultures he made of new bacteria in Petri dishes.

He was anxious to see the results, so he punched in the access code, entered the building and turned on the lights. It was quiet in the lab. Most of the animals were asleep and he was glad they wouldn't be a distraction.

As he walked by the large cage where Wilbur and Sadie were housed, he chuckled, and out of curiosity looked into the interior to see how the foretellers of terrorist attacks were doing.

To his surprise, neither of them was visible. After checking high in the branches of the phony tree, he turned on a set of lights overhead, but couldn't see either of them.

After walking around the cage, he picked up a flashlight hanging on the wall and entered through a small door. He shined the light around the interior and still couldn't locate the two fortune tellers, so he called out, "Where are you guys?"

Nothing moved and when there was no answer, he said aloud, "Strange, I wonder where they can be? Maybe somehow they got loose."

Climbing out of the cage, he searched the entire facility, but found no sign of them. Then he thought of Katie. "Damn her anyway. I bet she took them somewhere, maybe to the police. All we need is bad publicity. I better call Doctor Wilson."

(Seven)

At ten fifteen, Mona's cell phone chirped the refrain "There'll be a hot time in the old town tonight," a little faster than the composer intended. When she chose the tune, she thought it fit her life style, but lately it annoyed her.

It was late and she was busy tutoring her latest protégé, Mark Anderson, a blond-haired, blue-eyed, freshman with a marvelous body. She wondered who would be calling at this hour and started to ignore it, but at the fourth repetition of the song, Mark interrupted their rhythm, looked up at her and asked, "Aren't you going to answer it?"

Frowning to show she was upset, she said, "I suppose I should. Excuse me."

Getting up awkwardly, she moved to a nearby table where the phone lay, picked up the instrument, flipped it open and asked, "Who is this?"

From the tone of her voice, Jerry knew his boss was upset with him for calling so late, but he said, "Hi, Doctor Wilson. I hate to bother you, but two of the chimps are missing. I searched everywhere and can't find them."

Shaking her head at Jerry's incompetence, Mona asked, "Who are they?"

"Wilbur and Sadie," he said. "What should I do?"

Trying to solve his problem in a hurry and get back to Mark, she said, "Wilbur is good at finding places to hide and probably took Sadie along. Wait until tomorrow morning and I'll help you look for them."

Jerry surprised her when he said, "I have a suspicion Katie Adkins took them."

"Why would she do that?"

"The other day, she came up with a half-baked story of Sadie and Wilbur knowing about a terrorist attack. I blew her off and she wasn't happy."

After a moment of thought, Mona said, "I don't think Katie would do anything like that. Sadie and Wilbur are probably asleep somewhere and you couldn't find them. Go home and get some sleep, Jerry. It's late and you're tired. We'll find them tomorrow."

She breathed a sigh of relief when he said, "Okay, Doctor, I'm sorry I bothered you."

"Thanks, Jerry," she said, and then looked down at Mark who was still lying prone on her bed.

Noting he was still erect, she thought, "It's what I like about these first year students. They're full of vim and vigor and nothing stands between them and furthering their education."

Straddling him again, she asked, "Now, where were we?"

(Eight)

The next morning at eight a.m., Mona arrived at work and found Jerry waiting near the front door. His disheveled brown hair was hanging over his brow and a black mark on his left cheek looked like grease. It was apparent he hadn't located the two missing chimps, but she asked anyway, "Hi Jerry, did you find Sadie and Wilbur?"

He brushed back his hair and said, "No, and several workers helped me search for them. They aren't in the facility. I'm sure Katie has them. She was adamant about believing their story."

"I can't believe Katie would do something so irresponsible," Mona said. "Let's conduct one more search. If we can't find them, I'll call the police and tell them of your fears."

CHAPTER 7

(One)

It rained last night and this morning the sky was overcast. Because of a serious three-car pileup on the Interstate, Fad was late for work. Then he stepped into a mud puddle on his way into the building, looked down at his soggy shoes and said, "It looks like another lousy day."

As he walked into the squad room, the phone rang and he said, "Now what, can't I even have a cup of coffee before Mister Crime starts beating on me?"

There was no one else around. They were either on a coffee break or hiding out, so he said, "Aw, to hell with it. I have to get started somewhere."

Picking up the annoying instrument, he snarled, "Yeah?"

"Hey, Fad, how's it hanging?" Bert asked.

"Weak, limp and shriveled up. What's up, Bert?"

"Is Joe around?"

"Nah, Bert. The sign-out board says he's on a call about some guy shooting off bottle rockets in the park. I told him to let the Fish and Wildlife guys take care of calls like that, but you know Joe, mention shooting and he's on a tear."

"Yeah, I know. When he gets back, tell him our missing person showed up with a bullet in his head. We fished Larry Holgram out of the lake this morning. He was murdered."

"Damn," Fad said. "We hoped he would show up alive. It's going to be rough on his wife and their little girl."

"Yeah, I went out and told Carol about it. She's broken up and Claire will be in shock when her mother tells her about her father."

Telling it like it is, Fad said, "It's a world of hurt out there."

"Oh, there's one other thing, Fad. Tell Joe the blood in the research lab was Larry's. The results of the DNA came back just before we heard about him floating in the lake. It appears Larry was killed in the building with the chimps. That's why they were so shook up."

"Nothing surprises me anymore," Fad said, and then asked, "Why did I become a cop?"

Bert laughed and said, "To help your fellow man."

"Yeah, but who's going to help us?"

Beginning the old, worn out clichéd saying, Bert said, "Yours not to reason why…"

And Fad finished it in his own ironic way, when he laughed and said, "Only to crap on the very first try. Okay, Bert. Keep it high and dry, and don't drill any strange wells."

(Two)

When Joe heard the news about Larry, he said, "Damn. So the two cases are tied together. Great, now maybe I'll get to see the tall drink of water with the fabulous boobs and legs that won't quit."

"Is that all you think about?" Fad asked.

"What else is there?"

"Law and Order."

"It's a hell of a TV show."

"Ain't it the truth?" Fad asked. "I love the way the actors track down clues in no time at all. I wish one of the jerks would work with me on the graveyard shift to see how crime cases really go down."

"As if that would ever happen," Joe said.

Then the phone rang, Fad picked it up and heard, "Bert here. There's more bad news."

Shaking his head, Fad asked, "What else do we handle?"

"The beautiful doc Joe is always talking about called to report two of her chimps missing. I don't know what this has to do with Larry or whatever went on out there, but it's interesting. Plus it gives Joe a chance to go out and try to get in the doc's drawers while he interviews her."

"Yeah, in his dreams."

Turning to his partner, Fad handed him the phone and said, "It's for you, Joe."

As he listened to Bert's report, a smile formed on Joe's face and Fad knew he was thinking about the good-looking female doc, wondering if he could get into her pants. Maybe it would work out, but Fad wouldn't take odds on it.

"Okay, thanks Bert," Joe said and hung up.

When Joe looked at him, Fad said, "Looks like another trip out to the lab. You want me to come along?"

"Nah, you'd only cramp my style with the lady doctor."

"What style? You really think she'd go for an old fart like you?"

Raising his eyebrows, Joe said, "You never know, stranger things have happened."

"Yeah, maybe they do in Istanbul, but not here. Have fun. If you plan to stay overnight, give me a call."

Leaving the room smiling, Joe said, "Don't wait up, Daddy."

As he walked out the door and climbed into his cruiser, he was still laughing. Picturing Mona nude in his bed, he thought, "It'll be nice to see her again."

Lost in thought, he almost sideswiped another police car, and the driver shouted at him, "You drunk or something?"

"Sorry," Joe yelled back.

When the cop gave him a one-fingered salute, he chuckled.

(Three)

At nine p.m. on a dark moonless night, in the shadows of a large warehouse south of town, Claude waited for his payoff. It was against his principles to meet with his customers, but this job had turned out badly. Before parting with the remaining four hundred thousand dollars, his latest anonymous employer wanted to meet Claude to discuss the particulars and supposed repercussions.

Crickets chirping as they called for mates and the lapping of small waves against pilings were the only sounds besides a bull frog that sang his lonely song and was answered by another further away.

There was a smell of dead fish in the air and another more pungent aroma of fresh dog shit close by. After checking the soles of his shoes, he found no residue and was relieved.

SIGNS OF OUR TIMES

Claude wanted the money and an end to his career as an assassin. In his mind there were plans for retirement in Acapulco or wherever his fancy led him.

Twin beams cut through the night, as a dark brown Cadillac drove slowly through the gate and swung toward a loading dock where Claude had agreed to meet his client. Remaining in the shadows, he watched as Felix Mendez slipped from behind the wheel and stood beside the car.

As the door opened, the interior light came on and Claude saw Felix was alone in the vehicle. Waiting for a few moments before stepping out, he walked silently to where Felix stood smoking a cigarette and blowing smoke rings into the stillness of the night air.

He approached so quietly it startled Felix, who jumped backward and reached under his jacket.

Leveling his revolver until the red dot of the weapon's laser beam sight stayed centered on Felix's chest, Claude said, "Keep your hands in sight, please."

"So you're Mister Jones," Felix said. "You look more German than English. What went wrong with the contract?"

"You're not the one I talked to on the phone. Where's he and who are you?"

"He couldn't come," Felix said. "I'm his partner. Again, what happened?"

"In order to pull the job off within the time frame you indicated, I made a few adjustments. I'm sorry about the collateral damage, but it was necessary to make it appear to be an accident. Don't worry, I won't charge you extra for the woman and man."

Felix shrugged as if the two victims were insignificant as dead flies and said, "I hope your actions won't draw attention to our final plans."

"I don't know your plans, so how could my actions affect you? I did the job as you asked. All of the principals you wanted me to kill are dead. Now I'll take my money."

Felix smiled, as he said, "You seem to have the upper hand."

His smirk bothered Claude, and he asked, "What's so funny?"

Two shots broke the silence. The first bullet struck Claude on the right side of his chest and rocked him backward. The second one hit high on his right shoulder, knocking him off the loading dock and into a deep, water-filled drainage canal.

As he flew outward and downward, his eyes focused on Felix's face. The last thing he saw before he went underwater was that his smirk had grown into a large grin.

Speaking into the microphone under his shirt, Felix said, "Good work, Mohammed." Then he walked slowly to the edge of the dock and watched for a sign of Mister Jones, but saw none and said, "If you didn't kill him outright, he'll drown."

In his earpiece, he heard Mohammed laugh.

Meeting Felix here was Claude's second mistake. Not making sure of Claude's demise was Felix's first, but wouldn't be his last.

(Four)

It was still drizzling when Joe drove up to the research lab and parked in a handicapped space near the door. He figured his aching stomach qualified, as he thought, "Too many tacos with Jalapenos for supper last night, I'll probably fart fire later today."

Skipping his way through the small puddles, he kept most of the water out of his shoes, but one had a hole in the sole and by the time he got inside, his sock was soaked. Squishing his way to Mona's office, he knocked politely on the frame of the door.

With a smile that made Mona Lisa look like a five-dollar-a-night street walker, she said, "Come in, Detective Francone."

Trying to look suave and sophisticated and having it come off like the stain of catsup on a new white shirt, Joe said, "You can call me Joe. After all this time together, we must be friends."

Mona saw through his nonsense, but still thought he was cute, as she said, "Okay Joe. What can I do for you?"

Thinking, "I'd like to tell you what you could do for me, but it might get me punched out," he said, "I came about your missing chimps. Are they the same ones I saw the last time? Weren't they called Sadie and Willie?"

Automatically correcting him, she said, "Sadie and Wilbur. Yes, they're the same. Jerry believes Katie Adkins made off with them."

"Why would he think that?"

"She told Jerry what he thought was 'an unbelievable tale of Wilbur and Sadie knowing about a terrorist plot'," Mona said. "Jerry doesn't think chimps have brains, but they do. I wish I had known of Katie's fears, perhaps I could have helped her."

"Is there any way to know whether she has the chimps?"

"Only if we find them with her and we don't know where she is. Katie didn't come in this morning."

Pulling out his trusty notebook and pencil, Joe said, "Give me her address and I'll drop by to see her."

Before she could respond, his beeper went off and he said, "Excuse me."

After checking the call and reading a message to call in immediately, he remembered his hated cell phone was in his desk at the station, and asked, "Can I use your phone, Mona?"

"Sure," she said, handing him her cell phone.

When Red answered his call, Joe asked, "What's up, Red?"

"We've got a big explosion on Mulberry Street. A tanker truck blew up. If we can't get it under control, the whole damn block may go up in flames. I want you to go over there and take charge of the investigation. It looks like we have major casualties, dead and injured."

As he felt a sour taste in his mouth and his stomach acid started burning at the thought of what he would soon face, Joe said, "Damn, that's all we need. I'll get right on it. Is Fad there?"

"He's on his way," Red said. "Get going."

After flipping the phone shut, Joe stood up, put it on Mona's desk and said, "I'm sorry. We'll have to continue this another time. There's an emergency in town. Thanks for the phone."

"You're welcome," Mona said, her eyes sparkling. "I look forward to seeing you again."

"So do I," Joe said and thought, "I hope she means it."

(Five)

Sadie was terrified, cold, hurt and alone in a world she didn't understand. When the truck hit Katie's car, the impact threw Sadie out the open window and she landed hard on the asphalt road. The terrifying sound of the explosion came unexpectedly, and the blast blew her across the pavement and into a group of nearby shrubs.

It frightened her so much she lost control of her bladder and peed all over herself. Then the heat of the flames singed the hair from her back and a few drops of liquid fire fell on her right arm, blistering her tender skin. She looked for Wilbur, but couldn't find him anywhere.

In the excitement of the moment, no one noticed Sadie scamper away to a tall oak tree. Scurrying up the trunk into the highest branches, she stayed there for the remainder of the day, crying softly and licking her wounds.

Throughout the remainder of the afternoon, the sirens, noise from the exploding gas tanks and flames from the inferno a few hundred yards away startled her. As the day wore on and turned into dusk, she became groggy and fell asleep tucked into a fork of the tree where three branches came together.

A few hours later in the dark of night, Sadie awoke to pain and loneliness. Missing Wilbur, she cried softly as she scanned the underbrush for some sign of her mate. Finally hunger overcame her fears, so she climbed down from her perch and searched for food.

Making her way down back alleys and keeping to the shadows, Sadie avoided any contact with humans she saw on the sidewalks. Knowing stealth was her friend; she quietly removed the lids from several trashcans and rummaged through the contents until she uncovered the edible remains of vegetables or fruit. Her arm continued to ache and she licked it to ease the pain.

Three blocks away, in the form of a large Dumpster behind a grocery store, Sadie found the cornucopia of her dreams. With the ease of a thief at night, she scampered into the dark space. After finding a large broken wooden box half-full of out-of-date apples, pears and bananas, she ate until she felt her stomach would burst. Then she fell into a fitful sleep.

As the sun slowly rose in the sky, the warmth penetrated her hiding spot. Unfamiliar with her surroundings, Sadie came awake with a start. The blisters on her arm, now swollen with fluid, ached like the fires of hell. After breakfasting on the remains of last night, she looked around cautiously and saw no one or anything to frighten her. Climbing slowly out of the Dumpster, she made her way to some bushes behind a nearby aging apartment building.

Inborn survival instincts told her to stay close to her food source, so after burrowing into the interior of the brush, she made a nest from dead vegetation. Falling asleep again and dreaming of Wilbur and their comfortable cage, she whimpered softly and tears of pain and loneliness ran down her cheeks.

(Six)

Alice Grabowski was only eleven, but she was more upset than she'd ever been in her short life. One of Alice's seventh-grade classmates, Danny Shackley, was not only an ugly fat-headed dork, he was what her father, Harold, would label a "horse's ass".

Alice's mother, Dorothy, said Danny must have a crush on Alice because he continually teased her, but Alice thought Danny was plain mean and pig-headed.

Up until today, she managed to slough off all of his unwanted attention and mockery, but this afternoon after school was the final straw. He came up with a new idea and began calling her Alice "Grab-ass-ky". Several of his friends took up the chant and made her cry in front of them. She had never been so embarrassed in her young life.

Hoping for sympathy from her mother, she ran all the way home, but Dorothy wasn't there, so cursing the name of Danny Shackley under her breath, Alice went out on the back stoop to cry alone. She hated Danny so much it hurt and thought, "Just wait, I'll come up with something to pay him back—but what?"

It was too much for her young brain to contemplate, so feeling forlorn; she dried her eyes and sat with her knees drawn up under her arm. Resting her head on the soft platform they formed, she looked out into the trash-littered back yard of their small apartment and savored a bite of the apple she saved from lunch.

For years, Harold had tried his best to keep the back yard clean, but the grocery store down the alley didn't care and let their garbage blow where the wind took it. Most of it wound up in his open back yard and Alice thought, "Maybe if we had a fence instead of those stupid bushes, I could play out here without worrying about rodents."

Suddenly there was movement in the shrubs and she wondered if it was a rat. "I hate them because they carry all kinds of diseases."

She was about to jump up and run inside, when she saw a long hairy arm reach out of the brush and grasp an old worn-out baseball that had lain there for ages. Alice didn't believe it, but the first arm was followed by a second and then a hairy body.

A face with two sorrowful eyes looked up at Alice and her heart did a flip as she knew, "It's a monkey."

Afraid she might frighten her new guest, she asked softly, "Where did you come from?"

Sadie tipped her head to one side and studied Alice's face, and then finally making up her mind, she dropped the ball and signed, "My name is Sadie. What's yours?"

Looking at the monkey, Alice wondered what it meant by all those hand signals. The motions reminded her of sign language, something her teacher touched on during civics, but she wasn't sure because she never took the time to learn, and thought, "Besides, where would a monkey learn to sign?"

She tossed the half-eaten morsel of fruit at the monkey and asked, "Want a bite of my apple?"

Sadie jumped back and retreated into the brush, but a minute later her hairy paw reached out to grasp the fruit like it was a prized jewel. The arm and apple disappeared and Alice heard the sound of heavy teeth munching, as Sadie bit into the juicy treat.

When she had eaten, Sadie became brave enough to crawl back out of the vegetation. Sitting forlornly on her haunches, she looked up at Alice with the biggest eyes Alice ever saw and signed, "Where's Wilbur?"

Shaking her head, Alice said, "I don't know what you're saying, but what's wrong with your arm?"

Reaching down slowly, she touched Sadie's arm and she signed, "It hurts."

As she got up quietly so she wouldn't spook her new friend, Alice said, "Stay there. I'll be right back."

She went inside to the bathroom, found a big jar of green jelly her mother used for sunburn or scrapes and cuts, and carried it outside.

As she removed the lid, Sadie watched every move. Then beckoning with her fingers, Alice said, "Come here, sweet thing. I won't hurt you."

By the tone of Alice's soothing voice, Sadie realized in the midst of her sorrows, she had found a friend. She held out her sore arm and Alice said, "Let me put some of this on your blisters. It won't hurt and it'll cool them down. I can tell you're in pain. How'd you get these burns?"

As the cool jelly eased her pain, Sadie smiled a toothy grin and then without warning, jumped up on the stoop beside Alice and held her hand.

Surprised and happy to have such a lively new friend, Alice thought, "If old smart mouth Danny could see me now, I bet he would be so jealous."

As she examined Sadie's hairy body, Alice said, "Why your back is all singed. I can smell burned hair all over you. I wonder if you got hurt in that terrible fire yesterday. The papers say it killed some people. It's so tragic."

Sadie signed, "Hide, three, two, fire, X," but Alice had no idea what the gestures meant. She leaned out, patted Sadie's head and said, "Even with your burns, you're a pretty girl. What am I going to do with you?"

While showing as many teeth as she could and leaning heavily on Alice's knee, Sadie put her healthy arm around Alice and hugged her.

Looking at her new pet and knowing she couldn't part with her, but also aware of what Dorothy and Harold would say, Alice said, "Well, I'm going to keep you, it's for sure. But we have to hide you someplace until I can break the news to Mom and Dad. Come on; let's look at where you've been living."

The two new best friends walked hand-in-hand to examine Sadie's lair, while Alice's mind raced to figure out a way to make her guest comfortable enough to stay. Forgetting all about Danny, a smile lit her face as she skipped along with Sadie toward the alley and her hiding place.

CHAPTER 8

(One)

As Joe glanced at the burned remains of the monkey/chimp on the table in the morgue, Sarah continued their conversation by asking, "What's wrong with the fourth victim being a chimp?"

After shaking his head twice, Joe said, "It seems everything I touched this week has chimps connected with it. You wouldn't believe it if I told you."

Busy with her examination, and wishing Joe would leave, Sarah said, "Whatever."

Pointing toward the adjacent tables, Joe said, "Let's keep the news about the two gun-shot victims out of the papers for a while, Doc. It might help us catch the perps. And while we're at it, don't tell anyone about the chimp. The less these guys know about what we know, the better off we'll be."

"Okay, Joe, if that's the way you want to play it."

Flipping to a clean page in his notebook, he asked, "Have you got an I. D. on any of the victims?"

"Two of the six are still in hospital morgues and I'll get their names later. I'm sure the Chaplain will notify their next of kin. The truck driver on table one was named Ted Branski. He had a wife and two young kids."

Joe jotted down the info, and then he asked, "What about the women?"

"The driver of the Oldsmobile hasn't been identified yet," Sarah said. "The other woman was a young student at the University. We got her I. D. from motor vehicles when they traced her license plates. Her name was Katie Adkins."

He started to write the name down, realization struck him and he asked, "Katie Adkins? I just met her a few days ago out at the research lab while I was checking out a murder victim. She talked to the chimps out there."

"Talked to chimps?" Sarah asked. "How strange."

"Not really," Joe said. "Katie used sign language to communicate with them. Man, something weird is going on out at the lab. This is too much coincidence. The fried chimp must be one of the two reported missing this morning. I was out at the lab talking about them when I got the call about an explosion. Is there any way to tell if this is a boy or girl?"

"The usual," Sarah said. "He's a boy, or was. Now he's a roasted monkey."

"Now who's making sport with the dead?"

"It's my turn to apologize," Sarah said. "Do you know his name?"

"Yeah, it's Wilbur and his mate is named Sadie. I wonder where she is."

Sarah shrugged in helplessness, and said, "If Sadie's out there in the big city of Sulfur Springs, there's no telling. It sounds like you've got a major case on your hands. Who would want to kill two strangers to take out a student and two chimps? Somebody is really monkeying with your mind."

Smiling at her pun as he walked away, Joe said, "Cute, Doc—real cute."

When he got outside, he blew his nose hard to get rid of the Vaseline. Fresh air never smelled so good.

(Two)

Bert was up to his knees in robbery cases and needed a break. Someone was stealing every lawn ornament in town. So far, he counted sixty-eight separate reports. The burglary calls kept coming in at the rate of two or three a night, and he thought, "Someone must be going to open a new store soon. Why lawn ornaments? It beats me."

The phone rang and he hoped it was anything but another report.

"Please God, give me a break," Bert prayed silently as he picked up the instrument.

"Bert, this is Joe. Any chance you can walk up the hall for a sit down with Fad and me? We need to lay this thing out on the blackboard and see if we can make sense of it."

Glancing up at heaven to thank the Big Guy, Bert said, "Sure, I'll be right down. Pour me a cup of that stuff you call coffee."

"Thanks," Joe said.

"No," Bert said. "Thank you!"

(Three)

Fifteen minutes later, Bert, Joe and Fad gathered around a wooden conference table displaying so many cigarette burns, Joe wondered if they should rent a sander to make an even surface to write on.

Beginning the discussion, he said, "Okay, we're all on the same wavelength. Fad, you handle the chalk and we'll go over the time line to see what we have."

"No sweat."

Reading from his notes, Joe said, "Monday night Larry Holgram goes missing. A little after six p.m., he leaves his office, remembers he forgot his daughter's present and goes back into the building. That much we know from the records and our reluctant witness, Mister O'Reilly.

"Larry's upstairs about five minutes. Then suddenly he runs off the elevator, out the exit and into the building next door. Is that how you see it, Bert?"

"Yeah, while Larry was in his office, he was spooked. Either he overheard or saw something that made him fear for his life, and he ran."

"Supposedly no one else was in the building," Fad added. "If they weren't, who or what frightened Larry? I think Grady is lying."

Nodding, Joe said, "So do I, but we can't prove it, so let's move on. How did Larry get into the building next door? Did he have the access code? Doctor Wilson says almost everyone on campus or the Army base knows the combination."

"Which doesn't help a lot," Bert said. "It only narrows our suspects down to several hundred students, research lab staff and workers at the chemical facility."

Tapping his notebook again, Joe said, "Okay, here's another strange coincidence, Larry couldn't talk. He conversed in sign language. That much we know. Now comes the really weird part—the monkeys could also sign."

"They're not monkeys, Joe. They're chimps," Fad said.

"Okay, I stand corrected, chimps that sign. Mona said they're teaching them sign language and they're able to communicate.

"Then four days after Larry gets whacked, we have Katie Adkins as a victim of a fire/homicide and one of the chimps, Wilbur, fried medium rare. Katie just happened to work with the chimps and now they're missing, or at least one of them is. How weird is all of this?"

"Pretty far out," Bert said. "But it's beginning to make some sense. Katie had the chimps with her for some reason. That's how we wound up with Wilbur fried to a crisp."

"Yeah," Joe said. "Wilbur bought the farm, but where's Sadie."

"I just picked up on the 'Mona'," Fad said. "You two getting pretty cozy, Joe?"

Joe felt a blush on his cheeks, and tried to stop it, as he said, "It slipped out, but yeah, we're getting along fine. That reminds me, when Red called me, Mona was telling me a far-out story of Katie getting a message from Wilbur and Sadie about a terrorist attack. I have to find out more about that."

Looking up from his own notes, Bert asked, "What do you mean 'a terrorist attack'? Did Mona say where or when?"

"No. We were interrupted by the explosion and I had to leave."

Turning to Fad, Bert said, "Add it to the board. It's another piece of the puzzle."

The phone rang, Fad answered it, and after listening to the caller for a moment, he asked, "Can you hold on? I'll see if he's available."

Punching the 'hold' button, he turned to Joe and asked, "You know an FBI agent named Hefner?"

Joe chuckled and said, "No. Is he Hugh's son?"

Fad smiled and said, "I don't think so, but he knows you. He asked for you by name."

Picking up the phone, Joe said, "Sergeant Francone here, Agent Hefner, how may I help you?"

Without preamble, he asked, "Do you know Katie Adkins?"

"Yes, I knew her. She worked at the SCOU research lab, but she was killed in an explosion yesterday."

"I know," he said. "Two days ago, Katie called me and said she had two witnesses to back up her story of a planned terrorist attack on the United States, so we set up an appointment for yesterday morning.

"When she didn't show, I thought she was some kind of a kook. Then this morning, I read the official police report of her death and it didn't sound like an accident to me. Two people shot to death to set up a trap for her car was too coincidental."

Joe thought, "This guy is smart and a man after my own heart. I don't buy Katie being there as a coincidence myself."

"I like the way you think, Kris. I don't believe it was an accident either. Someone very clever set it up."

"Did Katie say anything to you about this supposed attack?"

"No. I heard about it for the first time yesterday from her supervisor, Doctor Wilson, who started to fill me in when I got the call about an explosion."

"We need to talk," Kris said. "What time would be convenient?"

"As we speak, two of my officers are with me and we're trying to lay out the time line. Why don't you drop by and give us a hand?"

"I'm on my way," Kris said.

"We're in room three oh three," Joe said. "I'll leave word with the desk sergeant to pass you up."

"It'll take me about fifteen minutes to get there. See you soon."

(Four)

Before they took a coffee break and waited for Kris to arrive, Joe filled Bert and Fad in on what Agent Hefner added to the pot.

As they shook hands and Joe introduced Kris to Fad and Bert, Joe sized him up. He was impressed with the agent's manner and appearance—young, slim and trim, probably twenty-seven or so, but looking older in a well-cut dark brown suit, white shirt and tan tie. He had blond hair, blue eyes and a quick smile.

Getting right down to business, he said, "Look, call me Kris. This is your show. So far no federal law was broken, but the FBI is always interested in any terrorist threat, imagined or real.

"Katie told me she had vital information she couldn't trust to send by e-mail or talk about over the phone. As I told you, she also said there were two witnesses to back up her story. Do you know who they are?"

Smiling, Joe said, "Yeah, we do, but you're not going to believe it."

"Why?" Kris asked.

"It's because they're chimpanzees, Kris."

"You've got to be kidding me,—chimps? Is that who or what Katie had for witnesses? She sounds more and more like a kook to me."

"No, Katie wasn't a nutcase. She worked with these chimps and taught them sign language. According to her boss, the chimps could speak to humans and each other by using sign language."

"Now I've heard everything," Kris said.

"Take a look at our board," Joe said, and brought him up to date on all they knew so far.

Concluding his briefing, Joe said, "The only thing I can figure is that during the short time Larry was in the building and before someone shot him, he passed on some sort of a message to Sadie and Wilbur."

Bert nodded and added, "They repeated it to Katie, who tried to tell her boss' assistant, Jerry Grimes, but he blew her off. It made Katie angry, so she called you, Kris. Does all of this make sense?"

"Sort of, but how did the perps who killed Larry hear about this in time to take Katie and the chimp out? And where's Sadie?"

"We don't know," Joe said. "We think Mister O'Reilly is lying about no one being in the building. There had to be someone Larry overheard or saw and it scared him enough to run."

"Then we need to talk to Grady again," Fad said. "He'll love to have me in his face for a second time."

Joe thought for a few seconds, and then he said, "Maybe we can turn you loose on Grady, Kris. He'll think you're some punk kid trying to make his bones, but maybe the title of FBI agent will sink in and he'll let something slip."

"First, let's go out and talk to Doctor Wilson," Kris said. "I want to find out more about what Katie told Jerry Grimes. If there's actually some sort of a terrorist threat to the U.S., we still don't know what it is or where it's planned."

As he shook his index finger at Joe, Fad said, "Look out Joe, or Kris will horn in on your territory."

"How's that?" Kris asked.

Laughing, Fad said, "Joe has staked out the fair maiden, Mona for his own. Don't get between them, Kris, or you might get trampled like a young bull elk during mating season."

"Fairly warned," Kris said. "I'll stay out of your way, Joe."

Joe's face was red, but he didn't care if they saw him blushing. Mona was some kind of woman and he wanted to stoke her fire, so he said, "You won't cramp my style, Kris. I'll give her a call and we can meet her later today."

"Good enough."

Heading for the door, Fad said, "I'm going by the medical examiner's office to see what else Sarah can tell us. You want to come along, Bert?"

Shaking his head, Bert said, "No, I have to talk to Carol Holgram again. Besides, I hate the morgue. I can't stand to watch someone cut up dead bodies."

"I don't blame you," Joe said. "Let's meet back here at four and compare notes."

CHAPTER 9

(One)

Claude dreamed he was on an ocean cruise and waves were rocking the ship. Then his head bobbed forward and his mouth filled with water. As his shoulder cried out in agony, he coughed and spat out the oily tasting fluid.

The pain brought Claude out of the fog he was in for the past fifteen minutes since Felix's companion shot him and knocked him into the water. It was luck alone that kept Claude from drowning.

Surfacing under the dock, the lapel of his coat snagged on a rusty nail sticking out of a creosoted piling. The shot to his chest knocked the wind from his lungs and his breath came in rasping gasps.

He tried to take in air as quietly as possible and heard the man he met talking to someone and the name "Mohammed". Then agonizing pain hit him like a bull moose on a rampage and he lost consciousness.

Once more awake and alert, he clung to his lifesaving pole with his good arm and checked his body for injuries. His chest hurt like hell, but he was glad he wore a flak jacket under his coat. It had saved his life.

As he tried to move his right arm, he experienced such pain it almost caused him to black out again. Knowing that either his shoulder or his arm was broken and useless now, in the fog of his semi-conscious mind, he remembered hearing Felix's remarks and his laughter as he thought he killed him.

Claude thought, "You should have made sure. Payback is hell. Now to get out of the water before I pass out again."

Reaching up with his left hand, he gently unhooked his coat from the nail. Then moving gingerly, he felt his way around the slimy post until he could see the lights across the canal reflected on the dark, dingy surface.

Twenty long feet across open water, a ladder was attached to a piling and led upward to the loading dock. He wondered, "Can I make it?" And then he thought, "I'd better or I'll die here in this cruddy canal."

Gritting his teeth, he struggled painfully out of his coat, letting it to slip off his injured arm and drift away. After he fumbled to loosen the straps and slip out of his flak jacket, it and his shoes sank into the depths.

Then, although he hated to do it, he got rid of his second gun, strapped to his left leg just above the ankle.

If the guy who shot him and the man he met were still on the dock, they'd have heard him by now. Except for the crickets, Claude didn't hear a sound, so it was a good bet both his assailants were long gone. The gun weighed too much to leave hooked to his leg, when he needed all the help he could muster and as little hindrance as possible to make it to the ladder.

Unhooking the straps, he let the holster and weapon slip down into the filthy water. Then letting go of his lifesaving pole, and using a one-handed dog paddle, he made his way across the stretch of water that seemed as long as an Olympic swimming pool.

He swallowed and spat out half the water in the canal before he grasped the bottom rung of the ladder and hung on. The pain in his arm had subsided some, so it might be possible for him to use his right arm to support himself.

It looked a long way up, but he had to make it. Hooking one leg over the bottom rung, he balanced awkwardly and then reached up to the third step, pulling his aching body out of the canal. Rivulets of oily water ran off his clothes and dripped downward, splashing quietly and making small concentric circles that spread across the oily surface.

Gritting his teeth against the pain he knew was coming, he turned and put the elbow of his injured arm through the opening. Then letting go with his good hand, he lunged upward and grabbed another rung all in one quick motion. The pain made him scream in agony, but he managed two more pegs and thought, "Only six more to go."

How he made it, he never knew, but after fifteen minutes of painful determination, he pulled his weary body over the top of the ladder. Panting for breath, he lay on the splintered wood of the dock, knowing that never in his life had he been so glad to be on solid ground.

After tearing off the right arm of his shirt and ripping it along the shoulder, Claude checked his wound and discovered it was a through and through. Entering three inches below his collarbone as a small pencil-sized projectile, the bullet had expanded and then exited out his back, leaving behind a jagged hole an inch and a half in diameter.

As he watched, dark thick blood seeped out of the opening and ran slowly down his back. He knew, "I need help soon, or I won't make it. Get up, Claude. Get moving and don't stop."

Gingerly pulling and pushing until he stood erect, he moved slowly down the dock toward the alley where he parked his car, as his wet soggy socks slapped against the wood, sounding like a washerwoman pounding damp clothing against a rock.

To no surprise, his vehicle was gone, taken as a souvenir by either Felix or his assistant. Pausing a moment to rest, he thought, "Enjoy it while you can. You're in for a big surprise when I catch up with you."

Staggering a few more feet, he leaned heavily against the wall of a warehouse to catch his breath. When out of the darkness, a woman's voice said, "You look like a drowned rat. What's wrong with you?"

The sound startled him and he reached for his gun, only to remember it was gone, drowned in the canal as he should have been.

Holding his hand above his eyes, Claude made out the dim form of a woman standing a few feet away in the shadow of the building. He replied, "I was shot."

Stepping out and reaching to support him, she asked, "Shot? Good God, who shot you?"

"Not a friend," Claude said.

Pointing in the general direction of the entrance, his unknown savior said, "I didn't think so. Come on, my car is over there. I heard sounds like shots or fireworks and wondered who was out here. I thought it might be some college kids and I was worried about them setting fire to the buildings."

"I'm glad you happened by," he said.

They took a few steps and she said, "I'll get you to a hospital."

"No, no hospital. They'll want to know who shot me and I don't want to tell them."

"You want to take care of the shooter all by yourself, right Mister Macho?"

"We'll see. Can you help me?"

Attempting to joke, she said, "I'm a sucker for a man who was shot. Okay, if you say so, I'll try to fix your arm. That's a nasty hole."

"Thanks."

Leading him to the passenger's side of a dark-red Pontiac Firebird convertible, she said, "Here we are. Let me get a blanket out of the trunk to put on the seat and wrap around you. I hate to ruin the upholstery with your blood, and you need something to keep you warm."

Holding on to the door for support while she popped the trunk, he asked, "Do you have any whiskey for a weak, wounded man?"

As she returned with the blanket, spread it on the seat and helped him sit down, she said, "I think I have some at home."

Then she pulled the wonderfully warm wrap around his legs and upper body and said, "This should help you until we can get some booze in you."

"Thanks again," he said and passed out.

(Two)

The report of the tanker truck explosion and associated casualties was big news for three days, remaining on the front page of the local paper until a house fire killed six siblings. Then the newspaper promptly forgot about the victims of a four-day-old accident, as the editor in chief, Ben Bernstein, told his staff, "Blood and guts sell newspapers. Start a fund for the victims of the house fire and run the old news on a back page."

Since it was not considered newsworthy of front page importance, the story of the authorities finding Larry in the lake was located on page three. What was one more killing to the general public who were immune to such daily carnage?

Being too "cool" to read the newspaper, Alice got her news from TV, what she heard in school and at the breakfast table, where for days her parents forced her to listen to the discussion of the terrible explosion.

It was all she could do to keep still long enough to satisfy her mom and dad that she was up on the latest news, before she could jump up from her chair and make a beeline for the back yard.

This morning, over the sound of the TV, she heard her mother say, "It's so terrible."

Knowing Dorothy expected a reply, she asked, "What?"

Dorothy shook her head and said, "Those poor people who were killed in the explosion a few blocks away. Just think, it could have happened on our street and we'd be homeless."

Looking up from the sports page of the newspaper, Harold said, "Thank your lucky stars it didn't."

Thinking she had fulfilled her daily news intake, Alice took her cereal bowl, spoon and glass to the sink and then slipped out the back door. Running swiftly down the worn path, she looked under the bushes until she spotted Sadie staring back and said, "There you are, sweet thing. Come out and let me see your arm."

Sadie climbed from under the shrubs, squatted by Alice's side and obediently held out her arm to let Alice inspect the burns. After the first two days, the blisters had broken and drained. The grease Alice placed on Sadie's burns helped to ease her pain and now they had scabbed over.

"They look like they're healing," Alice said.

Sadie bobbed her head up and down as if she really understood. Then for the hundredth time, she signed, "Where's Wilbur?"

"I wish I knew what you're trying to say," Alice said. "If I didn't know better, I'd think you could speak in sign language."

Sadie signed, "I'm hungry."

After seeing the same thing for enough times just before she gave her some fruit, Alice knew what she meant, so she handed her the last apple from the bin in the pantry and said, "Here. I hope mom buys more without asking what happened to all the rest."

As Sadie grinned and bit into the fruit, from behind them Harold asked, "What's that?"

Standing up and letting Sadie hide behind her, Alice said, "It's a monkey, Dad."

Harold had approached so quietly neither of them heard him. Now he looked closely at Sadie and said, "No, I think it's a chimp and you'll have to turn it in to the authorities. There's a story in the paper about two of them missing from the research lab at the Army base. There's a five hundred dollar reward we can put in your college fund."

Already knowing her question or any objections were useless when her father made up his mind and money was concerned; still, Alice asked, "Do I have to?"

"Yes, Alice, the chimp isn't wild and just because you found it, he doesn't belong to you. You know right from wrong. This animal can't live in the wilds of Colorado. It needs special treatment and food. Maybe it's got a mate somewhere that misses it. How would you like to be lost and all alone?"

Feeling ashamed for not considering such a scenario, Alice said, "I never thought about that. Okay, let's go call the police. Come on, sweet thing."

"Is that what you named it?"

Smiling at Sadie, Alice said, "I think it's a girl, and yes, that's the name I gave her. She really is sweet."

"In addition to the money, maybe you'll get to visit her as a reward."

"That would be nice," Alice said.

Rolling her eyes back into her head without letting her father see, she thought, "Parents!"

(Three)

It was another chilly, cheerless and dismal day as Joe parked his car and he and Kris walked to the research lab. Hanging forebodingly over the far-off mountains, a bank of dark grey clouds blocked the sun. Joe hunched over and pulled the collar of his old coat around his neck to keep the cold wind out.

When Jerry met them at the door, he shook their hands and then took them down the hall to Mona's office where he said, "Doctor, Sergeant Francone and an FBI Agent are here to see you."

"Thanks, Jerry, show them in."

As they stepped into her office, Mona said, "Hello, Joe. Who's your friend?"

"Doctor Wilson," Joe said, "this is Agent Hefner from the FBI."

Mona stood up, laughed and said, "Don't be so formal, Joe. Remember, we're old friends. Good afternoon, Agent Hefner. Please call me Mona. You're cute and I suppose you're married."

"Guilty as charged," Kris said. "Thanks for the 'cute' part, but I won't tell my wife. Please call me Kris."

Jerry turned to go, and Joe called after him, "Would you stick around for a few minutes, Jerry? I have some questions for you."

Wearing a frown instead of a smile, he said, "Sure."

Taking Joe's arm and leading him to the same comfortable recliner as before, Mona asked, "What brings you back out here, Joe?"

Noticing how Kris looked her over from head to toe, with a long pause on her breastworks, Joe thought, "Kris might be married, but he can still look. I knew he was my kind of guy."

After Joe called to make this appointment, he stopped off at his apartment. Instead of going to lunch, he shaved again, put on his best blue suit, a new, clean white shirt and a light-blue tie. He even went so far as to brush off his worn but still serviceable and comfortable steel-tipped black shoes.

The last time he was out here, he looked like a bum. Today he wanted Mona to see the real him, "whatever that might be."

As he sat down, he said, "Kris just joined our team. We're interested in the story about the terrorists Wilbur and Sadie told Katie. By the way, I was sorry to hear she was killed in the explosion on Mulberry Street."

"We're all saddened by Katie's death," Mona said, and Joe could tell she meant it.

Her eyes turned misty and she dabbed at them with a tissue as she said, "Katie was a real asset. She loved Wilbur and Sadie."

"Yeah, I know. Were you aware the two chimps were with Katie when her vehicle was hit by the truck? We found Wilbur's body, but not Sadie. Do you have any idea why they were with her?"

She shook her head and said, "No. The night before the accident, Jerry called me about ten thirty to report Sadie and Wilbur were missing. He thought Katie had taken them, but I told him I thought they were probably frightened and hiding somewhere.

"I didn't know about Katie's story or I would have been more concerned. We'll miss Wilbur too. Is there any report on Sadie's whereabouts?"

Turning to Jerry, Joe said, "No, but I'd like to know why you blew off Katie's story about the terrorists, Jerry. Would you tell me why in this day and age you didn't even consider it being real?"

From the beginning, Jerry was defensive and said, "Hey, I didn't have any idea Katie was going to get killed. I thought the chimps were putting her on. Maybe they saw something on TV to give them the idea. The smarter chimps like Sadie and Wilbur watch a lot of CNN and you know terrorists are the main theme."

Interrupting him, Kris said, "Yes, but it doesn't excuse your behavior. Now Katie is dead, along with one of her witnesses and the other is missing. If you let her act on her beliefs, maybe all three would be alive and we'd know what's going on. Now we're left with a mystery and perhaps a real terrorist threat we know nothing about. Thanks a lot."

Jerry's face turned red, but he remained defiant as he said, "I don't have to stand here and be insulted. I did what I thought was best for the lab and job security, and I still don't believe Wilbur and Sadie knew anything. You'll have to prove it to me."

"If we can find Sadie, maybe we'll get lucky," Kris said. "But tell us everything Katie told you, Jerry. Think it through and don't miss a word. Did she take notes and if so, where are they?"

"Yeah, Katie had notes, but I don't know where they are. Her memos are probably at her house or she took them with her."

As Joe did the same, Kris took out his notebook, and said, "Okay, tell us what Katie said. We'll look for the notes later."

Jerry spread his hands wide, and said, "Katie said they told her two men killed someone with a gun in back of their cage. These guys were supposedly terrorists who plan to attack the U.S. That's all she said, nothing more. She wanted to call the police, but I told her it was nonsense and she finally agreed."

"Again thanks to you, Katie took drastic action of her own," Joe said, and Kris nodded. "Are you sure that's all she said?" Joe continued his questioning.

"Yeah, like I told you, I didn't believe her story or want to hear any more about it. She asked me to talk to the chimps and I refused. I'm sorry."

Looking at him with contempt, Mona said, "You should be."

"That's all, Jerry," Joe said. "You can go."

Watching Jerry slink out of the office like a guy who knew he was in trouble with his boss, Joe got the idea if Mona had anything to do with it, he wouldn't have his cushy job much longer.

At the same time, Kris' and Joe's thoughts were identical; "It couldn't happen to a nicer guy."

When Jerry had shut the door behind him, Kris asked, "Did Katie say anything to you about this story, Mona?"

"No, I heard about it for the first time from Jerry the night he found Wilbur and Sadie missing. I wish she had talked to me before she took them, because I would have listened. I hope it's not too late to hear Sadie's story.

"On the same subject, I called the newspaper, told them two of our chimpanzees were missing and offered a five-hundred-dollar reward each for their return."

"Maybe Sadie will show up," Joe said. "But I wish you had checked with me before giving the story out. Now the perps will know Sadie is still alive, so we have to find her before they do."

Getting up reluctantly, Joe said, "I'll show Kris around the cage and then we'll take off. Thanks for your time, Mona. I hope I'll see you again soon."

Giving him another of her more-than-a-Mona-Lisa smiles, she said, "Stop by anytime, Joe."

(Four)

Dreaming again, Claude saw himself sanding at the small dark and smoky bar of the Zum Giesenend Restaurant in Osterath, Germany, watching Frau

Schmidt finish putting a frothy head on a large tankard of ale. In his mind he could smell the delicious liquorish taste of the schnapps he just drank and longed for another.

Then without warning, he came violently awake as someone poured a fiery liquid down his throat. Choking and coughing, he lunged forward, which brought such pain to his shoulder that he cried out in alarm, "What the hell?"

From out of the darkness above, a woman's voice said, "It's only the booze you asked for."

Looking down, he saw he was still seated in her Pontiac with a blanket wrapped around his legs. His sudden movement had caused part of the covering to fall from his shoulders and it bunched up in the small of his back against the car seat.

Turning his head slowly to the right, he saw for the first time a partial view of his savior. She was tall, about five feet seven inches, with a full head of long red hair. For a fleeting moment, a passing car shone its lights on her eyes and he saw their deep-blue irises.

The roofline of the car and the darkness partially hid her face, but from experiences in the past, Claude knew redheads only came in two styles, beautiful or plain. He didn't think she was plain, not with that hair and those eyes.

He tried to smile, and said, "Thanks again. I must have passed out."

"You're welcome. I couldn't carry you, so I went in and got a double shot of whiskey. I hoped it would bring you around so you can walk. Are you ready to try?"

"Let me finish the rest of the booze. It might help and sure can't hurt."

Taking the glass from her hand, Claude drank the remainder in one long hot gulp. Feeling the warmth of the liquid flow through his body, he said, "Two more of those and I'll let you examine me."

He tried to smile, but pain turned it into a frown, and she said, "No more curb service. If you need more liquor, you'll have to walk to the house. Take it easy and lean on me. You're still bleeding, but not as much. After I sew you up and cover the wound, I think you're going to be okay."

"It's going to take more than two drinks before I let you operate on me," Claude said. "I hope you've got ether or something to knock me out."

"I thought you were a big, macho man."

Getting shakily to his feet and feeling wobbly, he said, "Not that macho. Okay, I'm ready. Let's give it a bloody good go."

(Five)

At eight a.m., the phone on Joe's dresser rang and he reached out to grasp it. His mind was still foggy from the drinks he and Fad poured down last night at O'Grady's after work, so it wasn't functioning too well this morning.

His mouth felt like half the Russian Army marched through during the night. From the foul taste they left behind, Joe had the feeling most of them stopped to take a dump.

Picking up the receiver, he asked, "Yeah, what's up?"

Bert's voice sounded happy as he said, "It's me, with good news, buddy. Sadie has been found alive and well. Chalk one up for the good guys."

"Where is she?"

"A little girl named Alice Grabowski found her the day after the explosion," Bert said. "I guess she wanted to keep her, but her dad found out, saw the reward notice and called it in.

"Alice and her folks live about four blocks from the crime scene, over on Laurel Avenue—five twenty-six to be exact. I told them to keep Sadie inside until you got there. So far the press hasn't got wind of it."

"Thanks, Bert. I owe you one."

After writing the address down on his note pad and climbing out of bed, Joe's reflection in the mirror told him more than he wanted to know about how he looked. He thought, "Hung over and hanging out. I've got to go on a diet. What will Mona think?"

Laughing at his last statement, he smiled at his ugly, sorry-looking self in the mirror, but for some reason, his double didn't return the gesture, so he wondered, "I guess he's mad at me. Hell, I am too.

He tried to shave without cutting himself, but nicked his chin in two places and cursed aloud. Then he searched, but couldn't find his little white styptic pencil anywhere. Finally, he put small pieces of toilet paper on the cuts to stop the flow of blood, and knew, "It's going to be one of those days."

His blue suit was lying rumpled on the floor and it looked like he spilled a beer on the left leg of his pants, but it was better than his brown one. Besides, as hung over as he was, he really didn't give a damn what he looked like.

After brushing the suit coat off, he pulled on a clean shirt and climbed into the wrinkled outfit. Leaving his tie at home, he headed out the door.

It was a clear warm morning and small puffy white clouds dotted an otherwise empty blue sky. High overhead Joe saw two contrails from jets and wondered where they were headed. "I hope it's somewhere with sandy beaches and topless girls who serve tall cold drinks. I vote for anywhere but here, where they kill at the slightest provocation."

SIGNS OF OUR TIMES

After pausing at the corner Quick-stop for Danish and a leaky cardboard container of two-day-old coffee from the taste of it, he drove carefully over the rough streets, drinking the burned tasting liquid anyway, with only a few drops falling on his suit coat.

The roll contained raisins, which he hated because they reminded him of dead flies on a pile of horseshit. But rather than try to pick the little fruit pieces out and make a worse mess, he choked them down.

Twelve minutes after he left his house, Joe pulled up in front of the apartment building at the address Bert gave him, and said aloud, "Damn, I didn't get the apartment number."

Without thinking of the consequences, he promised himself, "No more booze on work nights." But as soon as he planted the thought in his mind, Joe knew it was a lie.

Too much liquor ruined his marriage and now it was about the only thing that kept him going when the job got tough. It was something his ex-wife, Shirley, never understood.

Climbing from the aging wreck which the city politely called a police car, he brushed about half of the crumbs off his suit jacket, and then walked to the main entrance where the mailboxes hung haphazardly on the wall.

Two of them had no names or numbers at all and he wondered, "How do they get their mail unless the mail man is a mind reader?"

One of the other two boxes, number four, displayed the name "Grabowski" hand-written with a black marking pen in neat letters.

Joe thought kindly, "It must be Alice's work."

Turning to his left, he made his way to the entrance of number four. After knocking politely, he waited for someone to open the door.

A young girl of nine or ten opened it until the chain caught, peered out at him and asked, "Are you a policeman?"

"Yeah, I am, Honey. My name is Joe. Are you Alice?"

"Let me see your badge and I. D.," she demanded.

"Sure," Joe said.

Reaching into his back pocket, he came away with his identification folder and billfold with his shield attached to the inside. After taking the I.D. card out of its holder, he handed it and the open wallet to Alice with the badge pinned to the flap, as he thought, "Been watching Law and Order, haven't you, kiddo?"

Her thin arm reached through the small space the chain allowed and took them. Then the door closed, but the lock didn't engage as she looked the papers over. Pulling on the door again, she held up Joe's picture to compare it to the apparition standing at her doorstep, and said, "You look a lot younger in this picture."

"Thanks a lot," Joe thought, but said, "Yeah, I probably do. That was taken a few years ago, but it's really me."

Handing the items back to him, she said. "Okay, I believe you. I'm Alice Grabowski, the person who called you. Are you here to pick up the chimpanzee?"

"Yeah, Alice; I am. Thanks for finding and taking such good care of Sadie. Was she hurt in the fire?"

Squealing in delight, Alice asked, "Is that her name? Yes, Sadie got blisters on an arm, and the hair on her back was singed."

From behind her, a man's voice said, "Open the door, Alice. Let the officer in."

Pushing the door shut again, Alice rattled the chain around as she removed it from its latch. Then the door swung open wide. Alice stood there wearing red flip-flops and a brown dress dotted with multicolored flowers.

Standing by Alice's side, Sadie waved, and Joe said, "Hi Sadie. How ya doing?"

She signed, "Where's Wilbur?"

Alice said, "Sadie's done that all the time she's been here. I think she's asking about her mate."

"Could be," Joe said.

Sticking out his hand, Harold said, "I'm Harold Grabowski."

As they shook, Joe said, "Pleased to meet you, sir. Thanks for calling. We needed to find Sadie in the worst way. I hope you'll keep this to yourself for a few days. She's an important witness to a crime and I don't want anyone to know we found her."

"Sure," Harold said. Then he asked, "Didn't the newspaper say something about a five-hundred-dollar reward?"

"Yeah, it did, but I'm not in charge of that. Don't worry. I'll make sure Alice gets it. As far as I'm concerned, she's a real hero."

"Did you hear the policeman, Alice?" Harold asked. "Maybe they'll put your picture in the paper."

Alice rolled her eyes, and Joe winked at her, but Harold didn't notice.

"That will have to wait for a while," Joe said. "You ready to go, Sadie?"

Looking up at Alice with sorrowful eyes, Sadie seemed reluctant to let go of her hand, but finally she did and grasped Joe's fingers with her paw.

"Good girl," Joe said as he showed Sadie his teeth, and asked, "How about a grin for me?"

Sadie grinned and her breath smelled of fresh bananas. Joe wondered what his breath was like and figured, "Russian crap, Danish, dead flies, horseshit and stale coffee. It's a great combination."

Sliding to her knees beside Sadie, Alice hugged her tight as small tears ran down her cheeks, but in spite of them, she attempted to smile as she cried, "I'll miss you, Sadie. I love you."

Sadie signed "I love you," and Harold said, "Hey, I know what it means. The chimp just said she loves Alice in sign language. Can you believe it?"

Joe said, "Yeah, I can. Sadie's a smart girl."

Harold stood there with his mouth hanging open like a Venus flytrap waiting for its next victim, as Joe reached down, patted Alice on the head and winked at her again. Reluctantly, Alice let go of Sadie.

As he walked Sadie toward his cruiser, Joe said, "Thanks again, Alice."

Sadie blew Alice a kiss over her shoulder and galloped alongside him, lurching back and forth like a drunken sailor out on a three-day binge in San Diego.

(Six)

In the converted kitchen area of a three-room cabin twenty miles north of Sulfur Springs, Felix sat at a work bench surveying his surroundings. With the sun hiding behind some dark clouds to the west, it was a cool evening and there was a smell of rain in the air. A light wind blew in the windows and the curtains flapped slowly, like sails on a pirate ship.

It was hard to explain why Felix associated with terrorists and planned mass murder on a scale unheard of before. He had a good job and until a drunk driver who was Jewish killed them, a beautiful wife and family.

Maybe it was the real reason for Felix's involvement. Ever since the accident he hated Jews and it warped his mind, but he didn't know it. All he wanted was revenge, and the murder of thousands, maybe hundreds of thousands didn't get through to Felix as being way beyond retribution.

In his madness, he knew all Jews were rich. Since only rich people could afford the high-priced tickets to the Cotton Bowl, accordingly everyone attending the game must be Jewish and therefore all the attendees should die.

There were a very few times when Felix felt some remorse, but then thoughts of his lovely wife, Carmen and their two small children, Roberto and Carlos, returned and his rage would block out any rational point of view.

As he watched the curtains flap, Felix was frightened and trying not to let it show. This morning he read the report of the missing chimps and the offer of a sizable reward for their return. But so far the newspapers hadn't reported anything about them being fried in the fire and Felix wondered why.

"Maybe I screwed up. Did Mister Jones do his job or did he miss them? I forgot to ask him about the chimps before Mohammed wasted him. It was stupid of me. If they're out there somewhere running loose, someone who knows sign language might recognize what they're saying and it's all we need."

The wind blew stronger and cooler, so he stood up, pulled a sweater down from a nail, put it on and continued to ponder. There hadn't been anything in the local rags about an unidentified man found in the canal either. Did the fish take care of Mister Jones or wasn't he dead?

"Damn, I should have made sure."

Catching the story about Larry Holgram on the third page, he was surprised Larry surfaced so quickly, and smiled inwardly at his pun.

But at the present time, Felix couldn't worry about such mundane things. Mohammed was on his case to get the nerve gas transferred into thirty-two of the thirty-six fire extinguishers he had purchased and it was going to take some time. One little slip and Felix would be dead instead of their intended victims, so he thought, "To hell with Mohammed. He's not going to risk his life by being here when I prepare the bombs."

Over the past year, Felix set up a small lab out in the woods in this tiny isolated cabin he owned. Now he possessed all the instruments needed to take the gas from the lab's container and allow it to flow one ounce at a time into the empty fire extinguishers.

Purchasing the equipment a piece at a time, one here and another there from ten different stores in six cities, Felix always paid cash and used phony I.D.

Mohammed and his terrorist friends had provided the unique detonators, primer cord and a small amount of C-4 plastic explosive to complete the devices. Each of the tiny, remotely controlled detonators was formed to resemble the seal attached to every fire extinguisher.

Just like the real item, the electrical inspection logo was imprinted on the face of the seal. The primer cord took the place of the waxed strings that ran around the handle and in and out of the seal.

A remote control box setting at the end of Felix's workbench would detonate the bombs simultaneously by a single command. The detonator would ignite the primer cord, which would set off the C-4 and blow the container apart, releasing the pressurized nerve gas into the air of the stadium.

SIGNS OF OUR TIMES

There were thirty-one entrances to the stands at the Cotton Bowl and the terrorists intended to have a bomb at each of them to cover the entire playing field, stands, plus the reserved and box seats.

"As the warm afternoon wind increases, it should spread the gas throughout the surrounding cities, killing thousands, perhaps hundreds of thousands," Mohammed said.

The location of the last bomb was in close proximity to the President's box, so the leader of the free world and his party would have no chance to escape. The site was Felix's idea and it enthralled Mohammed.

"No one will notice," he said. "It's brilliant, Felix."

Glowing with pride, Felix said, "I got the idea while watching re-runs of past Cotton Bowl games. The motorized stretcher used to carry injured players was always there, with a fire extinguisher located in the rear, and setting near the middle of the sidelines, very close to the Presidential box. If the other devices don't get him, this one will."

Even if the Feds were smart enough to discover the gas came from the lab in Sulfur Springs, Felix felt confident no one would be able to trace his movements or connect it to him. Before he left, he'd burn the cabin too destroy any evidence.

All these plans weren't bothering him. There was plenty of time to prepare the bombs. Mohammed would have to wait until he solved another problem.

The only weak link now was Grady. The cops questioned him and although Grady said he could handle the police, Felix had no further use for him. Now that the gas was out of the lab, Grady's services were no longer required.

Felix thought, "It'll be one less tie to me."

But how could he take care of him and not leave a body? Even though he fervently supported the IRA, Grady was a good family man. If he ran around on his wife, perhaps Felix could set up a phony sex scene and make it appear Grady was killed in an unfortunate accident while out with a prostitute, but he didn't think such a scenario would fly.

Mohammed wanted to waste Grady as they did Mister Jones, but it was too risky. Another killing even remotely connected with the chemical lab would surely make the Feds and everyone else suspicious, so Felix knew, "No, it has to be an accident and if possible, his body shouldn't be found. And it has to happen soon."

If the cops called Grady back in and got rough, Felix didn't know if he could keep his mouth shut. With two small kids, Grady would talk to save them, so Felix said silently, "Yeah, Grady has to go."

(Seven)

Claude and his companion staggered into her home together. Leaning heavily on her shoulder, he glanced around the living room, noting a cozy domestic scene. The room contained a fireplace with a small pile of logs at one side, a green upholstered couch with wooden arms and two comfortable-looking recliner chairs in a dark brown color.

Light came from two matching sea-shell-filled glass lamps on small pine end tables. Several paintings of ships and the sea hung on the walls. Light-green drapes framed a wide window in the front wall, which overlooked the canal where Claude was swimming a few minutes ago.

Stopping to rest and breathing hard, she said, "Well, we made it this far. Damn, I didn't think you were so heavy. Here, sit down in this chair, I can't hold you up much longer."

"Thanks again. What's your name? I can't keep calling you 'Hey you'."

"It's Carla—Carla Roberson. What's yours?"

Her smile faded into a frown as he said, "Just call me Mister Macho."

Claude took the time to study her from her head to her toes, and she stood there and watched as his eyes took in every aspect of her body.

Just as he thought, she was beautiful. While not gorgeous, she was more than pretty, with nicely tanned skin from her face to her feet. Her toes peeked out of leather sandals and displayed an even coat of light red polish to match her fingernails.

Her hands were not big, but were larger than average with long, slender manicured fingers. The skin of her face was smooth and tight at the base of her neck and he estimated her age as somewhere in her late twenties. She had curves in the right places, shapely legs, wide thighs and a nice set of breastworks.

When his eyes returned to her face, she asked, "Seen enough?"

"Yeah, you're a well-put-together package, Carla. And I mean it in a nice way. It's not a pass."

Her smile returned, and she said, "Thanks, but I'm not the one who needs to be looked at or after, it's you. We need to get your wet clothes off and then patch you up. How do you feel?"

"Like I was in a hatchet fight without a weapon," Claude said. "My shoulder burns like hell, but the rest of my body feels like I'm freezing."

Nodding knowingly, she said, "Hypothermia. Here, let me get those wet clothes off you. Don't be squeamish. I've seen men's bods before and you're nothing special."

"Now you hurt my pride. Go ahead. I'll help you all I can."

Between them, they got his pants off without much difficulty or pain. The shirt was easy; Carla finished ripping it from his back and good arm. Then she grabbed his bloody t-shirt and ripped it off too.

"Just like Marlon Brando in 'A Street Car Named Desire'," Claude said. "If you don't mind, I'll keep my shorts on."

As she wrapped a fresh warm blanket around his legs and put another over his left shoulder, she asked, "Bashful?"

He tried to tuck the second one around him, but required her help to finish. Then he said, "Thanks, that feels better. I'm warmer already."

Handing him a jelly glass half-full of whiskey, she said, "Here, take another drink. You'll need several of these before I can get to work on your wound. The good news is—it quit bleeding."

Pouring half the glass down his throat, Claude coughed as the liquor hit bottom. Within a few seconds he felt the warmth spread throughout his body. Looking down at where the bullet entered his chest area just below the collarbone, he couldn't see the exit wound, but could feel it.

Using Carla's makeup mirror and another smaller one, they gave him a good look at his injury. He tried to move his shoulder and although there was pain, there was no sound of bone grating on bone.

Flexing his fingers, he found they reacted to his mind's directions. With Carla's help he found he could swing his arm a couple inches each way. His chest was sore and painful to the touch, and she said, "You've already got a bruise there."

Claude couldn't tell her he wore a flak jacket and was shot in the chest too. She had enough on her plate already. So he lied and said, "I think it happened when I hit a piling as I fell into the canal. At first I thought my shoulder or arm was broken, but now I think it was shock. The bullet went straight through and I don't think it hit bone."

After studying the two openings for a few moments, she said, "That's my opinion too."

He finished the drink.

Carla poured him another, and said, "So, while we wait for you to get plastered, you want to tell me who shot you and why?"

"I can't tell you all of it. Suffice to say the other fellow and I had a disagreement over money and I came up on the losing end. I believe the jerk thinks he killed me. In fact, I'm counting on it."

"Oh, good," she said. "Then you can shoot 'the jerk' and someone can try to patch him up, right? When does it end?"

Claude moved without thinking, grimaced at the sudden pain, and said, "Hopefully when he's dead instead of me."

"Is it really necessary? Can't you go to the police?"

"No, I can't. Let's leave it at that. All I'm asking of you is some help and time for me to get well. Then I'll get out of your hair and let you live the good life again."

Carla's lips changed into a pout and she said, "And I'm supposed to smile, wave as you leave and go back to work like nothing ever happened, right?"

Sighing at her stubbornness, he said, "It's too complicated now, without getting you involved. Trust me. I don't want to see you hurt. Let's be ships that pass in the night and let it go at that."

"Drink your drink," Carla commanded, and Claude saw fire in her eyes. "I'll go get my sewing box. You know Mister Macho, I think I'm going to enjoy patching you up and watch you squirm with every stitch."

CHAPTER 10

(One)

After opening the door to Mona's office, Joe called out, "Here's Sadie" like he was Ed McMahon introducing Johnny Carson on the Tonight Show. His shout made Sadie howl like a coyote seriously looking for a mate. She galloped into Mona's office on all four limbs, jumped up on Mona's desk and scattered papers, pens and folders in all directions.

It wasn't the effect Joe was aiming for, but it did get Mona's attention. She said, "Hello you two. God, I'm glad to see you Sadie. Where have you been?"

Taking Sadie's hand, she helped her climb down from the desk.

Joe said, "I feel like Cinderella. Everyone gets noticed but me. Aren't you happy to see me too?"

"Grow up, Joe," she said, but smiled, so he knew she was glad to see him. "Where did you find our little lost girl?"

"I didn't. An eleven year old named Alice found her the day after the fire and kept Sadie hidden out back of her house. Her father finally caught on when all the apples and bananas in the house disappeared in a couple of days. He had her call us and I went out and picked Sadie up.

"By the way, Mister Grabowski's very interested in receiving the five-hundred-dollar reward."

"I'll make sure Alice gets it," Mona said. "Give me her address and I'll stop by to see her tomorrow."

He checked his notebook again and said, "Its five twenty-six Laurel Avenue, Apartment Four. You'll love the kid. Alice is cute as apple pie a-la-mode, and really broken up about parting with Sadie."

"I'll make it up to her. Now, you little dickens, we'll put you back where you belong."

"Where's Wilbur?" Sadie signed.

"What do I tell her? She asked about Wilbur."

"It would probably ruin her day to learn Wilbur went to the big jungle in the sky," Joe said. "I don't know. Maybe Wilbur is off visiting friends? Tell her anything to keep her happy. If she thinks he's coming back, she won't be upset and forget what Larry told her."

"I think it's cruel, but I agree," Mona said, so she signed, "Wilbur's on a trip to find a new home for you."

Sadie still looked forlorn, but instead of a frown, her grin returned and she signed, "For me?"

Lying and feeling like hell, Mona said, "Yes, you and Wilbur."

"Is there somewhere we can hide Sadie until we debrief her?" Joe asked.

"No, there's no place here. Don't you have any empty cells at the jail?"

"A cell for a chimp?"

Mona laughed and said, "You already have a lot of apes there. What's one more?"

"You got me. Yeah, I guess I could clear it with the boss. Red might not like it, but when I tell him why, I think he'll go along. Damn, I should have thought about it myself, but I was in a hurry to return Sadie and see you again. Oops, that slipped out."

As he blushed again, she said, "I'm flattered, Joe."

(Two)

The day after Sadie returned to the lab and Joe jailed her, Mona stopped by the Grabowski home to talk to Alice. She found her sitting on the back stoop with her legs hanging over the foundation, letting them swing back and forth.

Alice had a hand full of stones and Mona watched as she took them, one at a time from her left hand and aiming at nothing in particular, she threw them out into the littered yard.

She looked so forlorn it broke Mona's heart, so she said, "Hi, Alice, I'm

Doctor Wilson from the research laboratory. Thanks for finding Sadie. We missed her."

Without looking up, Alice said, "Not as much as I do."

She threw another pebble. It hit a tin can with a loud "ping" and ricocheted off into the bushes where Sadie hid just yesterday.

"I know what you mean," Mona said. "May I sit down with you? I love to let my feet dangle and pretend I'm a princess."

"Sure, go ahead, be my guest," Alice said, and then she asked, "Are you a real doctor? Do you go around cutting up monkeys, chimps or people?"

"No, I don't. I'm not that kind of doctor. The title in front of my name is sort of an honorary thing. It says I went to college and earned a fancy degree. There are a lot of my kinds of doctors in the world, but we aren't cutting anybody or anything up."

"That's good," Alice said. "I hate to think anyone would cut Sadie up."

"We'd never do that. Sadie is much too smart and valuable. She's as close to being human as you can get without being human. Do you understand?"

"You mean because Sadie can sign?"

"Exactly," Mona said. "We hope Sadie can help children to learn sign language and make it fun at the same time. Would you like to learn to sign? That way you could talk to Sadie."

"Would you teach me?"

Mona hugged her, and said, "Yes. You're a very special young lady, Alice. Everyone at the lab is proud of you. We know you didn't want to give Sadie up, but you knew it was best for her and did it. That makes you more grown up than a lot of older people I know."

Looking up, with joy replacing her sorrow, she asked, "When can I start? I'd love to see Sadie again and be able to talk to her."

"Why don't you have your father bring you out to the lab tomorrow morning at ten a.m.?" Mona asked. "I'll show you around and then we'll go see Sadie. They have her in protective custody, so she'll be glad to see you.

"By the way, we have your reward check. Your father says he has a college fund set up for you. Maybe someday you'll have a fancy doctor in front of your name and you can work with animals like I do."

As she hugged Mona, Alice exclaimed, "Oh, I hope so."

(Three)
Felix phoned Grady and asked, "So, how'd it go with the cops?"

Grady lied as he said, "No problem. A big black buck called me everything but a white man and tried his best to get me to say something, but I was cool. I told the story just like you said. After an hour of bullshit they let me go. The black son of a bitch thought he was tough, but I showed him."

Knowing Grady wasn't as macho as he acted, Felix thought, "I'll bet," but he said, "That's good. Do you think the cops will want to talk to you again?"

"I don't know, but if they do, they won't get anything out of me. They'll have to find me first. On Saturday, I'm heading for Mexico to do some deep pit caving."

"Is that smart?" Felix asked. "Won't the police think you're running away?"

"Nah, this trip has been planned for months and all my friends know it. Hell, I'm not cutting out. I'll be back next week. If the cops want to question me again, I'm up to it. I can beat them at their own game."

With a plan beginning to take place in his mind, Felix asked, "Are you going alone? I hear those caves are dangerous."

"A buddy of mine, Clete Palmer, is going along. We've explored a couple of the deep pit caves in Mexico before, El Sotano and Las Golondinas. We've got the right equipment and know what we're doing, so relax, we'll be okay."

"It sounds exciting," Felix said. "Where are you headed this time?"

"A cavern called Diablo's Hideout. Not many people know about it because it's out in the middle of nowhere. This cave is over four hundred feet deep and should be a blast."

"Have fun, but be careful," Felix said. "Call me when you get back."

"Will do," Grady said. "Lighten up, Felix. I was cool."

Not meaning it, Felix said, "Yeah. Okay."

After Grady hung up, he listened to the buzz of the phone for a few moments and pieces of his plan started taking shape. He put down the instrument, made some notes on a nearby scratch pad and a few minutes later, he said, "Yeah," again, but this time he meant it.

(Four)

Kris had been busier than a fire ant feeding his queen since the last time he saw Joe. After obtaining a search warrant for Katie's apartment, the next day, he and four other agents descended on her home.

To his bitter disappointment, they found no notes about the supposed terror attack. He didn't really expect to because he figured Katie would have them with her when she left to meet him and her memos burned in the fire.

Just in case the notes survived, they drove to the police impoundment yard to check the burned shell of her old crushed Volvo. The seats were nothing but charred and rusted springs with small pieces of burned upholstery clinging bravely here and there.

Fire had decimated the interior of the car and nothing salvageable remained. The vehicle smelled like burned flesh and Kris was glad when the inspection ended. If there were paper notes, they were long gone.

The next morning when he met Joe in the office, Kris told him, "The only thing we found was a melted twisted piece of plastic that looked like a handle for a leather briefcase."

"The fire did a number on Katie, Wilbur and everything inside," Joe said. "I remember it vividly. It was a hell of a mess."

"Yeah," Kris said. "Gasoline will do that. So where does this leave us?"

"This afternoon, Mona will be here with Alice and she'll ask Sadie what she knows. Then we'll follow the leads we develop from their conversation."

"If anyone can get the story from Sadie, it's Mona. She worked with Sadie since the start of the program."

"Sounds good," Kris said. "You want me to stick around?"

"Nah, there's no reason for you to waste your day here. As soon as we get anything, I'll phone and we'll go over it together."

Smiling, Kris said, "I think you want Mona all to yourself. Remember, when she walks in you'll have to watch the rest of the cops. They'll froth at the mouth."

Joe laughed and said, "Yeah, I know, but I can handle them. I guess you know I really like her."

Kris chuckled and said, "When you turn red around her all the time, it's self-evident. She's a good-looking woman and has a chest that won't quit."

Smiling as he remembered an old joke, Joe asked, "You know why men can't make eye contact?"

"No. Why?"

"It's because boobies don't have eyes."

(Five)

When she saw her friend behind bars, Alice cried out, "Oh Sadie, they put you in jail."

"I told you Joe has Sadie in protective custody," Mona said. "Sadie's not a jailbird. She's having a ball."

That was evident from the many banana peels and orange rinds surrounding Sadie where she sat on top of a folded down bed in the cell.

Mona thought, "Every cop in the building must be feeding her. I hope she doesn't get sick."

"Hello," Sadie signed to Alice. "It's nice to see you again."

"What did she say," Alice asked.

"Sadie says, 'it's nice to see you again'," Mona said. "Here, let me show you how to say 'Hello'."

Mona made the signs; Alice copied them, and asked, "How do I say 'I love you'?"

"Follow me," Mona said.

"I love you too," Sadie replied, and Mona said, "See how easy it is."

"I want to learn everything," Alice said.

"I'll teach you all the signs, but not today," Mona said. "I'll ask your dad to bring you out to the lab on week-ends and we'll work together. Would you like that?"

"Can I help teach the monkeys and chimps?"

"Sure," Mona said. "As fast as you learn, you'll take my place in a year."

"No, I won't. Look."

Alice signed, "I love you" to Mona.

Tears formed in her eyes as she said, "Thanks, Honey. I love you too."

Joe walked up and said, "It looks like you two are doing okay. I'm sorry I couldn't meet you, but I had to interview a witness to a robbery. I see Bert showed you where Sadie is. She looks like she's doing okay, doesn't she?"

"She's eaten way too many bananas," Mona said. "You'll be sorry about it when she has to go potty."

Joe laughed and said, "I'll send one of our rookies down here to deal with it. I'll tell the guys to knock off feeding her. Ever since she arrived, she's been a hit."

"Sadie's a lot more fun than most of the apes we have in here," Bert said.

"I told Joe she would be," Mona said.

Nodding his head toward Alice, Joe said, "We need to talk to Sadie about Larry."

Catching his drift, Mona said, "I think we've taken up enough of Sadie's time for today, Alice. Let me take you home now and we'll see her again real soon."

"Okay," Alice said, as she reached into the cell and waggled her fingers. Sadie jumped down from her perch and ran to meet her and Alice said, "Behave yourself, and remember I love you."

She signed the message to Sadie, who grinned and repeated it.

SIGNS OF OUR TIMES

"This is how you say 'goodbye'," Mona said.

"Goodbye," Alice signed, gave Sadie another pat on the head and turned to take Mona's hand.

Smiling at Joe, Mona said, "I'll be back shortly."

His heart did a jump through a hoop, and he knew he was blushing and Bert would see, but he didn't give a damn.

(Six)

Kris wasn't the only one who was busy. Felix felt like he ran the mile in three and a half minutes. His plan was taking shape, but it took some doing.

After driving his old pickup truck to a local sports shop, he rented a four-wheeled ATV and a ramp to load and unload the small vehicle. The dealer named Harry helped him load the ATV and tie it and the ramp down.

"Be careful," Harry said. "If you try to do foolish things, these vehicles are dangerous. This four-wheeled model is a lot more stable than the three-wheelers. Just don't try anything dumb like doing wheelies and you'll be okay."

"Thanks for the help and the warning," Felix said. "I'll see you next week."

At a local Wal Mart, he purchased a Ground Positioning System, (GPS), with receiver and antenna, plus the rest of the equipment he thought he would need.

He included some freeze-dried food in plastic packages that required no cooking, but in case the food wasn't as great as the labels proclaimed, when he got to the checkout, he picked up a handful of candy bars.

After loading everything aboard his pickup, he stopped and filled both gas and water cans at a local service station, drove home and parked and locked the vehicle inside his garage where it would be safe from pilfering. In his neighborhood, if you left a vehicle outside unattended for five minutes, nothing was sacred and everything was fair game.

Then he went inside his small home and called a local taxi. When it arrived ten minutes later, he told the driver, "Take me to the Swifty Rental place downtown."

"Sure Mac," the cabbie said.

Forty five minutes later, he returned home at the wheel of a dark-blue Chevy Cavalier, parked the car in his driveway, locked the vehicle and went inside to eat lunch.

Later in the evening as the sun set behind the mountains with an awesome display of brilliant colors, Felix emerged again dressed in dark clothes and carrying a pair of binoculars in a grey leather case.

After climbing in the rental car, he fired the engine up, drove across town to where Grady lived and parked across the street at an angle from Grady's place.

Using the binoculars, he watched Grady and his friend, Clete, pack equipment onto a double-cab, four-wheel-drive Dodge Ram. Grady's kids ran around causing havoc while his wife tried to keep them under control and away from the truck.

When everything was packed, they roped a blue tarpaulin across the top of the pile, moved the truck closer to the house and went inside. Thirty minutes later, Clete came out, got into a black Pontiac Firebird at the curb, tooted the horn twice and drove off.

Felix drove a few blocks until he came to a fast food place, stopped, went inside and ate dinner. While he read a local newspaper the place provided free, he lingered over a cup of hot coffee for an hour longer.

At nine thirty he got up, dumped the residue of his meal into a trashcan near the door and returned to his car. Driving slowly, he returned to where he parked previously and sat watching the house.

An hour after he saw the light go out in Grady's bedroom, Felix looked around for pedestrians and saw none. The neighborhood was quiet as a chocolate mousse. Dogs barked occasionally, but they were far off, which was a blessing. He hated them.

Leaving his vehicle at midnight and carrying the GPS antenna strapped to a heavy-duty magnet, he walked across the street and down the sidewalk to Grady's truck. After crossing the lawn to the Ram, he knelt down and secured the unit under and behind the rear bumper.

After lodging it close to the end, where it wouldn't shake loose on uneven ground, he tried to extract the unit by pulling on it with one hand, was unable to do so and thought, "Good enough."

Making his way back to the rental, he got in and picked up the receiver to check his work. When the small screen displayed the correct location of the antenna, he smiled, started the engine and drove away.

CHAPTER 11

(One)

When Mona walked in the door, Joe asked, "You ready to give it a go with Sadie?"

"Yes, I hope Sadie remembers whatever Larry told her. She's smart, but it's a shame we lost Wilbur. He was better at signing than she is."

Behind her, Joe saw four cops ogling her legs and drooling at the mouth. He thought "Kris was right."

Getting up and closing the door, he shut off their view, hoping they'd disappear before he and Mona headed downstairs to the cell block where Sadie held court.

Then he said, "Sadie's our only lead to Larry's murder and whatever's going on at the chemical lab. Do you want a cup of coffee or something to drink before we go see her?"

"No, I'm fine. I'm ready anytime you are."

Mona stood up and for a fleeting moment she gave Joe a glimpse of black panties, his favorite color besides red. When she saw his eyes on her legs, she smiled.

He blushed again, thinking, "Damn it anyway."

They made their way through an unusually crowded hallway to the elevator, where three other cops holding different reports, one of them upside down, climbed aboard with them.

The policemen didn't pay much attention to their paperwork. Instead, they studied their female companion. Joe stared at each of them and received large smiles in return.

Joe knew one of them, Hal Simmons, so he asked, "Seems a little hectic on the floor today, doesn't it, Hal?"

With a straight face he said, "Yeah, crime never takes a holiday."

The other cops smiled and nodded knowingly.

"You all headed for the basement?"

"Yeah," Hal said.

"That's strange. I thought Records was on the fifth floor."

No one replied as the group rode down three floors. Mona wore a smile, obviously enjoying Joe's predicament and the cops' attention.

When the door opened, Hal said, "After you, Miss."

Mona stepped out and the cops tried to blindside Joe, but he elbowed his way through them and grabbed Mona's arm possessively. She looked down at his hand and smiled. Joe blushed again, cursing his fellow officers under his breath as they followed them down the hall.

As they approached the empty cellblock housing Sadie, he said, "No visitors beyond this point. Doctor Wilson and I are going to question a witness. We don't need you clowns hanging around to bother us. Take off."

"Yes, Sergeant Francone," Hal said. As they turned and walked back toward the elevator, Joe saw one of them trip as he tried to get one more look at Mona's legs.

Joe thought "I hope you fall on your ass or break a leg."

He tightened his grip on Mona's elbow, and she didn't pull away.

(Two)

Two hundred feet down the shaft of Diablo's Hideout, Grady stopped his descent, turning slowly to look upward, downward and at the sides of the cavern he and Clete planned to explore. The cave was huge and deep, lined with rugged broken rocks, crevices, outcrops and pinnacles.

It was more fantastic than he thought it would be and he reveled in the fact that for the entire weekend, it was theirs alone to explore.

Above him, Clete lay on his stomach, looking down into the dark pit, trying to see Grady. The fierce sunlight above didn't penetrate very deep into the cave, so he could barely make out the outline of his buddy against the black rock.

Clete couldn't wait for his turn to ride the cable down into the depths to see the wonders of nature displayed as only she can. It appeared this cave was almost unknown and unexplored. There wasn't the usual litter and trash lying around the entrance.

After a long drive and the hectic traffic in Nuevo Laredo, they arrived here at noon yesterday. Clete was glad they had Grady's four-wheel-drive vehicle. The last fifty miles of their journey was over rough, torn-up gravel roads not meant for anything less sturdy than his Dodge Ram.

As soon as they found the cave, they set up the apparatus they had manufactured. It consisted of a long twenty-foot arm somewhat like a crane, with a sprocket at the end that allowed the cable from Grady's truck to pass through.

The rig had two pieces of heavy-duty aluminum, both twelve feet long, interlocking for four feet at the center, with eight titanium bolts to hold them together.

One end of the arm was attached to the front bumper of Grady's truck, on top of the winch and pulley unit. It held over seven hundred feet of study steel cable, capable of hauling over a ton of weight, more than enough for their use.

After the arm was constructed, Grady eased the Ram to within four feet of the edge of the cavern and parked it there.

Clete reminded him, "Leave the key in the ignition."

Everyone in the caving community knew the story of the guy who dropped the key to his vehicle out of his pocket on the way down into a deep pit cavern. After having to walk thirty miles through the hot desert to the nearest civilization, he and his companions almost died of dehydration.

Even though they knew their combined weight wouldn't cause the truck to stand on its nose, just in case, Grady and Clete loaded approximately three hundred pounds of rocks into the back of the bed. When it came to safety, there was a right way and a wrong way, and they only used the correct method.

After laying out his latest acquisition, Grady said, "Look at this. It's a remote control for the winch, with over a thousand feet of wire attached. As we descend, we feed it out with the cable. The remote control lets us stop wherever we want and then continue downward. I can even have the winch rewind to go up. No more quick one-way descents."

Looking the unit over, Clete said, "Hey, that's neat. I can't wait to try it out."

Jerking his thumb toward the setting sun, Grady said, "It's too late today. Let's get camp set up, eat a bite and get some shut-eye. I'm beat and want to be in good shape for tomorrow."

"You got it, buddy," Clete said. Grabbing the two-man tent from the bed of the truck, he started laying it out on the ground, and said, "Hand me the pegs and hammer."

(Three)
Two thousand yards away, Felix lay concealed behind a rock watching his quarry. With the GPS, it had been easy to follow Clete and Grady from a long distance behind. When they turned onto a rocky gravel road, he stopped his two-wheel-drive pickup, pulling into a grove of small trees.

As he watched Clete and Grady's progress on his receiver, Felix saw them travel farther on down the road. After unloading the rental ATV, he packed the gear aboard he thought he needed, hid the key to his truck under a nearby rock, started the engine of the ATV and drove off.

The road was rough, but knowing he had all the time in the world, he drove slowly. Strapped across the handlebars was a high-powered rifle and he carried a .38 caliber six-shot revolver in a harness under his left arm.

For the next two hours, Felix stopped periodically to check the location of Grady and Clete. When they stopped ten miles ahead, he thought, "They must have reached their destination. Grady said it was out in the middle of nowhere and he's right. I couldn't have asked for a better killing field."

Although Felix was of Mexican descent, even with the rifle and revolver hidden under his seat, there was no trouble as he crossed the border. He had his passport with him and a Texas driver's license, which was all the border guard required.

When a border patrol agent asked him about his citizenship, he answered truthfully, "United States".

Behind his truck, vehicles were waiting in line for blocks, so the harried agent waved Felix through without another thought or inspection, saying, "Drive carefully."

Driving slowly so he wouldn't kick up a dust trail, Felix doubted either of his prey would notice, but he hadn't lived this long without learning not to take any unnecessary risks.

When the receiver told him he was within a mile of their location, he pulled the ATV into a small gully and unloaded the supplies. Before he left, taking the key with him, he piled brush on his vehicle to hide it. Then he loaded up and headed out at a trot.

Now he saw Grady and Clete had completed their preliminary work prior to descending into the pit and were preparing a campsite. The sun was setting low on the horizon, but there was no indication of rain or clouds in the vicinity. After unrolling his sleeping bag, Felix laid it out and sat down on it to try the freeze dried food.

The first package said it contained beans and rice. Using a small knife, he cut off the top and poured in water according to the instructions. After sitting and waiting fifteen minutes while the food absorbed the water, he tried a bite and found it tasted like shit on a stick, so he threw it into the brush and grabbed two of his candy bars instead.

Washing the taste of the crap out of his mouth, Felix spat the water at the ground. Then grinning, he devoured the chocolate and nut combination as he thought, "I knew it was going to be bad, but not that foul. Damn it anyway, I wish I could have a fire, but it can wait until tomorrow."

He set his wristwatch alarm for 0500 hours, lay down in his sleeping roll and covered his head with his cowboy hat. In ten minutes he was sleeping like a wolf cub.

(Four)
"Hello, Sadie. How are you today?" Mona signed.
"Good," Sadie answered. "Where's Wilbur?"
"Still looking for a home for you," Mona lied.
"Good," Sadie repeated and grinned.
"Do you remember Larry?" Mona asked. "He talked to you a few days ago."
"Yes, bad man hurt Larry. Make loud noise, hurt ears."
"Yes, that's him. Did Larry ask you to remember something?"
"Yes."
"Can you tell me?"
"Bad man, fell X man is and Far East man," Sadie signed.
"Yes, I know they were bad men. What did Larry tell you?"
"Terror is, nervous gas, football game, kill president, thousand," Sadie signed.
"Where?"
"Cotton, food bowl, fall," Sadie signed. "Wilbur knows too."
"That's good. What else?"
"Hide, three, two, fire, X," Sadie signed, and then sat back to pick something from her coat.
"Is that all?"

"Yes, bad man, loud noise, Larry hurt, Wilbur and Sadie hide. Where's Wilbur? Sadie needs him."

Mona turned to Joe, who was writing furiously in his notebook as she translated Sadie's signs, and said, "I guess that's all. It's not much, is it?"

"I don't know," Joe said. "I don't like the part about 'kill the president and thousands'. It sounds like a terrorist plot to me. What do you make of the rest of it?"

"Let's ask Sadie to repeat it again and then leave her alone," Mona said. "I can tell she misses Wilbur and all these questions are upsetting her."

"Okay, but take it slow and let me compare my notes to what she says. Then we'll call Kris and see if we can decipher her story."

(Five)

It was time to speak with Grady again. Kris studied Joe and Fad's notes and then phoned him at home.

When Grady's wife answered, he said, "Good morning, Mrs. O'Reilly. This is Agent Hefner from the FBI. May I speak to your husband?"

"Grady's not here, he left yesterday for a caving trip down in Mexico."

"I'd like to talk to him. When will he be back?"

"He and his buddy, Clete, said it would be next week," she said. "Can I take a message?"

"Please have Grady call me at 555-7923, extension 45."

"I'll write it down and give it to him."

"Thanks," Kris said and disconnected.

Speaking to his partner, Ellis Crowder, Kris said, "Damn it, I hope Grady didn't skip out on us."

"I don't think he'd run and leave his wife and kids here."

"I hope you're right."

(Six)

Hearing a sound behind him, Clete turned his head and saw Felix standing there with a revolver pointed at his chest. Raising his hands in the air, Clete said, "Holy cow, man, I didn't know we were trespassing. Put the gun down."

"Is Grady at the end of the cable?" Felix asked.

"Yeah, he's about halfway down. How do you know him and who are you? Man, put the gun down, you're scaring me."

"Thank you," Felix said, and shot Clete in the chest.

From the force of the impact, Clete reeled backward, lost his balance and pitched off the edge of the cavern into empty space.

SIGNS OF OUR TIMES

(Seven)

After clamping his remote control to the cable, Grady pulled a flashlight out of his back pack to study the walls on the opposite side of the cavern. As the light shone into the darkness, it reflected off the wings of thousands of bats hanging upside down along the walls. As they breathed, their motion resembled a grey tide beating against a distant shore.

He heard a loud pop and a moment later, a pebble pinged off Grady's hard hat, so he turned his head upward in time to see Clete's body fall toward him. In self-defense, he threw up his arm and one of Clete's legs hit it, knocked the flashlight from Grady's grasp, breaking his arm in two places so fast he didn't have time to scream.

His eyes tried to follow Clete's descent into the void, but his buddy disappeared into the darkness in an instant.

In anguish, Grady cried out, "Oh my God!"

His damaged arm was useless. In absolute terror, he grabbed the remote control with his good hand and attempted to punch the up button with his thumb, but missed. Then above him, he heard the roar of the truck engine and wondered, "What the hell is happening?"

His second attempt at the control was successful. The cable began to retract and pull him up. He cried out, "Thank you, God!"

As he moved swiftly upward about fifty feet, Grady realized whoever was as the wheel of the truck was helping to pull the cable up by backing the vehicle. Suddenly the motor roared again, the cable slackened and the bottom dropped out of his world.

Looking up in horror, he saw his truck crash over the side of the opening with the motor screaming like some creature from the ice age. It flew across the cave, hit the opposite wall with a thunderous sound and fell toward Grady, as he dropped like a stone toward the bottom of the pit.

He experienced a moment of tremendous pain as his body hit an outcropping, and his shoulder was crushed. Half the bones in his body were broken by the impact. Then a moment later, his head struck a rock with such force it split his helmet in two and his neck snapped, killing him instantly.

Grady's torn and shattered body beat the truck to the bottom of the abyss by ten seconds, but his ordeal wasn't over yet. Although he never felt a thing, the wreckage of the heavy vehicle landed on top of him, spreading what was left of his lifeless shell over forty feet of the cavern floor.

Fifty feet above Grady's remains, Clete's body was skewered on a sharp pinnacle, spread-eagled upside down and backward. The knife-like rock had entered Clete's back and protruded from his stomach, while his legs hung were twisted in reverse over his head.

Looking like a Raggedy Andy someone discarded after too much use and abuse, Clete's torn, steaming guts hung out obscenely, as blood and gore dripped down the walls to join the smeared remnants of Grady in peaceful slumber.

As if they were insane creatures from Mars or Jupiter, thousands of bats beat their wings against the warm morning air and flew out of the mouth of the cave. As they hurried away from the source of their disturbance, their cries grew fainter.

Soon it was as still in the cave as a bingo parlor where the players waited for the next ball to be called.

At the edge of the gorge, Felix listened until the last pieces of the truck came to a noisy rest and silence returned. Then he reached down to the campfire, took a coffee pot from the coals, dumped cold coffee out of a nearby cup and poured himself a fresh hot cup.

"Damn," he said to the sky. "That's good stuff. I wonder what Grady and Clete have to eat in that cooler. I'm so hungry I could eat a jackass, hooves and all."

Turning toward the pit and thinking of his two victims, he made a bad pun as he said, "I don't think they're hungry, I just fed them a big piece of mountain goat."

CHAPTER 12

(One)

"I'll be back in a few minutes," Carla said. "Keep pouring the whiskey down. It isn't going to get any better."

"Yes, dear," Claude said. He felt the booze already. A few more and he'd be bombed. While she was gone, he managed to get two more under his belt.

"Although I don't have one on anymore," he thought, and smiled crookedly.

When Carla returned to the room dressed in a dark red two-piece swimming suit, he couldn't believe it. It wasn't a bikini, but it didn't leave much to the imagination. The tiny halter strained against the amount of lovely flesh it tried valiantly to cover, and the faint outline of her point of passion showed against the dark material of the bottom half. She was stunning and Claude didn't have to be half in the bag to recognize the fact.

"Okay," she said. "The first thing we do is get you under the shower. The canal did nothing to help your condition. No telling what's trying to get under your skin as we speak and they have two new openings to help them. Get up."

"That makes sense," Claude said.

"And all modesty aside," she said, "those jockey briefs have to go."

"My love, I think you'd do anything to get me out of my drawers."

"You're really something. Come on, stand up and I'll help you into the shower. I'll hold you up and help you wash."

Claude stood up slowly and said, "Anything you command, my love."

He thought, "The booze must be working, the pain isn't as bad."

Carla helped him walk through her bedroom and into a large bathroom and then commanded, "Get in the shower," and he obeyed.

"Now for the shorts," Carla said.

As she reached around Claude's legs to pull them down, her touch did something to him.

He became erect, and said, "Sorry about that."

As she fought to get his shorts over his manhood, she said, "I can't believe you. Gun-shot and half-shot, you still have sex on your mind."

"It's a natural reaction when I'm standing naked in a shower with a woman as beautiful as you."

"Well cool your ardor, Romeo. You're not getting anywhere with this one."

She turned on the shower, the cold water hit Claude's head and he yelled, "Damn!"

As she adjusted the control until the water warmed, she said, "It serves you right. Now stand still and let me wash you. Hang onto the towel bar and don't fall down."

"I won't," Claude said, and let her have her way with him. After the chill he felt, it was delightful to have the hot water course down his body.

Scrubbing him well, Carla raised suds over his back and chest, paying special attention to the wounds, which caused them to bleed again. Reddish water ran down Claude's legs and rolled in circles around his feet before exiting through the floor drain.

"Now that you're clean, it'll do your wounds a world of good," she said. "As soon as I put some antiseptic on the injuries they'll stop bleeding."

Carla continued to wash him, cleaning his hips and legs, front and back and it felt wonderful. To her amazement, but not his, Claude's erection remained stiff and hard.

Handing the soapy wash cloth to him and pointing at his penis, she said, "Here, you can take care of that."

Shaking her head in disbelief, she climbed out of the shower and began to dry her hair with a large, fluffy white towel.

Turning her back and reaching behind her, she said, "Stay where you are."

Claude watched in fascination as she undid the halter and let it drop to the floor. Next she reached down, slipped the bottom of her swimming suit off her shapely hips and legs. Then she stepped out of it.

With her bare back to him, she reached up on the back of the bathroom door, removed a terry cloth robe, put it on, pulled it around her and tied the belt in place. Then she looked up to see him watching her reflection in the mirror. He had discovered Carla was a natural redhead and with nipples as large as those, the breasts weren't implants.

Carla's face was flushed, and she asked, "Get a good look?"

Claude nodded. His head felt like it was made of iron.

"Now you," she said.

Pulling a clean towel from a small closet to her left, she wiped the water off his body, beginning at his back and working around to his front. As she toweled his chest, she never took her eyes from his.

He stepped out of the shower. She handed him the towel and said, "You can get your legs and other parts."

Pointing toward old faithful again, she said, "You really should do something about that."

"Don't I wish."

"You're a dirty old man," she said, but smiled and handed him a matching terry cloth robe.

"Those who shower and dress together tend to stay together," Claude slurred.

"Boy, you really are smashed. Good, it's time for me to see if I should have passed 'Sewing One Oh One' in high school."

(Two)

"Why white?" Claude asked.

"It doesn't have dye in it," Carla said. "You don't need anything to help infection. You already stand a good chance of catching something awful from the water you rolled around in."

After threading the needle, which looked like a harpoon to Claude, she laid it down on the small table she had placed between them and said, "You're not going to like this next procedure."

Pointing at the needle, he asked, "You mean your harpoon?"

"No, I mean the antiseptic. It's going to hurt."

"Shit," he said.

"No, that's what I'm trying to get rid of. Don't be a big baby, Mister Macho. Show me how tough you are."

"If you say so, dear," Claude said.

Poising the bottle over the worst wound, the one on his back, she said, "You might want to hold onto something."

Reaching across the table, he took hold of her leg with his good hand. She slapped it lightly and said, "Not that."

"You did say 'grab something'."

"God," Carla said, "I can't believe you," and poured the liquid from hell onto his wound.

Gritting his teeth, Claude did his best to keep from uttering the words he felt like saying, but finally gave in and exclaimed very slowly, "Son of a bitch!"

"Told ya," Carla said and laughed.

Through clenched teeth he said, "You're one heartless woman."

"And a few minutes ago you called me your love," she said. "What changed your mind?"

Claude was in too much pain to reply. Shaking his head, he moaned under his breath.

Attacking the other wound, she said, "Only one more to go."

"God damn it!" He yelled.

"That's all, my love," she said, teasing him.

"Or was she?" He wondered.

"Now we'll get out my trusty Singer sewing machine and stitch you up."

Continuing to shake his head, Claude cursed under his breath while Carla waved a piece of paper towel over his wounds to cool them. Finally after five minutes of pure hell, they stopped burning. He looked at the hole in front, saw it had stopped bleeding and thought, "She was right."

"What are you, a nurse?"

"No, I'm a librarian and get to read a lot of books. You're lucky—I re-read my first-aid book last week."

"Thanks," he said and meant it.

She looked into his eyes and knew it, as she said, "You're welcome. I think we'll only sew up the worst of the wound in back. I won't try to knit the skin together. It's too big a hole and would cause you more pain. The one in the front can be sewn together and won't leave a bad scar."

"You're the expert," he said.

Handing him the needle/harpoon, she said, "Here, hold this by the end."

"Am I supposed to do it myself?"

"No idiot. I'm going to sterilize the point the only way I know how."

Lighting a match, Carla held it under the point, which quickly turned black. Claude's end got hot in a hurry and he almost dropped it.

"Okay, hand it to me, but don't touch the point," Carla said.

"Gladly."

After carefully threading the needle, she said, "Well, here goes nothing," and stuck the needle/harpoon through the skin on his chest next to the wound. Surprisingly, it didn't hurt that much, just a stick like he got from a tetanus shot.

Fascinated at her handiwork, Claude watched as she continued sewing. When she finished, she tied a knot in the thread, cut it with a small pair of fingernail clippers and asked, "There, that didn't hurt much, did it?"

"No, you have a steady hand."

"It won't be as bad on your back. I'll close up a couple of small skin tears and pack some gauze into the hole to stop the bleeding and soak up any drainage. Hold still and I'll be done in a jiffy."

The sewing time was longer than a "jiffy", but again it wasn't bad. Carla snipped off the last thread and said, "There, all done. How do you feel?"

"Pretty good for the shape I'm in. I've been thinking about something and I need your help in one more matter."

Jokingly she asked, "You mean I haven't done enough? What now? You're not still thinking of sex are you?"

"No," Claude said, "My rental car," and didn't know if she was disappointed or not.

"The guy who shot me stole it, and I need to report the theft, but I can't in this condition. I also can't go into a police station to fill out a report if it's required."

"So what do you want me to do?"

"Call the number on the receipt in my billfold," he said. "Tell them you're my secretary and I've been out of town. I parked the car at the airport for an overnight trip and when I returned, it was gone.

"If they ask me to come in to fill out a report, tell them I'm out of town again and won't be back for a week. I'll pay for the rental up to today to square things, but since it's stolen, it's a police matter."

"Won't the police want you to fill out a report?" Carla asked.

"I hope by the time seven days pass, they'll find the car. I doubt they kept it. They probably moved it away from the canal so it wouldn't attract attention. If the cops found it there, they'd search the canal and they didn't want me found."

"Got it all figured out, haven't you?" she asked.

"No, not yet. I just don't want the police to think I stole the damned thing."

"Now you're getting grouchy," she said. "Okay, I'll take care of it. Now how do you feel?"

"Thanks," Claude said.

His eyes felt like each lid weighed a ton and he said, "I feel like someone shot me and then threw me in a cruddy canal. I need some sleep."

Smiling at his corny response, she helped him to his feet and said, "Lean on me. You can have my bed and I'll sleep on the couch."

"That's good of you. I'd object, but I'm too damned tired. Thanks for everything."

"Shush, lie down and go to sleep."

He started to thank her again, but his eyes closed and he was asleep in an instant.

Standing over him, Carla looked down at his still form and said, "Mister Macho my ass," but Claude was beyond hearing.

(Three)

Joe, Kris and Mona had been working for an hour as they attempted to decipher Larry's last words, what few of them there were. So far they'd made as much progress as a snail carrying an anvil across a railroad track.

Joe stretched and asked, "So, what can you make out of Larry's code?"

"Not a lot," Kris replied. "Was that all Sadie had to say or sign?"

"Yeah, Mona and I went over it twice and it was the same thing. I can get the part about killing the president and maybe thousands. At least it's my interpretation. Nothing else jumps out at me except for the two bad men and the fact the fire scared Sadie and she hid."

Suddenly the words began to make sense to Mona. From across the table she said, "I think the 'terror is' is supposed to mean terrorists. What do you think?"

"That's pretty good, Mona," Kris said. "How did you pick up on that?"

"Chimps have a pretty basic understanding of the English language, and we try to make it easy on them by using words that could mean two things or even three."

"Okay," Kris said. "I see your point. Take a look at the next two words. The 'nervous and gas' could mean nerve gas couldn't it?"

Clapping his hands together in joy, Joe said, "Yeah, you're right. Now we're cooking. What else jumps out at you?"

"Well, 'football game' is pretty self-explanatory," Mona said, "but it could mean any type of game."

"Why would it?" Kris asked. "I think if Larry wanted to say 'ball', he would have. He must have been specific for Sadie to say 'football'."

"Yeah," Joe said. "You're right again. Hey, take a look at the next line. Sadie said, 'cotton' and then 'food bowl'. I think Larry meant bowl, but Sadie substituted something she knew—her food bowl. Couldn't he have meant the Cotton Bowl?"

"It goes along with the next word, 'fall'," Mona said. "I think you're right."

"But what does 'hide', 'three', 'two', 'fire' and 'X' have to do with anything?" Joe asked.

"I'm not sure Larry told her those words," Mona said. "It may be in reference to the fire. Sadie might mean there were three of them in the car, two cars hit each other, the fire occurred and Sadie hid. I can't make any more sense of it."

"Me neither," Kris said. "What about you, Joe?"

"I don't know what it means, but Sadie repeated it twice, exactly the same way. It makes me think Larry told her those words. Do I make sense?"

"Yes," Mona said, "but Sadie might have added the words herself because she was frightened and missed Wilbur so much."

"Well, I'll keep working on it," Joe said.

"Me too," Kris added.

"Let's look at the first line again," Joe said. "I know Sadie was fascinated by the two bad men. I take it she doesn't know man from men, right Mona?"

"You're correct. It's a little too much to expect from a chimp. Remember what I said about using the same word for two meanings."

"Okay," Joe said. "So we have the bad men. I take it 'fell' must mean when Larry was shot. What's the X for again?"

"I don't know," Kris said.

"I don't either," Mona added.

"Then Sadie says 'is man and far east man'."

"The first 'man' is a man, just what Sadie says, probably from around here and white," Kris said. "The second 'far east man' could mean someone from Japan."

"What about an Arab?" Joe asked.

"They come from the middle east, Joe," Mona said.

"I know it, but does Sadie?"

"I see what you mean," Mona said. "Maybe Sadie got the direction mixed up or she substituted far for middle. I don't know. I wish Wilbur was here to get his version, but he's not, so we're stuck with what Sadie gave us."

"I go along with the Arab part," Kris said. "They're the ones that are our greatest enemies right now. Our relations with the Japanese are good. I wish we had a name to go with it."

Yawning, Joe said, "So do I, but we don't. Here, Kris, take along a copy of Sadie's story so you can study it. Let me know if anything falls out of your tree. We're stymied for now."

Looking at his calendar, Kris said, "The Cotton Bowl is a ways off, so it gives us some time to touch base with operatives in the field and see if they know anything. I'll put the word out and shake some trees myself."

Then remembering Grady and his inability to question him, Kris said, "Oh, by the way, I forgot to tell you that our buddy, Grady is down in Mexico."

Looking up from his notes in surprise, Joe asked, "You think he cut out?"

"No, Grady's wife said he and a buddy were down there caving. It's a hobby of Grady's. He's due back next week and I left word for him to call me. In case I'm wrong and he is running, I put his name on Interpol's 'Watch List'. I also notified our Mexican counterparts to be on the lookout for his John Doe."

"When you get Grady, shake his tree good," Joe said.

"I plan to."

(Four)
Felix ditched the rifle and revolver in a cistern on a ranch outside Nuevo Laredo. It was fairly easy to get them across the border from the USA. Who wanted to smuggle guns out of the states?

But getting the weapons back across the border was something else. If they were found on him or in his truck, he'd be in a world of hurt. The guns could be easily replaced with others. The United States was a cornucopia of firearms for sale anywhere and everywhere.

He made it back across with ease, but the border guards did give his truck a cursory search, so there was no doubt they would have found the rifle and pistol. If they hadn't, the dog that sniffed his vehicle would have.

The guards checked Felix's driving license, passport and contract for rental of the ATV, before they allowed him to cross the bridge, but his documents were in order and Felix looked innocent enough, (didn't he)?

Driving from the border straight through to Sulfur Springs, Felix stopped only long enough to return the ATV and ramps. Then pausing for gas and food, he headed northward to his hideaway in the mountains. Before anything else happened, he wanted to complete the transfer of the nerve gas. Mohammed would want to know where he was, so he picked up his cell phone and called him.

"Where have you been?" Mohammed asked, just as Felix knew he would.

"Tying up some loose ends. Grady won't be around to collect his portion of the money."

Mohammed was quick on the uptake and asked, "Will his body be found?"

"Hardly, Grady's four hundred feet underground, along with his truck."

"You'll have to tell me how you accomplished that," Mohammed said.

"Later. I'm going to the cabin to work on the product. Can you meet me there tomorrow afternoon at three? I want to test the detonators to see what they do to the containers before I load any of the cargo."

"Yeah, I'll be there. I want to see for myself. How long before the rest of the containers will be ready?"

"A week or ten days at the soonest," Felix said. "What's your rush? The game is still weeks away."

"Too many things have gone wrong lately. What if they find Grady's body? That'll lead them back to his place of employment and you."

"The chances of it happening are very remote," Felix said, chuckling at his pun.

"I hope so," Mohammed said. "I'll see you tomorrow."

(Five)

Felicity Jameson was a gamer. Only twenty-seven years old, Felicity stood five feet, seven inches tall and weighed one hundred and five pounds, with or without a wet t-shirt. Her brown hair was closely cropped and her breasts so small she was often mistaken for a young boy. But it didn't bother Felicity. In her short life span she did it all.

You name it and Felicity was there and accomplished it. Scuba diving off the great barrier reef with sharks that could swallow her in one bite, sky diving over twenty different states and three countries in singles and tandem chutes, hang gliding off the mountains of Switzerland, bungee-cord jumping from tall bridges and taller buildings and free-fall parachuting off mountain cliffs, to name a few.

But this was something new, dropping down into mother earth at the end of a slim steel cable in a place called Diablo's Hideout or the Devil's Hole, (take your pick). Felicity wasn't scared. Hell, to hear her tell it, nothing frightened her and all her friends could testify on her behalf she told the truth.

Her cousin, Bill Dougherty, came up with this idea after seeing a notice about the cavern in an obscure sports magazine. Bill was a spelunker, loving to crawl around in dark dismal caves. Felicity accompanied him once and wasn't sure if she had claustrophobia, but one time was enough. She toughed it out and never said anything, but whenever Bill mentioned it again, she was busy doing something else.

But they sprang this on her without warning and here she was, hooked to the end of a cable hanging off a long extension on the back of an old wrecker. Felicity thought she looked like a spider at the end of a thread of silk, and after glancing down into the shadows of the dimly-lit shaft, she felt about as insignificant.

The four of them, the owner of the wrecker, Jack, and Fred, (a moron from Louisiana), and Bill and Felicity, crawled over fifty miles of bad gravel road leading to the cave.

On the way, Fred kept them entertained by telling them he knew Elvis was alive and well, living with a Creole woman in a rundown shack near Houma. When it came to brains, Fred had about as many as a jackrabbit.

Felicity was sure the holes in the terrible road would blow out every tire on the damned truck and they'd be forced to call it off, but much to her surprise and disgust they didn't. So now it was time for her to show the boys she had a pair of balls too.

"Hang in there cous," Bill shouted from the rim. "It ain't no big thing. Be thankful we gave you first chance. Not everyone gets to do this."

"Thanks a lot," Felicity yelled back.

She heard his voice boom in her earpieces, "We'll take it nice and slow, fifty feet at a time. Use your microphone to let us know when to lower you. Keep us advised of what you see and use your flashlight to make sure you don't hit an outcropping."

Giving him the finger, she said, "If you're such an expert, why aren't you out here hanging in space? Oh, what the hell, go ahead and lower me down. The sooner I get there and back, the quicker you and your moron friends can do the same. Then we can get back to town and a cold beer."

"Let her go, Jack," Bill yelled, and Felicity dropped so fast it scared her and she forced back a silent scream. She'd be damned if she'd give the idiots the satisfaction of knowing they frightened her.

Then the cable stopped just as quickly and jerked upward again. It felt like her breakfast was coming up, and she had to choke it back down.

"You stupid son of a bitch!" She shouted into her mike. "What the hell was that? Take it slow, idiot."

"Sorry about that, cous," Bill said. "Old Jack don't know no moderation."

"He'd better learn. Let me down another fifty."

This time she dropped much slower and watched as the sun disappeared above her and she moved into darkness so thick she felt like it was a cold, uncomforting blanket. Turning on her light, she shined it on the walls, where bats by the thousands slept.

Forgetting about the open mike she said, "Damn, bats," and her skin crawled with goose bumps. If it was one thing she truly hated, it was those furry little balls of shit. The smell of their guano was rank and she gagged.

Bill laughed and said, "Yeah, there will be bats. I thought you knew."

Taking a couple of minutes to look down to make sure the idiots weren't going to drop her onto some pointy rock and cut her legs, she said, "Okay asshole—fifty more."

Spiraling downward again, she checked her progress with the light. When something glistened on a ledge, she saw a chrome strip laying there and thought, "That's strange. How did it get here?"

Then she saw some glass fragments on another shelf. As they reflected the glow of her flashlight, she thought, "That's weird."

She keyed her mike again and said, "Strange junk that glows down here, Bill."

"Someone is always messing up nature. Damn the litter bugs anyway."

Keeping her light moving, she ordered, "Let me down another fifty."

Now she saw more debris on several ledges, a piece of crumpled metal that looked like part of a truck fender and a chunk of chrome shaped like a bumper.

"If I didn't know better, I'd think someone junked a truck down here," she reported.

"Impossible," Bill said.

"Once more into the fray," she said, dropped fifty more feet and saw more junk, an abundance of broken glass and some frayed and torn seat cover material.

"More trash, Bill," she said.

"Can we pull it out?"

"You'd need a big wheelbarrow to pick it up and they're hard to find out here in the desert."

"You're a real comic," he said.

Shining her light down into the abyss, she spotted something large and shiny.

"There's something big gleaming down there. I bet it's a truck."

Cursing under his breath, Bill said, "Stupid assholes that screw up a cave deserve to be shot on sight."

Sounding more like a bidder at an auction than a cave explorer, she said, "Another fifty."

As she went down, Felicity rotated at the end of the tether and something brushed against her hair. It felt wet and icky and she thought, "Damned bat shit in my hair."

Turning her head, she saw Clete's legs hanging from the rock and his reddish-brown mass of flesh and guts suspended in air and time.

At first Felicity thought it was a giant spider, like the one she saw in a movie as a kid. Then the light lit up Clete's pulverized face and she recognized what it was, panicked for the first time in her life and screamed, "Pull me up! God damn it, Bill, pull me up! Pull me up!"

"What the hell's going on?" He asked.

She screamed louder, "You stupid son of a bitch, pull me up!"

Motioning to him to raise the cable, Bill said, "Damn, Jack, she's flipped out. Pull her up before she craps her pants."

When they finally hauled Felicity out of the damnable pit, she was still screaming and cursing. She continued to do so for fifteen minutes before they could calm her down enough to find out what she saw.

Every time Bill came close or tried to speak to her, she screamed and kicked at him. Never in his life had he seen eyes so wide, felt such terror in a person or heard his cousin use such foul language to describe his lineage.

Staring down the dark, foreboding shaft he asked, "What the hell's down there?"

In response, Felicity tried to scratch his eyes out and screamed louder.

"Who's brave enough to go down and see what's up?" Jack asked.

No one volunteered. They would wait until Felicity told them. It was a long fifteen minutes.

(Six)

"Well, let's see what you can do," Mohammed said.

Felix and he were at the base of a mountain overlooking the valley beyond, twenty miles from his cabin hideaway. They had to be this far away so the signaling device wouldn't set off the other detonators. All they were interested in was the four lying at the base of the mountain. It was simple. If these fire extinguishers worked, the others would.

Last night, Felix worked late pressurizing the four tanks to fifty pounds per square inch, enough to spray the contents into the air and spread it quickly after the containers ruptured. Then he installed the detonators, primer cord and a small piece of C-4 under the handle.

His hands shook and even in the cool evening air, sweat ran down his arms and dripped off his elbows. If he was this nervous working on them with no gas present, what would he do with the real thing?

"Probably shit my pants before it's all over," he thought.

Wiping perspiration from his forehead, Felix stood back and admired his work, thinking, "They look just like they should."

So he and Mohammed could trace the distance the liquid traveled after detonation, Felix filled them with water and dark-green dye. He knew it wasn't a fair test. "Nerve gas is much lighter and will travel a lot farther. But, I couldn't test the real thing. I do want to live to see another sun rise."

"Let's move back a couple hundred feet," Felix said. "I'm not sure how far the shrapnel will fly. I'd hate to kill either one of us."

Mohammed nodded and said, "Yeah, at this date and time, it would be a shame."

They moved farther down the mountainside until Felix felt they were safe. Looking around to make sure they were alone, he said, "Fire in the hole," and pushed the red button on the electronic signaling device.

The four explosions came as one and made much more noise than Felix thought they would. The sound echoed off the surrounding mountains like cannons at a state funeral.

Startled, Mohammed said, "Holy Allah, that was loud. I thought they'd just pop."

Shaking his head, Felix said, "The C-4 is more powerful than I thought. I'll have to reduce the charge in the real things."

"What difference will it make? Hell, leave it alone. The more noise, the more panic and the more people we'll kill."

"You're right," Felix said. "The dust is settling, let's go see what happened."

(Seven)

"What the devil was that?" John Kawalski thought, as the explosion below startled him out of a well-earned nap

John was free-climbing this side of the mountain alone all morning and wore himself out by the time he got halfway. But luck was with him and he found a nice niche he could crawl into and take a rest. Fatigue and the high mountain air got to him and he fell asleep, only to be rudely awakened.

Shaking his six foot frame loose from the crevice, he looked over the edge. Down below him, he saw two strange-looking dudes dressed for the street instead of the mountain. They were walking up a slight grade to a spot almost directly below him, where a cloud of dust still lingered heavy in the air.

Far below them, through an opening in the trees, John saw a shiny brown Cadillac setting just off the park road. It looked out of place, here in the wilderness of the mountains.

"Must be some city dudes," John whispered to himself and the mountain. "But who are they and what are they doing with explosives in a national forest?"

No one answered his question, but it was no surprise. Old John talked aloud a lot since his wife, Georgia left him two years ago and his friends had grown used to it.

They looked into his brown eyes, saw his clean shaven face and a crew cut so short John looked like Mister Clean, and knew he took up rock climbing in the hopes some day he'd fall and end his misery. They wished he might get over Georgia and make a new life with one of the eligible widows who lived in his small community.

John watched quietly as the strangers arrived at the dust cloud area. One of them reached down and picked up something. It was red and part of it reflected the sun like a gun shot across the clearing.

The first man handed it to the second and they nodded. Whatever they did with the explosives seemed to please them.

As if he was in a train tunnel high in the Rockies, John heard one of them say, "Look at the pattern of dispersal."

Then the wind picked up and he only heard part of what the other replied.

The first one picked up two other red objects and they nodded again. Then they pointed to the side of the mountain and down the hill in a circle.

From where he lay, John saw green streaks on the rocks and trees and wondered, "What the hell's going on?"

He shifted his weight to get a better view and dislodged some pebbles. Hurriedly he pulled his head back in, silently said, "Damn it," and remained hidden.

(Eight)
As Mohammed jumped backward and slipped to his knees, Felix asked, "What the hell was that?"

Looking upward into the sun, Mohammed said, "Some rocks fell from above."

He saw no movement and nothing on the side of the nearly-straight-up wall, so Felix said, "It's probably a delayed reaction to the blast. Have you seen enough, or do you want to stay here until the mountain falls down and kills us?"

"Let's go back to your cabin," Mohammed said. "I hate the mountains. They're too unpredictable. Give me the desert anytime."

Reaching down for some more fragments, Felix said, "Come on, help me pick up what's left of the containers and we'll get out of here."

(Nine)

High above their heads, John lay and listened to the clinking of metal on metal as the two strangers collected their hardware and started down the mountain. He remained hidden for another thirty minutes until he heard the far-off sound of a car engine starting. Then he climbed back down the mountain, not up it.

CHAPTER 13

(One)

As Felix thought, it required ten long, hard nerve-racking days and nights to complete the transfer of the nerve gas. At the end of that time, he was a mental and physical wreck. When he departed for Mexico, he took two weeks leave from the lab, and when it took so long to finish the hairy part of the job, he called to extend his vacation.

But now it was finished. Thanks to his careful preparation and steady no-nonsense approach, no gas escaped. After each container was filled, he was drenched in sweat and his hands shook so badly he had to take an hour or more to calm down.

As Felix thought of the consequences of his labors, he sometimes had second thoughts about this attack on America.

Deep in his heart, somewhere hidden behind his hate, he knew it wasn't anyone's fault except for the drunk who chose to wipe his family from the face of the earth. But still, for a reason he couldn't fathom, he maintained a deep-seated hatred of the Jewish faith, an overpowering loathing that drove him day and night.

The collateral damage the bombs would cause to every race and religion on the face of the earth didn't enter into the equation. Without realizing it, Felix had reached the brink of madness and instead of turning back, he crossed over.

Now the only thing remaining was to load the phony fire extinguishers aboard Mohammed's panel truck and when the Cotton Bowl rolled around, let him and his cronies complete the job.

When the bombs went off, Felix would be far away in Jamaica on vacation. Maybe afterward he might be questioned, but he doubted it. There would be such an outcry for reprisal they'd forget all about small fry like him.

Every day, Mohammed called to encourage him to finish, but at the same time harass him by saying, "We need to get the job done."

Almost at the end of his mental rope, Felix said, "I can't hurry the process. I'm exhausted and if I make a mistake, I'll die and they'll find the evidence. Have you thought of that?"

Knowing he was pushing Felix too far, Mohammed said, "Okay, calm down. I understand. Do your best and let me know when I can move the cargo."

So upon completion of the final container, Felix called and Mohammed was on his way. It was a beautiful day with a bright blue sky and small puffy clouds gently hanging overhead.

High above him, the symbol of America, a bald eagle, was drifting on the wind with his wings outstretched, and Felix thought, "He doesn't know it, but in the autumn, he's in for a big fall."

Chuckling at his silent pun, he lay back in his hammock and dreamed about the future. When he got his five million dollar payoff, he had great plans for a condo in the Caribbean and maybe one in South America.

Disappearing into the world of wealthy patrons, Felix would relish his vengeance. Dreaming of his future, he wondered, "Who was it who coined the phrase, 'Revenge is sweet'?"

(Two)
Joe had joined Bert in his office and now the two of them were up to their hips in paperwork. Over the weekend, the lawn ornament bandits had a ball, stealing so much stuff Joe wondered if they used a dump truck. The amount reported stolen was amazing and he wondered, "What the hell can they do with all this junk?"

The phone interrupted his thoughts and Bert seemed inclined to ignore it, so he leaned over, picked it up and said, "Yeah, what is it?"

"Guess what, Joe," Kris said.

"I'm not in the guessing mood today, Kris. It's been a lousy day with too much crime and not enough cops to take care of it."

"Well then, you'll be glad to know one of your boys won't be lying to you anymore."

"And who would that be?"

"Grady O'Reilly," Kris said and waited for Joe's response.

"Grady?" Joe asked in disbelief. "Damn, I wanted to question him again. How'd he buy the farm?"

Keeping him in suspense, Kris asked, "You remember I told you he headed south to Mexico to do some caving?"

"Yeah, I do. Don't tell me Grady fell down a cave and killed himself."

"According to the Mexican authorities, that's what happened," Kris said. "They found what was left of Grady and his buddy, Clete Palmer, down in a four-hundred-foot pit along with Grady's prized truck. It looks like someone goofed and the damned thing went in, taking both of them with it."

"Very convenient," Joe said, and then asked, "Do you believe that bullshit?"

Kris laughed and said, "Not really. We need to send someone down there to look at the remains and see what they can find that our Mexican friends can't. I volunteered. Do you want to go along, Joe?"

"I'm tied up with paperwork, but what about Fad? I think he can bust loose for a short vacation south of the border."

"I'd love to have him. I understand he speaks Spanish like a local."

"Yeah, he's a fountain of info, which will come in handy with the local cops. They dig someone who speaks their lingo."

"I'm heading down there in the morning by helicopter," Kris said. "Send Fad over this afternoon and I'll give him the particulars. Okay?"

Joe yawned and said, "Sure, he's been telling me I work him like Simon Legree, so he'll be glad to get away from the whip for a while."

"Thanks, Joe."

"Don't make me regret it. Bring back something to tie Grady to Larry's death."

(Three)

John finished his downward path on the mountainside with ease and now he stood in the center of what was a powerful blast area, where he could see a circular pattern of dispersal of a dark-green liquid among the rocks and small trees.

Reaching out, he put his finger on a few drops and it came away wet. Taking his life into his own hands, he tasted it and found it was nothing but water with dye.

Noting several overlapping circles, he knew more than one container had exploded. It was puzzling why anyone would come all the way out here to set off something so powerful. It made no sense.

As John lowered himself, the dust had settled and now he could see more than before. There were several pieces of red metal scattered about that must have been too small for the strangers to gather. Four or five chrome-plated pieces sparkled brightly in the sun and he thought, "I guess they figured they'd rust or in time the sand would cover them. Wait a minute, what's that?"

The sun glinted off a large piece of chrome that was blasted upward and outward and had landed on a shelf about head high, fifty feet from the center of the explosion. It looked like part of a handle, and for some reason it was familiar.

John thought, "I've seen it before, but where?"

Nothing came to mind, so he put it in his backpack along with several of the tiny red pieces of metal, and made the mental note, "There's residue of writing on a couple of them. I'll take them along and report this to the park ranger. Setting off dynamite or whatever they used out here must be a Federal offense. Hell, they could have hit me without knowing it. Damn them anyway. I hate people who screw up Mother Nature."

While John gathered his evidence, the sun slipped farther west and dark clouds moved into the vicinity. Now he was glad his climb was interrupted. If he was hanging off the cliff and it started lightning, he might fulfill the death wish his friends thought he had.

Shaking his head, he thought, "I've got a mystery now, so who wants to die before I solve it?"

(Four)

They were standing near the edge of the Devil's Hole, and Kris thought, "It's a good name for such a hellish place."

After he took a cautious look, Fad tried to stretch his back, which he thought might be broken after the hairy ride down fifty miles of piss poor road.

It shook Kris up too, but in a different way. Before they left, he ate tacos for lunch and the huge bumps along the way drove whatever was in them down into his lower bowel. Now he had to shit in the worst way.

When he found the Mexicans had a porta-potty on site, Kris was happier than a hooker with five customers haggling over her wares. It was a foul, evil-smelling plastic shed with most of the blue liquid splashed out over the floor, sides and especially the seat of the shitter.

But it was the best port the storm in his stomach had seen in many an hour, so he took a pleasing dump, as Fad stood upwind. (He was no dummy). Then they had walked out to see where Grady and his buddy took their dive, and Fad said, "Damn, that's a hole and a half."

"Yeah," Kris said. "Are you sure you want to go down there?"

Shaking his head in response to Kris' question, but then nodding in resignation, Fad said, "What I don't do for my country. Yeah, I guess we have to. The Federalies set this up for our benefit and to show the great cooperation between our two countries. How can we refuse?"

"The cage looks stout enough," Kris said.

As he climbed into the metal contraption and reached down to help Kris, Fad said, "Let's hope so."

From within, hidden in darkness, Inspector Hector Gonzales said in flawless English, "It's not as bad as it seems."

Wearing a spiffy tan uniform and a black hat with a spit-shined brim that would have pleased any drill sergeant in the U.S. Army, Hector said, "The pit is over four hundred feet deep, but we managed to pull out most of the wreckage. We found Mister Palmer speared on a rock formation. It wasn't a very pretty sight."

"I'll bet," Fad said. "Where was our boy, Grady?"

"We didn't know Mister O'Reilly was there until we moved the truck. Then we found him smeared over more than forty feet of the cavern floor. We had to use a shovel to pick up most of his remains. Our forensic scientists are still trying to put him back together. There are a lot of pieces missing."

"Good God," Kris said.

"I agree," Hector said.

"Yeah," Fad said.

Continuing with his unsolicited briefing, Hector said, "The truck was in gear, that much we know. It hit the far wall and bounced against several outcrops on the way down. We found pieces scattered all over the cavern. The strange thing is there was a stick or log inside the cab. There are no trees or limbs down here, so where it came from is a mystery."

"Maybe someone used it to push down on the accelerator, put the truck in gear and jump out before it went off the edge," Fad said. "It's been done before, even in movies."

"It's a possibility," Hector said. "We think when the truck went over, one of them, probably Mister O'Reilly, was hooked to the cable and going down into the cave. Mister Palmer wasn't wearing a harness like we found under the wreckage."

"How's his reconstruction coming along?" Kris asked.

"There was more left to him than Mister O'Reilly," Hector said. "But as I said, it isn't a pretty sight. When we get back to town, I'll take you to our morgue so you can see for yourself."

"I can hardly wait," Kris said.

"Well, here we are," Hector said as they arrived at the bottom of the pit.

Fad was amazed. He hadn't felt their descent, but knew it had grown darker and now it was lighter as they approached the bottom of the cave.

The police cooperation department went all out. There was a large diesel generator setting on the ground and a bank of lights circled the cavern. They could see damaged outcroppings and scars the truck made on its way down. There was a large pool of oily residue near the middle of the cave.

Pointing to a long, slippery-looking and brownish-red streak that ran from the sloped side of the cave to the middle, Fad asked in amazement, "That's all that's left of Grady?"

"That and very little else," Hector said. "We assumed it was him because it was his truck. We hope the few teeth we found will allow us to match his dental records. Mister Palmer conveniently had his driver's license in his pocket. Miracles do happen."

"We'll look around," Kris said. "But I don't think we'll find anything you didn't."

"Take your time, my friends," Hector said. "I get paid the same no matter where I am."

His black eyes smiled over his matching moustache, as he walked over to join some other Mexican cops gathered in a group, talking while they waited to be hauled out of the foul pit.

"Let's not spend too much time here," Fad said. "Damn, it must have been some fall."

"Yeah," Kris said. "I agree. I hope you rest in pieces, Grady."

"God, you're worse than Joe."

(Five)

This morning, when Mohammed arrived in his panel truck with a smile on his face and the dream of this moment in his heart, thirty-two red fire extinguishers were laying in a neat row on a soft cotton-filled mattress in the bedroom of Felix's cabin.

Smiling at the sight, he asked, "So it's all done, 'eh?"

Then his smile turned into an ugly sneer, as he said; "Now the Americans will pay for their invasion of my homeland and the many deaths of my people. Long live Saddam!"

Shaking his head at Mohammed's latest outburst, Felix asked, "Can't you lay off the political bullshit for a few minutes? Let's get this stuff loaded. I still have to set the place on fire to make sure no nerve gas escapes and they don't have any evidence to tie me to the attack."

"What's the matter, Felix? Are you getting cold feet at this point in time?"

"Hell no. I want my money and the chance to get revenge on the people who took my family from me. When they all die, I won't give a damn. I'll be living the good life in Jamaica, drinking rum and ginger ale on the beach and laughing my ass off."

Rubbing his hands together as if he were a gold merchant watching his ship come in, Mohammed said, "Good. I can't afford to have you go soft on me. Let's put them in my truck and I'll be on my way."

Holding his hands up like a traffic cop at an accident, Felix asked, "Where's my money?"

Pointing to a suitcase on the passenger's side of his truck, Mohammed said, "Right there. Don't you trust me, or do you want to count it before we load?"

"No, I believe you. I'll help you pack the containers and get you on your way. Then I'll tally my reward and set the cabin on fire. Make sure you're a long ways away so no one will see your vehicle and connect you with the fire. I'll be right behind you."

They spent the next thirty minutes carefully carrying each fire extinguisher from the cabin, one at a time to the special packing cases in Mohammed's truck. Each box had sixteen soft foam rubber holes and there were four inches of thick padding around each opening. The containers fit snugly inside without touching each other.

When they were finished, Felix held out a small plastic case with an empty compartment where the batteries should be, and said, "Here's the signaling device. It takes two C-type household batteries, like these."

After displaying them to Mohammed, Felix turned and threw the batteries into the interior of the cabin.

Mohammed asked, "Why did you do that?"

"Don't even think of putting the batteries in place until the minute before you set off the bombs," Felix said. "That way you won't hit the button by mistake and set them all off in the back of your truck or wherever you store them."

"Good thinking," Mohammed said.

Handing him a heavy suitcase, he added, "Here's your money."

After he opened it, Felix saw neat stacks of hundred dollar bills arranged across the entire interior. It was more money than he had ever seen in his life. With his back to Mohammed, he said, "Thanks, I'll count it later."

"You're welcome," Mohammed said, and shot him twice in the back.

The impact of the bullets drove Felix to his knees. The case slipped from his hand, he fell forward across it and gasped, "I should have known."

"Yeah, you should have. You tied up your loose end with Grady, now I took care of mine with you."

Turning his head to stare at his killer, Felix's last thoughts were, "It's a good thing I planned for this eventuality. I'll see you in hell, Mohammed."

Although he was speaking to a dead man, Mohammed said, "Thanks again." But to make sure, he stuck his right foot under the body, rolled it onto its back and then shot Felix in the forehead.

Reaching down, he took the suitcase before it got bloody, carried it to his car and put it on the floorboard on the passenger's side.

He walked back, grabbed the body by the feet and dragged it inside the cabin. Then he walked to where Felix had conveniently placed a five-gallon can of kerosene.

As he poured the flammable liquid throughout the interior of the cabin, he made sure to thoroughly drench Felix's body. Then he stood back and threw a lit match into the cabin.

With a loud "whoosh", fire erupted from the doorway and two windows. Flames licked at the furniture, and the curtains that waved so gallantly a few days ago caught fire and were consumed in a few seconds.

Mohammed didn't stick around to view his handiwork. Climbing into his vehicle, he quickly drove away.

(Six)

After another long, bone-jarring ride over the same road, but different bumps, rocks and holes that threatened to swallow their range rover, Kris and Fad made it back to Nuevo Laredo in time for a quick dinner. (This time Kris stayed away from tacos.)

After two rum and Cokes, his stomach felt better. Then Hector drove them to the morgue where Earnest Winslow, the forensic scientist they brought along was waiting.

Pulling up and parking outside the lab, Hector said, "I'll stay with the car. I saw the remains earlier and I just ate dinner."

Inside the foyer, standing by Earnest's side was his Mexican counterpart, Jose Martinez, a tall, thin dark-skinned doctor in a white coat with several blood spots on one arm. It was apparent they were recently diving around in the body parts, (what few remained), of either Grady or Clete.

"What'd you find, Ernie?" Kris asked.

"Not much. There wasn't a whole hell of a lot to work with in the first place."

Fad shook his head and said, "Yeah, we heard. So there's nothing here, 'eh?"

With a smile on his face, Earnest said, "I didn't say that. You asked me what I found. Now ask Jose what he discovered."

Knowing he'd been had in a grim reaper kind of sick joke, Kris asked, "So what did you find, Jose?"

Seeming to enjoy Ernie's humor, Jose smiled and said, "It's a good thing Mister Palmer landed the way he did. If he hit right side up, the pinnacle would have blown his breastbone away and I never would have found this."

When he held up a crushed piece of metal in a plastic bag, all the lawmen knew it was a bullet.

Fad asked, "He was shot?"

"You bet your ass," Earnest said. "And whoever did it sent the truck over the side to hide the evidence. The doer was plain stupid. He could have kicked or thrown Clete off and we'd have thought it was an unfortunate accident."

"Sometimes we get lucky," Fad said. "This looks like one of those times. Great work, Jose."

"Thank you. Here, you'll want to take this with you."

After handing Kris the plastic bag, he said, "Good luck finding the perpetrator."

"The gun is in a ditch or river," Fad said. "The shooter wouldn't risk trying to cross the border with it."

"You're right, Fad," Kris said. "But now we can tie Grady to Larry's death and we know there's something unexplained going on at the chemical lab. Katie, Larry and Wilbur didn't die in vain."

"Yeah, but we've got a long ways to go to stop whatever the terrorists have in mind. We better get our asses back north of the border and go to work."

Kris nodded and said, "Yeah, you're right. Tell Hector we're ready to go and I'll call the pilot to fire the bird up. Thanks again, Jose, and you too, Ernie."

CHAPTER 14

(One)

Claude slept for four hours and Carla snooped for four minutes. While he rested, she went through his clothes. Claude's pants pockets held the keys to a GM model car, a dollar seventy-six cents in change and a wallet containing two thousand, five-hundred and sixty-seven soggy dollars.

Inside the billfold was a damp German driver's license in the name of Claude Werner, a matching temporary driver's permit for the United States, the rental slip for the Chevy he was worried about, two credit cards from German banks in the same name and nothing else. Whoever Carla's guest was, he traveled light but had money. In her short lifetime, she'd never had that much cold cash in her purse.

Claude's ruined shirt held absolutely nothing—zip, zero nada. He wore a fairly expensive foreign made watch, most likely Swiss, with a leather band. There were no rings on his fingers and he didn't appear to need glasses.

Taking the nearly dry rental receipt, Carla called the 1-800 Number and told the lies the way he asked. The rental agency bought it and she breathed a sigh of relief.

The lady who Carla spoke to was named Sharon and when they had finished their transaction, she said, "Please have Mister Werner call us when he returns."

"Yes, ma'am," Carla said sweetly. She hated to be called ma'am, and it probably pissed Sharon off, but Carla didn't care, she was tired.

As Claude snored softly, she glanced over at his still form and watched his chest rise and fall in rhythm with his breathing. The front of his robe had come undone and she admired his muscular body from head to toe.

The thought came to her mind, "At least he's not hard any longer," and she laughed at her powers of observation.

Although she was twenty-seven, Carla was never married. Over the years, she had her share of men and enjoyed sex, but never met the perfect partner.

Now she mused, "Maybe I never will," but she kept hoping.

It was beyond her comprehension, as to why she was helping this complete stranger. It wasn't like her. She was usually prim and proper and did the right thing. She should be on the phone speaking to the police, telling them she had a man in her bed with a gunshot wound. But for some reason, she couldn't pick up the instrument and make the call.

When she heard sounds like firecrackers, she went down to the warehouse a block away. She thought she could handle any teenaged kids who were setting off fireworks, but when she saw Claude, "If it's really his name," and he told her he was shot, she was intrigued, not wary.

Now it appeared she was in this thing up to the top of her pantyhose. Moving quietly to the bed, she shook him gently until he awoke and said, "Sorry to disturb you, but you need to take some antibiotics. I have some Cipro with an out-of-date label, but it's always worked wonders for me, so let's try a couple. Here take these and I'll hold the glass."

His eyes were heavy with sleep as he said, "Thanks. I need to go to the bathroom. Can you help me up?"

"Yeah, come on you big baby."

After she helped him to his feet, he stood there unsteadily until he got his balance and she asked, "Can you make it or do you want to lean on me?"

He winked and said, "I'll give it a bloody good try".

He shuffled off slowly and she followed in case he needed her help, but as he went into the bathroom, he said, "You won't have to hold my hand or anything else."

Catching the innuendo in his remark, she said, "You bastard," but she smiled.

Carla heard the sound of his urine hitting the bowl and it went on for a minute or two before he finished. Then the tap water ran as he washed his hands. When he came out the door, she said, "You need to drink a large glass of water to replace the fluids you lost. It'll help you heal faster."

After emptying the glass she handed him, he said, "You're the doctor."

"No, I'm just the librarian. Back to bed and sleep for you. I have to do the same. Don't be Mister Macho and try to do it all yourself. Call me if you need anything. I put the Cipro and a glass of water by the bed. Take two more every time you get up to go to the bathroom and drink another glass of water."

Slipping back under the covers, he said, "Yes dear, and thanks Carla. You've been wonderful."

"You're welcome, Claude."

"Been snooping, 'eh?"

"Yeah, but we'll talk about it in the morning. Get some sleep. Good night."

"Sleep well yourself."

For some reason, although she was worn out from the excitement of tonight, it took Carla a long time to fall asleep and then she dreamed of Claude in a very sexy way. Looking forward to the days ahead, she knew she would wake with a smile on her face.

(Two)

The smoke drew John's attention to the cabin in the woods. After his adventure high in the mountains twenty miles north, he spent several days traveling all the back roads, searching for something to tie the two strangers to what he found. If he saw either of them, John knew he would recognize him. He had made steady progress in eliminating the roads leading off the main highway, but until now, he wasn't this far south.

As he pulled up fifty yards away from the cabin, it was burning intensely. Half the roof was caved in and there would be no saving anyone who hadn't got out by now.

"Is anyone here?" He shouted twice, but received no answer.

Then he noticed the brown Cadillac was setting fifty feet from the conflagration.

"Damn, that's the car I've been searching for," John thought. "Where's the guy I saw up on the mountainside? I hope he's not inside the cabin."

The left side of the vehicle was taking the brunt of the tremendous heat. Smoke rose from the paint as it burned and curled off, and he thought, "Whoever owns it better hope it doesn't explode."

The words weren't out of his mind when it did just that, and the force of the explosion knocked him off his feet. Smelling singed hair, he knew it was his. Crawling back to his car, he jumped inside and roared away backward from the two towering infernos.

He picked up his cell phone to call Parks and Wildlife and let them know about the fire, but he was too late. They were already on the scene. He watched as two yellow tanker trucks and a red pickup pulled into the driveway.

The tankers hosed down the house and car, while the driver of the pickup walked over to where John sat, looked at him inquisitively and asked, "That your place?"

"No. I was passing by, saw the smoke and got here about a minute before the car blew up. It almost took me with it. I was stupid, standing so close to the fire."

"Yeah, and your hair's singed too. You see anyone around?"

"No. I called out a couple of times, but got no answer. If anyone was inside, they're history."

Peering in his window, the guy said, "You can say that again. Haven't I seen you before?"

Sticking his hand through the opening he said, "My name's Wally."

"John Kawalski," he said, shaking Wally's hand. "Yeah, I do a lot of free-climbing. We may have seen each other at the office when I signed up for a permit."

"Yeah, that's it. I knew I saw you somewhere. It looks like they've got the car out, but the cabin's going to burn to the ground."

"I hope no one was inside," John said.

Wally grinned and said, "In an hour or two, we'll know if we've got barbecue."

"You have a weird sense of humor."

As he ambled away, Wally said, "Before it gets blown off by the hose, let me get the license number off the Caddy."

(Three)

Wally used the registration he found in the Cadillac to trace the identity of the badly burned body discovered in the cabin to Felix Mendez. The postmaster serving that address also told Wally who lived there. It was as easy as that. The hard part was finding someone to notify.

John and Wally drove into town to see what or who they could find. According to Mister Mendez's neighbors in Sulfur Springs, he was a loner after his wife and children were killed by a drunk driver.

When he heard the latest news, Wally said, "Man, this guy had a rough life."

"Yeah," John said. "It looks like it, but if Mister Mendez was such a loner, who was the other guy with him? Something doesn't add up."

Wally shrugged and said, "There was a hell of a lot of technical equipment in the cabin, mostly scientific gear. He had lots of beakers and some type of a pressure tank that blew about halfway through the fire.

"We thought Mendez might be cooking 'meth', but it wasn't the right type of gear. I'll ask the neighbors where he works and check there. Maybe his boss will know his next of kin."

(Four)

Claude had been laid up for a week and was itching to get out and find what he could about the man he met at the canal and the guy he spoke to on the phone. They weren't the same. The man on the phone was probably the one who tried to waste him. Of the two, he may have been the better shot, but Claude thought, "He was good, but not thorough in his work. It'll be my turn soon and I'll show him a thing or two."

Carla was fantastic. For the first two days she stayed home "sick", but then he told her, "Now that the initial shock is past, I can heal by myself. I'm getting better every hour, and with a few days rest and recuperation, I'll be back on my feet."

Presenting her side of the argument, Carla said, "You need some physical therapy for your arm and shoulder."

"You can help me at nights and on weekends. There's no reason for you to risk losing your job. I've been enough of a burden. Give me time to heal and I'll get out of your life."

Finally giving in, she said, "Okay, but I'd like to know more about you. I know you're from Germany, but where? And what do you do for a living?"

"I lived in a little town near Dusseldorf called Osterath," Claude said, and then told her the story he cooked up in his sleep. Some of it was true, but the rest was fiction.

"I was a banker for several years. Then I took up day trading and quit when I made a million dollars. Now I'm semi-retired and looking for new investments. That's what I was doing when I hooked up with a crooked person and got shot."

"And when you're healthy, you plan to look him up and do the same to him, right?"

"That was all 'Mister Macho' talk," Claude said. "Do I look like a killer?"

"No," she said. But then she asked, "But what's the description of a killer? It would be nice if we could tell one from his appearance, wouldn't it?"

"Yes. Then maybe I wouldn't have done business with this guy."

"Do you know his name?" Carla asked.

"I'm sure the one he gave me was phony," he said. "I should have done a better job of checking him out."

"Yes, you should have. I'm glad to hear you aren't out for revenge. That's a cold, bitter road."

"You're right," Claude said. "Let's talk about something else. What's for dinner?"

"I'll bring back some chicken from KFC," she said. "I have to run into town and buy you some clothes. The canal water did a number on your pants and I threw out what was left of your shirt, t-shirt and shorts."

"Not my shorts. After you worked so hard to get me out of them, I thought surely you'd keep them as a trophy."

"Hardly," Carla said, but laughed anyway. "You have a one track mind. Stop it or I will turn you in."

"Okay, but you can't blame me for trying. You're a beautiful woman."

"Thanks, but I'm not in the mood."

"Maybe later?" He asked.

"Don't get your hopes up, Romeo. Take your antibiotic and lie down like a good little boy. Get some sleep while I'm gone."

As Carla walked toward the door, Claude said, "Yes, dear," and smiled behind her back.

(Five)

Fred, the rent-a-cop on duty at the front entrance, wouldn't let Wally or John into the building. After pointing to the same miserable chairs Bert tested not too many days before, he said, "You'll have to wait over there until I call Mister Witte. He's Mister Mendez's supervisor."

As they tried the seats, Wally shrugged and John sighed. After two attempts, they looked at each other, gave up and remained standing with their arms folded until Mister Witte arrived and asked, "How may I help you?"

Not one for pulling punches, Wally said, "I'm Wally Taylor, a Ranger from Oak Creek Canyon State Park. We believe one of your employees died in a fire yesterday. A cabin burned, we found Mister Mendez's car outside and there was a man's body in the ruins."

Appearing shocked, Hershel said, "For the past two weeks Felix has been on leave. Four days ago, he called in to extend his vacation because he was working on an important project. Are you sure it's him?"

"The body was severely burned and we'll have to locate Mister Mendez's dentist to match the teeth with his dental records. But yeah, we're pretty sure it's him."

"Oh, my God," Hershel said. "This is our second tragic loss in less than a month. The man who worked next door to Felix, Larry Holgram, was murdered recently. Now we have this. What's next?"

Without thinking, he moved to one of the wobbly chairs, sat down and said, "I have to catch my breath. Have you notified the Sulfur Springs police?"

"No," Wally said. "First, we wanted to find Mister Mendez's next of kin and notify them."

Turning to his other visitor, Hershel asked, "Who are you?"

"I'm John Kawalski. The other day I saw Mister Mendez set off explosives in the state forest. I was first on the scene of the fire, so I came along to see if I could help."

"That's decent of you," Hershel said. "But explosives, it doesn't sound like the Felix I know. I think you have the wrong man. But to answer your question, as far as I know, Felix has no relatives living here. Not too long ago his wife and children were killed by a drunk driver and Felix had a hard time adjusting to life without them. There were times he appeared bitter and inconsolable."

"I don't blame him," John said. "Mister Mendez had a lot of trouble on his plate in such a short time."

"I think I should call the police," Hershel said. "They'll want to know about this."

Turning to leave, Wally said, "I'll let you handle it. Maybe they can find Mister Mendez's kin and tell them of his demise."

Hershel shook his hand and said, "Thanks for letting me know. I'll take it from here."

When Wally looked at him and asked if he was coming along, John said, "I'd like to stick around and meet whoever the police send."

"Are you going to be all right by yourself? I have to get back to work."

"Yeah, don't worry, Wally, I can rent a car. Thanks for bringing me along. My mystery is getting deeper every minute."

CHAPTER 15

(One)

When Mohammed arrived in Fort Worth to deliver the bombs and helped carry them into the rental storage space, he could tell something was wrong. His controller, Hushan, was angry and when Mohammed thought about it, he had a right to be. It was stupid of him to kill Felix.

When Hushan was mad, his black eyes bore through you like an electric drill. His moustache twitched as if he had a spasm in his lip, and his face turned red.

Hushan was one of a chosen few to have met with Osama Bin Laden in Saudi Arabia and kissed his hand. Now as he looked in scorn at Mohammed, he wondered why he ever recruited the idiot.

After Hushan's brother, Mustafa was sentenced to death for his part in terrorist attacks against their sworn enemy, the United States; Al Qaeda operatives pursued him as a potential leader of a sleeper cell. At the time they met with him, Mustafa was languishing in a prison, so Hushan was anxious to avenge his brother and easily swayed to join their organization.

Over the past three years, Hushan had found a number of individuals anxious to repay debts, real or imagined against their own government. It was amazing and rewarding at the same time, but occasionally he made a mistake by recruiting a man who was only in it for the killing.

Now Mohammed had shown his true colors and it was time for Hushan to ream his ass or get rid of him. Knowing he still needed him for a while, Hushan chose the former option.

Frowning knowingly, George, the guy employed as a fireman, and who would be the one to put the bombs in place, stood by quietly out of the way of any shit that might splatter.

Hushan asked, "Why did you have to eliminate Felix so soon, Mohammed?

"The plan was for him to die later, just before we settle the score for my brother and the many others the Americans have killed in their invasion of our homeland. How can you be sure Felix didn't leave something behind to incriminate you or our organization? How could you have been so stupid?"

In a lame defense, Mohammed said, "I'm confident he didn't. Felix was a loner and I never saw him take notes."

"But you can't be positive, can you? And Felix eliminated the guard who could have let you in to check his office. Between you, I don't know which one is the bigger idiot. But there's nothing you can do now, that avenue is closed. Pray to Allah the fool didn't leave anything behind to wreck our well laid plans."

"I can still get into Felix's house," Mohammed said. "If there's anything there, I'll find it."

Standing on the balls of his feet, Hushan seemed to tower over Mohammed as he said, "Don't be seen."

He was tall, but when he did his little trick, Hushan seemed taller than Allah himself.

Stuttering a little in his haste to make amends, Mohammed said, "I won't. Here, this is the signaling device to use when you set off the bombs. Felix warned me not to install the batteries until just before you use it.

"Remember, all of the bombs are set on the same frequency and will go off at the same time. If you push the button by accident, you'll kill yourself and those around you."

"Thanks for the warning," George said. "I'll remember it."

Suddenly changing the subject, Hushan asked, "Where's my money?"

"Still in the suitcase on the floorboard," Mohammed said. "The fool didn't even look beyond the first layer. I put one-hundred-dollar bills on stacks of fives and tens and the lower rows are strips of paper."

"The four hundred thousand is all there?" Hushan asked.

Smiling, Mohammed said, "It's the same money I saved by getting rid of Mister Jones."

Hushan was still not in a good mood. He frowned as he said, "Good. Go outside and get the case, George."

Trying to get back in his good graces, Mohammed said, "That's it then. I'll search Felix's house and let you know what I find."

It didn't work. Hushan was still upset, as he barked, "Then go, do it and keep me advised. Learn to control yourself or your future will be very short indeed. We have no place for fools in our organization. Allah go with you."

"And with you," Mohammed said as he walked to his car and drove away. His sweaty shirt grew cold from the air conditioner, so he shut it off and rolled down the window, but the hot breeze did nothing to cool his feeling of trepidation.

Turning to George, Hushan said, "The idiot will be the end of us. He's a loose cannon and I don't trust him. The stakes are too high in this game we're playing, but he doesn't know it's not a game. Take the bombs and move them to your garage."

"Sure," George said.

As he bent over to pick up one of the heavy cases, a large black widow spider tattooed on his left bicep quivered in its web and seemed to grow larger.

For all of his bluster, Hushan was deathly afraid of spiders. Despite his efforts to avoid it, goose bumps rose on his arms and a chill ran down his back.

Hushan didn't think George noticed, but he did, and smiled behind Hushan's back.

(Two)

Bert finished logging all of the lawn ornament bandits' newest crimes and the list of stolen items was longer than any other he had ever seen. When the phone rang, he put the paperwork down, picked up the headset and gave the standard greeting.

"Sergeant Collins, this is Hershel Witte out at the chemical laboratory. We spoke a few days ago about the strange death of Larry Holgram."

"Oh yeah, Mister Witte, I remember you. How are things going? Do you have any new information to report on Larry's disappearance and murder?"

"No," Hershel said, "but there's been another strange new death in our organization. Felix Mendez, who had the office next to Larry, was killed in a mysterious fire at his cabin up in the state forest at Oak Creek Canyon."

"Felix Mendez?" Bert asked. "Wasn't he one of the men I spoke to?"

"Yes, come to think of it, he was."

"That's a strange coincidence," Bert said.

"Yes. I think so too. A ranger named Wally Taylor and a man named John Kawalski came down from Oak Creek Park to see me about notifying Felix's next of kin. As far as I can tell, Felix didn't have any in town, but after talking to the two gentlemen I thought I should let you know what's going on."

Bert added the names to his notes and asked, "Has anyone been in his office?"

"No. Felix was on vacation for two weeks and called in four days ago for an extension of another week. He said he was working on an important scientific project at his cabin and needed extra time to finish it. It's all very strange and Felix's death is a mystery.

"Mister Kawalski remained behind to talk with you about a strange occurrence he witnessed up in the forest. He thinks it might be important."

"I'll talk to some of the other officers who are working on the case and we'll come out within the next hour or so," Bert said. "Will that be satisfactory?"

"Yes. Mister Kawalski says he doesn't mind waiting."

"Fine, we'll see you shortly. Keep everyone away from Felix's office."

(Three)

Over the intercom, Bert asked, "Are you too busy to run out to the chemical lab again, Joe? Hershel Witte just called in to report another of his employees was killed in a suspicious fire up in Oak Creek Canyon Park."

"That's strange," Joe said.

"Yeah, the word strange came up about ten times in our conversation. He has a guy from Bed Rock waiting to talk to us, a Mister John Kawalski, who says he witnessed something strange."

Pausing for a moment and chuckling softly, Bert said, "Hell, there I go, sounding like Hershel. Anyway, they're waiting for us at the lab. You think Kris or Fad will want to sit in on this?"

"I'll send Fad for a search warrant for Mister Mendez's office. You did say Felix Mendez, didn't you? Why does his name sound familiar?"

"He was one of the guys I interviewed out there. Let me check my notes."

Joe heard Bert shuffling papers and a drawer being opened and closed. Then Bert came back on the line and said, "Yeah, he worked in the office next to Larry on the left-hand side. Said he didn't know a thing. Hadn't been to work that night, left early, it says in my notes. Not too friendly with Larry and he didn't know sign language. Very vague about the last time he saw Larry alive."

"Good notes," Joe said. "If Grady let him in for some reason, maybe it's who Larry heard. It makes sense."

"Yeah, but who was Felix Mendez talking to? Grady said, 'No one came in', remember?"

"Yeah, and I'd believe Grady if he swore on a pile of Playboys. He was lying and we all knew it. Look where it got him, spread over half of Mexico. But to answer your question, yeah, I'll call Kris and clue him in. He can meet us there. Fad and I'll be down your way as soon as I call Kris."

"See you in ten minutes," Bert said.

(Four)

Claude was restless. It was a beautiful clear, crisp late summer day and he had just returned from a two-mile walk, but that wasn't what he needed. Carla was working again and he missed her company. His chest was almost healed; the wound scabbed over on both sides and the pain less each day. He hated to think what kind of crap floated around in that cruddy canal.

He was lucky to have no infection, but Carla and her Cipro were to thank for that. She called her doctor and got a refill, so Claude was set for the next thirty days.

It was difficult to spend so much time with such a good-looking woman without feeling something for her. He was afraid he was falling in love.

That wouldn't do, as he thought, "Time to cut and run."

But it could wait for a little while longer, so he said aloud, "Time to call my controller instead."

Picking up the phone, he dialed the number from memory and heard the call switched through several lines and computer centers until he got a recording that said, "Leave your name and number and I'll call you back."

"This is Mister Jones. It's urgent I talk to you. I'm at a secure location. Telephone number 555-3241. Call immediately."

After hanging up, he held his hand over the phone. Within thirty seconds it rang, and the voice of his unknown controller said, "You have two minutes."

"I had trouble with the payoff for the last contract," Claude said. "They tried to kill me. I need to know who set up the hit on the Adkins girl."

"Impossible," his controller said.

Claude insisted, "It's not impossible. I told you, he tried to kill me. I need a name and address."

"I thought you were going to retire."

"Not until I settle the score. Are you going to help me for old times sake or not?"

After a moment, his controller relented and said, "Mohammed Alta, Denver. It's spelled, A, L, T, A, and that's all you get. Do you need help or supplies?"

"No, I prefer to work alone. Thank you."

"Remember, this is it. I don't know you and won't answer your calls. Your time is up."

The line went dead, and Claude thought, "Denver. No wonder they could reach me so soon. I was there on vacation when the controller told me he had a rush job. I wonder if Alta is listed in the phone book or does all his business by cell phone. At least now I know who I'm dealing with, but I have to find his partner."

As was his habit each day, he read through the Sulfur Springs newspaper Carla brought in from the front lawn, hoping to find a clue to his assailants. So far he'd had no luck, but today his fortune changed.

Glancing casually at the Obits, the face of Felix Mendez jumped out like a snake in the grass and Claude said, "Damn, it's him."

"Killed in a mysterious fire in his cabin at Oak Creek Canyon State Park," he read aloud. "It looks to me like Mohammed got rid of his flunky, which is too bad. I was looking forward to killing him nice and slow, after I got every bit of info he knew about 'his plans'."

There was a postscript to the death notice informing readers to turn to page four for a story on the fire. Following the instructions, he read a write-up three columns long. It was interesting information and he went over it twice, noting the name of the man in charge of the investigation was Sergeant Joseph Francone.

After thinking for a few minutes, he picked up the phone, called the precinct and asked for Sergeant Francone.

"I'm sorry, he's out of town for the day," the operator said. "Can someone else help you sir?"

"No," Claude lied. "It's all right. Joe's an old friend. I was passing through town and wanted to say Hi."

"What's your name, Sir? I'll pass your message on to Sergeant Francone."

"That's all right, operator, I'll call back later. Thank you."

"You're welcome," she said, and her tone of voice said she was miffed because Claude wouldn't identify himself.

"Tough titty" he thought and hung up.

(Five)

The heat in the lab must have been set at eighty. It was cool outside, with a threat of rain or an early snow in the air, but this was ridiculous. As soon as they got in the door, Bert and his companions started shedding clothes the way a dry Christmas tree drops its needles after the holiday is over.

Fred had instructions to take them to Mister Witte, so there was none of the bullshit chair sitting this morning. Glancing at the waiting area, Bert noticed there were two new seats available, but the other sad old ones still set there looking like they'd rather be in the dump.

As they shook hands and he introduced his fellow officers of the law, Bert said, "Thanks for calling, Mister Witte. This is Sergeant Joe Francone from our office and Agent Kris Hefner from the FBI. Both of these gentlemen are working on Larry's case and would like to see Mister Mendez's office."

"My partner should be here shortly with a search warrant," Joe said. "We'll wait until he arrives to make entry."

"This is John Kawalski," Hershel said. "John came all the way from Bed Rock to speak with you, so I'll leave you alone and let him tell you his story. When your partner arrives, have my secretary notify me and I'll accompany you to Felix's office."

"Felix Mendez," Kris said. "That name's been running around in my head since I first heard it. Does it ring a bell with you, Joe?"

"Funny, I told Bert the same thing. No, I didn't know him. I'd remember a name like that."

"Go ahead, Mister Kawalski, tell us your story," Kris said.

"Hell, call me John. I'm a rock climber, like to go out and free-climb shear cliffs by myself. My friends tell me I've got a death wish and maybe I did, but I'm over it now. I have a mystery of my own to solve."

Wishing John would get to the point, Joe asked, "And what's that?"

"I was climbing a few days ago and was about half-way up an escarpment when I got tired and took a little nap in a crevice I found. An explosion woke me up and I peeked over the side to see this Mendez guy and another dark-skinned individual walk up to a cloud of dust to check out what they'd accomplished by setting off a device. I think it must have been dynamite or C-4."

"How do you know that?" Kris asked.

"I worked with the stuff in Vietnam. We used to knock down trees with C-4 and det cord. It would cut through a six foot diameter hardwood like a knife."

"Yeah," Bert said. "I heard about that."

"Anyway, I stuck around until they left and climbed back down to see what the hell they were up to. It's illegal to set off explosive devices in a state park. Hell, they could have started a big forest fire."

"And what did you find?" Joe asked.

"Lots of pieces of metal painted red and some chrome fragments too. The biggest thing I found was a curved handle I know I've seen somewhere before, but just can't place."

"What did you do with the evidence?" Kris asked.

"I turned it in to the head ranger up at the park, Ezra Parrish. He has it."

"Is that all?" Joe asked.

"No," John said, "there's more. I thought I'd snoop around on my own, maybe find this guy and ream his ass out for setting off explosives in the park. I rode up and down every path and gravel road out there searching for his car, but didn't get lucky until I saw the smoke from the fire in which this Mendez guy died.

"I was the first one there and the cabin was already too far gone for anyone to get out alive. His Cadillac was burning about fifty feet away, and like a dummy I stood too close. It blew up and almost took me with it. I had to get a crew cut because it burned half the hair off my scalp."

John rubbed his head to prove his point.

Joe asked, "Where did you find Felix's body?"

"Just inside the door and it was pretty gory. He was lying on his back, well-done and charred on the outside. The local coroner came out, pronounced him and took his body into the town of Bed Rock. They've got Felix refrigerated, waiting for his next of kin to claim what's left."

"We need to get our forensic people up there," Kris said. "This is too much of a coincidence."

"Yeah," Joe said. "I'll bet we find a slug or two in Mister Mendez. Man, his name is driving me crazy. Why is that?"

"I don't know, but here's Fad," Bert said.

(Six)

"Go ahead, Hershel, open it up," Joe said. "Here's the warrant for your files in case anyone from the family wants to raise a stink."

"Thank you," Hershel said. "If you don't mind, I'll just wait in my office."

"That'll be fine, sir," Kris said. "We'll try to be as neat as we can."

"You first, Fad," Joe said. "Take Polaroid shots of the entire office before we tear it up, so we can put it back together again before we leave."

"Sure," Fad said. He stepped to the door, opened it and began to take a series of photos. After changing the film pack once, he said, "I think that'll do. Come on in. Whoever this Mendez guy was, he was neat."

The office looked like one out of Good Office Keeping Magazine, (if there was one). Since the door was closed after Felix left for vacation, there was a light sheen of dust on the desk, but other than that it was as neat as Bert's mother's place.

"Take each drawer separately," Joe said. "Let Fad document the contents with the camera. Then take each item out one at a time and don't miss a thing."

(Seven)

Two hours later they were almost finished. The heat was their enemy until Fad climbed up on the desk and shut the vent.

"If he hadn't been able to close it, we'd probably be searching in our skivvies by now," Bert thought.

All the drawers were checked and the file cabinet gone through like it held the Japanese codes for World War II, but they found nothing. Fad worked on the computer, trying to open Felix's files and found his way into most of them, but not all.

"The lab boys will have to break his entry code," Fad said.

"Did you check under the desk drawers?" Joe asked.

"Yeah," Kris replied, "twice. There are no envelopes or anything suspicious looking."

Bert was looking through some books on the window sill. Most of them were technical manuals, but one title got his attention. It was a plain Jane book with a red cover titled: "Terrorists Are Among Us" and it seemed out of place.

"Hey," Bert called, "look at this."

The others gathered around and he said, "Check out the title. It looks like it doesn't belong there. Everything else is technical crap only a chemical scientist could or would read."

"Yeah," Joe said. "Take a look inside. It's your find."

Holding the book by its binder, Bert shook it and a small envelope fell to the floor.

"Bingo," Kris said.

"Don't pick it up with your bare fingers, Bert," Joe warned. "Fad, you got some gloves?"

"Yeah, four pair of them. Here Bert, try these on."

Slipping his large hands into the gloves, Bert pulled until they slid onto his fingers and said, "Kind of small, Fad."

"Your tax dollars well spent again."

Stooping down, Bert picked up the envelope by one corner, and asked, "Now what?"

Indicating a letter opener on the desk top, Joe said, "Use his knife to slit it open. Dump it out and spread it open on his desk. Try not to touch it any more than you have to."

"Roger," Bert said. "Looks like notes."

"Read them," Kris said, pulling out his notebook to write down the contents.

Joe beat him by two seconds, smiled over his pencil and said, "Never take notes in ink, Kris. You can't change them later."

"I'll remember that," Kris said, holding up his hand to display a fancy thin-lead pencil in his fingers.

Bert read the note. "It says:" 'Mohammed, possibly lives in Denver, terror attack on U.S., Cotton Bowl, nerve Gas Agent to be used. Thirty-two containers disguised as fire extinguishers. Kill the president and as many Americans as possible.'

"That's all?" Kris asked.

"Hell," Joe exclaimed, "that's a bunch!"

"Wait a minute," Kris said. "Felix Mendez—Sadie told us his name and we didn't know it. Remember, 'Fell X Man is'. Damn, why couldn't we figure it out?"

"Because we didn't speak to him, Bert did," Joe said. "And his name never came up in on our brainstorming session, remember?"

"Yeah, I do. Hey, you were right about the Arab. Sadie must have substituted 'far' for 'middle'."

"Yeah," Joe said, "but we didn't know about this Mohammed guy then."

"Boy," Fad said. "We screwed up big time."

"Yeah," Joe said, "but Felix left us the plan. Now we know what to expect. We can find this guy and put him away for life or get the death penalty. Now all we have to do is locate this Mohammed."

Looking at him inquisitively, Fad said sarcastically, "Oh yeah, Joe, that'll be easy. There can't be more than two or three million Muslims who are named after their spiritual leader."

"But even if you do catch him, what happens to the nerve gas?" Kris asked. "That is if they have it. How could they do it and not have it detected?"

"I don't know, but we need to talk to Hershel to find out what's been going on here," Joe said. "If they do have the gas, you're right. Just catching this Mohammed won't make sure we retrieve it. Damn, disguising it as fire extinguishers, that's some idea."

As he looked over his notes, Kris was quiet and then suddenly said, "Shit."

At his outburst, the others looked at Kris in surprise, and Joe asked, "What?"

"We had it all the time. Look at Sadie's story. 'Hide three two fire X'."

"I don't believe all of this," Joe said. "You're right, but how the hell would we have ever figured it out?"

"Probably never, but Larry was pressed for time. He did the best he could."

"Too bad it wasn't enough," Bert said. "Carol will be happy to hear he died serving his country."

"You can't tell her about this," Kris said. "Look, the FBI is assuming jurisdiction of this case right now. Since you're already knowledgeable of the particulars, you'll stay on as my assistants. I'll notify my boss and he'll clear you working with us with your supervisor, and we'll get all the help we need. But until then, we have to keep this hushed up.

"We need to know how much gas is in each of these containers. Talk to Hershel, Joe, and find out if there was some missing, no matter how much over a long period of time. If there was, you'll have to tell him what we think Felix and the others are planning and swear him to secrecy."

"You better get your ass up to Oak Creek Canyon State Park and Felix's cabin," Fad said. "He was doing something up there besides sucking his thumb or jerking off. Your forensic scientists need to be sharp."

"See if you can talk Hershel into going, Joe," Kris said. "Tell him we need him along to show us what Felix was doing. He'll be able to determine if it's connected with nerve gas."

"I'll get him to go by putting the fear of God into him. If Hershel thinks some nerve gas is missing and Felix was working with it, he'll break his balls to get there."

"I'll leave it up to you, Joe," Kris said. "Fad, get on the computer and try to get a line on this Mohammed. Bert can help you. I'll drive up to Felix's cabin and secure the scene before anyone walks off with anything."

"Before you leave, Kris, ask John about what he saw," Joe said, "Maybe he can describe what the equipment looks like."

"Good idea. I'll see you and Hershel up there post haste."

"I haven't heard that expression in years. Keep it up and I might learn English from you yet, Kris."

"You can use it to impress Mona."

"I haven't seen her in two weeks and she's right next door. Too bad I don't have time to check on our romance."

"Later Joe," Kris said. "Get with it."

"Yes sir, your Agentness," Joe said and bowed, but Kris missed it. He was already out the door and down the hall.

CHAPTER 16

(One)

Shivering as he sat inside the medical examiner's office in Bed Rock, Kris waited for an answer to his request. It was chilly outside, but here it was colder than three day old snot blasted onto a snow bank by a boozer with a bad head cold.

"Why do they keep it so cold inside these places?" Kris asked silently and then answered his own question, "To prevent the spread of germs."

From the looks of things, the germs were winning.

Across the desk, the good Doctor Amos Witherspoon sat with his face wrinkled up into a frown, trying to come up with a reason to reject Kris' demand for an autopsy on Felix Mendez. The clothes on his tall lanky frame were layered, so he didn't notice the cold.

Amos wore an old, decrepit grey sweater with the elbows showing thin over a white jacket, which in turn covered a two-piece set of dark-green scrubs. The legs were short and Kris saw cotton long-johns peeking out from under them.

Doc Witherspoon's face displayed four or five day's growth of beard and a bulbous nose that glistened amber from the booze he consumed on a daily basis.

Later Kris would tell Joe, "The old geezer's nose was so round and red you could have painted a three on it and used it to play pool or left it alone and played snooker, take your pick."

A set of crooked tobacco stained teeth with a few gaps here and there peered out of Amos' thin mouth. When he spoke, his breath issued forth booze fumes he had tried in vain to cover with a large swig of mouthwash.

Suddenly he hacked up a goober of phlegm, turned and spat it into a soiled sink that Kris would never want to wash his hands in, no matter how long and hard he scrubbed it. After wiping his chin on the arm of his sweater, Amos asked, "Who's going to pay for it, you young whipper snapper?"

It was obvious Kris' FBI credentials hadn't made an impression on him, but Kris was persistent and said, "The Bureau will, but if for some reason they don't, the city of Sulfur Springs will. Sergeant Francone will arrive later today and confirm it. Our forensic team will also be here in a few hours to assist you."

"Assist me my ass," Amos said. "I've cut people up and down for years and I don't need any help. If the yahoo that's taking up my valuable cooler space," Amos paused, jerked his thumb over his shoulder to indicate the morgue behind him and continued without taking a breath, "was shot, I'll know in a few minutes. Your guys will only be in the way and question my every move. Tell them to take a hike."

"I'd appreciate it if you'd let them observe your procedures and gather any evidence."

"They can watch and I'll give them any slugs I find, but that's all," Amos said. "Now I want your name, address and badge number. I was stiffed by the government before."

Taking a card from his billfold, Kris entered the requested info on the back, handed it to Amos and thought, "Finally, thank God and Greyhound. Now I can be gone." Standing up, he stuck out his hand, which the good doctor ignored like it was the carrier of the Asian bird flu.

"Thanks" Kris said, (and didn't mean it), turned and walked out the door to where John sat in comfort in the nice warm car.

He had told John he could ride home with him when he found out the rock climber planned to rent a car for a one-way trip to Bed Rock. Kris knew it would cost John an arm and a leg, something a human spider couldn't afford. Since Kris was going there anyway, he'd appreciate John's company and conversation.

After they were on the road for a half hour and exhausted about every subject known to man, (John could talk and did), John said, "If you have time after you finish your other chores, I want to take you up the mountain to where those two guys did their blasting."

"First, I have to stop by and arrange for an autopsy on Felix Mendez," Kris said. "Then I'll go out and secure the scene of the fire. I hope no one's been there collecting souvenirs."

"I doubt it," John said. "It's a long ways out in the woods and not too many people know the road exists. Plus there wasn't a hell of a lot left anyone in his right mind would want."

"Good. After Joe and Hershel get there to check the place, I'll be glad to go with you. I want to see if the red metal pieces could be part of a fire extinguisher."

"Damn," John exclaimed and slapped his forehead with his right palm. "A fire extinguisher, that's what the handle I found came from. I knew I saw it before. Why would those two jerks blow up fire extinguishers filled with green water?"

"What green water?" Kris asked. "You never mentioned it before."

"Hell, I forgot about it. Yeah, the fire extinguishers were filled with water and green dye. It was spread out over a fifty foot radius and made interesting overlapping circular patterns on the rocks and grass."

"So there was more than one," Kris said.

"You catch on quick," John said. "Yeah, that was my impression. I only heard one explosion, so they must have set them all off at once."

"Interesting," Kris said. "Now I can't wait to get up there to see it."

(Two)
Two hours later, as Kris and John stood outside the ruins of the cabin that looked like the blackened bones of a whale who beached himself here eons ago, Joe and Hershel drove up in Joe's old beat-up squad car.

It resembled a reject from the junk yard and was covered with a thick coat of dust. It was apparent that on the way up here Joe didn't let any grass grow under his feet or on his vehicle, although if you spread some seed on it now, in three days you'd have a portable lawn.

Kris and John hadn't entered the cabin. They conducted their investigation from afar. The place was a charred shell, but if enough remained perhaps Hershel could tell them what Felix was up to. If anything was missing, Kris chalked it up to theft by pack rats or small ground squirrels. There was an overabundance of them in the vicinity.

It rained a couple of days ago and there were no fresh tracks in the mud or charcoal, so no one was here since the firemen departed.

As Joe and Hershel climbed from the car, Joe stopped, stared at the ruins and said, "Not much left, is there."

"Hopefully there's enough for you to work with, Hershel," Kris said. "Go ahead. If you need help moving anything, shout and we'll do it."

"Thank you," Hershel said and walked through the remains of the doorway. A scarred and charred quarter panel of a burned door hung forlornly from one blackened hinge like the tongue of a dog after a long run through a park.

They watched as he moved slowly around what was left of a table and picked up several beakers and chromed, smoke-stained pieces of metal. Suddenly he stopped and said, "Oh my."

"What?" Kris asked.

Pointing to a section of plywood that was still halfway intact, only charred around the edges, Hershel asked, "Can you move this piece of roof?"

It was covered with tarpaper and grey shingles soaked by rain or still retaining the water pumped on the fire by the local foundation savers, and concealed whatever he wanted to see.

"Sure," Kris said, and asked Joe and John, "You want to give me a hand?"

They went into the cabin with him and helped lift the heavier-than-it-looked piece of roofing. Under it was a four-legged contraption about three feet high, four feet long and three feet wide. On top of that was a badly bent arrangement of bars which had contained thick glass at one time, but now had melted into clumps, forming strange obscure patterns.

One side had pitched forward and remained almost undamaged. There were two large holes in the center, approximately eight inches wide, from which hung the charred and melted remains of two long rubber tubes with gloves attached to the ends. They could see three fingers attached to one, but the other was beyond recognition.

"Christ!" Hershel exclaimed. The unexpected curse was out of place for such a mild-mannered man.

Kris asked, "What is it and what did he use it for?"

Pointing to a long slender container with a hole in its side resembling a tank used by welders, Hershel said, "Felix had an air-tight chamber and it was attached to the ruptured pressure tank over there."

Hershel's explanation went over Kris' head. He looked at the others and saw they were as perplexed as he.

"You care to explain it in layman's terms?" Joe asked.

"A bigger unit similar to this is in our lab," Hershel said. "It's used to transfer dangerous material from one container to another."

Forgetting about John being present, Joe asked, "Like nerve gas?"

"Yes. I can't believe this. How did Felix fool us all?"

"Nerve gas," John exclaimed. "What're you talking about?"

"Shit," Joe thought, knowing he opened his mouth at the wrong time and now the crap was about to splatter.

All he could do was hope he didn't catch the full brunt, as he said, "That's what they burn in the chemical lab you visited, John. What you heard when I opened my big mouth was classified and I should have my tongue cut out for letting you know about it, but now you do.

"So you have two options open to you. You can keep your mouth shut and forget I said anything, or you can spend the next few months in 'protective custody' in the slammer in Sulfur Springs. I'm sorry, but what we're dealing with here is so secret no one else knows about it."

"Hell," John said. "You know you can trust me. I'll never tell a soul. Remember, I want to find out why these guys were messing up my woods. I want to nail their asses to the wall as much as you do; comprendere?"

"Okay, John," Kris said and shot Joe an unforgiving look.

Joe blushed and looked away as Kris said, "I'm sorry Joe let his mouth run away with his brains, but now you know and I doubt it would keep you quiet if we put you in jail. Thanks to you, we know a lot more than we did. Stick around, but keep your mouth shut."

"I said I'm sorry," Joe said.

"Okay, Joe," Kris said. "We all make mistakes."

Hershel interrupted them and said, "If we can get back to what I was discussing, that's a container from our lab laying over there."

Pointing to a scorched metal container resembling something you hooked up to a milkshake machine, but which had a rounded top and a small opening at the apex, Hershel said, "It held up to thirty-two ounces of fluid, but it's empty now."

"Thirty-two, there's that magic number again," Kris said. "It's the number of fire extinguishers in Sadie's message. Felix must have put one ounce in each of them."

"Sadie, who's she?" John asked. "And why thirty-two fire extinguishers?"

"Now who opened his mouth?" Joe asked.

Looking as if he'd like to kick his own ass up into the treetops, Kris said, "Damn, that's what happens when we have civilians around and don't pay attention. I apologize for my remarks earlier, Joe.

"John, lawman or not it looks like you're in this thing up to your ass, like it or not."

"It's okay with me," John said. "If I can help my country, all you have to do is ask."

"You gentlemen will have to excuse me," Hershel said. "I need to sit down. You don't know how lucky it is Felix didn't slip up and let some of the gas enter the atmosphere, or kill himself and a lot of others."

"How many people could be killed by an ounce of nerve gas?" Kris asked.

"Thousands," Hershel said sadly. "If the wind was right and it was released in a heavily populated area like New York, perhaps hundreds of thousands."

"Or Dallas/Fort Worth?" Kris asked.

"Are those the targets?" John asked.

"I keep opening my mouth when I shouldn't," Kris said. "I guess it's contagious. But yes, John those are the targets of the bombs we think Felix put together up here."

Turning to Joe, Kris said, "Joe, you might as well fill John in and see about getting him deputized or some legal status, now that he knows most of what's going on."

"I'll take care of it," Joe said.

Hershel walked to Joe's car and sat in the front seat. His face was ashen and he looked like he might throw up as he asked, "Are we finished here?"

Taking pity on him, Kris said, "Yeah, I think you've told us enough. I'll get the local cops to provide security up here until the forensic team arrives. They can gather up everything and bring it down to Sulfur Springs. There isn't any chance of anything dangerous getting loose, is there?"

"No. The fire would have destroyed any remaining gas, although I believe Felix completed the transfer and moved the final product elsewhere. I didn't see any evidence of anything like fire extinguishers in the wreckage."

"Me neither," Joe said. "Yeah, Felix moved it or got it ready to go and someone got rid of him and stole it. Man, these guys are ruthless. They kill without losing any sleep over it."

"It's typical of a terrorist," Kris said. "No quarter asked and none given. We're going to need all the help we can get to find the gas before they use it."

"Jesus," John said.

"Yeah," Kris said. "We could use His help too."

"What's our next move?" Joe asked.

"John is going to take me out to where he saw Felix and his partner set off the explosive devices," Kris said. "You want to come along?"

"Is the autopsy all set?"

"Yeah, the local doc reluctantly agreed to do it. By now our forensic team should be in town to observe. He won't let them assist him."

SIGNS OF OUR TIMES

"Then sure, I'd like to go with you," Joe said. "Three pairs of eyes are better than two. I'll drop you off at a hotel in town, Hershel. We should be finished by tonight and after the forensic team gets here, they can take over. In the morning we'll head back to Sulfur Springs. Is that okay with you?"

"Yes, that's fine. I still can't believe how Felix fooled us all. We wrote off the small amount of missing gas from a series of canisters as a mistake in the calculations when they were initially filled many years ago.

"Things back then were hectic and not as controlled as they are now, but it's no excuse. I'm responsible for checking such details and I let it slide right by me. I'll never forgive myself if anyone is killed by these terrorists."

John had listened to everything with an open mind, but he was shocked to find he was now involved in such a horrific plot to kill thousands of his fellow Americans.

Shaking his head as if it would make the horror go away, John thought, "My mystery is about to make me sick to my stomach."

(Three)

Claude's fantasy dream came true and he couldn't believe it. He and Carla became lovers so casually it seemed a natural thing to do, but was it fair to her for him to take advantage of her love with his lies, one after the other?

"No, it wasn't," he admitted silently, but he couldn't help himself. Carla was like a tonic he needed to exist. One taste and he wanted more.

It was several days since he was shot and met her. His wounds were healed sufficiently to allow them to start a routine of physical therapy in the evenings after Carla came home from work and on the weekends.

At first it was pure hell, bending his arm and shoulder to the max, but with steady repetition things improved. Now it only hurt for a short time and when Claude really got into it, then the exercises became pleasurable.

Carla bought him several outfits with his money. Claude never asked for an accounting. What he had was hers without asking. He knew he owed her more than money alone could repay. There was a lot more cash where the few thousand he had with him came from.

"If only she knew how he earned it," he thought. "God, how can I explain it to her?"

Letting the thought go to a hidden corner of his mind, to be dealt with at a later time, he remembered two days ago when he was doing some free weights and Carla sneaked up behind him, wrapped her arms around him and kissed the back of his sweaty neck.

"Ugh, she said, "too salty."

Claude turned and she met his mouth with hers. Her tongue searched for his in frantic haste and he couldn't believe it. They broke apart and he pulled her around to sit on his lap. The move hurt his shoulder, but he hid it as he said, "I've wanted to do that since I met you. Why the sudden change in your attitude?"

"Shush, no questions," she said, curling into his arms as he kissed her deeply.

They made love through the evening and into the night.

At first, she asked, "Is this hurting you?"

"Only in my heart," he said. "I thought about you every night and wanted to crawl into your bedroom and beg you if I had to. I think I'm falling in love with you."

"I feel the same way, but I'm afraid it's only lust after all this time together. I hope it isn't, but if it is, I understand."

"There's a lot about me you don't know," Claude said. "Some of it's ugly and I can't talk about it, but there's more good than evil. I just hope I can show you that part of me."

"You already have. As for the bad, I've had it happen to me before, so I'm no stranger to it. If you ever feel like talking, I'm a good listener. If not, it's okay. Let's enjoy what we have. If it ends we'll know it at the same time."

"You're a very perceptive woman."

"I guess it's the librarian in me," Carla said. "In my spare time I read too many romance books. During the past few days I had some exotic dreams about you."

"Were any as good as this?" Claude asked.

"No," she said. "You weren't really in my arms."

For the rest of the night, there wasn't much time for conversation. If Claude died tomorrow, he'd remember their first night forever.

(Four)

"Over here," John said.

He led them up a steep climb from the parking lot three quarters of a mile away and then up to heaven by the looks of it. By the time they reached the top, Joe was puffing like a locomotive that needed more steam.

It was cooler in the mountains, but Joe was sweating like an orangutan in heat. He glanced over at Kris and saw beads of perspiration hanging on his brow, but he was breathing naturally and Joe thought, "Kris hasn't said a thing and doesn't even look winded. But then, he's not an overweight fart like me. God, where's the top of this hill?"

At the sound of John's remark, Joe looked up from where his face was dragging the ground, about to be stepped on by his own feet, or so it felt, and saw they had reached the crest.

It leveled off and the soil was sandy with stones lying scattered about. It looked as if the boulders fell off the mountain and landed here to rest for eons, before another ice age took over and moved them along.

Pausing for a moment to get his breath, Joe thought, "It must be nice to be a rock. It's all downhill for them and then they get to rest for as long as God wants them to."

Pointing upward and outward, John said, "It rained since I was here last. Most of the dye was washed away, but you can still see some faint traces of it. See?"

The spots seemed to ask to be joined together like a puzzle in a kid's book at a local restaurant. As he walked over to the steep cliff and looked at a slight line of light-green dots, Kris said, "I see what you mean. Where were the bombs set off?"

Pointing to a small depression in the soil, John said, "Right there. It was deeper, but it looks like the rain filled it in too."

"Yeah," Joe said, reaching down to pick up two dime-sized pieces of red metal. "It uncovered more fragments."

The small remnants were hot to the touch. He moved them from one palm to the other to keep from being burned and said, "Damn."

"The sun warmed them up," John said. "It does that up here where the air's lighter."

"Put them in your pocket, Joe," Kris said.

"Yeah, and burn my nuts off. No thank you, I'll wait until they cool down."

"Whatever," Kris said; studying the patterns and trying to determine how many containers were tested. He was sure there was more than one and said, "I think they brought three or four of the fire extinguishers here to test. See how the dispersal patterns interlock and overlap? I estimate four of them. Does it leave thirty-two more or just twenty-eight?"

"I believe they come in a box of twelve," John said, "or thirty-six for three boxes. It works out conveniently."

"See, I told you John would earn his bread," Kris said. "Okay, so we still have thirty-two to find."

Kris asked, "From the size of the depression you saw after they set the bombs off, John, could you tell if it was dynamite or C-4?"

"I'd say C-4. Dynamite is too unpredictable. It takes more to do the job than they could reasonably hide on or in a fire extinguisher."

"I see your point," Joe said. "I know a little about plastic explosives and a small piece of C-4 goes a long way. I wonder how they set them all off at the same time."

"The must have a signaling device hooked up to a set frequency," John said. "They only have to push the button once to have the bombs all go off simultaneously."

"I think we've seen everything there is to see," Joe said. He put the cooled pieces of metal in his pants pocket and said, "Let's head to town, find a place to down a few brews and talk this over. We need to come up with a viable plan."

"There you go again, using big words," Kris said. "It must be the high altitude. It allows your brain to breathe."

"Up yours," Joe said and started back down the hillside. From the way Joe rolled down the mountain, it looked like he'd make a good rock, but he knew he wouldn't lie around and rest on his laurels the way they did.

(Five)

After breaking in through the back door of Felix's residence, for the past thirty minutes Mohammed searched the place like a berserk bulldozer. Paper, books, technical documents and the contents of every drawer lay scattered on the floor. So far, he found nothing and he didn't think he would, but Hushan said to search and search he did.

Moving into the bedroom, he tore it apart, making more noise than he realized. The sounds traveled across the alley to where Harriette Johnson sat on her rear stoop smoking a joint, rocking back and forth to music only she could hear.

Her short, kinky black hair swung to and fro in time with her movements and she asked aloud, "What the fuck's going on over there? It sounds like someone's tearing the little Mexican's place apart."

Harriette was no angel of mercy or Good Sam, but she was protective of her neighbor's junk. If someone could rob the Mex's crib and get away with it, hers might be next and she had a good stash of hash on hand she didn't want to see walk away.

She got up, went inside, phoned 9-1-1 and left an anonymous message about a possible B and E at four seventeen Elm Street. The operator asked for more info and Harriette hung up thinking, "If they want to know more, they can damn well come out and take a look."

If she was wrong, Harriette wasn't going to have them hassle her for making a false report. In her present half-drugged state, she forgot when you called the emergency number; they knew instantly where it came from.

Hunkered down behind her fence, she peeked through a crack to watch what would happen. The noises of mass destruction continued to resound throughout the house across the alley and she thought, "Damn, the cops better hurry or there won't be anything left."

She took another hit, and it may have fogged her mind for a moment and she might have drifted off for a while, because when she looked again, a cop was walking up to the back door and she thought, "Go get 'em, Lone Ranger."

Then the door seemed to flake off some green paint, and the cop dropped like he'd been pole axed.

Silently, Harriette said, "What the fuck? Jesus, the perp shot him through the door. I didn't hear the shots, so he must have used a silencer. What a set of balls."

The door swung open and Harriette ducked down to make sure the doer wouldn't see her and waste her too. When she got the courage to look again, the shooter was kneeling down by the cop, whose legs twitched like he was dancing the Mambo.

"Help, police!" The doer yelled.

It startled her as she wondered, "Why's he calling for the cops? Shit, he just shot that one. What is he, crazy?"

Looking through the crack again, she saw a uniformed cop who must have been the other one's partner run around the corner with his gun drawn. He looked down at the murderer, who knelt by the first cop's side like a guardian angel.

Pointing down the alley at a car pulling away, the shooter said, "He shot him."

The dumb cop bought the lie, took his eyes off him, turned and looked the way the doer pointed.

Harriette watched in horror as the killer pulled his gun from under his legs and pumped two shots into the second cop's back. A string of blood drops flew through the air like red raspberry Jello and the cop dropped like a stone.

Standing up, the doer calmly shot the first cop in the head. Then he moved to the other cop and did the same thing.

In her stoned condition, Harriette thought she said "No", in her mind, but she must have said it aloud, because the killer looked her way.

Getting a quick look at his profile before she dropped to her stomach,

Harriette started to crab-crawl away toward her back door. She prayed, "Jesus, Joseph and Mary, don't let the fucker get me and I'll never touch another joint."

Harriette reached her steps, but instead of going up them and into her house, she crawled under the stoop and hid behind the concrete riser. A moment later she heard the fence groan in protest as the shooter leaned on it.

Her heart raced, and her breath came in ragged gasps, but she put her hand over her mouth and held her breath for what seemed like an eternity until she heard the fence groan again and footsteps running down the alley.

Staying where she was until ten minutes later, when she heard the scream of sirens, she figured, "some other Good Sam called it in."

In the future she'd be damned if she'd pay any attention to what was going on outside of her yard. Forgetting her oath to God, Harriette lit another joint, took a deep hit and waited for the cavalry to arrive.

(Six)

It was late evening, almost ten p.m., when Joe's cell phone rang in his hotel room. He thought, "It figures, I get settled back against the headboard with a cold one in my hand and some idiot has to call me."

Looking at the plastic monster from hell with disdain, he was sorry he had it. He hated it with a passion and usually left it in his desk drawer, but he was out of touch without it up here, so take it he did.

Two hours ago they finally received the autopsy report from the doc and found out Felix took two .38 caliber slugs in his back and one in the head. He was dead before the fire turned him into toast.

The damned phone chimed again, like the bells in Big Ben, beckoning Joe to answer, as he thought, "All right, you son of a bitch, I heard you."

Sitting the brew down carefully on the back of the dresser, he picked up the noise maker, flipped the top up and said, "Yeah."

The caller said, "Joe, this is Bert."

Joe knew instantly there was big trouble in store because he could hear Fad in the background saying, "Damn it, damn it, damn it".

"What's up Bert?" He asked.

"The shit hit the fan here. Two cops are down over at Felix's house. Whoever popped them also shot them in the head to make sure they were dead."

"Damn!" Joe exclaimed. "Who was it?"

"We don't know, but we think the shooter was this Mohammed character.

We got an anonymous call from a junkie over on Watson Street. She lives behind Felix's place and heard whoever shot the cops tossing the place and called it in. Fad sent the two rookies from A Squad over there for a look-see, and now he's blaming himself."

"Son of a bitch," Joe said. He couldn't believe how casually these guys wasted someone. Two more dead and they were his fellow officers.

He thought, "Damn this case anyway."

Bert said, "Yeah, that's what we're dealing with here, some real smart and lucky sons of bitches. The neighbor says the shooter popped the first cop through the back door. Then he kneeled down by the cop's side and called for the police real loud.

"The cop's partner came running, and the killer told him someone else shot his partner and pointed down the alley. The rookie fell for it and the shooter wasted him too."

"Son of a bitch," Joe repeated. His heart was beating so fast he thought he'd pass out.

He turned, sat down on the bed, took a deep breath and asked, "Is there any description of the doer?"

"She only saw his profile. Said he had a moustache, swarthy, dark complexion, about six feet tall, maybe a little shorter. Wore dark clothes, nothing she remembers. When they found her under her back stairs, she was whacked out of her mind. She says the doer came after her when she cried out in alarm as he gave the cops the coup de grace."

"Good thing she hid and got away or we wouldn't know this much," Joe said. He was calmer now, but would hate to see what his blood pressure would register on the pump right now.

"Yeah," Bert said. "You better come back ASAP. Fad's broken up about this. I hope he doesn't go off the deep end and tie one on. It wasn't his fault."

"I'm on my way," Joe said. He shut the phone, jumped up from the bed, threw open the door and ran down the hall to Kris' room.

(Seven)

As he drove toward Denver and his occasional home, Mohammed was running scared. Although he'd worn gloves so there wouldn't be any prints at Felix's place and he knew there was no way to trace his gun because he never used it before, he wondered how the police had found him so quickly.

There was no way for him to know the master plan wasn't compromised. All he knew was somehow they had found him and he was more afraid than at any other time in his life.

For a moment, he wondered, "What would Hushan say now? Hell, he'll waste me as a liability. No, I won't contact him until I'm sure what happened."

Using the cover of a carpenter on a crew that built Big Burger Hamburger joints all over Colorado, with a home base in Sulfur Springs, Mohammed moved around a lot, but could take time off when he was needed by the organization, which was a plus.

To avoid being seen, he took all the back roads he knew and made good use of a map to find the ones he didn't. He hadn't spent much time at the trailer since he rented it, but it seemed like an ideal place to hole up now.

Six months ago, he leased the dump and paid for a full year in advance, which pleased the shit out of the pimply-faced bastard who owned the shack. The main reason Mohammed had the trailer was to give him an address for his driver's license and other documents.

He belonged to one of those so-called "sleeper cells" you heard so much about, but never imagined you'd find in your own back yard.

Having no close friends, he stayed with other members of the organization only when it was necessary, and it didn't happen often. No one asked any questions. They kept their mouths shut and let you stay until you moved on.

No one in this "game" knew Mohammed's last name. It was one of the rules and a good one for everyone concerned. Most members used phony first names too, and he tried it for a while, but sometimes forgot to answer to his alias. Knowing the time may come when he might slip up; he eventually reverted to using his real moniker.

As far as he knew, there was no way to trace him to the trailer, so Mohammed felt safe in going home. He doubted if the heat would work after his long absence, even though he kept the bills paid by having them sent to a mail box in Sulfur Springs.

A few minutes after nine p.m., he made it there safely, parked at the end of the trailer and pulled his weary frame from the car. He felt like he'd been rode hard and put away wet, a saying he picked up one night in a bar down in Texas. Mohammed liked the way it sounded and thought it had sexual connotations, even though others didn't seem to perceive it that way.

Looking up and down the street, he didn't notice anyone sitting in parked cars and thought, "I'm probably worried about nothing. I thought someone cried out when I wasted the cops, but maybe I was hearing things. I didn't see anyone in the yard across the alley. Besides, I doubt if anyone got a good look at me. I wasn't there three minutes. Damn, Mohammed, calm down."

Walking inside, he found the thermostat set at fifty degrees and the house not much warmer. After turning the heat up, he went to the closet, got a coat and put it on while he waited to see if the damned furnace would turn on. It did and he uttered a sigh of relief.

After lying down on the bed to rest a while, before he knew it, he drifted off to sleep. For someone who killed as many times as he did in the past few days, it was a peaceful slumber.

CHAPTER 17

(One)
When Claude phoned Sergeant Francone again the following morning and finally reached him, he sounded tired, as if he hadn't slept for a day or two.

"Sergeant Francone, how may I help you?" Joe asked, but his voice cracked and Claude knew something was wrong. Claude hadn't watched TV this morning or read the newspaper yet, so he knew nothing about two policemen being shot to death the previous afternoon, so he said, "This is Mister Jones. I want to confess to a murder."

Thinking he had another nutcase on his hands, Joe sighed and said, "Listen my friend, two cops were killed last night and I'm not in the mood to listen to bullshit."

"This is no bullshit," Claude said. "Does the name Katie Adkins ring a bell?"

"Damn," Joe thought. Sucking in wind, he snapped his fingers loudly and Fad looked his way. While making a motion with his hand to tell Fad to trace the call, Joe said, "Yes, it does."

He tried to stretch out his words, but his caller wasn't buying it, because he said, "Don't take the time to trace my call. I'll be gone in a few more seconds. Are you interested in speaking with me?"

"Yes, I am."

"Then give me your cell phone number and I'll call you later. No tricks, Sergeant or you'll never hear from me again."

"Okay," Joe said. "The number is 555-7269. You got it."

"Yeah, I'll call you soon. I think we can help each other. Keep it in mind if the name Mohammed means anything to you."

Hearing Mohammed's name from this guy threw Joe for a loop, but he was a professional and quick on the uptake, so he asked, "Mohammed? There are millions of rag heads out there named Mohammed. You got a last name on him?"

Joe didn't fool Claude. He heard his quick intake of breath when he mentioned Mohammed and asked, "You mean you don't know his last name?"

There was silence on the line as Joe tried to think of a quick comeback that made sense, but his mind went blank.

"I'll be damned. You don't, do you?" Claude asked.

"You son of a bitch," Joe said.

"No, I'm not and I'm not Mohammed, so stop thinking that way. I'll talk to you later."

The line went dead, and Joe shouted in frustration, "Damn it anyway!"

Everyone in the room looked at him, and Kris asked, "What's up?"

He had followed Joe back to Sulfur Springs last night in his rental car doing close to one hundred miles an hour, with Joe's siren blaring, and both of their cars' warning lights flashing all the way. When he called his supervisor, he had approved Kris sticking around to help, so he'd been awake for nearly twenty-four hours.

Joe said, "The bastard who shot Katie called me and told me he wanted to confess. Then he laid the name Mohammed on me. Can you believe the balls it took for him to call?"

"What'd he say?" Kris asked.

"He wants to talk to me later on my cell phone. I guess he thinks there's no way to trace it."

"Not if he keeps moving around," Kris said. "This guy is smart. Did he say anything else?"

"Yeah, when he mentioned Mohammed, he sounded like he was pissed. I could read it in his voice. He says we may prove helpful to each other, whatever the hell it means."

Fad ran back into the room, and said, "Not enough time for a trace, Joe."

"Yeah, and he knew it. Damn, can you believe this?"

Kris shook his head and said, "You'll have to hear him out, Joe, even if he's a murderer. Any lead we can get on Mohammed is more than we've got now."

"Yeah I know," Joe said and laid his head on his arms on his desk. "Damn, I'm tired."

"Why don't you knock it off?" Fad asked. "You're no good to us when you're beat.

"The same thing goes for you, Kris. Head for the sack and get some rest. If this asshole calls you later, you need to be fresh to deal with him."

Nodding, Kris said, "You're right, Fad. Come on, Joe, follow me to the rental place and I'll drop my car off. Then you can let me sack out at your place and we can both be there when this guy calls. Did he give you a name?"

"Yeah," Joe said. "Mister Jones, know how many of those there are?"

"Too many, and it's phony," Fad said. "Get the hell out of here, both of you."

Sitting back on the couch, Claude looked at the phone resting in its cradle, and thought, "They don't know his last name. I'll be damned. I've got a bargaining chip two miles wide and four deep."

(Two)

Two days later, Claude's plans were complete. All he needed now was a car, a cell phone, the equipment on his list and his guns. Then he'd pay a visit to Mister Mohammed Alta.

As he thought, "Payback time, partner. I told you it would be hell;" he turned to Carla and said, "I need to borrow your car. I may be gone for a day or two, but I'll be back. I have something important to do."

She was leaning over the sink as she did dishes from supper and asked, "What, chase down the guy who tried to kill you? I thought you were over it."

"I am," Claude lied. "I took your advice and called the cops. They're interested in this guy for more than one reason, but I can't tell you about it. It's a matter of national security and the police made me promise not to divulge anything."

Carla turned, put her wet hands on her hips and asked, "Are you for real? Do you expect me to believe that bullshit?"

"Yes, I do and it's not bullshit. Did you read the paper about the guy killed in the caving accident?"

Wiping back two strands of hair that had fallen over her eyes, she said, "Yes. What's he got to do with you?"

"What about the guy who was murdered and dumped in the lake?"

"Yes. I read about him too. Where's this going?"

"One final question," Claude said. "Did you hear about the guy who burned to death in his cabin up in the state park?"

"Again yes, I read the stories. What are you driving at?"

"They're all related," he said. "They worked at the nuclear laboratory."

"The cops told you all this? Who are you, Claude, an undercover agent?"

"No, they only told me a portion of it. I knew one of the men for some time, the guy who was talking to me when I was shot. He's the one who burned, so I'm not trying to find him anymore. The cops want my help for a while to identify the shooter. He's a suspect in the killing of those two cops. Now do you believe me?"

Finally making up her mind to believe and trust him at the same time, she said, "I don't think you could make all that up. Okay, here're the keys to the car. I can catch a ride in and back with Sherry until you return. Will you be okay?"

"Yeah, I'm not in any trouble, if that's what you mean. I have to run up to Denver to take care of this and some other business matters. I'll be back as soon as I can and I'll call you every morning at six. Oh, that reminds me, I also need to borrow your cell phone. I lost mine in the water."

Handing it to him, she said, "Call me tonight and let me know what's going on."

"I will, don't worry," Claude said and kissed her eyelids. "You know I love you."

"Yeah, I do." She smiled, and asked, "Do you have to leave right now?"

"No, I've got time for a quickie."

"You bastard," she said, but took his hand anyway and led him to the bedroom.

(Three)

Despite Claude's apprehension and for all of Mohammed's secrecy, it was easy to find the address of the elusive Mohammed Alta. All it took was a call to information.

Mohammed's landlord listed his phone number when they came around asking for info. Mohammed wasn't aware of it as he never took the time to check the phone book. Even if he had, he figured no one knew his last name, so why worry? It would prove his undoing.

"Do you have a listing for Mohammed Alta?" Claude asked. "The last name is A-L-T-A, first name Mohammed, the way it sounds."

"Hold one, please," the operator said.

Fifteen seconds later she said, "I have a Mohammed Alta at twelve, thirty-three five Hill Avenue, Lot Number five. It's 555-2244."

"Yeah, that's him, thanks operator."

"You're welcome, sir. Thank you for using A T and T."

Laying the phone on the seat, Claude continued driving toward Denver. He stopped in Sulfur Springs long enough to pick up his equipment from a locker-sized rental storage place, along with more cash from an ATM. It felt good to be armed again. He missed the feel of his guns against his chest and ankle.

After turning into the parking lot of a Super Wal Mart store, he locked the car, walked inside, grabbed a cart and headed to the hardware department, where he spent an hour finding and buying all the items on his long list of supplies. He completed his shopping trip by pausing in the fishing equipment aisle to pick up one very necessary item.

After double checking his purchases, he had a funny thought, smiled wickedly and then pushed his heavily loaded cart with a squeaky wheel across the store to the meat department. He bought a package of foot-long hot dogs and squeaked his way to a checkout stand, where he paid cash for everything.

"Doing some home repairs, 'eh?" The senior citizen at the checkout asked.

"Cleaning up some loose ends," Claude answered.

"Have fun," he said.

"I intend to."

Claude's next stop was a store specializing in kinky sex apparel and associated trinkets involved in that type of sport, where he bought four pairs of sturdy handcuffs with keys.

"Going to chain the old lady to the bed?" The proprietor asked.

"It wouldn't be the first time."

"Good for you," the guy said.

Shaking his head in disgust, Claude walked out.

(Four)

Hushan threw the paper down on his desk and cursed the day he recruited Mohammed to be his right-hand man, as he thought, "This idiot is leaving a trail of bodies and killing indiscriminately. Now it's two policemen. My God, what was he thinking? And he killed them outside Felix's home. Will the police make the connection? We may be doomed."

Picking up his cell phone, he dialed the number of the fire station on Butler

Avenue. When they answered, he asked for George Schroeder and as he waited for George to come on the line, he knew, "Mohammed must be stopped. I should have killed him myself when he delivered the bombs. He's of no use to us now, so it's time for him to disappear."

(Five)

After Kris and Joe left, Fad was almost sorry he told them to take off. They were now understaffed and hurting. Everyone was pulling their weight and working long hours as they attempted to find new leads on their two hottest cases, the killing of two of their own and the associated plot to kill thousands at the football game, which wasn't far off.

On top of that, they were trying to get through the tremendous backlog of burglary reports attributed to the Lawn Bandits. For one reason or another, the burglars had stopped their rampage three days ago and there had been no new reports in that period.

Looking around the room, Fad noticed Bert wasn't there. Then he remembered he hadn't shown up the two previous days either and he wondered, "Where the hell can the old fart be?

As he turned to ask Red about his absence, the phone rang, so he grabbed it and answered in the prescribed manner. To his surprise, it was Bert, who asked, "Hey, Fad, What's up? Been getting any?"

"Where the hell have you been, lard ass?"

"Man, I've been more harried than a hooker with lockjaw and six guys waiting for blow jobs."

"Doing what?"

"You wouldn't believe me if I told you," Bert said. "Tell everyone there that the drinks are on me at O'Grady's tonight at nine. I have something to celebrate and I want you all there. Bring Kris along. I think he'll enjoy what I have to say."

"You're right, I can't believe it. You're going to buy a round of drinks? That's a first. What's the reason?"

"I'll tell you tonight," Bert said.

"Okay, but I just sent Kris and Joe home. They got a call from a guy who says he knows about Mohammed, so they're working on it.

"The rest of us will be there. We could all use a break from the caseload. Your Lawn Ornament Bandits have created so much paperwork that we may have to go out and chop down our own trees to get the paper."

(Six)

Nine o'clock rolled around and Bert was a no-show. No one seemed to care, they were into the booze and relaxing as only cops can do. Finally at nine twenty, Bert made his grand entry dressed in a formal uniform with all his medals and ribbons.

His black shoes were shined and the bill of his cap reflected light like a billboard. Attached to his chest was a large blue ribbon with a number one in the middle, and he carried a large cardboard box full of whirly-gigs with a sign attached to one side that read: "Three for five dollars. Guaranteed to scare the shit out of your moles. Get them while they're hot."

Pointing to the blue ribbon, Fad said, "What did you win, Bert?"

"The jackpot,—you remember the Lawn Ornament Bandits? Thanks to yours truly and a sweet little lady named Grace who drives a snazzy BMW, they're history."

"You caught them?" Red asked.

"Yeah, it turns out the dumb assholes were decorating their own lawn and house with the stolen items. Grace drove by and saw her two pet ceramic frogs setting in their lawn. Even though the perps painted black rings around their eyes, she knew them on sight. She phoned it in and I went out on the call.

"The frogs were hers all right, had her name on the bottom. We got a search warrant and I've been hauling stuff out of their house for the last three days. You won't believe the evidence room. It's packed to the ceiling."

"Congratulations," Red said. "What's with the whirly-gigs?"

"Hell, we had so many of those I figured I'd sell them and put some money into the Police Benevolent Fund."

Moving to Bert's side, Red whispered in his ear and asked, "You aren't serious, are you?"

"Time out," Bert yelled over the noise in the bar. "I need to take a leak."

Talking in a hushed tone, he said, "Come along with me to the head, Red, and you too, Fad. We need to talk."

As they followed Bert toward the men's room, the door swung open and a slightly inebriated black cop named Lou Harris walked out.

When Lou saw the trio, he asked, "Hey Fad, are these two white honkies from the KKK? Did they finally catch up with you?"

Fad smiled knowingly and said, "Nah, I've been having some trouble with my heart. I need to take a leak and the doctor told me not to lift anything heavy. These two friends kindly volunteered to come along and hold my pecker for me."

SIGNS OF OUR TIMES

"Damn Fad," Lou said. "You're doing your part to uphold our highly exaggerated reputation. Hang on tight, gentlemen."

Lou staggered away, and Bert led his two companions into the men's room, where he turned to face them and said, "To answer your question, Red, hell no, I'm not serious. You know we can't sell evidence. It's against the law and we need the stuff to nail the lawn bandits' asses to the wall.

"I bought the whirly-gigs myself out of my own pocket. The story about bagging the lawn bandit perps is true, but the rest is pure bullshit. I'm out to have some fun with the rest of the guys.

"They've worked their asses off trying to catch this Mohammed or whoever wasted our two rookies. Fad, you, Joe and Kris are about out on your feet from working the terrorist threat. Now you and the other guys need to laugh a little before everyone goes back to the same old grind.

"Play along with my nonsense and we'll have some fun. What the hell can it hurt?"

Red laughed and said, "Good idea, Bert. We'll back up your play. Come on Fad; let's see what Bert has planned."

They returned to the bar where several of the more inebriated cops were wearing the whirly-gigs on their uniform caps.

Bert shouted above the noise, "My evidence room is open for any and all bidders."

Red and Fad spread the word about the gag among their closest friends.

Going along with the joke, Fad asked, "Got any other good bargains, Bert?"

Turning his hat around on his head, Bert pulled a cigar out of his pocket. After sticking it in his mouth, he took a stance like a car salesman giving his best pitch, and asked, "Ya wanta buy a good used birdbath real cheap? Hardly ever been swum in and has a fresh new coat of bird shit. We've got twenty-seven of 'em, so I can make you a good deal."

"Nah," Fad said. "I'll wait until you get desperate and the half-priced sale rolls around."

Bert frowned, wiped his brow and said, "Too bad, because I'd throw in a couple of Gnomes and maybe a full set of the seven dwarfs for another five dollars."

"How many of those do you have?" A half-bombed Ernie asked.

"Thirty-six," Bert said.

After he attempted to do the math in his liquor fogged mind, failed badly and didn't realize it, Ernie said, "It doesn't compute, someone's missing. Poor Dopey and Sleepy, they were my favorites."

From the bar where she was feeling no pain, almost like one of her customers, Sarah said, "The perps probably dropped some and broke 'em."

"I could use a big pot for my back patio," Red said.

Bert bragged, "We hold our big truckload sale in two weeks, don't miss it."

"You got any Snoopy stuff?" Sarah asked. "He's my favorite."

"Only two and they're collectors' items," Bert said. "I'm thinking E-bay, a bidding war and big bucks."

"How many cases did you clear?" Red asked.

"One hundred and ninety four. Now you know the reason for the blue ribbon. I'm number one."

"Let's give him an ovation," Fad said.

The entire bar gave Bert a one-finger salute to tell him he was number one in their books.

Ignoring their signal, Bert said, "Drinks are on me."

Fad shook his head and his mouth dropped open in mock disbelief as he said, "Now there's a first to go with your number one, Bert."

Turning to the bartender, he added, "Make mine a double, Clyde."

Standing at the bar and enjoying the nonsense, Red caught sight of a rookie patrol officer named Willie Clancy. He had been looking for Clancy for some time, so he shouted over the noise of the bar, "Clancy, come here."

Ignoring the fact that rookie cops do not address their superior officers by their first names, even in a cops' bar, Willie asked, "What's up, Red?"

"I had an interesting inquiry from the coroner about one of your reports. He wants to know what part of the body a "yet" is in."

"Hell, Red, I don't know. Am I a doctor?"

"No," Red said, "but you aren't much of a report writer either."

"What do you mean?"

Pulling the report in question from his pocket, Red pointed to a sentence he had highlighted in yellow, and said, "You wrote, 'Mrs. Bellows was shot by her husband and the bullet is in her yet'. You should have used the word 'still'. There is no 'yet' in the human body."

Setting his drink down on the bar, Willie reached for the report and said, "Here, let me change it."

Taking it from Red's hand, Willie moved to the bar, crossed out the word 'yet' and changed the sentence as Red had suggested.

Then he handed it back to Red, who read the change and said, "You stupid jerk. Now it reads 'the bullet is in her still'. Was Mrs. Bellows a bootlegger? The sentence should read, 'the bullet was still in her body."

"Gee, Red, I changed what you told me to."

"See me in the morning, Clancy," Red said. "You're going to take a grammar class."

Turning to Bert, Red said, "Trying to find brains in a rookie cop is like trying to catch fireworks with a butterfly net."

(Seven)

At nine thirty sharp, when he dialed Joe's number, Claude was sailing along at seventy miles an hour on the outer loop around Denver and didn't think there was anyway the cops could trace him. But he kept it short and sweet when Joe answered on the first ring and asked, "Is that you, Mister Jones?"

"Yeah, Joe, it's me. Listen close. I have the last name for Mohammed and I'm willing to trade you that info for what's going on out at the chemical lab. Is it a deal or not?"

"What do you mean?" Joe asked.

"I'm not stupid," Claude said. "I know all about Felix, Larry and Katie, and their ties to the lab and the chimps. I need to make amends for Katie. I shouldn't have taken the job, but I was greedy. I'm hanging up now. Think it over, Mohammed's last name for info. You have ten minutes to make up your mind. I'll call again and if you don't deal, you can find him yourself after I get done with him."

"Don't hang up!" Joe shouted, but he was talking to a dead phone, so in disgust he said, "Damn."

"No chance of a trace," Kris said. "He's on the move. What did he want, Joe?"

"He wants to trade us the last name of Mohammed for information on the lab. I've got ten minutes to make up my mind. If I don't tell him, he won't call again. What do you want me to do?"

Squinting up his brow, so it looked wrinkled and soft like the outside of a prune, Kris said, "He's got the upper hand. Go ahead, make a deal with the devil. If Mister Jones can give us Mohammed, we're better off than we are now. We don't have a clue."

Joe grinned momentarily, but then it changed into a frown as he said, "Don't I know it. Okay, let's trade. He seems to want to help in order to make up for Katie. Maybe our hit man has a conscience after all."

"Let's hope so," Kris said.

(Eight)

Mohammed was tired of sitting on his ass in his little trailer, chain-smoking cigarettes and watching TV. Last night he slept the sleep of the dead. He didn't realize how tired he was when he walked in, but now he knew, "It's a damned good thing the cops weren't after me. As far gone as I was, they could have driven a tank in here and I never would have heard them until they shot my ass off."

Today, Mohammed was feeling good. From all indications and reports on TV, there were no leads in the double slaying of the policemen in Sulfur Springs. His worries of yesterday were in vain and he thought for a moment of calling Hushan to see if he knew anything, but decided not to when he remembered his last warning. He wasn't sure the freak wouldn't waste him just on general principles.

In case he was wrong, Mohammed remained in the trailer all day, afraid to show his face. Occasionally, he checked outside by peeking between the slats of the blinds to see if anyone was watching his place or seemed suspicious. So far it was all clear and he didn't think there was anything to worry about, but it was always best to play it safe.

There weren't many street lights in this part of town and the cheap-assed landlord must have supplied forty-watt bulbs in the lamp over the door outside. It barely lit the stairs and didn't reach out into the yard. It was the dark of the moon and Mohammed's property was as black as a coal miner's ass at midnight, five hundred feet under mother earth.

At eleven, after watching the late news, hunger got the best of him. For breakfast, he had two cups of stale coffee along with a power bar from an unopened but out-of-date box. At noon he ate four, three-month-old candy bars and drank a coke. No wonder he was starved.

Checking outside one last time, Mohammed saw nothing out of the ordinary, so he opened the door and walked out. He stopped on the small stoop to look around as he stretched his tired back. Everything appeared cool, so he walked to where his car was parked at the end of the trailer.

As he turned the corner, a piece of pipe came out of the darkness and hit him in the middle of the forehead. He saw stars and the force of the blow knocked him to his knees.

Through the fog of near unconsciousness, he heard a somewhat familiar voice say, "That's for Katie, you bastard." Then whoever it was, hit him in the back of the neck with the same pipe and it was lights out. Mohammed never heard Claude say, "And that's for Larry Holgram."

SIGNS OF OUR TIMES

With his knee on Mohammed's back, Claude looked around to see if anyone heard his attack. The trailer park was as dark as the inside of a buffalo's ass and as silent as a mosque before prayer time. No dogs barked and no one came out to check out the noise.

Slipping a pair of handcuffs on Mohammed's wrists, Claude ratcheted them down as tight as he could. He didn't give a damn if he cut off Mo's circulation—that was the least of his worries now.

After stuffing a rag in Mo's mouth, Claude wrapped duct tape around his head until he looked like the mummy in the movie. He made sure Mo's nose passages were clear, he didn't want him to croak, not yet. Then he used more of the multipurpose tape to wrap Mo's lower legs together.

Leaving him lying on the gravel and grass-speckled driveway, Claude walked two blocks down the street to Carla's car.

He drove quietly to the side of the trailer, parked, got out and popped the trunk. The light came on, so he hit it with the knuckle on his right hand and it shattered. His hand hurt and he saw he drew blood. Sucking on the cut, he tasted the warm sickly-sweet fluid.

Then he dragged Mo to the trunk, where he struggled to load him, torso first. Mo's shoulders finally cleared the opening and his head struck the bottom of the trunk with a sound like a ripe watermelon dropped into a cardboard box. After lifting Mo's legs, he bent them to get the body into the space.

It was tight, but Claude didn't give a damn about the uncomfortable ride his prisoner would have. He eased the trunk lid down slowly until he heard the lock engage, took one more look around and picked up his pipe. He threw it into the back seat, got in, fired up the engine and backed out onto the deserted street.

(Nine)

While Kris listened, Joe made his deal with Mister Jones. Claude didn't say much as Joe told him a short version of what was about to go down if they didn't catch the terrorists.

"That's it," Joe said. "Now what's Mohammed's last name and where is he?"

"It's Alta," Claude said. "That's A-L-T-A. He lives at twelve thirty-three five Hill Avenue, Lot five in Denver, but Mo isn't home right now."

"Damn it, we had a deal."

"We still do," Claude said. "I'm going to do what you can't or would be too squeamish to do, so hang in there by the phone and more info will be forthcoming. Thanks for trusting me, and I assure you the story is safe with me. I'll call back."

When he heard the buzz of a dead phone in his ear, Joe said, "You dirty bastard." Then turning to Kris he said, "I hope Mister Jones didn't stiff us, Kris."

"I don't think so. I'll check out the name and address. If it's legit, we'll take a S.W.A.T. team out there."

"From what he said, you won't need to," Joe said. "I think he's got Mohammed and is rubbing our noses in the crap because he could catch him while we couldn't. Hold off on the cavalry charge. If anyone's watching, it would tip our hand. The nerve gas is our priority. Now that we know his name, we can always catch Mohammed."

"Just the same, I'm going to send one of our undercover agents to watch his house. If someone shows, he'll try to find out who they are."

"Your guy better be good," Joe said.

"He looks like a wino out on a binge and dresses the part. In that area of the city, he'll blend right in."

(Ten)

While Mohammed slept, Claude was busy, but now the stage was set, and he slapped Mo awake. They were in a broken-down and deserted barn on an abandoned farm in the countryside east of Denver.

The nearest neighbor or highway was miles away, so screams wouldn't be heard here. Years ago, Claude had hunted here and remembered it as a place where he and Mo could talk privately and not be disturbed.

As he regained consciousness, Mohammed moaned and attempted to move his arms, but they wouldn't respond. Turning his head, he saw he was staked out like a human sacrifice, naked and alone.

His legs and arms were stretched to their maximum. His wrists and ankles were hooked to handcuffs, which were attached to plastic covered steel cables, leading to four fence posts pounded into the dirt.

The area around him was illuminated by a three cell flashlight with a large lens lying nearby on the frayed green plastic seat of a bent and battered chromed chair.

When he tried to move his body, he felt grit and pieces of straw under him, and he didn't get far. The only range of motion he had was in the cheeks of his ass and they didn't do much except roll from side to side.

SIGNS OF OUR TIMES

A figure of a man came into his limited area of vision, reached down and picked up the flashlight. Then he turned, held it under his chin so Mohammed could see his face, and asked, "Are you comfortable?"

Now that the fog was lifting from his sore head and neck, Mohammed recognized Claude as Mister Jones, and thought, "It's the hit man. I didn't kill him after all. What's he going to do?"

Fear clamped its heavy hands on his heart and he tried to speak, but the rag in his mouth only allowed him to make choking sounds.

Noting the terror in Mo's eyes, Claude grinned evilly, and said, "Probably not, but you look surprised to see me. If I was you, I'd be pissing my pants in fear. Are you?"

Mohammed tried to put on a game face, as he shook his head and defiance shone in his eyes, but his quivering hands told Claude it was an act, so he said, "You will be, I guarantee it."

Reaching behind him, Claude pulled on a short cord attached to a gasoline generator. It started immediately, roared for a minute and then hummed gently.

Hanging from a rafter, a small light bulb came on overhead and illuminated a twenty-foot circle with Mohammed in the middle, staked out like a virgin princess at a cannibal bake off.

Picking up an electric nail gun from the ground, Claude plugged it into one of the three remaining receptacles on the generator, and asked, "Ever use one of these? It packs a hell of a wallop. Let me demonstrate."

Not waiting for an answer, he picked up a scrap piece of half-rotted two-by-four from the floor, held it in his left hand and tapped the nail gun with the board.

It made a hollow ringing sound, and then he pushed the tip of it against the board and pressed the trigger. The gun went "pow" and the board flew out of his hands.

Laying the nail gun aside, Claude picked up the wood. He held it in front of Mo's eyes so Mo could focus on the round brass nail countersunk deep into the rotting wood, and said, "Isn't that amazing? It went all the way in with just one quick motion.

"What do you say, Mo, let's talk about the bombs. Where are they?"

Although he couldn't speak, when he heard the question, Mohammed's startled eyes betrayed him.

With one swift move, Claude reached down, ripped the duct tape from Mo's face with a cruel flip of his wrist and pulled the filthy rag out of his mouth.

Turning his head, Mohammed spit blood and phlegm onto the ground and choked out his answer, "You'll never find them."

"I think you'll change your mind, Mo old buddy."

Taking his time, Claude picked up a wider piece of plywood and placed it under Mo's left hand. Then he spread Mo's fingers and held them flat against the board with his left hand, while reaching for the nail gun with his right.

As Mo watched, Claude moved the nail gun from one finger to another and sang a silly parody of a child's fairy tale, "This little piggy went to market and this little piggy took a walk."

Then before Mohammed realized what was happening, Claude pressed the nail gun to Mo's index finger and fired a one-inch nail through his fingernail and bone.

The pain was instant. Mohammed's screams filled the barn, and he tried in vain to pull his hand free.

Claude held it tight, looked him in the eyes and asked again, "Where are the bombs?"

Through clenched teeth, Mohammed said, "Go to hell."

Claude shrugged and continued to sing his ditty, "And this little piggy said no, I won't talk."

Then he fired another nail into the joint of Mo's thumb and Mo screamed again, only louder and longer.

When he didn't get an answer, Claude continued singing and asking the same question, but Mohammed hung tough and wouldn't talk.

During the next ten minutes, Claude worked his way through the fingers on Mo's right hand and then fired a single nail through the joint of Mo's big toe.

Although sweat broke out on Mohammed's face and head, and the pain was evident by the way his body twitched at the end of its tethers, he somehow managed to resist.

Between the torture treatments, Mohammed's mind raced. "I was prepared for death and the reward of the promised virgins in heaven, but this is worse than death. When will it end?"

His thoughts were interrupted when Claude grabbed him by the hair, twisted his head upward and said, "I can keep this up all night or until you run out of digits, Mo. Let's see, what other place will hurt like hell? What about your elbow?"

Claude shot another nail into Mo's elbow joint. Mohammed thought his arm would fall off. He had never experienced such pain and his screams became almost constant.

When he still resisted, Claude moved the tool to Mo's shoulder and said, "This is for the bullet you put through mine."

After he shot another nail into the bone, he paused a moment to think and listen to Mo's screams. Then he smiled and said, "On second thought, that bullet hole was two, so here's one more to even the score."

Mohammed heard bone crunch and the pain was unbearable. His whole body was on fire.

Smiling like a ghoul who was hungry for more blood, Claude said, "Damn, you're one tough dude."

Pausing again, he asked, "What's an Arab's favorite part of his body?"

Looking deep into Mo's eyes, Claude answered his own question, "Oh yeah, your cock. Let me show you something special I brought along."

As Claude moved out of his sight for a few moments, Mohammed kept screaming and moaning between the stabs of pain. It was obvious that his tormentor was enjoying his torture routine and it would continue for some time.

When he returned, Claude was hiding something behind his back.

Mohammed tried to steel himself for whatever lay ahead, but the pain was already getting to him. He didn't know how much more he could take.

"I have a surprise for you," Claude said, and pulled a fish-cleaning board from behind his back. "Guess what I have in mind for this little jewel."

Mohammed screamed, ""No, you wouldn't."

"You wanta bet? Let me give you a demo on what's going to happen if you don't talk."

Reaching into his shirt pocket, Claude pulled out a hot dog wiener, and asked, "Does it look like something you know? It's bigger and longer than yours, Mo, but watch closely."

After placing the board on Mo's chest so he could witness the proceedings up close and personal, Claude clamped the wiener down at one tip and it split open. Pinkish meat and sickly-looking fluid squished out and ran off the board, onto Mo's bare chest.

Staring up at the tool of the devil which his tormentor held, Mohammed couldn't take his eyes from it.

Smiling wickedly, Claude pushed the nail gun down on the wiener and in quick succession, fired two nails into it. Pieces of meat flew through the air, but the majority of the hot dog remained speared to the board.

Smiling knowingly at Mo, Claude asked, "One more time Mo, where are the bombs?"

Not believing Mister Jones would really do what he said; Mohammed remained defiant and spat out, "You'll never know motherfucker."

Shaking his head at Mo's stupidity, Claude dumped the ruined wiener on the floor and said, "Okay, you asked for this."

Reaching down between Mo's legs, Claude grabbed Mo's limp penis with his left hand. With his right, he moved the fish-cleaning board between Mo's legs and laid Mo's flaccid manhood on it.

As he clamped Mo's tender foreskin to the board and picked up the nail gun again, his victim screamed in fear and pain.

Then Mohammed felt the cold steel tip of the nail gun on his penis and fainted.

Two minutes later, Claude slapped Mo awake again.

Moaning in pain and humiliation, Mohammed looked down between his legs. Old trustworthy was still with him, but the pain from the clamp was excruciating.

"You fainted, Mo and would have missed all the fun and pain," Claude said. "For the final time, where are the bombs? Tell me, or I'll nail your prick to the board so hard, you'll never be able to get it loose."

Mohammed had reached the end of his endurance. The pain from his wounds was bad enough, but he knew he couldn't go through the type of torture Mister Jones had in mind.

When he looked into Claude's eyes, Mohammed knew he was serious.

He gave up and shouted, "Allah may never forgive me, but I'll tell you! They're in a storage area on the outskirts of Denver."

To emphasize his point, Claude tapped Mo's penis with the nail gun, and asked, "What's the name of the place and the number of the unit?"

Cold shivers ran up Mohammed's back and he felt faint again, but between quick gasps of air to relieve the mind numbing pain, he managed to reply in short sentences, "Store and Go. Unit number ten. Four twelve Oak Street. The key's in my pocket."

"Who's your contact?" Claude asked.

"A man named Hushan. He lives in Fort Worth. That's all I know. We only used first names so no one could talk."

"Well, maybe not everyone," Claude said, temporarily removing the nail gun from between Mo's legs.

Believing his ordeal was over, the flood gates opened and Mohammed poured out his guts.

For each good answer he received, Claude used a pair of long-handled pliers to pull a nail from Mo's body.

As he spelled out the entire plan in detail, Claude listened to each statement, compared Mo's info with what Joe and his buddies had already discovered and realized it checked out. As a bonus, Mo disclosed the first names and addresses of three other men he stayed with at various times.

The last terrorist he gave up was the man who worked in the fire department and planned to switch the fire extinguishers a week prior to the big game.

"His name is George, that's all I know. He's a stocky German who hates Jews and he's a big shot in the Aryan Brotherhood. He works for the fire department in Fort Worth, close to the Cotton Bowl, but I don't know the station number."

"Is there any other way to tell who George really is? You said you only used first names."

"He has a tattoo of a spider in a web on his left arm. He thinks it's sexy."

As he pulled the last nail from his index finger, sweat ran down Mo's face in rivulets and he looked like he was going to faint again.

Smiling at the relief on Mo's face, Claude said, "That worked out rather well don't you think—the last bit of info and the final nail."

Through his pain, Mohammed actually said, "Thank you, thank you."

"You're welcome," Claude said, and fired a two-and-a-half-inch nail through Mo's penis, pinning it to the plywood.

Screaming in agony, Mohammed passed out again.

(Eleven)
When Joe answered his call, Claude said, "Your boy is about ready for delivery. The bombs are in a storage area on the outskirts of Denver. The address is four twelve Oak Street, Unit ten. Check out a guy named George in the fire department in Fort Worth, Texas who has a tattoo of a spider on his left arm.

"Hushan is the name of Mo's contact. No last name and no address except Fort Worth. That's it. I'll call you later so you can pick Mo up.

"I nailed him good and he may have thoughts of cutting out, but I don't think he'll go off half-cocked. I guarantee he'll be willing to talk."

"Where are you?" Joe asked.

"Later Dude," Claude said and hung up.

"Son of a bitch," Joe said, but he was smiling.

"What's wrong?" Kris asked.

"Not a damned thing. Let me fill you in."

(Twelve)
When Mohammed woke up, his hands and legs were free. The cruel clamp

was no longer attached to his foreskin, but to his dismay, his penis was still nailed to the terrible board, which was now pegged to the ground with a steel stake driven through it. There was no way he could dislodge it without tearing his penis off.

"Oh most merciful Allah," Mohammed prayed and moved without thinking. In the middle of his prayer he changed to a different God. "Oh, sweet Jesus it hurts. Please make it go away."

His left shoulder, arm and hand were swollen, and he couldn't move them. Every small twitch of his body pulled his penis against the horrible nail. His manhood was already swollen around the brass shaft and a small trail of blood was dried on top of the board.

Looking to his right, Mohammed saw Claude standing a few feet away and watching him. Then he noticed a box cutter by his right side with a two-inch blade, and instinctively picked it up in the hopes of using it as a weapon. The movement caused him extreme pain and he cried out. He couldn't believe the pain one nail could cause.

Turning further to the right, he saw a handgun just out of reach behind him. In his present condition he knew he couldn't reach it, so he tried to remain as still as possible as his mind raced and he wondered, "What the hell is going on?"

"Ah, so you're back among the living," Claude said. "I see you found my little present to you. How's your pecker, Mo? Sore, I'll bet."

Through teeth that wouldn't unclench, no matter how hard he tried, Mohammed gasped, "You bastard."

Claude laughed and said, "You really didn't think I wasn't going to pay you back for trying to kill me, did you? This is how I see it, Mo. You have three choices."

"One, you can try to pull your prick off the nail, but there's an awfully big head on it – the nail, not your dick. I'm afraid it would do a number on your cock and cause it to bleed severely. We're a long way out in the country and you'd have a hell of a time finding a doctor before you bled to death.

"Number two, you can use the box cutter to cut your prick free from the nail and get to the gun, which has only one bullet in it. That way you can do the honorable thing and put yourself out of your misery. But you still have to do some serious surgery on your cock. It's my favorite, but I don't think you'll take it.

"Or number three, you can sit still, hurt and bleed a little and wait for the cops to find you. I called them a minute ago and told them where you are. It'll take them a while, but if you don't move around too much and if the medics aren't too pissed at you for wasting those two cops, they might pull the nail out of your cock and you'll be free of pain. If it was up to me, I'd bend it in a circle and leave it there to remind you what a prick you really are.

"I'm leaving now and I hope I hear the gun go off before I get out of here, but it's your choice Mo. Take care now, don't go off half-cocked."

Still laughing, Claude walked out of the barn, paused for a few moments and listened carefully. He had time to spare because he hadn't called Joe yet, but he would when he got out on the highway.

"Let the son of a bitch sweat a little more. Not Joe, but Mo," he thought and laughed again.

All he heard was Mo screaming in Arabic and knew he was cursing him. But Mo was too late; Claude knew he was already doomed.

CHAPTER 18

(One)

As he walked in the door Carla said, "So you're back. Did you get your man?"

"No," Claude lied.

Then he hugged her to his chest and kissed the top of her head as he said, "I told you, the cops will take care of him."

Curling into his arms and returning his caresses, she said, "I missed you."

She could feel his heart beat and the warmth of his body reassured her of his love. After all these years of searching, his arms felt like home to her and she said, "Umm, that feels good."

"I thought of you every minute I was gone. And to prove it, I stopped in Denver and bought you something."

Looking into his eyes, she asked, "What?"

"It's a small token of my love for you. Someday, I'll buy you a bigger and gaudier one to impress your friends."

"You can't mean a ring?"

"Why not, don't you want to make an honest man of me?"

"It's supposed to be the other way around," she said. "Show me."

Reaching into his pocket, Claude pulled out a small square blue box tied with a thin red ribbon and handed it to her.

As tears ran down her cheek, she untied the bow and let it slip to the floor. Then she paused a moment to look into Claude's eyes once more before carefully opening the lid and peeking inside.

Hoping he'd come back tonight, she'd prepared a fire in the fireplace. Now the small stone in the ring, which was shaped like a heart, sparkled with red and yellow highlights as it reflected the light from the flames.

When she looked up again he said, "I thought it would make you happy. Don't cry."

"It's what women do when they're extremely happy," she said, reaching up and kissing him tenderly. "I've never seen anything so lovely, Claude, thank you."

"Then I take it I can consider myself engaged?"

As she slipped the ring onto her finger, she said, "Yes, you idiot."

Pointing at her hand, he said, "I think I was supposed to do that."

"Now I'm the idiot."

Taking the ring from her finger, she gave it back to him and said, "Please do the honors."

After he did as she asked, he hugged her to him again and thought of what he'd just done. All the way from Denver, he'd struggled with his inner feelings and the type of life he led up to this moment.

Now he knew he was a fool to become a paid assassin and realized the name said it all—he was an ass twice and in over his head.

Although he hoped his time with Mohammed was the end of his deadly career, from the sounds of things there was much to be done in a short time. Now the fate of thousands lay in his hands and those of a few courageous police and FBI agents.

Fate was fickle, but sometimes you got the chance to make amends for past transgressions. Perhaps this was his opportunity to square things with the Big Guy in the sky.

If He allowed it to happen, Claude would spend the rest of his life with Carla and raise kids instead of hell. It was up to them both, he and God, which was an unlikely alliance.

Breaking into his musings, Carla looked up and asked, "What's wrong?"

"Nothing, I was just thinking of how lucky it was I got shot."

"How could that have been lucky?"

Smiling again, he asked, "What chance was there I'd stop in your library and meet you?"

"I don't know, probably none."

"Because I was shot, I got to meet you. That makes it the luckiest day of my life."

Holding up the ring for him to see, she said, "And today is the greatest one of mine."

(Two)

Lying in the dim light, Mohammed tried to stay as still as possible. Every move he made was pure torture to his body, mind and soul.

As he waited for the law to arrive, his mind kept saying, "Come on. Come on." He was clenching his teeth so hard his jaw felt like it was broken.

Despite his efforts to remain still, the cold ground made him shiver and small stabs of raw pain ran through his body. Tears ran down his cheeks and he shook his head from side to side trying to block the sight of his speared manhood from his memory and swearing silently, "God it hurts, you son of a bitch, whoever you are."

After Claude left, Mohammed lay still digesting his words and options, none of which was acceptable. He'd be damned if he was going to give Mister Jones the satisfaction of hearing the gun go off. Staring at his hand that held the box cutter and then looking down between his legs, he knew. "No, I couldn't do it."

Even though it caused him more pain, he threw the knife as far as he could. He was close to the brink of exhaustion and madness was waiting only a step away.

Then from deep in his memory, he remembered one of his cohorts saying "Life sucks, but the alternative is unacceptable", and it calmed him somewhat, but the agonizing pain persisted.

Thinking ahead, he knew the days and years in the future would be terrible. There would be prison time for sure and the hatred of his fellow inmates, and then when Hushan and his men pulled off the horrific attack, perhaps death at their hands. But he played the game and lost and now his fate was in the hands of Allah.

Another involuntary muscle spasm hit him and Mohammed screamed out in agony.

(Three)

Over a speaker phone, Joe said, "You wouldn't believe it, Fad."

He and Kris had driven up to Denver first thing this morning after Mister Jones phoned them the night before.

SIGNS OF OUR TIMES

Today they were using a back office at the Denver Police Station for their work area and planned to stay in town as long as it took to solve the problems they faced.

"We got the call from Mister Jones, who gave us the location of Mohammed," Kris added. "We called the Denver cops and when they got there they found Mohammed with his pecker nailed to a fish-cleaning board that was staked to the ground.

"He was lying in the middle of a pool of light in an old barn. We've seen the pictures the cops took and it's like something straight out of the Omen."

"I'm sorry I missed it," Fad said. "Too bad they didn't leave him there."

Joe said, "The cops said Mohammed was babbling like a baby. Whoever this Mister Jones is, he did a number on our boy. Mohammed sang our song and he kept on talking, even after the EMS crew pulled the nail out."

Kris laughed and said, "Let me tell you, they were anything but gentle when they learned this was the guy who offed the two cops."

Joining in his laughter, Fad asked, "Where's Mohammed now? I'd like to ask him a few questions myself."

"Mo's pecker didn't look too good to me and a doctor is looking at it now. I think surgery is on tap for Mohammed. But for now we're keeping him under wraps. No one gets to speak to him except us."

"Why?" Fad asked.

"Because the bombs weren't where he said they were," Joe said.

"Man, oh man," Fad said. "I didn't think we could trust this Mister Jones."

Although Fad couldn't see it, Joe shook his head and said, "I don't think he knows the bombs weren't there. When he called, he sounded real upbeat and made all kinds of puns when he said, 'he'd nailed Mohammed and he wouldn't be going off half-cocked'.

"It was a sign of a guy who was sure of his work. I don't think Mohammed could have faked it, not with the pain he went through. Hell, if it had been me, I'd be singing opera.

"Mohammed doesn't realize someone moved the bombs. He was really pissed because he spilled his guts before Mister Jones nailed his prick to the board.

"I think the leader of this group of morons saw the report of the cops killed on TV and thought Mohammed was a liability."

Kris added, "Or they didn't trust Mohammed and moved them without telling him."

"So where does it leave us?" Fad asked.

"Second in line at a suicide pact with only one bullet in the gun," Kris said. "We've only got forty days to find the bombs. If we don't, we have a big task ahead of us. Can you imagine trying to cancel that yearly event and having to evacuate Dallas and Fort Worth?"

Shaking his head again, Joe said, "No, I can't, and I hope Mister Jones will help us prevent it from happening. You know, although I don't approve of his methods, you can't fault the results."

Nodding, Kris said, "Yeah, I agree. Mister Jones isn't like us. He's not affected by any constraints of modern civilization. He does what he feels is necessary to achieve the most direct response to his questions. Then he only asks once before he takes dire action to show you how serious he is. Just ask Mohammed."

Fad said, "I know what you mean. No matter how he might despise torture, if the average guy on the street knew what Mister Jones was accomplishing, he'd cheer the guy on. Our elusive friend understands terrorists don't answer to anyone for their actions, so why should he?"

"He gave us another lead, and Mohammed confirmed it," Joe said. "The guy named George in the fire department in Fort Worth is the only viable resource now. Everyone else is either dead or in custody except him, the head honcho and whatever idiots are following him."

(Four)

After stopping across the street from Mohammed's trailer, George parked his SUV under the umbrella of a large live oak tree. He was a well-built young man, with blond hair and blue eyes, heavily muscled and proud of his German heritage. If it was up to him, the Germans would have won World War II and be running the world.

The rag heads George fooled around with weren't the chosen race, but were the ones leading the fight against impure America. If he could help them in any way and they were successful, perhaps it would lead to world cleansing. As far as he was concerned, too many Jews and blacks were running things now. Their day would come.

Sitting quietly and chewing gum, he watched the trailer for fifteen minutes. A dim light on the porch cast shadows on the concrete stoop and a car was parked at one end. No lights were lit inside, so perhaps his target was asleep.

Checking his watch, he saw it was fifteen minutes after midnight. No one was around, except for a dirty drunk with a ragged beard, sleeping on a damp bus stop bench on top of some folded newspapers.

SIGNS OF OUR TIMES

Dressed in a long filthy Army coat with the stripes of a Private First Class on one arm and torn threads on the other where the matching insignia should have been, the bum had a large stain near his groin, telling George the wino had pissed himself in his sleep.

Wrapped in his coat, the drunk's arms hugged a half-full bottle of cheap wine like it was the teat of a beautiful woman. George heard him snore through his nose. One of his shoes had a loose sole hanging over the heel and it flapped in the light breeze like a dog's tongue as he licks water from a bowl.

Carrying a pry bar under his arm, George climbed down from his vehicle, walked to the bench and nudged the drunk with it. The boozer smelled like yesterday's vomit and urine mixed together. He snorted and one hand slipped off the bottle, but he didn't wake.

Leaning closer, the odor of an unwashed body wafted up to attack George's nostrils and a scent of liquor was strong on the bum's breath. Shaking his head in disgust, George thought, "Where do they come from, and why do we let them live?

If it was another night, he would enjoy beating the shit out of the degenerate, but he had other chores to accomplish. If the idiot was there when he finished, he'd kick him in the balls just for the hell of it.

Taking his time, George crept toward the trailer and up the stairs to the landing, took a rag from his pocket, wrapped it around the small bulb and unscrewed it from the light fixture above the door. Trying the door, he found it was locked, so he put the pry bar between it and the frame and pushed with steady pressure until the door popped open.

With his gun drawn, he moved hastily into the darkness within and stood with his back against a wall. The smell of stale cigarette smoke hung in the air, and although it was chilly outside, he felt the sweat of his own fear run down his back.

This was something new. George hadn't actually killed anyone with a gun before, and as a lump of phlegm stuck in his throat, the metallic taste of terror made him want to spit in the worst way.

The dim light from a street lamp let him to see there was no one in the living room or kitchen. He paused a few moments to see if anyone heard him enter, but there was no sound, so he crept quietly to the bedroom. The worn linoleum floor squeaked and he stopped, but the silence was unbroken, so he continued on.

The bedroom door was open and George peeked around the frame. In the dimness he saw the bed was mussed and the ash tray full of cigarette butts, but there was no sign of Mohammed.

After checking the rest of the trailer, he cursed when he saw the evidence of Mohammed's recent occupancy, the empty candy bar wrappers and bent soda can. A roach cracked under his heel as he stepped on the insect and ended its life, and he asked silently, "Where are you, you fool?"

After he turned on the lights, double-checked everywhere and found nothing, he suddenly thought, "Mohammed's car's still here. Perhaps he took a stroll, but at this late hour?"

George doubted it. On the way here, he hadn't seen any fast food places or even a convenience store in the neighborhood.

More nervous than he would admit, George turned off the lights, walked out and tried to close the door, but the lock was broken. Giving up, he let it hang open. Then as if it was mocking him, it swung back and forth in the breeze.

Foolish in his anger, George kicked the door and it hit the frame with a noise like a gun shot, rebounding to hit him in the leg.

Rubbing his sore knee, he silently cursed his stupidity, "That wasn't smart, asshole."

After screwing the light bulb back into the socket, he looked around the outside area. To his surprise, the drunk had moved on. Except for the crumpled newspapers and an empty wine bottle, the bench was empty.

He thought, "I must have disturbed his sleep and he's looking for more cheap booze. He was lucky. In the mood I'm in, I'd have beaten him half to death. Damn you anyway Mohammed, where are you?"

In case his quarry was sleeping there, George walked slowly toward the car with his gun drawn. The vehicle was unlocked and Mohammed wasn't inside.

As he turned back to the trailer for a second look, George noticed scuff marks in the driveway and thought, "Something or someone was dragged for a short distance. There's a set of tire tracks not matching the others. Was I too late? It looks like it. Hushan isn't going to like this."

Loping off to his truck, George climbed in and as he drove away, he squealed the tires. He didn't see the drunk hiding across the street behind another trailer, with a smile on his dirty hairy face and a Glock, fifteen-shot automatic pistol in his hand—one similar to those issued to FBI agents in the field.

(Five)

After waiting two days for Mister Jones' call, when his cell phone rang and Joe answered, he could tell his caller was in a good mood, but it didn't last long.

"Good morning, Sergeant," Claude said. "How are you?"

"Not so good," Joe said. "You lied to us."

"What do you mean?" Claude asked, sitting up on the couch from where he was lying and watching the morning news on TV.

"The bombs weren't where you said they would be."

"My God," Claude said. "I was sure Mo told the truth."

"I don't think he knew they were gone," Joe said. "Hushan probably heard of Mo's latest killings and moved them. You have to admit he's a liability now."

Smiling at Joe's use of his nickname for Mohammed, Claude said, "Yeah, but it leaves us both in a bad situation. There isn't much time before the Cotton Bowl."

"We know it," Joe said. "Are you having more ideas of torturing someone to give you info?"

"No, I think gentle persuasion would work better."

Since he heard the news about the bombs, Claude's mind was racing and he was already working on a plan, so before Joe could say anything more, Claude said, "I'll get back to you," and hung up.

Mister Jones brought out the worst in him, and without realizing it, Joe said, "Son of a bitch."

"Who was it?" Kris asked.

"Mister Jones again,—he's still out there running amuck."

"What do you think he'll do next, nail Hushan's dick to a board?"

"No, he said something about using gentle persuasion. Let's wait and see what he comes up with. So far, he's way ahead of us in the clue department."

Kris nodded and said, "While we wait, we've got our mysterious 'George' to check out. Our undercover agent reported a big, blond-haired guy with a crew-cut and driving an SUV did a B and E on Mo's trailer last night after midnight. He got the license number and it checks out to a George Schroeder, who lives at fourteen seventy-nine Mocking Bird Lane in Fort Worth."

"It must be him," Joe said. "The Fort Worth cops checked the employee listing for the fire department and his name popped up. He works at the Butler Street substation.

"I think we should take a good look at George," Kris said. "It's time to move our operation to Fort Worth."

(Six)

Walter "Specks" Washington was a young black man who earned his street smarts early. With his long, kinky hair braided into cornrows, Specks wore thick glasses and a slim goatee to try to hide a bad case of acne.

Loving hip-hop music, he thought he was God's gift to the rap movement sweeping the black community and spilling over into mainstream America. Specks spent most of his day dreaming of making the big time while doing dirty part-time jobs no one else would.

When he was younger, Specks tried a little pot and even took a toke of coke one night, but it made him sick instead of high, so he never touched the shit again. Now that he was twenty- one, his old man kicked him out of his house and told him to find his own crib, saying, "I'm tired of supporting your deadbeat ass."

Today Specks was trying to earn enough bread to pay the rent on a small one-bedroom apartment with a shared bathroom down the hall he found a couple of weeks ago. Every time he went to take a dump, he found shit on the stool or someone had pissed all over it or on the floor. The smell was enough to make you puke, but it was all he could afford.

He could have turned to pushing dope, but he was no dummy, the white powder was killing the blacks. He'd joined the far-out organization of old Hushan to further his people, not harm them. If Specks had his way, the dopers would have their nuts cut off and served to them for their own dinner.

His thin lanky frame shivered in the cool afternoon air and goose bumps flitted over his arms. He was tired, half-starved and ready to call it quits, but he couldn't until he saw George turn into his driveway in his big SUV, go inside and check out his apartment.

After George came back out to give Specks the high sign everything was okay, then and only then could he take off. That wouldn't happen for a couple more hours. George worked the day shift and didn't get off until six p.m.

As he tried to stay warm, he thought, "All this for a lousy twenty frigging dollars an hour. I wonder what George has in his apartment that's so cool I have to spend my time guarding it.

Today wasn't too bad, for part of the day he had some company, some of his buddies from the street who enjoyed rapping and making up new tunes. They spent part of the afternoon sitting on the curb across from George's joint, trying to outdo each other about what they'd do when they made their first million.

Franklin, an old friend from school and "Twist", an older wino took a few hits off a joint and tried to talk Specks into it, but he said "no" and meant it. After a few more war stories, they took off for greener fields and left him alone.

Now he wished he had told one of them to watch the place for him while he took a piss break. His bladder felt like it was on fire and if he was lucky, he might take a dump and get rid of the pizza he ate last night. Cheese always stopped his bowels up and he had a hell of a time passing it.

He wondered, "Should I take the chance? If Hushan finds out I left my post, he'll have my ass, but I have to piss. To hell with it, no one's been here all day. Who's going to know?"

He could go to the pool room a block south, but the old fart behind the counter didn't want anyone but customers using his crapper, so it left only McDonalds, a block and a half the other way.

Specks took off at a run, but he was out of shape. After the first block, he slowed to a brisk walk. Although it was cool, by the time he got there, he'd worked up a sweat.

Then he found someone was in the can and had the door locked.

Standing in the hall fidgeting, Specks thought, "Probably someone jerking off while reading a sex book. Come on, asshole, get it over with and come. Wipe off your dick and get the hell out of the shitter."

Finally after a three minute wait, a Spic about fourteen walked out with a grin on his face and a paper towel in one hand. "Sorry," he said and threw the wadded paper at a trashcan. He missed and said, "Shit," but didn't pick up his litter.

Hurrying into the bathroom, Specks locked the door and dropped his drawers. He sat down, emptied his bladder and strained to pass some of the thick stool he knew the cheese created. After a full minute, he finally heard a small splash in the bowl, wiped and pulled up his pants.

As he walked by the counter on his way out the door, the smell of hamburgers and fries got to him and he thought, "What the hell, a man's got to eat, don't he?"

There was no one in line, so he hurried to the cash register and waited until a young mulatto teenybopper with a nametag reading "Sally", a mixture of black and Hispanic heritage, ambled over to take his order. Sally concentrated on working her gum from one side of her mouth to the other and it was a moment before she said, "Welcome to McDonald's, how can I help you?"

"A cheeseburger and fries," Specks said.

"Ya want anything to drink?"

"Yeah, throw in a small coke and can you hurry?"

Looking nervously over his shoulder, he saw the street was empty, but he couldn't see all the way to where he was supposed to be.

The cash register hummed and spat out a long white receipt, and Sally said, "That'll be three dollars and twenty-seven cents," as she smacked her gum.

After handing her four wrinkled one-dollar-bills, he waited until the cash register told Sally how much change to give him. He knew she couldn't figure it out on her own and he was right.

When she finally figured out how much she owed him and handed it to him without counting it out, she walked to the window behind her and found a cheeseburger and fries baking under a yellow light.

Specks had no idea how long they'd been there, but he was in a hurry, so he thought, "To hell with it."

After Sally packaged them up and gave him a cup for his drink, he ran to the fountain, filled it half full with ice and pushed the mechanism to active the spigot. The foam took forever to dissipate and in his haste, he didn't wait to fill it completely to the top.

As he hurried out the door, he tried to suck some of the soft froth off the top. It spilled on his new stone-washed jeans and he cursed again.

Five minutes later, he reached his post and let out a large sigh of relief. No strange cars were on the street and George's place looked like it did when he left.

Sitting on the curb, he ate his lunch, crumpled up the napkin and wrapper from the burger, put them in the sack and took the time to walk across the street to throw them into a small dumpster outside of George's apartment house.

(Seven)

From a block away, Claude spotted the guy watching George's place. The black kid was leaning against a lamp post, looking bored, but kept staring across the street at the apartment building where George lived.

Claude knew, "Unless he's peddling dope or paid to be there, a young black wouldn't be out alone on the street in the cool air; not in this part of town."

This guy wasn't doing the bop most dealers did and wasn't paying attention to the traffic on the street, so Claude thought, "No, he isn't a doper. He's a guard."

Instead of continuing on up the street, he pulled up the collar of his jacket, turned the corner and circled the block. On the corner, he found a pool room with a coffee shop and bar to one side. He walked in and took a stool at the counter where he could look out the window and down the street. The black kid was still there, stomping his feet to keep them warm.

SIGNS OF OUR TIMES

At the pool table closest to the door, an old man played a solitary game of eight ball, shooting bank shots, looking like he was trying to find a sucker to hustle. Seeing Claude watching his action, he asked, "Care to shoot a little pool?"

"Don't mind if I do, old timer," Claude said. "It's been quite a while since I held a cue in my hand, so don't laugh if I scratch or flub a shot."

"You wouldn't try to hustle an old man out of his social security, would you?"

"Not me," Claude said. "Rack 'em up."

While keeping an eye on the kid up the street, he shot pool for two hours, losing more games than he won. A couple of other blacks joined the guard, one young groupie and an older boozer who held a bottle of cheap wine in one hand and a rolled joint in the other. They hung around for another hour until they exhausted the booze and the hash. Then they took off and left the guard alone again.

From where Claude stood, he saw the black guard shifting his feet around and crossing his legs like he had to piss. It was the sign Claude was waiting for. He watched while the young black looked around and then took off at a lope toward the McDonalds down the street. Then handing the old man twenty dollars, he said, "Thanks for the games."

"Thanks yourself. You play pretty good for someone who hasn't held a stick in a long time."

Shaking the old man's hand, and his head at the same time, Claude said, "Yeah, but you'd take me, nine times out of ten. Maybe I'll see you again and we can play some serious pool."

Walking out, he moved quickly down the opposite side of the street to George's apartment building. A fast look around told him the black kid was the only lookout, so he took a small brown satchel from his pocket, selected a pick and within a minute he was inside.

Closing the door behind him, Claude did a quick search of the living room that was furnished with worn out junk in the style of the fifties and a ragged carpet that stunk of stale cigarettes and spilled beer.

Next came the bedroom with a sweat-stained, unmade bed and soiled sheets knotted at the bottom. A swastika flag and a picture of Hitler hung over the bed, and a bedside table was littered with well-creased propaganda pamphlets from the Aryan Brotherhood. Claude was satisfied of two things—George wasn't married and he was a slob.

A .45 caliber automatic in a shoulder holster, with two full clips attached to the straps in individual leather pouches, hung from a wooden peg in the bedroom closet. Claude took the rig and hid it under the sagging couch in the living room.

Then he checked the kitchen, which smelled of day-old bacon grease and had dirty dishes and cups in the sink. The residue of scrambled eggs clung to one plate while another held tomato stains looking like spaghetti sauce.

The only interesting item in the entire joint was a certificate issued two years ago, signifying George Schroeder was a licensed jet pilot. George must be proud of it, as the diploma was framed in dark oak with non-glare glass.

Moving on to the garage, under a tarpaulin in the far left corner he found what he was looking for—two large black suitcases, each of which held sixteen fire extinguishers.

Opening the top case, Claude felt the hair on his arms and the back of his neck rise. It scared the devil out of him to think, in the middle of Fort Worth, there for the taking was enough nerve gas to kill everyone for miles around.

Claude's hands shook as he closed the case and pulled the cover back over the cases to where it had been.

Sweat rain down his back as he thought, "How brazen or stupid can they be?"

Checking his watch he noted it was five fifteen. If his information was right, his target would be home soon. Walking to the bedroom closet, he pushed the clothes to one side and leaned against the wall out of sight with the door half open, the way he found it.

He heard the clock on the bedside table ticking off the seconds, but he didn't mind waiting. In fact, he looked forward to meeting George—up close and personal.

CHAPTER 19

(One)

Today Sadie was to be sprung from prison. Only she and the rookie cops assigned to clean up after her were glad to see her depart. When you cleaned up monkey shit once, you never cared to do it again, especially after too many ripe bananas. Word was passed around the station that the next guy who overfed her would find his car full of chimp do do.

Bert came up with the brilliant idea of videotaping Sadie's "testimony", as she signed her way into fame with the help of Alice and Mona. Alice was becoming quite adept at signing, so Mona let her be the star of the show. But now, it was finished and everyone stopped by to say goodbye to the little widow chimp.

Mona told Sadie that Wilbur had died, and they could tell it broke her up by the way she moped around her cage this morning, but she perked up when Alice arrived to take her "home" to the research lab.

"Sadie will be okay," Mona said. "When she sees the other chimps and monkeys, it'll be like old home week."

"And I'll visit her every chance I get," Alice said.

"Sadie's free to go," Joe said.

He flew back last night to pick up some clean clothes and clear his desk before returning to Fort Worth. At least it's what he told Fad.

Fad laughed and asked, "Who do you think you're fooling? We all knew you wouldn't miss a chance to spend time again with the lovely Miss Mona."

Grinning like Sadie, Joe said, "The thought did cross my mind."

Later Joe and Mona shared a few moments alone and made the most of them.

"I'm sorry I haven't been able to see you," Joe said. "I've been in Fort Worth and I have to head back tomorrow. Kris and I will be there for some time."

"I missed you, Joe," Mona said, and if anything, her smile was even brighter than before. He could smell her perfume hanging in the air and being this close to her gave him an involuntary erection.

"When we get done with this job, I hope you'll let me take you out to eat, or dancing or something," he said.

Patting his groin possessively, Mona said, "Definitely something. We wouldn't want that to go to waste, would we? It's too bad you have to leave tomorrow morning."

Grinning knowingly, Joe said, "Yeah, but we have tonight."

"Do you think you could tear yourself away from the paperwork you mentioned?"

"It can wait," he said.

Taking her arm possessively, he poked his head around the door to Fad's office and said, "I'll be out of the office until tomorrow morning. If you want me, try my cell phone."

"Okay," Fad said, and thought, "Yeah, as if you'd answer it. Get some, Joe."

(Two)

Claude heard the garage door motor activate, followed by a high-pitched squeal like a rat with its tail caught in a trap, as the door struggled against gravity and rose reluctantly into the air. George's SUV sounded like a freight train switching cars in a rail yard as its diesel motor pulled it into the garage.

The noise of the engine died, and the truck door opened and slammed shut again. Claude heard George walk through the door into the kitchen, and then the sound of his footsteps echoed through the house as he took a cursory look into each room. When he was satisfied, George walked back to the garage, and Claude heard him say, "See you tomorrow, Specks."

The garage door squeaked downward again and thumped against the concrete. The motor whined for an instant longer and then silence. As George walked into the bedroom, he was whistling a merry tune and his shirt was half off, when Claude pushed open the closet door and strode out, gun in hand.

Struggling to get his arms untangled, George asked, "Who the hell are you?"

"A friend of Mohammed's and Hushan's," Claude said, waving the gun to tell George to have a seat on the unmade bed.

"I've never seen you before. What's your name?"

"Mister Jones," Claude said, and saw the change in George's eyes.

His irises had been narrow, but now they widened in fear or cunning as he said, "I heard of you."

"I thought you might. Just before I killed him, Mohammed said to tell you hello."

"Jesus," George said. His hands shook and he clasped them together in front of him to hide it.

"He won't be much help to you," Claude said. "But don't be so nervous. I'm not here to kill you. I want you to deliver a message to Hushan."

"How would I know someone named Hushan?"

"You have his merchandise stored in your garage," Claude said. "Why try to bullshit me?"

"What's the message?" George asked, and looked like he was getting bolder.

"Turn around, lie down on the bed and put your hands behind you," Claude said. "Don't do anything stupid. Your gun isn't where you think it is, so use your head. I told you I don't want to kill you,—at least not yet."

George looked into Claude's eyes and knew he was telling the truth, so he turned over and did as Claude asked.

Taking a pair of handcuffs from his pocket, Claude slipped them around George's wrists, snapped them shut, held his gun alongside George's head and said, "Tell Hushan he'll get his merchandise back when I get my four hundred thousand dollars, plus two million more for my trouble. I'll give him five days to get the money together. Then I'll call to let him know where the exchange will take place. You got all that?"

"Yeah, I got it. You know you're a walking dead man, don't you?"

"Not yet, Georgie Boy," Claude said and hit him in the back of the neck.

George slumped to the floor, unconscious. Claude made sure he was out of business, tied his legs together, stuck a rag in his mouth and taped it shut. Then he walked out to the garage and made sure the door was unlocked.

Returning to the front door, Claude walked out boldly as if he owned the joint. Walking briskly, but not running so he wouldn't attract any attention, he made his way two blocks down the street and another half-block to the right to where he had parked Carla's Pontiac.

Firing up the engine, he drove back to George's apartment, backed into the driveway, climbed out, raised the trunk lid and then the garage door.

(Three)

Specks turned to watch the fancy red Pontiac Firebird drive by. It was a while since he saw anything so sweet. It didn't belong to anyone around here, with the possible exception of a drug dealer he didn't know. They were the only ones who could afford something that nice.

He was seated on the stoop of Helen Sanchez's porch, curled up near the door with his back resting against the jamb, trying to work up the nerve to ask her out.

Helen sat on the top step, concentrating on putting the final touches to her bright red fingernail polish, looking bored.

Specks heard Helen put out if you treated her right, but he never had the courage before to ask her out on a date because she was twenty-five and probably thought he was a kid.

Pointing to the car, he said, "Look at that."

Using her wrist to brush her brown hair back out of her grey eyes so she wouldn't spoil the new polish job, she said, "Neat-o".

She wore a yellow halter top under a jade-green short jacket and Capri pants in a darker shade of olive. Her pert nipples pushed against the material of her thin bra and the sight of them gave Specks an erection that made him wish he was older.

As the car drove down the block, his eyes followed it in envy, but he was surprised when the vehicle stopped and backed into George's driveway.

As he watched, a big white guy got out, popped the trunk, raised the garage door like he lived there and disappeared inside for a minute. Then he came out carrying a large black suitcase lying on its side. It must have been heavy, because he used both hands to support the case and struggled to get it into the trunk.

"What the fuck is he doing?" Specks asked aloud.

"Watch your dirty mouth," Helen said and frowned.

"Sorry," he said. "I meant the white dude carrying stuff out of George's crib. Look."

Helen turned as the white guy came out again with another case and lifted it into the trunk. Then he closed the lid very slowly and carefully as if the cases contained glass or something very precious and fragile.

Specks stood up and began to walk down the stairs, but then the white dude got into the car, started the engine and turned his way. Ducking back into the darkness of the doorway, Specks stared at the license number on the front bumper and said, "Colorado plates, Eight Four N Six Four Five. Help me remember it, Helen. Write it down somewhere."

"With what? I don't got no pen."

"Use your lipstick. Eight Four N Six Four Five, you got it?"

"Yeah," Helen said, "but repeat it just to be sure, and you owe me six bucks for a new tube."

"Eight Four N Six Four Five," Specks said as he checked the numbers and figures she'd scrawled in big block style on the stoop. "Yeah, you got it all right. Stay here, I'm going to check on George. Some weird shit is going on."

(Four)

Just after he and Mona completed their second round in the sack, Joe's cell phone rang. The first time was frantic and the scratches on his back would be a reminder for several days. The second was slower and more romantic.

As he thought, "Mona is a tiger and I've got her by the tail," Joe laughed at his own pun and was reaching for her left breast to see if the nipple was as firm as it appeared to be, when the jingle interrupted him.

"I have to answer it," he said. "Sorry."

"We have all night," she said.

Thinking it was probably Fad yanking his chain, Joe snarled into the phone, "Yeah, what is it?"

"Hello, Joe, this is Mister Jones," Claude said.

Joe sat up in bed, reached for his suit coat to get his pen and notebook and said, "Yeah, I recognized your voice. What's up?"

"I thought you might want to do a little horse trading.'

"What do you have to trade?"

"Thirty-two fire extinguishers," Claude said, and Joe heard him laugh.

"You don't mean it, you got them?"

"Would I lie to you?"

"You did once," Joe said.

"I didn't lie, they were in the storage area, but Hushan got scared and had George move them."

"You know George, do you?"

"Yeah," Claude said. "You might say he and I are good buddies. He thinks I'm a knockout."

"What do I have to trade that you want?" Joe asked.

"How about an unconditional pardon or immunity from prosecution for any and all crimes I may have committed on your turf, including Katie and the others?"

"You've got a large pair of balls," Joe said. "What makes you think you can get away with it?"

"Check with your FBI buddy and his bosses," Claude said. "I'll bet they won't care about me if they get the fire extinguishers back. In fact, if you'll listen I've got a good idea."

"Go ahead," Joe said. "What do you have to lose?"

"I think you should talk to someone at the chemical lab and see if they can siphon out the nerve gas and replace it with something harmless. If so, I can trade them back to Hushan for the money he owes me and he'll believe the plan will still work.

"That way Hushan and his friends will go ahead with an innocuous attack and it gives you time to find the names of all of the players and capture them."

Joe wondered if innocuous meant the same as ineffective. He hated people who used big words, but he said, "I don't know how long it would take to do something like that. How much time do we have?"

"I gave Hushan five days to get my money together," Claude said.

"So it's all about the money after all."

"Not really, but a man has to live. If everything goes the way I hope it does, I plan to retire and never be heard from again. If not, I'll have fun playing the game to its conclusion."

"What if he double crosses you and tries to take you out?" Joe asked.

"I have a fool-proof way to make the switch. I'll have the upper hand and my campaign platform is the best. Trust me."

Joe thought, "There he goes again, making up puns I can't figure out," but he said, "Okay, I'll make some calls about your immunity, but it may take a while."

"I'll call you at 0800 hours tomorrow, but no traces, Joe. If we have a deal, I'll tell you where to find the cases and you can return them to me later. Don't go back on your word. Before you pick up the merchandise, I want the offer of immunity in writing."

"If I can get it, you'll have it," Joe said. "God, I hope this works. Just knowing that stuff is out there somewhere makes me sweat. You're sure you know how to handle it?"

"Like a baby, gentle and easy," Claude said. "I've talked too long. See you tomorrow."

"Who was it?" Mona asked.

Joe checked the time on his watch on the bedside table and said, "A murderer who wants to make a deal. In the next ten hours I have to convince my superiors and a hell of a lot of other important people to go along with him. I'm sorry baby, but we'll have to cut this session short."

"There'll be others," Mona said and kissed him. "Go save the world."

As he began dressing, Joe said, "God, I hope so."

(Five)

When his leader answered, George said, "Hushan, the merchandise is missing. Your paid assassin got in my apartment and knocked me out. When Specks woke me up, we found the cases were gone.

"You fool. Why didn't Specks see him enter? There are only two ways in, the front door and the garage and he was supposed to watch them both."

"Specks had to take a piss and was gone a few minutes," George said. "Mister Jones must have been watching and got in during that short time frame. He was hiding in my closet and I didn't see him."

"You're both idiots!" Hushan yelled. "Now years of work and planning are ruined. If you weren't the only pilot we have for the emergency escape plane, I'd shoot you myself."

"Mister Jones left a message for you," George said.

"What?"

"He's willing to trade the cases for the four hundred thousand dollars you owe him, plus another two million for his trouble. Was it smart for Felix and Mohammed to try to kill him? Now we've got him on our case. They should have paid him off."

Hushan said, "It's my fault. They did it on my orders. Did anyone see this man?"

"Yeah, the good news is, Specks got his license number. It's a Colorado plate, Eight Four N as in Nancy, Six Four Five. I can get a buddy on the police force to check it out for me. You want me to do it?"

"Yes, you fool, why wouldn't I? You should have done it already. Call me when you know where he lives."

"Okay," George said. "Are you going to make the deal?"

"We'll see," Hushan said. "We'll see. Tell Specks he did a good job getting the license number, but if he ever leaves his post again, I'll take personal pleasure in tearing his head off his skinny body."

"Yes, sir," George said. "I'm sorry about this Hushan, but there is some good news. Mister Jones told me he killed Mohammed after he gave him my address. At least we won't have to worry about the police getting to him."

"Sometimes there's a rainbow behind the clouds," Hushan said. "I'm pleased to hear the good news. Losing the fire extinguishers was not your fault George, but do me a favor. Kick Specks' ass so he learns a lesson. Do it after you tell him how proud I am of him."

"You got it," George said.

(Six)

It was six a.m. and early for a phone call, but Claude knew Carla didn't sleep late and never left before seven thirty. He dialed her number and a mental picture of her naked body danced in his mind. God, he missed her.

When she answered on the second ring, he said, "Hi Babe, do you miss me?"

"Yes, when are you coming back?"

Claude left two days ago, heading for Denver to help the cops again, according to his story, but Carla was getting worried and wondered if he was telling her everything.

"A few more days should do it," he said. "A new development came up and I have to stick around to see how it plays out. I really wish I could tell you about it, but I can't. You'll have to trust me."

"As long as you swear you're not going to kill someone, I believe you."

"Pile up the Bibles, Babe. I really am helping the police and when this is all over, with the bad guys in jail, I'll tell you everything. Then you'll be proud of me."

"I am now," Carla said, "and I love you."

"I love you too, you know that."

"Yeah I do, but I have to hear it every day or I get frightened," she said. "Oh before I forget it, the rental car agency called and you're off the hook. The police found the car in a mall parking lot with no damage, so everyone is happy."

"That's good news."

Smiling at his reaction, she said, "Okay, take as long as you need to get this over with and then come back to me. I'll be waiting."

"See you soon," Claude said. "I'll call again tomorrow, same time."
"I'll be here."

(Seven)
"The car is registered to a woman, not a man," George said. "Her name's Carla Roberson and her address is three sixty-three Wharf Avenue in Sulfur Springs."

"She's probably Mister Jones' girl friend," Hushan said. "Remember, he drove a rental car and we took it."

"Yeah, the next morning I dropped it off in a mall parking lot."

"Get your ass in gear, George. Come by and pick me up. We need to take a trip to Sulfur Springs to meet the lovely Miss Roberson."

"Give me ten minutes to throw some clothes in a suitcase and I'll be there."

(Eight)
After they were ushered into his office and seated in front of his desk, Kris' supervisor, Cowboy "Hoot" Henninger said, "You've been busy, Kris and you also made some pretty important decisions on your own. You sure this Mister Jones is legit?"

His first name really was Cowboy. His rodeo dad gave it to him a year before a renegade bull put him six feet under the cow shit speckled arena dirt. Cowboy got his nickname when his third grade teacher saw his name and said, "That's a hoot." It stuck and Hoot was what everyone knew him by. He didn't really give a damn about the Cowboy moniker anyway.

Hoot was dressed sharp in a tan pair of Dockers and a matching shirt. Nearly sixty-five, he had a full head of snow-white hair under his Stetson and as many wrinkles on his brow as his years. He was suntanned, skinny and looked taller than his five foot six inch height.

Kris thought the cowboy hat did that for him. Hoot was his immediate supervisor, in charge of the entire district including Denver and Sulfur Springs.

In answer to his question, Kris said, "So far, Mister Jones has panned out, and he's our only lead to the nerve gas. I had to make a snap decision to let him in on the story, but if I goofed, I'm sorry."

"No," Hoot said. "I backed you up one hundred percent. I'd have made the same decisions. No apology is necessary and I'm glad you kept us informed."

"Thanks Hoot."

"So, where are we now?" Hoot asked.

Referring to his notes, Kris said, "Our Mister Jones came up with a somewhat complicated plan, but I think it will work. He wants to trade the cases with the nerve gas containers to us for full immunity.

"We get the guys at the chemical lab to drain out the gas and replace it with something non-lethal. Then Mister Jones takes the cases back and trades them to this Hushan character for the money he has coming. I guess Hushan stiffed him on his fee for taking out Katie and the chimps."

Hoot frowned and asked, "Why would we let Mister Jones do that?"

"If the terrorists think they've still got the real thing, they'll go ahead with their plans," Kris said. "It gives us time to either infiltrate their organization or find them by tracing their movements and telephone calls.

"Then just before the big game, we perform a raid and pick them all up."

Hoot sat back in his chair and thought for a moment, and then he said, "His plan is kind of far out, but I like it. Can we replace the gas in five days?"

"We only have four days left, but Mister Witte out at the chemical lab thinks they can do it in three. They have more equipment there and it's far superior to what Felix had in his cabin."

Turning to Joe, Hoot asked, "How do you vote in this, Joe?"

"You guys have jurisdiction now. I'm just an interested bystander."

"Yeah," Kris said, "but your cell phone number is the one he calls."

Shrugging and acknowledging the fact, Joe said, "I established a rapport with Mister Jones and I think he's telling the truth. Hell, when he tries to trade them back to Hushan, he's the one taking the chance, but I say let him try. We know the main characters now, and with luck we can probably round up most of them, but if this works we'll get them all."

Hoot nodded and asked, "And you, Kris?"

"I say go for it."

"Let me talk to the director," Hoot said. "This has to come down from the top. He's the only one who can make this type of decision and has the juice to get the immunity approved and drawn up in a hurry."

"I don't want to tell you your business, Hoot," Joe said, "but you'd better be quick."

"Take a seat in the outer office and I'll get on the horn."

"Yes, sir," they said in unison.

(Nine)

As they sat waiting in the outer office, Kris said, "That's seventeen I've seen today."

"Seventeen of what?" Joe asked.

Pointing toward a red cylinder hanging on the wall by the door, Kris said, "Fire extinguishers. I've never thought about them as much in the past. They're just there and I guess we all get used to having them around, but not actually seeing them. This case has changed all of that. Now I'm counting fire extinguishers whenever I notice one and it's amazing how many there are."

Joe nodded and said, "You're right. I've been noticing them a lot more myself."

CHAPTER 20

(One)

He and Hushan were seated in his SUV, easing down the blacktopped lane toward the dock area on the same canal where Mister Jones was unsuccessfully ambushed, when George said, "That's the address over there on the left."

Pointing down the road, Hushan said, "It's only a block from the warehouses where Felix and Mohammed first met this Mister Jones."

"The place looks deserted," George said.

"Maybe she works," Hushan said. "It's only four thirty. We'll sit and wait. Pull up under the shade of that tree so the sun won't heat up the car."

Thirty minutes and half a pack of gum for George later, a white Buick drove down the lane and stopped in front of the house. Carla climbed out with a small stack of books in her arms, shut the door, leaned back in the open window to say something to the female driver and then watched as Sherry made a U-turn and drove away.

She took no notice of the truck at the side of the road. Someone was always parking there to fish in the canal. Carla didn't blame them, it was a warm day and she wouldn't want to come back from out in the sun to a hot vehicle. She walked quickly through the white picket fence with a gate hanging permanently open on one hinge and up to her door.

Reaching into her purse to find her keys, she heard a sound behind her and turned to see a swarthy Arab type older man and a young white man walk up the path to her door.

At the sight of them, the caution light in her brain was lit bright orange, but she asked, "Can I help you?"

Smiling, Hushan asked, "Do you own a red Pontiac Firebird?"

Dropping her books, Carla tried to put the key in the lock before they reached her, but she fumbled with the chain and it was too late.

They were on her in a heartbeat, one at each side, and the same man said, "I believe the answer is yes. Here, my dear, let me help you with your key."

After taking the ring from her hand and finding the right key on the second attempt, he opened the door. George pushed her rudely into the living room and held her arms tight against her side as he said, "She's something else."

His eyes ran over her body and his hands reached up to cup her under her breasts. Carla pushed at his hands and struggled to get away, but he was bigger and stronger.

Hushan grabbed George by the arm and squeezed until it hurt as he said, "Control yourself, you fool. We can't trade damaged goods."

Then he stared into Carla's eyes and asked, "Where is the elusive Mister Jones?"

Carla lied, but her eyes gave her away as she said, "I don't know who you're talking about."

"I think you do," Hushan said. "Sit down."

When Carla didn't immediately respond to his request, George pushed her down into a straight-backed wooden chair.

"Your friend has been up to no good," Hushan said. "He has something of mine and I think he'll be willing to trade it for you."

"I think he'll want his money more than her," George said.

Hushan was amazed and asked, "Look at her. Would you prefer money to this?"

"Hell yes," George said. "Two million dollars will buy me a covey of quail like this one."

"You're not a romantic and something tells me Mister Jones is," Hushan said. "But perhaps you're right. The merchandise is the important thing. We'll go ahead with the trade as planned, but send him a video of our guest so he'll consider giving us the money back."

Addressing Carla, he asked, "What do you think, my dear? Will he trade for you?"

"I still don't know who or what you're talking about," Carla said. "You have the wrong person. Let me go."

Pointing to her eyes, he said, "No matter how you try to hide a lie, the eyes always give you away. Tie her up and gag her, George. It's a long ride back to Fort Worth. Let's see how she likes it on the back floorboard under a blanket."

George frowned in defiance and said, "Hell, put her in the trunk."

"Carbon monoxide from the muffler might kill our passenger," Hushan said. "Do as I say, George."

"Thanks for using my name."

"That's the least of your worries," Hushan said. "Mister Jones knows your name and where you live. Let's hope he hasn't shared the information with anyone else."

Thinking of the implications of his remarks, George said, "Jesus."

"And Allah too, George," Hushan said. "Pray to them both."

(Two)

Five minutes before Claude walked in his door, Charles "Gordo" Gordon was seriously considering suicide. For his young age of thirty, Gordo was fifty pounds over his prime weight, growing balder by the year and stone cold broke.

Although he tried faithfully to reduce his debt, he still owed more than thirty thousand dollars on his college loans, another forty-two thousand and change on his run-down home on the wrong side of town and was two months behind in the rent on his law office.

Married for a short time, Gordo fathered one child, a boy named Thomas and then found out the kid wasn't his. Wanda, his cheating bitch of a wife was getting it on with his best friend, Louis, and Gordo was the only one in town who didn't know about it.

Two days ago his car, a fifteen-year-old wreck, finally gave up the ghost, and each day Gordo had to walk fourteen blocks from his home to his office.

Knowing his legs, heart and mind couldn't take much more of this, Gordo sat in his small office in a run-down mall at his beat-up desk with a plastic top cracked on one corner. Looking at his reflection in a mirror on the wall that was peeling silver from the back, he felt just like it, old and used up, and his life reflected nothing but trouble.

Born of mixed blood lines, Creole, French, Spanish and maybe a little

SIGNS OF OUR TIMES

African Black thrown in for good measure, Gordo grew up on the mean streets of New Orleans. He got his street smarts early, but by the grace of God, he had a good mother who made him study hard, no matter how much Gordo wanted to run with the pack and chase whores on Bourbon Street.

She stayed on his ass and Gordo graduated from high school in the top ten percent of his class, went on to college and then law school, where he managed to pass by the skin of his teeth and the good favors of a kindly professor who liked Jazz as much as Gordo did.

From there, he was hired by a firm in Dallas that went belly-up a year later when they lost a large lawsuit against one of the partners for sexual misconduct. Gordo was out on his ass when he was just getting started.

Deciding not to place his fortune in the hands of others, he opened his own small law office near the outskirts of Fort Worth, but it wasn't working out. Maybe eating a gun was the way to go.

Looking up at the tall white man, who walked up to his desk in a nice blue suit, Gordo smiled and asked, "What can I do for you, sir?"

"That depends," his guest said. "I'm looking for a good lawyer. Are you one?"

"I think I am," Gordo said. "I try hard."

"Let me ask you a few questions. Then we'll see if you want to take my case."

"Have a seat and fire away," Gordo said, moving a steel and plastic chair from where it sat by the wall and putting it in front of his desk for his guest.

"If I hire you, you're bound by the Lawyer/Client privilege, aren't you? In other words, you couldn't tell anyone including the police what I look like, where I live, what I told you etcetera. Am I correct?"

Gordo wondered, "Who is this dude and what's he done?" But he said, "Yeah, once I agree to take your case and you pay me a retainer, I'm your attorney for life. I can't talk about you to anyone or tell them anything you say to me."

"Good," Claude said. "Let me explain my situation and you tell me if you're willing to be my attorney."

"I'm listening."

"Okay, here goes. The police would like to charge me with a crime, but they don't know what I look like. I'm not saying if I'm guilty or not, but I have something they want so badly they're willing to grant me immunity for any and all crimes I may or may not have committed. Are you with me so far?"

"Yeah," Gordo said. "I follow you."

"What I need is a go-between," Claude said.

"What do I have to do?"

"I hope the police will grant the immunity, but I can't pick up the documents or they'll know who I am. I need you to act as my intermediary, receive the papers, check them over for authenticity and tell me when they're approved and final."

"That's all?" Gordo asked.

"Yeah, that's it for now. If things work out, I'll make some big bucks from this deal. I'll need someone to handle my investments and keep his mouth shut about my business. What about it?"

"What kind of retainer are we talking about?" Gordo asked.

Pulling a stack of bills from his inside pocket, Claude laid it on the desk and asked, "What about fifty thousand now and a hundred and fifty more when I get the papers?"

"God damn," Gordo said. "Did I hear you right, fifty thousand?"

Sensing somehow he's made a new friend, Claude said, "Yeah, and the rest later. How about it, are you my attorney?"

"You bet your ass," Gordo said. "Let me get a contract drawn up."

Forgetting any thoughts of suicide, he repeated, "God damn."

Gordo was back in business and things were definitely looking up.

(Three)

The next morning Claude phoned Carla at six a.m., but she didn't pick up and he was worried. Every fifteen minutes until eight, he tried again. Then he called the library where she worked.

When an elderly lady answered the phone, he asked, "Is Miss Roberson there?"

"No," she said. "Carla hasn't shown up and she didn't call in either."

"Could she be sick?" Claude asked.

"When Carla left yesterday afternoon she was fine. Who is this?"

"If she comes in, tell her Claude called," he said. "I'll call back later in the day."

He thought, "Something's wrong. When we spoke yesterday, Carla said she would be there. She wouldn't miss work unless it was an emergency."

Taking a chance, Claude dialed Joe's cell phone. When he answered Claude said, "Joe, this is Mister Jones."

"The approval isn't back yet."

"That's not why I'm calling. I need a favor."

"You do?" Joe asked. "What's in it for me?"

"You might save someone's life."

"You running around with your nail gun again?" Joe joked.

"No," Claude said. "A friend of mine may be in trouble. I want you to check on Miss Carla Roberson at three six three Wharf Avenue in Sulfur Springs."

"Is she your girl?"

"No," Claude lied. "She's just a friend. I tried to call her and she doesn't answer. It's not like her. If our mutual friends found out about her, she's in trouble. Please, I'm asking you as a personal favor."

"That's the first time I've heard you say 'please' since we met," Joe said. "Okay, I'm in Fort Worth, but I'll have somebody drive out and take a look. Call me in a couple of hours and I'll let you know what they find."

"Thanks, I appreciate it."

"I'll have the word on your immunity by this afternoon. Maybe when you call, you can kill two birds with one stone."

"Don't mention the word kill," Claude said. "I'll talk to you later."

"Getting squeamish when it comes to your friends, 'eh?" Joe asked, but he was talking to a dead phone.

Hanging up himself, he said, "Damn Mister Jones anyway. He always gets in the last word."

(Four)

In the middle of an empty rundown warehouse that reeked of rotten vegetables and wino's urine, Carla sat on a straight-back wooden chair, staring into the lens of a video camera Hushan held in his hands.

"Smile," Hushan said, and she frowned.

George said, "He said 'smile'," and slapped Carla's face, as he thought, "I don't give a damn if I'm on the tape. Mister Jones knows what I look like and I also know who he is. If he sees me hit his chick, maybe he'll be pissed enough to let me have a crack at him, man to man."

"You bastard," Carla said.

George had to admit she was one tough broad. He wished Hushan hadn't put her body off limits. Man, what he could teach this redhead. Maybe later, if things worked out the way Hushan hoped they would.

"This is your lucky day, Mister Jones," Hushan said for the camera. "As you can see, we have your girl friend. She's a lovely woman and has a very nice ring. Hold up the heart-shaped diamond, George, so I can focus on it."

Grabbing Carla's left hand, George twisted it around to display the diamond Claude gave her. She sobbed and tears ran down her cheeks.

"Good," Hushan said. "As you can see, we have treated her kindly so far, but if you don't meet us at the old rock quarry on the west side of Fort Worth off Boulder Avenue at nine o'clock tomorrow night with our money intact, there's no telling what we may do to such a lovely girl. George would love to have her, but for now, I've forbidden it.

"Do I make myself clear, Mister Jones? Meet me at the rock quarry off Boulder Avenue, at nine p.m., the day after you receive this video. Don't be late."

After shutting the camera off, Hushan said, "That should do, George. Tie our guest up and then go out and get her some food. We can't afford to let her starve."

(Five)
"Your friend wasn't there," Joe said. "My guy said it looks like she left in a hurry. The front door was ajar and a stack of books was scattered outside on the stairs. There wasn't any sign of forced entry and no struggle as far as he could tell."

Hating himself, Claude said, "Damn, Hushan and his men may have her. When I picked up the nerve gas, I drove her car to George's garage. Someone may have seen me and got the license number. I was stupid."

"Yeah," Joe said. "If they have her, you were, but what do we do now?"

"If my immunity comes through, we go through with the transfer."

"We got it an hour ago," Joe said. "How do you want to handle the paperwork?"

"Take it to my lawyer, Charles Gordon, at the Landmark Mall on Stewart Street, Suite number four. When he Okays it, I'll call and give you the location of the containers. Make it fast. We don't know what Hushan will do and I need to make some plans."

"Okay," Joe said, "you got it. "It's on the way."

"Stick by your phone," Claude said. "I'll call soon."

(Six)
Claude was more afraid than at any other time in his life and his mind was racing. They had Carla and it was his fault. He cursed himself and the life he led and wondered, "How could I have been so stupid as to involve her in my troubles? Why didn't I leave when I was healed and let her get on with her life?"

No, he had to fall in love with her when he had no right to. Now Carla might pay for his error with her life. If so, he couldn't live, and many people would die before he did.

Clenching his fists together, he thought, "Calm down, Claude, and think. Make plans for any eventuality. If you outthink them, these guys can't win, they're not that smart."

Taking a deep breath, he cleared his mind of negative thoughts and began to plan.

(Seven)
When Gordo answered, Claude said, "This is Mister Jones. Do the papers check out?"

"Yes, they do, Mister Jones. You're a free man. I have them here for you."

"They'll have to wait for a while," Claude said. "Later today, along with your final payment, I'm sending you a sealed envelope by courier. Should anything happen to me, it contains instructions I want you to follow. Can you do it for me?"

"Sure thing, Mister Jones. You were a life saver to me and I'll do anything you ask."

"Thanks, Gordo. In case I don't see you again, it's been a pleasure knowing you."

"Thank you. Whatever you have to do, I wish you good luck."

(Eight)
"Joe, this is Mister Jones. I got the word from my lawyer. Thanks."

"You're welcome, where are the containers?"

"They're in a storage locker at 'Store and Go' on Winterhaven Drive, unit thirteen for good luck. The key is at my lawyer's office. When you've replaced the real containers with phonies, put them back in the same place and I'll have Hushan pick them up."

"How are you going to handle your switch?" Joe asked.

"I'm going to get the money and tell him where the bombs are. If they have Carla, he'll tell me about it after the swap is made and he has his merchandise. Then we'll see."

"Call me if you need any help," Joe said. "You're a free citizen now, so you can call for the police if you need them."

"Thanks, Joe. I may take you up on the offer. I'll talk to you soon. Good luck on transferring the gas."

CHAPTER 21

(One)

"Sergeant Francone, this is Hershel Witte out at the chemical laboratory on Camp Shaffer."

"Yeah Hershel, what can I do for you? How's the transfer coming along?"

"Fine, but that's not what I want to speak to you about. How many containers did you say there were?"

Joe's blood ran cold as he said, "Thirty-two. Why, how many did you receive?"

"Only thirty-one," Hershel said. "One of the cases had an empty space. At first I thought you made a mistake in the number Felix prepared, but then I remembered Agent Hefner saying thirty-two, so I thought I should let you know."

"Thanks, Hershel," Joe said, but didn't mean it.

Normally, Joe wasn't a religious man, but now he prayed, "Please don't let it be true."

And then he thought, "Damn, I can't reach Mister Jones. He calls me. I wonder if he knows."

Getting up from his desk and suddenly feeling much older, Joe walked wearily back to the rear of the building where Kris had taken up residence as the agent in charge.

Kris was leaned back in his chair with his feet up on a drawer and it looked like the long hours finally caught up with him. His chest rose and fell as he slept and Joe was tempted to let him sleep, but knew he had to wake him.

"Kris," he said a little louder than he normally would have. Startled by his call, Kris' feet fell off the drawer and his body pitched forward as he came awake and asked, "Yeah Joe, what is it?"

Sounding like James Lovell on Apollo 13, Joe said, "We have a problem. Hershel called from the lab and says they only received thirty-one fire extinguishers. That means one is missing and unaccounted for."

At the news, Kris blinked twice and ran his hands through his hair as he tried to focus his blurry eyes on the matter at hand. Then he said, "Holy shit."

"My sentiments exactly," Joe said. "Do you think Mister Jones knows?"

"He didn't say anything about one missing, did he?"

"Not in any of our conversations. Ever since the exchange, he's been quiet. I suppose he'll call before he and Hushan meet to let us know what's going on. I'll ask him then."

Looking at his hands, which had suddenly begun to shake, Kris said, "God, I thought we had this thing licked. If we can't find the missing container, we'll have to cancel the Cotton Bowl and evacuate both towns. Imagine the nightmare that will create."

"I don't know if we can cause that kind of panic," Joe said.

"What alternative is there?"

Shaking his head, Joe said, "I don't know, I just don't know."

(Two)

Locked in a small room, with a folding Army cot for a bed, two thin sheets and a lumpy pillow for bedding, a wooden folding chair to sit on, and a chipped white chamber pot with a roll of toilet paper for her "necessities", Carla was so tired she didn't know up from down.

A single sixty-watt bulb hung from a ceiling fixture on a white, plastic-coated wire. The light remained on twenty-four hours a day. Since there were no windows in the room, she wasn't sure if it was day or night outside.

Time lost all meaning to her, so she guessed at the hours and days spent here by the number of meals they gave her. Today no one came in to empty her "toilet", and the smell of her urine and stool was almost overpowering in the overly-warm cubbyhole where she was confined.

Carla wore the same outfit she had on when they kidnapped her, a brown skirt and white blouse. Her captors didn't even have the decency to supply her with a change of clothes or underwear.

Neither of the garments fared well. After three days, they were wrinkled and stained. How much longer her jailers intended to hold her before they tried to trade her for their two million dollars was anyone's guess.

Besides her love for him, the only hope she could cling to was that Claude was working on a scheme to get her away safely. She knew his heart must be torn because he felt he betrayed her by using her car.

Hushan offered the information to her the day he kidnapped her, when he said, "If your boyfriend wasn't so cheap and rented a car, we wouldn't know who you are. The least Mister Jones could have done was change license plates. He's not as smart as he thinks he is."

"Wait until I get a chance to even the score," George bragged.

Although George was well built and had muscles, Carla didn't think he could take Claude in a fair fight, but she didn't want to find out.

As she prayed, "Please let Claude and me get out of this in one piece," Carla heard footsteps outside the door and a key rattled in the lock. Determined to show resistance as long as she was able, she stood up with her fists clenched.

As Hushan walked in the door, trailed by his ever-present shadow, George the goon, he said, "Good morning, Carla."

George nodded in her general direction, but she didn't return their greetings.

Pointing to her chamber pot, Hushan said, "My God, it stinks to high heaven in here. I'm sorry, Carla."

Turning to George, he said, "Take the pot and empty it, George. See if you can find some antiseptic spray to cleanse the place."

Grumbling under his breath, George picked up the foul container and walked out the door. He banged the chamber pot against the door frame and some fluid spilled out.

"Clean that up when you come back," Hushan said sternly.

When he was out of sight, Hushan said, "I think George did that on purpose, Carla, and I shall chastise him later. I apologize for his rudeness."

"Thank you," she said.

Waving his hand as if it was nothing, he said, "You're welcome. For your information, we'll be leaving soon. Tonight is the night to settle all old debts. I hope your friend will cooperate and we get our goods.

SIGNS OF OUR TIMES

"Tomorrow night we'll make the trade for you in return for our money. I would hate to harm such a lovely woman as you, but if I must, I will.

"Remember my warning. Do as you're told and things will go smoothly. Make waves and you'll pay the consequences."

The news of her impending release brought small tears of relief to her eyes as she said, "I understand."

Hushan noticed, handed her a clean handkerchief and said, "Keep it."

"Thanks," she said and wiped her eyes.

Returning with the empty pot, a damp mop, and some insect spray in an aerosol can, George said, "This is all I could find."

He dropped the pot near her bed and it made a hollow ringing sound. Then he soaked up the liquid with one swipe of the mop and leaned it against the wall out in the hall.

When he sprayed the room with an odor reminding her of the repellent used in an outhouse at a country school where she once taught, Carla remembered it never killed any of the wasps. To the contrary, they seemed to thrive on it.

The memory brought a smile to her face and a little joy to her heart.

"We'll be back shortly and let you know how the exchange went," Hushan said. "Before we leave tomorrow, I'll give you a few minutes to freshen up in my bathroom."

A battler to the end, Carla said sarcastically, "You're too kind."

(Three)

Tonight was the dark of the moon. With a heavy cloud cover and possible thunder showers forecasted, it would be hard for anyone with a rifle to see without a night scope.

The afternoon of the exchange between he and Hushan, Claude phoned Joe and when he answered, he asked, "Hey Joe is everything ready for the big exchange?"

"I'm glad you called," Joe said. "We have a small problem. One of the fire extinguishers is missing."

Joe heard his quick intake of a breath before he asked, "What do you mean, one's missing? There were supposed to be thirty-two. I saw them in George's garage."

"Are you sure?" Joe asked. "Did you open both cases?"

"No. I didn't want to take the chance that George might notice the tarpaulin was moved. I only looked in the top one and there were sixteen in that case, so I assumed there was the same number in the other. I guess I goofed."

"You have no idea where the missing one is?"

"If I did, it wouldn't be missing, would it?"

"Don't be a wise ass," Joe said. "This is serious."

"Don't I know it? What will Hushan think?"

Believing Mister Jones didn't know the answer, sweat broke out on Joe's brow, as he asked, "Do you think he'll take the time to count them in the storage area?"

"No, but the shortage is bound to come up soon after they move them to their final destination. Hell, what's one less to Hushan if he thinks he still has the real thing?"

"The problem is who has it?" Joe asked. "If we can't account for all of the bombs, we'll have to cancel the football game, clear both cities of millions of people, causing a panic the likes of which I don't even want to think about."

Sounding sincere, Claude said, "We do have a problem, and just when I thought we were in the clear. What do you want me to do?"

Grasping at any chance, Joe asked, "Do you know any more of Hushan's men? Can you get to them to see if they know anything?"

"Yeah, I do and I can try, but I have my hands full tonight. The exchange should go well, but after that, it might be a different story. If I'm still alive tonight and Hushan does have Carla and wants to trade for her, I'll call you and discuss some plans I have for that party."

"Good luck," Joe said and meant it. A lot was hanging on the outcome. Sweat ran down his brow as he thought of the consequences if Mister Jones couldn't pull it off.

(Four)

When Claude phoned, Hushan said, "I've been waiting for your call. I have your money. Are my goods safe and ready to be returned to me?"

"Good and yes," Claude said. "Meet me tonight at midnight at the Wheeler Street entrance in front of the Tyler Building in downtown Dallas. Come alone and bring the money in one suitcase and no tricks. You don't get the location of the merchandise until I get the money."

"I'll call you on your cell phone before I arrive and wear a red rose in my lapel so you can recognize me. Are my instructions clear?"

"Completely, Mister Jones. I look forward to finally meeting you face to face."

"Until tonight, Hushan," Claude said and disconnected.

(Five)

As Claude walked up to the sleek blue and white helicopter setting on its pad at a small airport on the west side of Dallas, the pilot leaned out of the front seat and asked, "Mister Jones?"

Bending unnecessarily under the slowly moving blades and approaching the cockpit, Claude said, "Yes, that's me."

Sticking out his hand to shake, the pilot said, "My name's Paul—Paul Stokes. I'm the one you talked to about leasing the helo."

Handing him a manila envelope full of cash, Claude said, "Nice to meet you, Paul. Here's your money, ten thousand dollars in cash, just as I promised."

Taking the envelope and sticking it under his seat without counting it, Paul asked, "This trip isn't illegal, is it?"

"No. All you have to do is take me to the top of the Tyler Building in downtown Dallas and land on their helicopter pad at fifteen minutes before midnight.

"I'm meeting a friend there for a short discussion, which shouldn't take more than twenty minutes. Then you'll fly me back here. Very simple and very legal, I assure you."

Tilting his head to one side, Paul said, "Sounds strange, but who am I to question your motives. As long as the police don't come looking for me, its okay with me."

"On the return trip, I'll have a large suitcase weighing about fifty pounds. It won't be a problem, will it?"

"Not at all," Paul said. "It should fit easily into the passenger compartment. You can ride up front with me if you choose to."

Checking his watch, Claude said, "Fine, it's now eleven. Can we get there in time?"

Paul did a quick calculation and said, "Yes, if we leave in the next ten minutes."

"Then let's go."

(Six)

Pacing the sidewalk from the curb to the entrance and back again, Hushan waited for his phone to ring. Across the street in an office overlooking the door, he had stationed George with a high-powered rifle equipped with a night-vision scope.

Two blocks away, Specks sat in a rental car monitoring another cell phone.

If Mister Jones made a run for it, and George didn't get him first, Specks could cut him off.

A strange sound seemed to come from somewhere around the building, but he didn't see anything, so he shrugged and continued pacing. As he turned toward the entrance again, his phone rang. He answered it and said, "Yes."

Mister Jones' voice echoed in his ear as he said, "Keep walking and when the window washing platform gets there, put the suitcase on it and stand back. When I have my money, I'll send it back down with a shoe box and the location of the merchandise will be inside."

Frowning at the thought, but knowing he had been outfoxed, Hushan said, "You sneaky bastard."

Glancing up, he saw the platform hanging ten feet above him. As he watched, it dropped slowly to the sidewalk, bounced lightly as if it was rubber and then rocked gently from side to side.

In his earpiece, Claude's voice ordered, "Put the suitcase on board."

Gritting his teeth and grimacing, Hushan did as he was told and watched the platform begin to rise into the dark sky. For as large as it was, it moved quickly and he lost sight of it as it reached a height above the street lights. They blinded his night vision and he couldn't tell how far up the platform was.

Pulling the second phone from his pocket, Hushan speed dialed George's number. When he answered, Hushan shouted, "He's on the roof. Can you see him?"

"No, it's too high."

"Can you see the window washer's platform?"

"Just barely, it's at the top of the building. Wait, it's coming back down."

Cursing aloud, Hushan stood on the balls of his feet and waited for the platform to return. He'd been outsmarted and it felt like he'd been kicked in the balls.

Up above he heard the beat of a helicopter's blades as they bit into the night air and saw a dark shape flutter off the roof and away into the darkness. Cursing again, he said, "As Allah is my God, tonight was yours, but tomorrow night will be mine."

CHAPTER 22

(One)

After Paul dropped Claude off at his car, he considered opening the suitcase, but knew he should wait until he got to his motel room. His feeling of trepidation continued to haunt him.

Hushan had said nothing about Carla over the phone and made no threats when he gave up the money. But Hushan was too smug. Something in his voice told Claude he thought he had the upper hand.

As late as it was, traffic was light, so it was an easy trip from the small airfield to the Embassy Suite Motel off I-45.

Although he knew it was stupid of him, Claude still drove Carla's Pontiac because it made him feel closer to her. Thoughts of what she must be going through tortured his mind, but he knew he must separate the memory of Carla from his conscious thoughts, or he might make a mistake that would cause her death.

After pulling into a parking spot near the front of the motel, he shut the engine off and sat for a moment staring at the suitcase on the front seat beside him. It was like a silent partner in a business deal gone bad, something you didn't want to face, but knew you had to sooner or later.

Easing out of the car, Claude reached across the seat, pulled the brown leather case across the fabric and hooked his hand through the handle. Surprisingly, if the money was all there, it wasn't as heavy as he would have imagined.

The polished glass doors to the motel slid open as Claude approached. The clerk on duty, a Vietnamese girl about twenty years old with slanted eyes and long black hair, smiled shyly at him.

Walking through the entrance, he made his way to his room on the first floor, noting the hallway smelled of disinfectant and the lingering odor of a pepperoni pizza someone ordered for delivery not too long ago. The two scents didn't blend well.

Sounds of passionate coupling came from the room next to his, and he tried to smile, but a picture of Carla and he in her bed came to mind and he couldn't. His reflection in the mirror showed a tired but determined man staring at a suitcase, almost afraid of what he would find inside.

Shivers ran through his shoulder blades and down his arms as he reached for the case and pushed the two sliders. The lid popped up and he helped it open the rest of the way. The money was there all right, but so was a video tape with an envelope taped to its side.

The message was signed in large letters with the name "Hushan" and said, "Before you revel in your wealth, Mister Jones please view the attached."

Taking the tape, Claude put it in the video player setting under the TV in the built-in cabinet by the dresser. He turned on the TV and waited for the picture to appear before he hit the "Play" button.

A blank blue screen was replaced with a picture of Carla seated on a wooden chair in the middle of an empty warehouse. As George stood next to her and held her down with one hand on her left shoulder, she looked frightened.

Claude heard Hushan say "Smile," but Carla frowned.

George said, "He said 'smile'," and slapped her face

Claude's fingernails dug into the handles of the chair in which he was seated and he cursed the day he let George live to deliver his message.

"You bastard," Carla said, and Claude felt her courage in those two words. He thought, "You'll pay for that, George."

Listening carefully to the rest of the tape and Hushan's instructions, he winced when George twisted Carla's wrist around to display the diamond ring he gave her. It made his blood pressure rise and he felt a pounding behind his ears, warning him to calm down and think rationally.

The screen went blue, so he rewound the tape and watched it in its entirety again. Carla's tears and the condition of her clothing made his eyes mist. Wiping them away with the back of his hand, he attempted to calm his emotions.

When he felt he was in control again, he got up and turned the TV and recorder off, popped the tape out and threw it into the trash can next to the desk. Then he picked up the phone and called Joe.

(Two)

It rained the following night, a hard pouring torrent blocking out any stars and adding to the darkness of a moonless night. Earlier in the day, Claude and Joe scoped out the quarry from a police helicopter and got a good feel for the layout.

At six a.m. they finally met in the parking lot outside police headquarters. Joe looked nothing like what Claude pictured him in his mind, but his intelligent eyes told Claude this man was no fool. Although Joe's clothing hung from his overweight frame like wrinkled curtains too large for a small bay window, Claude knew he could take care of himself in any situation.

As they shook hands, Joe said, "So you're the elusive Mister Jones. Do you have a first name?"

"It's Claude. Thanks for meeting me. If I was you, I wouldn't have."

"I'm not too happy about Katie and the drivers of the other vehicles," Joe said. "You got away with murder and it goes against my grain."

"When Saint Peter and I meet, I hope my actions to save thousands of innocent people might wipe it off my ledger."

"Yeah," Joe said. "I took it into consideration when I agreed to help you. You were more than helpful to us in this investigation. If it weren't for you, we'd still be clueless."

"Thanks," Claude said.

"I've got an unmarked helicopter set up to check out the site," Joe said. "I figure Hushan might have someone out there watching to make sure it's not a trap, but an early flyover by an aircraft shouldn't shake him up too much. As dumb as these guys have been so far, he probably won't even notice."

"Thanks again," Claude said. "Let's take a look and then we can make our plans."

That was earlier, but the downpour changed the situation. He and Joe couldn't expect any help from the air because the helo was grounded by the weather. They also agreed too many people on the scene would spook Hushan and he'd call the meeting off.

Although this wasn't an FBI case, they cleared their plans with Kris, who said, "You're in charge here, Joe. I can't help you in an official capacity, because it would taint the charges if you make any arrests, but if you need me on my personal time, I'm available."

"Claude thinks he and I can take care of it and I agree."

Shortly after they returned from the flyover, Joe introduced Kris to their one-time foe. He could tell Kris was uncomfortable around Claude. Hell, he didn't blame him.

Although Kris liked Claude's looks and the way he carried himself, Claude was still a murderer. Well, maybe an ex-murderer, pardoned and given immunity, but it still went against his beliefs.

The most important item now was to get an innocent woman freed from the clutches of Hushan and his cronies. Claude confessed to Joe that Carla was more than a friend, something he knew from the beginning. It didn't take many smarts to figure it out. Claude was too worried when he called to ask Joe to check up on her.

(Three)

The rugged worked-out, worn-out and deserted quarry looked like a graveyard for giants. Huge broken blocks of different-colored stone were lying on their sides like toppled tombstones or standing like silent sentinels strewn about the landscape in no logical sequence.

Piles of gravel were interspersed with boulders the size of cars. Water was everywhere—in a deep pit lake created by the removal of the marble, in small wide pools where large machines scooped out the sand and in shallow puddles underfoot.

Jagged streaks of burning white lightning cut through the night, while thunder crashed and echoed from the high walls of the unnatural canyon the quarrying had created over the years. A bent and battered fence once surrounded the area, but it had been trampled to the ground as thrill-seeking teenagers found the place and took it over for illegal and dangerous, swimming, necking, joint smoking, partying and screwing in the back seat of their cars.

Shattered Styrofoam coolers, beer and soda cans, torn, stained and soaked pizza boxes, wrappers from every fast food place in town and used condoms floated in the puddles.

Large rivulets of rainwater cut through the mud to move the trash along toward the larger pools and lake. They gathered there atop the muddy surface like the debris of toppled sailboats caught in a hurricane.

SIGNS OF OUR TIMES

Claude pulled up to the wide, muddy entrance in Carla's car, where a double-wide woven-wire gate was hanging from its posts, reminding him of the maw of a giant whale as it fed on plankton, or the mouth of a great white shark on the attack.

There was no other vehicle in sight, so it appeared he was the first player in the game to arrive. He backed the Pontiac in close to the ruined fence and shut the engine down. Sitting quietly for a few moments and listening to the rain beat on the roof, he watched the lightning flashes against the black sky.

Then after pulling his collar up, he grabbed the grip of the suitcase in his right hand, the door handle in his left and climbed out into the maelstrom. The wind tugged at his jacket as the suitcase swayed and beat against his legs.

Walking quickly, Claude splashed through puddles and mud toward a group of cracked blocks of granite a hundred feet away and stopped behind the largest. Dropping the case to the soggy ground, he pulled out his weapon, a Glock fifteen-shot automatic pistol. It felt warm in his cold hand, like an old friend.

Somewhere above him, Claude knew Joe was watching his back. He hoped Joe could see through the spray and foggy mist surrounding them. Claude's hair was stuck to his scalp and his coat was already soaked through. Cold water ran down his spine and made him shiver.

He thought, "Come on, Hushan. Let's get this over with, one way or another."

Rising and falling as the driver made his way down the rocky road to the quarry, twin headlight beams cut through the inky darkness. Then the car stopped at the entrance gate and the lights flicked off and on. Claude didn't know what it meant, but he hoped it wasn't some teenagers out for a thrill tonight. It wasn't the time or the place.

Picking up the suitcase, he moved farther back into the jumble of man-sized rocks and boulders at the rear of the U-shaped bowl of the quarry. By the light of an occasional lightning strike, he saw the muddy, oily and litter-laden surface of the lake behind him. Large drops of rain splattered against the surface and created a pattern of interlocking concentric circles among the trash.

A car door opened and Claude heard muffled voices. Then a shout echoed hollowly against the sodden cliffs, "Mister Jones, show yourself."

Claude stepped halfway out from his hiding place, but remained in the shadows and shouted, "I'm here, show me Miss Roberson."

A flashlight came on and whoever held it shined it on Carla, who stood huddled against the downpour, clothed only in the outfit Claude saw her wearing in the video. She was already drenched, with her soaked thin blouse stuck tight against her breasts as the wind tore at her.

As Carla threw her arms up to shield her eyes and face from the onslaught, Claude swore under his breath. "You bastards."

The light went out, he was temporarily blinded, and Hushan shouted, "The money, where is it?"

Holding the suitcase high in the air, Claude answered, "Right here."

Over the noise of the wind and rain, Hushan yelled, "I'll send George over to get it. When he starts back, I'll send Miss Roberson on her way to you. No tricks. Do you understand?"

"Yes," Claude called and watched as George held open his coat to show he was unarmed.

Claude thought, "I'll believe it when cows give chocolate milk," and kept his gun sight held tight on George's chest as he walked slowly to where Claude waited.

Using the toe of his left foot, he pushed the suitcase away from the rock he stood behind so he wouldn't get too close to George. If the opportunity arose, he wasn't sure he could restrain himself from cold-cocking him.

As he approached with his hands held high above his head, George said sarcastically, "Nice to see you again. That's a nice piece of fluff you've got. I enjoyed my time with her."

Gritting his teeth, knowing George was only trying to provoke him into showing himself, Claude kept his temper, thinking, "There can't just be two of them. A third guy must be out in the rocks waiting to pop me. Where is he? Think, Claude."

Keeping him covered, Claude said, "Pick up the case with your right hand, Georgie Boy and keep the left one in the air. If you as much as blink, I'll take great pleasure in shooting you in the balls. Don't start walking until I tell you."

George smiled at him, but didn't reply. Picking up the case as instructed, with his left hand held high, he turned his back to Claude.

"Start the woman," Claude shouted, and the flashlight came on again so he could see Carla begin walking toward them, stepping carefully over rocks and trying not to stumble. She took two steps, and Hushan shouted, "Stop."

She did and stood there shivering in the cold, as Hushan shouted, "Let George go."

"Go ahead, Georgie boy, but go slow," Claude said. "Keep your hands where I can see them and stay away from Carla. Walk in a circle to get back to your friend. If you get within ten feet of her, I'll shoot you in the back."

George snarled, "And Hushan will kill your girlfriend."

"Yeah, but you'll die first. Do what I told you."

"Okay, asshole," George said. "Your day will come."

Ignoring George, Claude watched as Carla matched him, step-for-step on her agonizingly slow journey toward Claude. Then she stumbled and fell headlong into the mud and water. It startled Claude and he involuntarily stepped out from behind the rock.

"Look out," Joe yelled from behind him.

Two shots boomed out in rapid succession. A bullet ricocheted off the stone close to Claude's head and several chips hit his face.

A scream came out of the night and Claude heard a thud like a body hitting the roof after a suicide jumper decides to end it all.

At the sound of Joe's shout, George took off at a run toward the car. Claude snapped off two quick rounds in his general direction, but wasn't able to get a good sight picture because of the impact of the chips on his cheek. He felt warm blood flow down his wet face, but ignored the pain and looked for Carla.

She was still down on the ground, with her arms reaching out toward Claude and pleading for his help.

Another shot rang out and Claude heard the bullet impact against the rock a foot above his head.

The rain continued to beat down in sheets, making it difficult to see what was happening. Two quick shots came from behind him and Claude knew Joe was covering him.

The side windows of Hushan's car shattered into a cascade of glass chips as Hushan and George dove behind the vehicle to return fire.

Carla began to crawl toward Claude, and then he saw the impact of two bullets as they hit on either side of her, throwing up mud and dirt.

"Stay where you are, Miss Roberson," Hushan shouted.

Carla put her arms over her head and screamed in fear.

Joe pumped two more rifle shots into the car and more glass shattered. Either George or Hushan stood up over the hood and returned fire with an automatic rifle.

More shots ricocheted off the walls, but as far as Claude could tell they hit nothing. Behind him, Claude heard the sound of falling rocks as they struck the surface of the lake.

He thought, "Joe must be moving to a better location."

Suddenly Hushan shouted, "Hold your fire."

With his voice whipped by the wind until it was faint to Claude, Joe asked, "Do you give up?"

"No," Hushan said, "but I have a proposition."

"What?" Claude asked.

"It seems we have a stalemate. Let us go and you can have the woman."

"No way," Joe replied, and Claude figured Joe was caught up in the heat of the moment, not remembering the main reason they were here was to rescue Carla.

He started to override his comments, but he wasn't quick enough as Hushan shouted, "Then we'll do it the hard way."

Claude wasn't prepared for what happened next.

George and Hushan stood up quickly, and George sprayed the rocks around and behind Claude with a full thirty-round clip, while Hushan shot Carla in the back.

Forever afterward, the sounds of the bullet smacking into Carla's body and her scream of pain would remain in Claude's memory.

Stunned, he fell to his knees and shouted, "You bastard! Now you'll die."

"Perhaps, but the woman you love will bleed to death before then," Hushan shouted. "Let us walk away and you can call for an ambulance. Keep up the battle and regardless of what we do to each other, she'll die."

Behind him, Claude heard Joe say softly, "I'm hit, Claude. Let 'em go and take care of Carla."

Claude turned to see Joe lying back against a boulder, with blood flowing from a wound in his upper right chest area. Not wanting his opponents to know it was now two to one, with the odds in their favor, he whispered, "Are you okay?"

"Yeah, I got the bastard that was behind you, but George put one in my chest. I can't help you much, so let 'em go."

"All right," Claude shouted. "Go. We'll meet again."

As they climbed into their car and drove off, he heard Hushan shout, "I hope so."

(Four)

The night before, there wasn't time to thoroughly check the bombs in their packing case. By the time Hushan got the location from the shoe box and drove to the storage area, it was late, so he took a fast look into the top case, saw the fire extinguishers nestled in their foam encircled spaces, smiled and latched the top.

SIGNS OF OUR TIMES

Turning to Specks and George, he said, "Carry them to the car, and then let's get the hell out of here."

"Take one, Specks and I'll get the other," George said.

Grabbing hold of the top case, Specks complained, "Damn, they're heavy."

Smacking Specks on the side of his head with his open palm, Hushan said, "Quit whining, you skinny bastard."

After hurrying outside, Specks struggled to get the case in the trunk while George stood by, offering no assistance.

As low man on the whipping post in this funky organization, Specks was growing weary of the bullshit he was expected to take.

At first it was fun and exciting, working to put the "man" down, and maybe kill off a bunch of honkies, but the longer he hung with Hushan, the more he grew to hate him.

Hushan had decided no one could protect the bombs better than he. He also had learned not to trust anyone else, so they drove to his house and unloaded the cases in his garage.

As he sat and watched George and Speck performing the manual labor, Hushan thought, "Too many of my underlings are dead. If they keep killing each other off, I won't have anyone left."

Afterward, they walked into the kitchen for a drink and Hushan went over the plan for the next night.

He said, "I'll drop you off early Specks, so pack a lunch and take along a cooler of soft drinks. You'll have all afternoon to find a spot where you can take out Mister Jones.

"Then tonight, George and I will try to get him out in the open, so you can nail him. Are you up to making your bones?"

Not sure he meant it, Specks said, "Yeah Hushan, I'll get rid of him for you."

In the past, Hushan had asked him to do a lot of strange things, but never murder. But maybe if he pulled this off, he'd get a promotion to Hushan's right-hand man or at least be on a par with George.

With Felix and Mohammed out of the way, it seemed reasonable to Speck's feeble mind that he'd be next in line after the guy with the spider tattoo.

They slept-in the next morning, so they'd be fresh for the evening's work. If Hushan was successful in recovering their money, it would go a long way toward paying for their retirement in Aruba, the place he decided to go after they set off the bombs.

Knowing Fort Worth and Dallas would be ghost cities, contaminated and littered with dead bodies, when he thought about it, shivers ran up Specks arms. But he was looking forward to the sandy beaches and the dark-skinned natives he read about in a travel folder. They could have the cold weather in northern Texas.

(Five)
At one in the afternoon, Hushan and George drove Specks out to the rock quarry and dropped him off. In his back pack he carried a small cooler with six soft drinks, a package of chips and three sandwiches in a plastic sack. The ice was already melting and Specks hoped it wouldn't make the food soggy.

Low-hanging, ugly grey and black clouds covered the sky, making it a dismal, muggy day. The weather was warm for the time of year. As Specks climbed up through a rock chimney in back of the small lake, he was sweating while he listened to rap music through his ear phones.

The sides of the steep cleft were cracked, providing hand and foot holds, but the rock was crumbling and it scared the shit out of him. As he crawled slowly up the narrow slit, the rifle he carried was heavy on his shoulder and swung around like a pendulum. Looking down, he saw he was more than fifty feet off the hard rock floor of the quarry. If he fell, they'd need a spatula to pick up what was left.

Finding a ledge jutting out of the cliff, Specks climbed out onto it and discovered it gave him a good view of the surrounding area, including the gate and piles of rocks and boulders to the rear.

He didn't look to his left or he would have seen Joe staring at him through the peep sight of his rifle. Joe was on another ledge, seventy-five feet away and hidden behind a large flat rock sticking out of the side of the cliff.

Taking one last look, Joe ducked back down out of sight. There was a small cave to his rear, so he climbed in and settled down for a long wait.

Specks laid the rifle down on the ledge, turned up the volume of his disc player and snapped his fingers in time to an old rock and roll tune from the fifties. Sometimes he got tired of the rap crap and turned to Elvis and the Righteous Brothers for variety. Reaching into his cooler, he pulled out a cold diet soda, popped the top, leaned back against the wall, took a large hit and waited.

Two hours later it started raining and Specks was miserable, until Joe killed him just after he drew down on Claude. Then, as he screamed and fell off the ledge, his lifeless body crashed down hard onto the floor of the quarry and he felt nothing.

(Six)

The nasty wound was not in Carla's back, it was high on her left hip and bleeding badly. When Claude reached her side, took her into his arms and tried to stem the flow of blood, she was unconscious, with her eyes rolled back in her head.

Joe was on his cell phone, trying to reach his fellow officers, but the storm was interfering with the transmission lines and he couldn't get a signal.

Claude heard him shout, "Damn, I can't get out.

Joe tried to stand up to move around until he could make a connection, but he was too weak. Sliding back down to a sitting position, he asked, "How is she?"

"Hushan got her in the hip and it's bleeding badly," Claude said. "I can't make it stop. I think he hit an artery."

"They got us good. Can you put a tourniquet on it?"

"I'll try," Claude said, as he pulled off his sodden jacket, squashed it together to make a wet pillow and lay her head on it.

Carla was still unconscious and her breath was ragged with pain, so he used strips of cloth from his shirt and tied them around her hip. Then with the barrel of his gun as a fulcrum, he turned the cloth as tight as he could, but the blood still coursed in red rivulets down her leg.

Watching as the artery spurted out more, he yelled, "It isn't working, Joe."

"I still can't get a signal. You'll have to drive up the road until you can get one. Haul me over there and I'll try to help her while you're gone."

"I don't want to leave her!" Claude cried.

"If you want to save her life, you have to."

Knowing he was right, Claude kissed Carla's face and tenderly wiped some of the blood from her cheeks that his fingers left there. Then he raced to Joe, helped him to his feet and they staggered to where Carla lay to find she was now awake and moaning softly.

Taking her hand in his, Claude said, "God, I'm sorry Babe."

"Go," Joe said. "Get help fast. I'm not doing so well myself."

Squeezing Carla's hand gently, Claude smiled at her and said, "I'll be back. Hang in there. I love you."

She tried to smile through the pain, but couldn't, so she nodded and lay her head back down on his coat.

Taking the cell phone from Joe's hand, Claude ran through the rain, stumbling through the mud and puddles until he reached Carla's car. After jumping in, he managed to get the key in the ignition with his shaking fingers and fired up the engine.

He stomped on the accelerator, but the car acted as if it was running over huge bumps, refusing to move very far before it stalled. Then he noticed the vehicle leaned to one side.

Climbing out, Claude found the tires on the right side were slashed and knew the Pontiac wasn't going anywhere.

Turning, he ran up the rocky road to the top of the hill and the highway. At this time of night, it was deserted with no one in sight and no headlights from either direction. Claude began jogging down the road, trying the cell phone every time he was winded and stopped to catch his breath. Nothing, there was no signal.

The storm continued to roar around him and hard rain pounded his skin as he splashed through wide muddy streams rushing across the blacktop and crashing into the ditch.

When he saw the friendly lights of a gas station up ahead, he thought, "Thank God!"

His aching lungs and feet told him he had run five miles, when in reality it was only three, but determined to make it; he struggled on only to find the station was closed.

Picking up a broken piece of a yellow concrete car-stop, he threw it through the plate glass of the front door. Then after pushing the splintered remains out of the way and cutting his hand, he reached through and opened the dead bolt and lock.

He searched, found a phone behind a littered counter and dialed 9-1-1. When the operator answered, Claude felt like crying, but managed to choke out the story of an officer down and tell her of the second victim. He knew the report of a lawman being shot would receive priority over any other call.

After he gave the operator his position and the location of the quarry, she said, "Stay on the line."

"How long will it be before anyone gets here?" Claude asked. "The two victims need medical attention immediately."

"Six minutes to your site," she said, "and three more to the quarry."

As tired as he was, knowing he couldn't make it back to the quarry in less than fifteen minutes, he decided to wait, and said, "Have an officer pick me up and take me to the quarry."

"On the way," she said and repeated unnecessarily, "Stay on the line."

Leaning against the wall, Claude slid down it until he was seated, laid his head down on his arms across his folded-up knees.

As tears ran down his face he prayed, "Please God, don't take her from me!"

SIGNS OF OUR TIMES

(Seven)

As they drove away, Hushan said, "They're on to us, George. That was too close. Mister Jones had help. There were two of them."

Still pumped up, with adrenaline flowing through his veins like oil from a west Texas drilling rig, George asked, "What do we do now?"

With an evil smirk, Hushan said, "We can't wait until the Cotton Bowl. We must strike now."

"Whoa!" George exclaimed. "We're not prepared to do that, are we?"

Speaking as if he was talking to an errant child, Hushan said, "The original plan was to fly low over the stadium in a helicopter with the signaling device. Even though they may be on to us, we can use the same plan with a few changes."

Perplexed, George asked, "Like what?"

"We place the fire extinguishers around Fort Worth and Dallas on main streets we can locate and follow in a small aircraft, setting the bombs off one at a time or in groups.

"We can still kill thousands, perhaps hundreds of thousands. The only juicy target we won't hit is the President, but we can embarrass his administration so badly the people will rise up and call for his impeachment."

George persisted in questioning his leader, as he said, "It sounds good, but how do we make our escape? The gas will carry for miles."

Showing his brilliance in planning, Hushan said, "We meet at the airport and you fly us to Aruba as planned. We can beat the gas to the plane and be safely on our way."

"I hope you're right," George said. "It's too bad we can't settle up with Mister Jones. I'm sure they got Specks. I heard his body hit the ground."

"We'll let the gas take care of our enemy," Hushan said. "What a fitting end for the man who supplied it to us. Don't you think its poetic justice?"

"Yeah, I like the idea, but hey, I just thought of something. I can't go home. Mister Jones knows where I live."

Sitting back in his seat with a smile on his face, Hushan bragged, "Now you see the wisdom in storing the gas at my place. Good leadership always conquers adversity. Head for my home. There's work to do."

(Eight)

Its lights flashing red and blue against the force of the still raging storm, the state police patrol car bounced down the rocky road to the quarry. The driver, Sergeant Bill Fisher, didn't let up on the accelerator as they left the highway.

Bill knew his passenger wanted to get to the crime scene as fast as humanly possible.

Pointing to where three blue and whites and two ambulances sat with their light bars lashing out into the darkness, Claude said, "Down there."

Near the center of the muddy quarry, two of the vehicles kept their spotlights on the scene, where a blue blanket covered one still form on the ground and three EMS personnel knelt by whoever it was, while medics worked on another person lying on a gurney.

As the police searched for any other victims, Claude saw several flashlights moving among the rocks and columns of stone. When the car slid to a halt, Claude crossed himself and prayed Carla and Joe were going to make it, jumped out the door and ran to the gurney. Looking down, he saw Joe with pain showing in his face, but there was something else, sorrow too.

Looking at Claude, Joe shook his head and tried to speak, but choked up and covered his mouth with a knotted fist.

"God, No!" Claude cried out to the heavens above. Turning quickly, he knelt by Carla's body, grabbed her cold still hand and wept.

One of the medics said, "I'm sorry, but we got here too late and she bled to death. Sergeant Francone tried to stop it, but he couldn't. Whoever shot her hit the main artery in her leg and shattered it, so a tourniquet couldn't stop the flow."

"I'm sorry," he repeated, patting Claude's back.

As if the clouds were joining in his grief, rain poured down on Claude's head. Continuing to hold her hand, his shoulders shook with fury and shock, so the medics stood back and let him have his private moment with Carla.

Stroking her face tenderly, he said, "Forgive me."

Then as he traced her eyes and mouth with his fingers, he remembered when she was alive and so full of love for him.

One of the medics asked quietly, "Can we move her now? We'd like to get her out of the rain."

"Thanks," Claude said, standing up to watch as they lifted Carla tenderly onto another gurney, covered her from head to toe under a clean white sheet and rolled her body to a waiting ambulance. By the time the medics got there, the sheet was soaked, but when they put her inside the vehicle, they replaced it with another dry one.

As he turned to where Joe lay watching him, it was apparent Joe made the medics wait until he could speak with Claude and tell him what Carla said before she died.

SIGNS OF OUR TIMES

With tears running down his cheeks to mix with the rain, he said, "I'm sorry I couldn't save her. Carla told me to tell you she'd be waiting for you in heaven. I don't think she was in any pain toward the end. She smiled, turned her head and was gone. I thought you should know."

Claude's eyes were overflowing and he let the tears course down his face as he sobbed uncontrollably.

Reaching out with his good hand, Joe grabbed Claude's and held on. They may have been old enemies, but now their grief was shared like brothers.

A medic said, "We have to get you to the hospital, Joe."

"Can I ride with him?" Claude asked.

"Sure, let us load him and you can climb in the back. I know he'd like your company."

Turning to walk to the other ambulance, Claude said, "I'll say goodbye to Carla and be with you in a minute, Joe."

Carla's body lay like a rag doll, cold and still. Although he knew she was gone, he hoped somehow she could hear him, so he knelt by her side, took his hand in hers and said, "I'll see you very soon. I'll always love you. Goodbye for now."

Steeling himself, Claude stood up and walked away without looking back.

(Nine)

The next day Hushan and his men were busy planning where they would place the bombs.

While George laid out a map of both cities and they marked likely spots for each of the fire extinguishers, Hushan said, "Be sure to mark parks or any baseball diamonds. We can hang them on posts, put them in trash cans or out in the open and no one will notice. They're something people see every day and it doesn't register on their subconscious."

"What about some of the tall buildings?" Ali Zabara asked. He was a small Arab who lost his family to American bombs in Afghanistan and vowed reprisal, even if it meant his own death.

After sneaking across the porous Canadian border, Ali joined Hushan in Fort Worth and now worked at a gas station. He was a good candidate for a suicide mission, but Hushan hoped everyone here would survive to fight again.

"If we set them off high in the air, the gas will be caught by the wind and spread faster."

"A wonderful idea," Hushan said. "Do it."

As he walked in with one of the cases, George said, "Look at these babies."

He raised the lid, stared down at the contents and began to count, "One, two, three," and went on until he reached fifteen and then stopped abruptly.

Hushan waited for him to continue to sixteen, but instead, George turned and headed toward the garage for the other case.

"Wait, George," he said. "Are you sure you counted them correctly?"

"Yeah, there are fifteen. Why?"

When George shrugged as if he thought Hushan was stupid, he walked to the case and checked them himself. There were four rows and four containers in each row except the last. There was one empty space

"There should be a total of thirty-two," Hushan said. "Bring in the other case and check it."

After carrying in the second case, George opened it and said, "Sixteen here, none missing."

"God," Hushan cried. "Someone has taken one. When was the last time you checked the cases, George?"

"Hell, I never opened them. Just having them around scared me. I didn't want to set one off by accident. Maybe Mohammed took one."

"Why would he?" Hushan asked. "He never mentioned anything to me and I know he wouldn't do such a thing without my permission. He knew they were too dangerous to handle indiscriminately. Who can have it?"

George shrugged again and said, "Not me, but what about Mister Jones? They were in his possession for five days."

Hushan frowned and asked, "Why would he take only one? Besides, there is no way to set it off by remote control unless you have the signaling device. To detonate it manually would mean his death too. No, he's too smart, so it wasn't him."

"Then who has it?" George asked.

"Perhaps Felix only filled thirty-one," Hushan said. "It's apparent no one opened the cases until now. Why worry about one extra anyway? We have plenty."

George patted the top of one of the cases and said, "True."

(Ten)

As the ambulance skidded on the wet pavement, Claude hung onto Joe and his gurney to keep him from sliding off and onto the floor. The vehicle slowed, the tires regained their grip on the road and they continued their conversation as Joe said, "You mentioned a black kid that guarded George's place. Was he skinny with cornrows and a thin goatee?"

"Yeah," Claude said, and then he asked, "Was it him you shot back there?"

"His description matches the one of the shooter that I gave to the cops. I only saw him once, when he set up camp on a ledge about seventy-five feet away."

"Thanks for taking him out," Claude said. "He came close."

Wiping his face with a towel he found on a shelf, Claude felt his cheek. There were several small open sores, which made him look like he had measles.

Smiling through his pain, Joe said, "You made them bleed again."

Holding the towel against his bloody cheek, Claude said, "It looks like you'll make it, so when we get to the hospital I'm going to take off. Thanks again for taking care of Carla while I was gone. I'm glad she had a friend like you with her when she passed on."

Already knowing the answer, Joe asked, "Got some unfinished business to take care of?"

"You might say that. Be aware, from this point forward all bets are off. Tonight death walks the streets of Fort Worth and Dallas, and his name is Claude Werner."

"So it's your real name."

Smiling, Claude said, "Yeah, you might need it for my tombstone before the next couple of days are over."

"Are you sure you don't want my guys involved?"

"Yeah, I don't want any more collateral damage. Carla was the last innocent person I killed. There won't be any more. From now on only the guilty will die."

Joe nodded and said, "I can't officially sanction your efforts. If they ask me, you never said a word and just disappeared. Go slow, but get the bastards for me too."

"Keep your cell phone handy," Claude said. "If I can, I'll give you a blow-by-blow account."

CHAPTER 23

(One)

After the answering machine picked up, Claude heard George say, "Ben, this is George. We're leaving for Aruba tomorrow at four in the afternoon and I need you as my co-pilot. It's a matter of life and death. Your life if you're not on the plane with us. I think you know what I mean. Meet me at the airport at three so we can preflight the aircraft."

Ben wouldn't be going anywhere tomorrow. His body was lying next to the phone in a pool of blood. He was one of the men Mohammed gave up and Claude kept secret from Joe and the Feds. Ben's black hair glistened in the lamp light and the matching irises of his dead eyes stared up at the ceiling as if he were counting flies. Five of his severed fingers lay in a row by his side.

Nearby, Claude sat in a recliner wearing only his underwear, as he wiped his hands, listened to the message and thought, "It always pays to hedge your bets and get good odds."

After George hung up, Joe looked down at Ben's body and said, "It's too bad you're already dead, but don't worry, I'll take your place."

Looking at his shirt where it lay on the couch next to him, he saw there were some small blood splatters on the collar. He hoped anyone who noticed would attribute the blood to the cuts on his face.

SIGNS OF OUR TIMES

Before holding his question and answer session with Ben, Claude removed his own clothes to avoid such an accident. But sometimes flying blood tended to travel great distances. This was one of those times.

Feeling he had been too soft with Mohammed, Claude knew now was the time to get down to business. He didn't have time to fool around with niceties.

When Ben answered the door in his pajamas, Claude hit him in the head with a large ball peen hammer, knocking him unconscious. Ben fell to the floor, and blood from a nasty cut ran down his brow.

After locking the door, Claude tied Ben's hands behind his back by wrapping his wrists with duct tape and then used the same to immobilize his bare legs. In the kitchen he found a pretty pastel towel with small hearts embroidered on it, ripped it in two, stuffed half in Ben's mouth and taped it in place.

Letting him sleep for a few minutes, Claude walked around the farm house and checked the rooms.

The kitchen was clean and smelled of roast beef. He discovered a plate with leftover meat was stored in the refrigerator under an aluminum tent. Using a very sharp butcher knife he found in a wooden holder by the stove, Claude cut a slice and ate it while he inspected the living room. He took the knife with him.

On the coffee table were several books and magazines. The main theme of most was aviation and planes. A framed certificate was on one wall, very similar to the one in George's home, but this one indicated Ben Romero was qualified as a pilot of reciprocating aircraft.

An overflowing ash tray sat on the floor, next to a worn reclining chair, but besides the pilot's license, there was nothing else interesting in the room.

Moving on to the bedroom, he found a .38 caliber revolver in a holster in a drawer and a .12 gauge shotgun leaning against one wall with one shell in the chamber and three in the slide. Ejecting them all, Claude put the cartridges in his pocket, but left the empty weapon in place. He took the handgun with him for possible use later in the day.

The closet contained nothing but men's clothes, so there was no woman living here and Claude thought, "Good."

He didn't want anyone stumbling upon them in the next hour or so. After that it wouldn't matter, he'd be gone and Ben would be dead.

Ben was still where Claude left him, so he moved the recliner closer to where he lay and then slapped Ben's face until he regained consciousness.

Ben stared at Claude with fear in his eyes and they seemed to ask, "Who are you?"

In answer to his unspoken question, Claude said, "I see you're wondering who I am and what I want. You may have heard of me, I'm Mister Jones, and I'm here to ask you some questions."

The name registered. Ben's eyes flickered and grew larger until they seemed to bulge out of his face.

Continuing to smile, Claude said, "Nice farm you have here. It's far enough out in the country to have clean air and the noises of the city won't bother you, right?"

Ben didn't try to answer. His head remained still with his eyes following every move Claude made, as he continued, "It also works against you in times like these, Ben old buddy. No one will hear us as I work with you.

"Now, I'm going to ask you a question and you're going to give me an answer by nodding or shaking your head. Do you understand?"

When Ben wasn't fast enough to comprehend he was supposed to nod his head, Claude did it for him by grabbing his hair and rocking his head back and forth, as he asked again, "I said, 'do you understand?'"

This time, Ben nodded and Claude said, "Good. Here's question one: "Do you know a man named Hushan?"

Ben shook his head and Claude said, "Liar."

Reaching behind him, he took the hammer and with one cruel swing, he broke Ben's big toe on his left foot.

As Ben tried to scream, he choked and Claude said, "Oh, now you're having second thoughts about your answer, aren't you?"

Reaching inside his coat jacket, Claude pulled out a small pair of pruning shears. When he saw the tool, Ben's eyes got larger and he nodded his head so fast he looked like a bobble doll.

Opening and closing the shears with an ugly sounding "snap", Claude continued to play Jeopardy, and asked, "Okay, once again, do you know Hushan?"

Ben nodded and large salty tears ran down his cheeks.

"What about Georgie boy? I think his name is George Schroeder. You know him too?"

Another nod and more tears.

"Good, now we're getting somewhere. Do you know where the bombs are?"

The question evoked a frightened look from Ben, but no response. He looked like he would piss his pjs.

Bending down and looking deep into Ben's eyes, Claude said, "I'm going to take the tape off now, so you can answer some more questions."

SIGNS OF OUR TIMES

Ben nodded, but wasn't ready when Claude ripped the tape off. Large chunks of hair and some skin from Ben's bottom lip came along with the strip. A small trail of blood ran from his torn lip and dripped onto the collar of his sleepwear.

Spitting out the towel, Ben took a large gulp of air.

Claude asked, "Where are the bombs?"

With the gag gone, Ben suddenly became belligerent and stubborn, as he shouted, "Kill me if you will, but the bombs will avenge me. Allah be praised!"

Reaching behind Ben with his pruning shears, Claude calmly snipped off Ben's index finger.

Blood spurted and Ben screamed in agony.

Holding the still pink finger in front of Ben's face, Claude repeated his question, "Where are the bombs?"

Through his torn lips and clenched teeth, Ben spat out, "Go to hell."

"Not quite yet," Claude said, and clipped off Ben's middle finger.

It took four fingers, a thumb, and some coercion on Claude's part before Ben would talk.

After lining up the digits in front of Ben so he could see the end result of his stubbornness, Claude said, "Come on, don't be stupid, Ben. Tell me what I want to know and I'll call the cops and an ambulance. Maybe the doctors can sew your fingers back on. I'm not after small fry like you. I want the big boys.

"I'm tired of cutting off fingers and getting nowhere. The next thing I snip off will be your dick."

Seeing the certainty in Claude's eyes, Ben suddenly began to sing like Elvis.

Looking at his digits lined up in a row, as his body shook with pain, Ben shouted, "At George's home in Fort Worth."

"What's the address?"

"Fourteen seventy-nine Mockingbird Lane."

"What do they plan to do with the bombs?"

"Kill the President and many others at the Cotton Bowl," Ben said, and spat at Claude. "I hope you'll be there."

"I doubt it," Claude said.

Waving the pruning shears in the general direction of Ben's crotch, he asked, "How do they plan to escape?"

"We have a plane at the Harris County Airport—a small jet. George is the pilot."

"And you? "What's your role in all of this?"

Between sobs of regret and pain, Ben said, "I was to help put the bombs in place by posing as a fireman. Then I would be the co-pilot on the trip to Aruba."

"I saw your license, very impressive," Claude said. "What's the tail number?"

"F W dash four seven one four."

Claude asked him a few more important questions and when he had the answers, Ben pleaded, "Please call the ambulance. I'm bleeding badly."

Looking down grimly at Ben, Claude asked, "You never got the chance to meet my fiancée, did you? Your friends Hushan and George killed her by letting her bleed to death. You're a cohort of theirs Ben, so that makes you guilty by association. What's good for the goose is good for the gander."

Grabbing Ben by his hair with his left hand, Claude raised Ben's head and using his own butcher knife, Claude calmly slit Ben's throat. Ben's piercing scream turned into a bloody gurgle.

Either the knife was sharper than Claude thought, or he exerted a little more effort than necessary. Ben's head was nearly severed from his body.

Claude had all the info he needed, and it was obvious Ben didn't know about the loss of the fire extinguishers. Looking down at his handiwork, Claude thought, "Ben must not be a member of the inner circle, but now there's one less flunky."

After getting some towels from the bathroom, Claude began to clean up. Suddenly the phone rang. He continued to wipe his hands as the shrill tone sounded four times, the answering machine picked up and he heard George's message.

(Two)

Signaling winter wasn't far away, it was a typical fall day in the Dallas/Fort Worth Metroplex. High above, thin clouds resembling wispy cotton balls, raced across a light blue sky tinted grayish-green by the exhaust fumes of thousands of vehicles on the untold miles of concrete cutting through and around the twin cities.

In the middle of the mid-day traffic, one of those automobiles held three men dressed as firemen, on a mission they hoped would bring the hustling and bustling cities to a standstill for years to come.

Another vehicle held a man with bloody sores on his cheek, who intended to keep the cars, buses and trucks running.

As he climbed back into the SUV, Ali said, "That's four of them."

SIGNS OF OUR TIMES

When George couldn't reach Ben by telephone, Ali took his place. He wore one of George's extra uniforms and it fit him badly. Ali was slimmer and three inches shorter than George, but no one had paid any attention to him at the last four stops.

Three of the targets were rooftops a mile apart, where the terrorists simply laid the container out of sight behind a chimney. The fourth was a baseball diamond used by the local softball league teams in the evenings. During the mornings the diamonds were deserted, so they screwed in the hanger and put the fire extinguisher outside the announcer's booth behind the backstop. There was a lot of open ground and a brisk breeze was already blowing in from right field toward home plate.

Hushan sat in the passenger's seat, puffing on a filtered cigarette as he "supervised" the placement of the devices. It seemed manual labor was beneath the dignity of the leader of the pack, but George didn't mind.

He'd seen the money in the case waiting for them at Hushan's and knew when the job was finished part of it would be his. He couldn't wait to get his hands on one of those dark-skinned babes in Aruba. A friend told him the young tourist chicks on spring break also gave pussy away. If so, when the ships docked, George would be standing in line.

The next stop was another high rise two miles away, so George stepped on the gas and sped away.

"Slow down you fool," Hushan ordered. "Don't attract the police. Don't you think they know about us by now?"

"Sorry," George said.

When they reached the fourteen-story tower, George climbed out and said, "'I'll get the next one. Hand me one of those things, Ali."

Reaching into the case, Ali pulled out a fire extinguisher. The chain to the ring on the handle caught in the foam and he pulled harder. When it finally came free, and as he handed it to George, the ring fell out of its holder.

In his haste to catch it, he knocked the fire extinguisher from George's hand and the container hit the concrete curb with a loud "clang". The handle flew open and gas escaped in a cloud of green smoke, as Hushan shouted, "You've killed us all!"

He dove down in his seat as if it would stop the gas from getting to him.

Ali seemed transfixed in the rear with his eyes bulged out and his mouth agape in fear.

Trying frantically to escape, George dived to the sidewalk and crawled behind the truck. He turned, watching in horror, as the fire extinguisher expanded its contents into the air and the deadly green cloud spewed out, spreading across the pavement.

As a gentle wind blew the gas farther down the street, several bystanders looked at George inquisitively, wondering what the firemen were doing. The small crowd watched as the cloud slowly dissipated around them and sank to earth.

After holding his breath as long as he could, Hushan exhaled loudly and inhaled a small amount of air. Then he peeked over the dash at the pedestrians on the sidewalks and saw none of them was affected by the gas.

The few of them who stopped to wonder about their actions, moved on and shook their heads at the antics of the firemen. They didn't think it was appropriate for public servants to roll around on the street or set off fire extinguishers on a public thoroughfare.

From the back seat, Ali said in awe, "They don't work." Staring into space he unknowingly repeated, "They don't work."

Transfixed by the scene, which would dwell in his mind for as long as he lived, Hushan said, "I know."

As he recovered from his shock and climbed back into the driver's seat, George asked, "Did you see that? The bomb went off and nothing happened."

Comprehension of the past few days finally made its way into his mind, and Hushan said, "They switched the contents on us. They knew all along and played us for fools. We've got to get away."

(Three)
Joe's cell phone rang, and the nurse handed the hated contraption to him. Even with the aid of narcotics, his chest hurt like hell. He wondered who was calling him so early in the morning, then realized it could only be one person and asked, "Yeah?"

"Hi Joe," Claude said, and then he asked, "What do you do when there are bad apples in your crop?"

"What is this, twenty questions? Hell, I don't know."

"You prune out the branches that don't produce," Claude said.

"What are you now, a gardener?"

"Yeah, I thought it would be a nice change of pace."

"I wish I knew what the hell you're talking about. Come on, give me a break, my chest hurts and all this talking isn't doing me any good."

"One down and several more to go," Claude said. "Stay tuned. You can find this one on Old Potato Road in Irving, seventeen hundred block, big farm. He's not going anywhere and might need a hand when you get there."

"I hope you're not hitching up for more than you can plow," Joe said.

"I'm not. How are you doing?"

"The doc says I'll live. I lost some blood, but they've been feeding me so much steak I'm worried I'll grow horns and start chasing heifers."

"Mona wouldn't like that. Has she heard about your heroics?"

"Yeah, I'm a real war hero. She's sitting next to my bed, wondering who I'm talking to."

"Give her my love and take good care of her when you get out," Claude said. "Good women are hard to come by."

"Are we going to see you again?"

"I doubt it. I'm going on a one-way ride tomorrow. I'll call you after I land and let you know how the flight was."

"Where you headed?"

"To the promised land," Claude said. "Oh, before I forget it, you can rest easy about the missing fire extinguisher. I know where it is and I intend to return it to the proper people. If I don't get the chance to say it to your face, thanks for everything."

"Good work," Joe said. "Everyone will be glad you found it. Remember what I said. Go slow and watch your back."

"Via Con Dias my friend."

The line went dead and Joe said, "You always get in the last word."

Reaching up to pat his hand, Mona chuckled at his statement.

(Four)

Acting like a big shot, Hushan ordered, "Take the trunks out to the airport, George, and we'll meet you there at four."

They spent the remainder of yesterday and all this morning, disposing of the fire extinguishers in Dumpsters along a back alley and packing items Hushan felt they must have with them if they were to begin anew in Aruba. It seemed to George that Hushan was taking everything but the frigging stool in the bathroom.

Shaking his head as he looked at the pile of boxes, he said, "By the time you get there, I'll have the preflight done and the engines warmed up. Don't be late and don't forget the money."

Hushan wasn't about to let him take the money suitcase to the plane and George thought, "Maybe he thinks I'd take off without him," and knew, "He's right."

Hushan stopped packing for a moment and asked, "Did you get in touch with Ben?"

"I left him a message. Don't worry, Ben will be there. When I called him, I thought we'd be running away from the nerve gas and told him so in a round about way. He'll know what I mean and be there on time with all his shit too. I hope the plane can haul all this junk."

Wiping perspiration from his brow with an already stained handkerchief, Hushan said, "Believe me, it's all necessary. Get going, George. I'll stop by and pick up the others, but I won't bother with Ben. He lives too far out in the country and if he doesn't make it, it's his funeral."

"And you wonder why no one thinks you're a great leader of men," George thought, but he kept his mouth shut, knowing Hushan still held the purse strings.

Before he left, he said, "Remember to tell the assholes no more than one suitcase apiece. They can carry it on board and pack them in the back of the plane. Your junk will take up all the space underneath. Anymore weight and we'll never get off the ground."

After he carried the last load to his SUV and packed it in, George fired up the engine and spun the tires in the gravel as he sped away. He hated to give up this little toy, but maybe he could find a Hummer for sale in Aruba. He knew a vehicle like it would impress the chicks.

(Five)
Hidden behind a generator and its wheels, Claude stood across the tarmac watching George finish unpacking his truck and loading the boxes and trunks into the underbelly of the small eight-passenger jet setting several hundred feet from the nearest building.

As George put the last item in place and locked the compartment, his jacket swung open. Claude saw he wore the .45 rig Claude hid under the couch and thought, "I'm surprised. From the way his house looked, I didn't think George did any housework. He probably stumbled across it by accident, but it's nice to know how he's armed."

No one else was with Georgie boy and it pleased Claude to no end. Although his plans covered many scenarios, it would be easier to accomplish this way.

Maybe there was a God and He was helping. Just in case, Claude looked skyward and mouthed, "Thank you."

He could use all the help he got in the next few hours and he thought, "It could be our alliance isn't so ungodly after all."

Climbing into his undersized tank, George moved it to the side of a hangar.

SIGNS OF OUR TIMES

As Claude watched, he got out, patted the hood and said something. He thought sentimental Georgie boy was telling his ride goodbye and wondered if his eyes were misty.

As George strolled across the tarmac with his hands in his pockets like he was playing a quick game of pocket pool, Claude thought, "I wouldn't put it past him. Dream about those Aruba girls all you want, Georgie. That's all you're going to do."

Something on the tarmac caught George's attention and he bent over and picked up a piece of tinfoil from one of his gum wrappers. He must have dropped it while he was loading Hushan's junk and his luggage. He didn't want it to get sucked up into the engine.

Walking slowly around the aircraft, George pulled the safety pins, counting them to make sure he had them all. Everything looked fine; the stabilizer moved correctly, the tires looked like they contained sufficient air and all the other memorized points of the preflight checked out satisfactorily.

Climbing up the thin steps that folded down out of the side of the aircraft, George checked the passenger cabin. It was clean, as it should be for what they paid the service company.

Fresh white linen covers were fitted over the top of each seat and the lap belts were laid across each cushion to form a neat X. It reminded him of a game of tic-tac-toe, where only one person played and won every game.

Whistling a catchy tune, the title forgotten, George opened the small door to the two-man cockpit and climbed into the left-hand seat. It felt warm from the sun shining in the three small windows. As he sat and looked over the instrument panel, he reveled in the mystery of flight and his ability to control it.

The fake wood glowed with a fresh coat of polish and the dials shone like diamonds in a coalmine against the ebony finish. There was a faint aroma of flowers in the air, probably something new the cleaning crew used. The scent masked the smell of oil and aviation fuel, two things of which he never grew tired.

Glancing out the window, he saw no one in sight. If Ben was coming he would arrive shortly, so he pulled out his pre-flight list and began to check off every item. When he reached to tap a dial, his shoulder holster got in his way. Shrugging out of the rig, he removed it and hung the weapon over the back of his seat. There would be no need for it now.

Feeling the plane shudder slightly as someone climbed the stairs behind him, George asked, "Is that you, Ben?"

Not waiting for an answer, he continued with his thoughts of the future. "I wonder if I'll have any trouble smuggling the gun into Aruba. Probably not, the cops down there let just about anything go on. Look at the young chick that's been missing for months. Aruba's police force must be a joke."

George chuckled at the thought, but his laughter stuck in the front of his throat, as he felt the cold steel of a revolver at the base of his neck.

The thought flashed though his mind, "It isn't Ben."

The familiar voice of Mister Jones resounded in his ears, "Hello, Georgie boy. Going somewhere? Thanks for taking your gun off, it saves me time. Keep your hands on the wheel."

George felt the holster slide off the seat and saw his unwanted visitor slip the weapon down to the floor on the right side of the co-pilot's seat. Keeping his gun in place as he reached behind him, Mister Jones pulled the cabin door shut and locked it. Then George felt him remove the pistol and turned his head to watch his visitor climb into the right-hand seat.

Claude smiled, pointed with his Glock at the door and said, "Ben told me you like to be by yourselves when you take off and land. He says you won't let anyone watch from behind."

Through a mouth suddenly gone dry with fear, George managed to choke out, "Where's Ben?"

"I'm afraid he's not going to make the flight. The last time I saw him, he was looking for a handout in his living room. We played a game of chance and he lost to four of a kind and a thumb for a kicker."

The answer didn't make sense to George, but without being told, he knew Ben was dead.

He pleaded, "Please don't kill me!"

"I have no intention of killing you, Georgie boy," Claude said. "All I want you to do is fly me and your fellow terrorists to Aruba, where you'll all be arrested. Do what I say and you'll live. Disobey me and you die."

Reaching into a small black case George hadn't noticed him carry on board, Claude pulled out a red fire extinguisher, and asked, "Look familiar?"

Claude hated to lie to Joe. He'd had the fire extinguisher since the day Carla went missing. He told Joe he would give it to the proper people and thought, "Well; they'll arrive shortly, so in that respect, I didn't lie."

As he stared at the container and knew it was the one missing from the case, George's hands shook on the wheel. It rattled and he asked in fear, "Is it for real?"

"The only one left," Claude said. "You see what I mean about killing all of you if you don't follow my instructions? I understand death by nerve gas is terrible. I hope we don't have to find out."

"But you'd kill yourself too," George said.

"Yeah, but it would be worth it to watch your skin peel off and the gas work on your lungs."

"Okay, you win," George said. "I'll do it. I'd rather spend years in a jail in Aruba than here in the USA when they find out what Hushan intended to do."

"Now you're being smart," Claude said. "I didn't think you had it in you. But just in case, I'll keep the fire extinguisher ready to use. I know a little about flying, so finish your checklist and warm up the engines before Hushan arrives."

(Six)

It was a meeting of the entire law enforcement community. The only ones missing were the Royal Canadian Mounted Police and a Bobbie from London. Joe's hospital room looked like a wake for a fallen cop, but he was still alive. Booze flowed like, well, booze when there are cops around. Joe held a half-full cup in his hand and listened to the buzz around him.

They were celebrating his recovery, but mostly they were reveling in the good news of the retrieval of the last nerve gas container. The relief they felt was like a heady tonic flowing through the crowded room, cheering them all.

"I can't believe what your buddy did to the guy out in Irving," Bert said. "I've seen blood before, but this was more than I thought one man could hold."

"Do you think Claude got the info about the last bomb from Ben before he cut his throat?" Kris asked.

"I don't know," Earnest said. "Would you talk if he cut off four fingers and a thumb? I know I would."

"Did he really do that?" Joe asked.

"Yeah," Sarah said. "They were lined up like soldiers on parade. They have them on ice down in the morgue along with his body. His blood tank is a little low."

"Now I know what he meant by 'needing a hand'," Joe said, chuckling. "Claude is something else."

With his Stetson jutting out over his face, Hoot asked, "What's he going to do next?"

When Kris thought about it, he couldn't remember ever seeing Hoot without the hat.

"I don't know," Joe said. "He said something about taking a one-way flight, but the way he makes puns, I don't know if he means on a plane or up some stairs."

From a chair near the door, Fad said, "I guess we'll have to wait until we find the next body or bodies to see what other tools he knows how to use. Claude's mighty handy with a nail gun, hammer, knives and pruning shears. What's next, a Roto-Rooter?"

"Either that or a jackhammer," Bert said.

Joe chuckled, then grimaced, and said, "Quit it you guys, you're going to make me drop a stitch."

"You're not too slow with the puns yourself," Fad said, lifting his drink in a salute. "Here's to Claude Werner, if it's really his name. Staple one for me buddy, right in the balls."

(Seven)

George and Claude watched as a brown Cadillac pulled up alongside the plane and then parked fifty feet away. Five people stepped out, and to Claude's surprise one of them was a woman of oriental or Arab descent. From this distance he couldn't tell which, but it really didn't matter anyway.

As they made their way to the plane and up the stairs, struggling with the weight, they all carried suitcases of different sizes, colors and designs.

Claude signaled George to remain silent and he nodded his understanding.

As the passengers stowed their gear and buckled up, various sounds and muffled voices filtered through the door. The clink of metal on metal from the seat belts was followed by the sound of someone pulling the stairs upward and locking them in place.

Knuckles rapped on the door and a voice boomed out of the speakers overhead. It was Hushan using the intercom to communicate with George.

He said, "We're all aboard and the luggage is stored away. Did Ben make it?"

Claude nodded for George to answer, so he picked up a microphone from where it hung on the instrument panel, and said, "Yeah. Get buckled in. We're set to go."

"Next stop Aruba and sandy beaches," Hushan said, and they heard his microphone click as he hung it up.

After putting his mike back where it belonged, George started the right-hand engine. It caught and the sound began to build as he fed it more fuel. Then he repeated the sequence for the left one.

When both motors were running smoothly, George synchronized their rhythm, contacted the tower through a voice-activated headset, as Claude listened through the co-pilot's earpieces, and then he taxied the plane toward the runway.

On the threshold, after receiving their final clearance, he let off the brakes, advanced the throttles and the plane roared down the runway into a clear blue sky.

"Wheels up," George said, pushing the correct knob to retract the struts into the fuselage. The small plane flew like a bullet, rocketing rapidly upward until they reached their assigned cruising altitude of eleven thousand feet.

"Nice flying," Claude said, as he heard the air traffic controller give George the final clearance, altitude and heading for Aruba. He checked the instruments and saw the dials were in the green, right where they should be.

George reached for his shirt pocket and Claude nudged him in the side of the head with his gun. Slowly pulling out a pack of gum, without saying anything, George asked if he could chew some.

"Be my guest," Claude said.

After opening two sticks, he folded them in half and put them in his mouth. His teeth moved back and forth as he tried to gather enough saliva to moisten the gum, but his mouth was dry. He felt like he was feverish, but knew it was only nerves and the cause was his having to sit next to the red fire extinguisher.

For the next hour as they flew over the outskirts of Houston and out into the blue of the Gulf of Mexico, they remained silent.

There was a lot George wanted to ask Mister Jones, but he was afraid to open his mouth. He kept his weapon aimed in George's direction with his right hand and used the other to caress the metallic side of the fire extinguisher as if it was a young girl's breast. George shook his head at the sight and wanted to puke.

(Eight)

Twenty minutes later, Claude said, "Engage the auto-pilot."

George did as he said, took his hands off the wheel, leaned back in his seat and asked, "What now?"

After taking out a pair of handcuffs and a roll of duct tape from his briefcase, Claude said, "Put your hands behind your back."

Looking up from his seat, George asked, "Is it necessary? I'm not going to do anything."

"I'll feel better if you're incapacitated until we get close enough to land," Claude said. "I'll untie you when we get there. Besides, I have some work to do."

As they snapped shut around his wrists, George felt the cold steel of the twin discs. Claude bent his arms behind him into a very uncomfortable position and then hooked the handcuffs around a seat brace so he could hardly move. Knowing there was no way Mister Jones was going to worry about his well-being, George toughed it out.

As George's cramped muscles contracted back and forth under his shirt, the spider in his web seemed to grow bigger and move toward the center of his handiwork. It was a shame he couldn't see it.

Kneeling by his side, Claude pulled George's legs backward, wrapped them together and then to the seat with duct tape so George couldn't reach any of the foot pedals. Claude was thorough in his work. Then he stood up and reached for the fire extinguisher.

George watched in fascination and disbelief, as Claude tore the det cord and phony seal from the handle. When he saw Claude pull the pin, his eyes bugged out and he screamed silently, "God, he can't let go of the handle, not now!"

Through a mouth suddenly filled with thick saliva, he asked, "What are you doing?"

When Mister Jones didn't answer immediately, sweat broke out on George's brow and a wintry chill in his shoulder bones spread to his arms in the form of goose bumps. His stomach rebelled and he felt bile rise in his throat.

Finally Claude said, "It's payback time."

Stepping close to the door, he undid the latch and opened it wide enough to allow the fire extinguisher to pass through. Then he pushed his arm and the container into the passenger cabin.

Over his hand and the top of the devilish device, Claude saw Hushan glance up and their eyes met. Fear wrapped its icy hands around Hushan's throat and a silent scream stuck in it.

Claude squeezed the handle and the nerve gas erupted from the nozzle in a thick grey cloud that drifted toward Hushan and the other passengers/terrorists. After keeping the handle down until he felt the pressure lessen, Claude dropped the bottle into the passenger compartment and then shut and locked the door. The last thing he saw before his view of the cabin was blocked, was Hushan's horrified face as he clutched his throat with both hands.

SIGNS OF OUR TIMES

When he heard the canister spew forth its deadly contents, George screamed in fear. Knowing in a few minutes the gas would seep through the space between the door and its frame and they were both doomed, he cried out, "You said I'd live!"

Claude smiled wickedly and said, "I lied. Did you think that after you and Hushan killed the only person who ever meant anything to me, I'd let either of you live? Damn, Georgie boy, I gave you more credit than you deserve. It's time to meet our maker."

Ignoring George's screaming and his trashing around as he tried to break free of his bonds, Claude sat down calmly in his seat, reached up, turned off the automatic pilot and pushed the steering wheel forward. As the plane began to dive at a steep angle, he held the wheel in the forward position and sat back to watch the show.

Fifteen hundred feet above the ocean, as it hurtled toward the surface and destruction, the plane sliced through a shaft of golden sunlight and the rays illuminated the interior of the cockpit with a heavenly glow. In that split second, everything moved in slow motion as if it were a dream.

In his mind, Claude saw Carla in a snow white gown holding her hands out to him and beckoning him onward. A feeling of peace came over him and he never felt so strong or so free in his entire life. He smiled and it was still on his face as the plane hit the water, the wings broke off and the fuselage plunged into the depths.

Their seats snapped off at impact, but George and Claude were already dead and felt nothing as their bodies were crushed against the instrument panel. Behind them in the passenger cabin, the seats containing the tormented bodies of the five terrorists ripped from the floor and hurled forward, together with their luggage and every loose item in the compartment.

The combined weight of their remains and other equipment shattered their bodies, breaking and pulverizing them in an instant. The congealed mass of unrecognizable flesh, bone and debris hit the wall and door to the cockpit, broke through and continued on to fill the small space to overflowing. Some oozed out the broken cockpit windows and was absorbed by the water.

The bullet-like projectile of the plane continued on its downward spiral until the weight and force of the water overcame its forward velocity. Then it slowed and stopped for a few moments and began to rise. Water seeped into the hollow shell through rents and tears and it paused again, floated in negative buoyancy for a minute. Then it turned over and slid downward into the dark-blue abyss.

The nerve gas not absorbed by the congealed mass seeped out slowly and dissipated into the ocean, to be diluted by the cold water until it became harmless.

The one-way flight to hell was over for Hushan and his friends, but Claude wouldn't be calling Joe to report on it. He was too busy holding Carla in his arms.

(Nine)

The door to Joe's hospital room opened slowly, and a fat man walked in wearing a thousand-dollar suit, but still looking like a gypsy drifter from Louisiana. He carried a new leather briefcase in his left hand, with a suspicious round bulge at one end, as if the case held a bottle of booze.

Joe was finishing reading the story about the plane crash and looked up to see who his visitor was.

"Sergeant Francone?" Gordo asked.

"In the flesh and bandages," Joe joked. "What can I do for you?"

"My name's Gordo and I have a letter for you from Mister Jones. He asked me to deliver it to you if anything happened to him. I see you're reading the story of his demise."

"Yeah," Joe said. "It was something. What a way to go."

When the report of the crash reached the FBI and Kris recognized the owner of the plane as Hushan Ziare, he, Joe, Fad and Bert had figured it all out, or at least they thought they had.

Kris thought he knew the name Ziare from somewhere, but it hadn't yet registered that Hushan was the brother of another terrorist who was now residing in a federal prison for his part in a hijacking of a cruise ship not too long ago. It would be another month before Kris made the connection.

Now maybe this letter would close the case and ease everyone's mind, so Joe asked, "Who are you, a lawyer?"

"Yeah," Gordo said, "and thanks to our mutual friend, a rich one."

"Good things come to those who sit on their fat asses and wait, even lawyers," Joe joked. "No offense."

"None taken," Gordo said, and laughed with him. "Anyway, here's his letter."

Joe took his time and read the letter carefully. Then he re-read it. It was fascinating and as a tear ran down his cheek, he said, "It looks like Sulfur Springs will be getting a new library.

"It says here Claude gave everything in his bank account to Carla for her love, and to cover the other provisions of his hand-written will he had notarized a few days before he died.

"In case Carla died, Claude wanted a library built in her memory."

"Four million should take care of it," Gordo said.

"Damn, he had that much in the account?"

Gordo smiled and said, "Yeah, that and a lot more. He left me three hundred thousand to insure the remaining monies are received by his beneficiaries.

"Alice Grabowski gets the same as I do for her college education. A million each in sorrowful retribution and to atone for his foul deeds goes anonymously to each of Nora Smith's twins and Ted Branski's two children. The last million goes to Claire, Larry Holgram's daughter."

More tears ran down Joe's cheeks and he said, "I take it Claude told you the whole story in the letter he mentions he gave you."

"Yeah, he did. It's strange, he was a killer and now he's a hero."

"It's too damned bad he won't get credit for saving nearly a million innocent lives," Joe said. "They're keeping that part of the story out of the papers. If I was you, I'd burn any evidence of it, including his letter. Thanks for dropping by, Gordo."

"There was one other thing he wanted me to do."

"What's that?"

As he held out a bottle of expensive French wine, Gordo said, "For you and Mona."

When Joe opened the attached envelope, there was a small card inside that read, "Go slow, marry the girl, live long and prosper."

It was signed simply, "Claude".

Shaking his head, but laughing at the same time, Joe said. "I'll be damned; he got in the last word again."

The End